Vengeance

Book Four of the Falling Empires Series

By

James Rosone & Miranda Watson

D1521908

Disclaimer

This is a fictional story. All characters in this book are imagined, and any opinions that they express are simply that, fictional thoughts of literary characters. Although policies mentioned in the book may be similar to reality, they are by no means a factual representation of the news. Please enjoy this work as it is, a story to escape the part of life that can sometimes weigh us down in mundaneness or busyness.

Copyright Information

Table of Contents

Chapter One
The Great Escape

Geneva, Switzerland

Johann Behr was practically beside himself when he'd heard his friend Roberto was missing. At first, it was suspected that his disappearance was related to a robbery or even a kidnapping for ransom. But when three days had passed and his body hadn't turned up and no one was demanding money for his return, Johann became paranoid that he might have been snatched up by the Americans.

When French and Brazilian intelligence looked into the matter, they discovered that Roberto's name didn't appear on the Air France passenger manifest, despite the fact that several flight attendants claimed he was on the plane, sitting in first class. To further compound the mystery, there was no record that he had ever purchased a ticket. Even the airport security cameras, which should have captured him leaving the plane and walking through the airports in Geneva, Paris, and Rio, all lacked any images of Roberto. It was like he had been electronically erased.

The French firmly believed that the only way this was possible was if another foreign intelligence agency was involved. Johann knew that the only countries that had this level of sophistication were the Russians, the Chinese, the Israelis, the British, and most certainly the Americans. The thought of the Americans interrogating Roberto was unnerving—if he broke under their questioning, he could expose their entire scheme.

Johann placed several calls to Erik Jahn, Peng An, Lance Solomon, and of course, Marshall Tate. They all agreed to pony up millions of dollars as a reward for information leading to Roberto's safe return. Peng and Erik also dispatched a small army of PMCs, bounty hunters, and intelligence specialists to Brazil to aid the local government in finding their most prominent citizen.

Despite all this, Johann still had to carry out the duties of UN Secretary-General without letting anyone know of his inner turmoil. If their conspiracy were to come to light, it would not only be the end of his political career, it would destroy his legacy, and it could topple the entire United Nations organization.

His assistant poked her head into his office. "Mr. Secretary, the coalition partners have arrived. I have them taking their seats in the briefing room." She was a young, beautiful twenty-something—he liked a little eye candy for the office. She was also a trained BND operative, which

Johann used to his advantage frequently to acquire more information on selected individuals.

"Thank you, Monika. I think I lost track of time," he replied. He stood up and walked toward the briefing room just down the hallway from his office.

Upon entering the room, Johann made his way around the table to personally shake each person's hand and greet them. He made sure that each member was given a moment to speak with him before the meeting started. It was his way of trying to keep them all on his side.

Finally, he sat down and brought the meeting to order. "Ladies and gentlemen, we have a lot to discuss, so let's get down to it," he announced.

The Russian Defense Minister opened it up. "The weather is finally warming, which means the polar sea lanes are opening back up. We've dispatched a number of ice breakers to try and clear us a passage through them. It's a much shorter journey from Russia and Norway through this route than it is traveling further south around Greenland. It's also not currently patrolled by the US Navy."

"The challenge isn't moving ships through the area," said General McKenzie via video teleconference, "it's finding a port that hasn't been bombed by the Americans or that won't be bombed when they learn we have a ship in port."

"Let's not forget that we've also taken a vast majority of the American satellite system offline," the German Defense Minister countered. "The few remaining satellites they have, as well as their airborne reconnaissance assets, are mostly focused on the Chinese front. That works to our advantage."

"I agree," asserted the Russian Defense Minister. "The Chinese have finally entered the war and it's drawn all of America's surveillance assets away from Canada to Mexico and the Pacific. We can and should use that to our advantage."

With a stern look on his face, the Dutch Defense Minister bellowed, "I think the bigger question we have to ask is how many more forces are we willing to commit to this conflict before we pursue some sort of terms to end it?"

The Dutch might have been the hardest hit during this war. More than half of their ground forces in North America had been either killed or captured. Their government was taking a beating in the public opinion for their continued support of this war against a once-strong ally. The Americans had also paid several of their major ports and industrial centers a visit, thoroughly bombing some of them beyond repair.

"I think we have come too far, invested too much, and lost too many soldiers not to see this through to victory," the Norwegian Minister of Defense replied. He paused for a moment before adding, "With the severe losses we've sustained in Canada, we may need to consider shifting our forces to the southern front. I'm not sure we're going to be able to supply and support our northern front, given the continued American blockade of Canada and their relentless attacks against their ports and airports."

The French Defense Minister angrily shouted, "So you would have us abandon our forces? That would condemn our northern armies to defeat!"

"Our northern armies have *already* been defeated. We just haven't accepted it yet," the Norwegian insisted. "We can't break through the blockade, and we can't use the civilian or military airports. How are we supposed to keep our forces supplied? The weather is turning to spring and the Americans have nearly pushed our forces back to Canada. If we adjust our efforts now and send our replacement forces to join the Chinese in the south, we may still be able to defeat Sachs."

Several of the defense ministers in the room nodded in agreement.

Shaking his head in disgust, the French Defense Minister barked, "Had the Germans not surrendered the bulk of their forces in Chicago, we wouldn't be in this situation."

"How stupid are you?" exclaimed the German Defense Minister. "Our forces got surrounded in a city of several million people. We had no way to resupply them and no means to break them out. When we told Sachs we'd turn the city into an American Stalingrad, they sent their stealth bombers to systematically destroy the German power grid." He paused for a moment as he angrily shook his head. "We didn't have a choice. The Americans were destroying three power plants a day, and they were going to continue to do so until we ordered our troops to surrender."

Johann held his hand up, trying to calm everyone down. He didn't need another blow-up in one of these meetings like what had happened with the Chinese several weeks ago.

"Gentlemen, we're all on the same side. Let's not forget that. Germany was backed into a corner. The division commander got outmaneuvered and was summarily trapped in the city. He also shouldn't have threatened to turn the city into a smoldering ruin—that forced the Americans to pursue a drastic response, which ultimately led to the division having to surrender. Now, let's move past that and figure out how we can support this growing militia force and the Chinese operation in the south."

"I think I have a few ideas on how we can speed some of that up," the Russian Defense Minister offered.

The rest of the meeting was spent discussing a path they hadn't fully embraced at the outset of the war but that looked more appealing by the day—the use of private military contractors.

****

April 8, 2021
Rio de Janeiro, Brazil
CIA Safe House

"I sure hope this works, Seth."

Smith was unusually nervous. The man was usually cool as a cucumber, but not today.

"It'll work. These guys have done this many times. We just need to be ready and at the marina when they tell us to be."

Breaking into the conversation, Ashley asked, "What about the rest of us? How are we going to get out of the country?"

Looking at Ashley, Smith explained, "Already been covered. The Assistant Secretary of State for Western Hemisphere Affairs is arriving today. She's going to be meeting with the Prime Minister tomorrow. While she's in the meeting, the Regional Security Officer from the embassy is going to drive you guys in their diplomatic vehicles to the Assistant Secretary's private plane. You'll all get on and when she's done with her meeting, she'll head back to the airport and join you. She'll fly you out under her diplomatic cover."

"That'll really work?" Ashley asked, a bit skeptical at the idea.

Smiling, Smith replied, "This isn't the first time we've done this, Ashley. Yes, it'll work."

"OK. Then how do you want us to approach the embassy?" she asked.

Smirking at the question, Smith replied, "Ashley, they aren't actively looking for you or anyone else yet. It's not like your cover's been blown. You guys will just walk up to the embassy, present yourself and the Marines will let you in. Coordinate with the legat if you're still concerned about it. He's your friend. He can help you if needed."

Blushing, Ashley quickly replied, "Sorry. I guess I'm just not used to all this cloak-and-dagger stuff. I got swept up in worrying about how you two are getting out of here with Lamy."

Seth sighed. "As long as our cover isn't blown or they catch wind that we have Lamy with us, we should be fine."

****

Mid-Atlantic

Commander Jett looked at the new orders with a bit of skepticism. *What are they up to?* he wondered.

"Change to our orders?" asked his XO as he entered the CIC.

Nodding, Jett handed him the paper.

"USS *Laboon* is to make best possible speed to coordinates…and wait fifty miles off the coast of Rio de Janeiro, Brazil," he read. "Hmm…sounds like secret squirrel stuff. But all the way down there?" the XO asked. He handed the orders back to the skipper.

"Ours is not to reason why but to do or die, XO. Get us turned around and let's make best possible speed to our new coordinates," the skipper ordered. In just a few moments, the ship was racing to try and be in position at the appointed time.

****

Norfolk, Virginia
Chambers Field

Lieutenant Calland watched several of his sailors help load two of their rigid inflatable boats into the back of an Air Force C-17 Globemaster. The giant cargo plane could fit both of their RIBs inside, along with the crew.

Walking up to SB1 Ross, Lieutenant Calland asked, "Is everything set? The boats are all rigged up and ready?"

SB1 Ross looked at the LT as if to say *we know what we're doing, sir*, but he held his tongue. He knew the man was just doing his job.

"Everything's all set, sir. We've even brought some extra gas with us in case we need to extend our range to link up with the *Laboon*."

Lieutenant Calland nodded. "Good job, Ross. Your team is on it as usual. Do you have any reservations about the pickup location?"

Ross shrugged. "Not really. This doesn't look like it's going to be a hot pickup, so we have that going for us. I think bringing extra fuel is going to give us more options in case the ground team has to make a last-minute change."

"OK. Just wanted to get your opinion on it." Calland paused for a second as a couple of the special warfare combatant-craft crewman yelled at one of the Air Force loadmasters over something.

Turning to look back at his men, Ross responded, "If you'll excuse me, sir, I need to go see what kind of trouble my guys are stirring up."

Smiling, the LT headed back into the office next to the hangar. As soon as he entered the room, someone told him, "This is going to be a tricky mission, sir."

Surprised, Calland turned to look at the senior chief who'd made the statement. "What makes you think that, Kavanaugh?"

"Twenty years experience doing this kind of crap."

"OK, Chief. What's your concern?"

"First, this is really short notice. We normally have a few weeks to plan a mission like this—not twenty-four hours. A lot could go wrong. Second, we have no air or naval support once we're inserted. Third, unlike most of our missions, they're sending six SEALs with us. That means they think this mission could go south, which is why they're beefing up our security and firepower. Fourth, I'm not sure if you're aware of what's going on in Brazil right now, but there's a nationwide manhunt to find the general director of the World Trade Organization, who also happens to be a Brazilian national. My money says he probably has something to do with this little last-minute mission that's been cooked up."

Lieutenant Calland paused for a moment to think about that. He suddenly felt a bit less sure about this mission than he had just a few minutes ago. Finally, he replied, "Those are good points, Chief. I don't have an answer to that other than to say we've been given a mission and it's our job to make sure it happens. Just stay on the men and let's work to make sure everything goes smoothly and we get our people home."

"Will do, sir. Just wanted to put some of that out there between you and me. That aside, if the ground team is able to get a boat and meet us at the pickup location, this mission should be a walk in the park."

****

Six hours later, the crew was loaded up in the back of the C-17, ready to get airborne. The boat crews and six SEALs accompanying them were ready to pick up this high-value package.

When the rear door to the aircraft closed, the pilots applied power to the engines as they raced down the runway. They had a long flight ahead of them—some seventeen hours when they included the midair refueling they'd need to make in addition to the surreptitious flight path around Brazil.

Lieutenant Calland heard from the pilot that they'd be changing their transponder to appear like they were a US Navy P-8 flying an antisubmarine patrol. It would give them a cover for flying around the land portions of Brazil and explain why they'd be flying below ten thousand feet from time to time. Once the aircraft had delivered them, it would turn around and link up with another refueler before it made the long trek back home.

Now it was just a matter of waiting until they reached the insertion point.

****

CIA Safe House

Rio de Janeiro, Brazil

Sitting low in the rear passenger seat of the SUV, Seth couldn't believe how quickly things had fallen apart. Shortly after Ashley Bonhauf and the other members of their team arrived at the embassy, someone had caught on to who they were and connected it with the disappearance of Mr. Lamy.

An unknown surveillance team had been camped outside the embassy, taking pictures of every person who came and went since Roberto Lamy had gone missing. Somehow, someway, they'd managed to piece together who Ashley was, as well as the other FBI agent, the two people from the NRO, and the DoD rep. Once they knew their identities, they looked at the aerial surveillance of the embassy and backtraced where Ashley and her crew had originated from. That eventually led them right back to the safe house and the urgent warning Smith had received to get Lamy the hell out of there.

Fortunately, Seth and Smith had already strapped Mr. Lamy into the third-row seat of the BMW X7 50i when the local station chief told them to get out. He'd said he had a source in the security service who tipped him off that a raid was being mounted to capture the people they suspected were holding Mr. Lamy. They had minutes to get out of the compound before it would be surrounded and they'd be trapped.

A local Agency guy sat in the driver's seat, wearing a sport jacket, expensive watch and black sunglasses. He sported a stylish modern haircut. He looked the part, like he belonged in this rich exclusive neighborhood driving this extremely expensive SUV.

Smith and Seth sat low in the back seats as their driver drove through the neighborhood toward an alternate safe house they'd try to hole up in until the rendezvous time.

As they drove, four police cars whipped past them with their lights on, but no sirens. Trailing behind those vehicles were several large trucks, presumably carrying a SWAT team.

Staying low, Seth shot Smith a nervous look. "That was close," he said.

"Yeah. Way too close. There's some serious assets being used to track us if they found the house this quick. I'm not even sure the alternate site is going to be safe."

Keeping his eyes on the road and his head straight, the driver suggested, "I think we should drive you guys to the marina and get you on the boat. Now that the authorities have a lead, they're going to really turn the screws on us.

They'll shut down the bridges and toll roads. It'll make it nearly impossible for us to drive back in the city if we leave."

Seth glanced at his watch, then looked up at Smith. "We could do that, but we're going to be more than three hours earlier than the original pickup time."

Smith stared for a moment at Mr. Lamy, who still had a piece of tape covering his mouth. "It's still going to be light out when we get to the marina," he said nervously. "He could be a problem."

"I can give him a sedative," Seth countered. "He'll be a lot more cooperative."

Sighing, Smith finally relented. "Take us to the marina. We'll try to make it work."

The driver nodded and immediately grabbed his phone.

"Antonio?" the driver asked. "Yeah, we're coming early. We need the boat fueled up and ready for us to leave in thirty minutes."

Meanwhile, Smith pulled out his encrypted smartphone and placed a call back to Camp Perry to inform General Lancaster of the situation. When he hung up, his expression was grim.

"Lancaster isn't sure if the Navy can pick us up ahead of schedule. Unfortunately, we're going to have to sit out in the water for several hours if we want to avoid being cornered at the marina."

****

Off the Coast of Brazil

The C-17 pilot gave control of the aircraft over to his copilot so he could take a quick bio break and head back into the bay to find the Navy lieutenant in charge of this mission. He spotted the only guy with bars on his collar and walked up to him.

"Sir, can I talk with you privately for a second?" he asked.

Lieutenant Calland got up and followed him toward the ladder that led to the flight deck. "There's been a slight change to our plans. Apparently, something's gone seriously wrong for the team on the ground and they need to exfil several hours ahead of schedule. We've got enough fuel to hold off on refueling while we increase speed to get you guys in position, so I wanted to let you know we'll probably be dropping you guys off close to two hours ahead of schedule."

Calland acknowledged the information and passed it along to his guys. "Also, listen up—there've been some updates in our rules of engagement since we've been in the air," he announced. "You are now authorized to use deadly force to protect the package, who just happens to be none other than Roberto Lamy, the Director-General of the World Trade Organization—that's right, the very man that the entire government of Brazil and half a dozen intelligence agencies are aggressively trying to find in Rio de Janeiro."

Several of the guys let out a soft whistle, realizing the firestorm they were about to jump into. If the guys on the ground had been compromised, then they might have to shoot their way out of the country.

****

Off the Coast of Brazil

As the captain of the USS *Laboon* sat in his chair in the CIC, an ensign walked up to him with a paper in hand. "Sir, we just received a flash message from NMCC," the young man announced.

Raising an eyebrow at the news, Commander Ross took the piece of paper and read it over.

This is not good, he thought.

He grabbed the phone that connected him to the bridge and spoke to the XO. "I need to speak to you right away," he insisted.

A few minutes later, his XO walked up to him. "I heard we got a hot message," he remarked.

Commander Ross nodded. "We did. There's been a change to our mission timeline and the rules of engagement. We need to get to the extraction point two hours early if possible. We've also been authorized to use deadly force to protect the package. Here, look at this," he said as he handed the XO the orders.

The XO silently read the contents of the papers for a moment. His left eyebrow rose. "Isn't this the guy they've been talking about on the news?" he asked. "Didn't our intelligence summary say the entire country was looking for him?"

"Yeah, it did," Ross confirmed. "I wasn't sure why it had been included in our intelligence update the other day, but I understand now. We're supposed to link up with the recovery team getting him out of the country and then escort him back to NAS Mayfair. From there, he'll be flown to Norfolk."

"This could be tricky if the Brazilians catch wind that he's being smuggled out by boat."

"Agreed. When we get to the exfil point, make sure our shooters are on deck in case they need to provide some small-arms cover. Also, tell the air boss to have his helos armed with Hellfires. Not sure we'll need them, but I'd rather have them loaded and ready than need them and not have them."

****

Rio de Janeiro, Brazil
Marina Da Gloria

"We're coming up to the marina," Rich told Seth and Smith. "I'm going to park us under those trees near the entrance. You guys stay here and get him ready while I go check on the boat."

He parked the vehicle, leaving them the ignition fob in case they needed it for some reason.

Seth opened his small black backpack and retrieved his leather pouch with his concoction of interrogation drugs. He pulled one of the syringes out and filled it up a quarter of the way with the happy drug. He then turned to face Mr. Roberto Lamy.

He snapped his fingers to get his attention. "The drug I'm about to give you is going to make you feel super relaxed. This isn't going to hurt you in the least. Now, when I take this tape off your mouth and give you this drug, we're going to walk with you to a boat that we'll take out to sea."

Roberto's eyes went wide when he heard the words *boat* and *sea*. He tried to say something but couldn't with the tape on. Seth reached over and pulled the tape off so he could say his piece.

"I've told you what I know. Please don't kill me." He started whimpering and crying, fearful of death.

Smith looked at Seth as if to say *shut him up already*.

Seth gently tapped Mr. Lamy on the cheek. "Look at me, Rob. We're not going to kill you. We're actually trying to save you. Those people you told us about, they're trying to kill you to shut you up. What we're going to do right now is move you to a boat and get you out to sea. We're going to link up with some folks who are going to get us out to a US destroyer. They'll escort us back to the US, where we can get you moved to a safe location. There you'll be able to testify under oath as to what's been going on," Seth explained. He hated wasting time like this and telling him so much, but he knew if he could convince Roberto that he needed to cooperate with them if he wanted to live, it would go a long way towards making this great escape go a lot smoother.

Roberto took a couple of deep breaths and stopped sobbing. "OK, I understand," he answered. "Just keep me alive. If you can keep me alive and get my wife out of the country like we agreed, I'll tell your court everything I told you."

Seth moved closer to Mr. Lamy and reached for the man's left arm, lifting the sleeve of his polo shirt and injecting the liquid into his deltoid muscle. A few seconds later, the drug went to work. His eyes glazed over a bit, and he became a lot more docile.

Just then, Rich approached the BMW. He opened the driver's-side door and climbed in.

"I just checked on the boat. It's ready. We got a full tank and we're all paid up. We probably have another twenty minutes until the sun's down. Do you want to sit tight here for a bit until it's dark or get going?"

Smith glanced over at Seth. "What do you think?" he asked.

"I think the sooner we get him on board and get out of the marina, the better. We have no idea if the Brazilians are going to lock down the marina or the harbor. For all we know, they could search every boat trying to leave Rio."

"True. I just hope James and Julia are able to play a convincing enough role back at the house to buy us some more time," Smith said nervously.

"They will. I saw Julia giving James goo-goo eyes the last couple of days. They'll make it look convincing. Their story will hold," Rich said in their defense.

Julia was a local asset that helped them manage the safe house, and James was one of the JSOC operators on Task Force Avenger. When they'd had to leave the safe house, Smith had thrown together a quick exfil plan—Julia and James would stay behind at the safe house and pretend to be fooling around in the pool when the police raided the place. They'd pretend to be a couple who had rented the place from a friend. Their job was to slow the police down and give Smith and Seth more time to get away. The ambassador would work on securing their freedom later.

"All right. Then let's get him out to the boat," Smith said, the decision made.

******

Rio de Janeiro, Brazil
CIA Safe House

Michael Dwyer, a man from an Irish security firm that had been hired in a roundabout way by Johann Behr to locate Mr. Roberto Lamy, walked up to the palatial estate, observing all of the activity carefully. The police were bringing out some electronic equipment, presumably to analyze evidence on site to see if they could find anything useful.

Upon entering the front room of the estate, he was drawn in by the rich decorations. The walls were inlaid with mahogany, and there was intricate crown molding along the ceiling. Walking further down the hallway, Dwyer entered an ornately adorned living room with large overstuffed leather couches and two leather chairs. The room opened into a kitchen that a master chef would be envious of. The eating area and kitchen flowed to a covered patio that led to an infinity pool, overlooking the city below and the ocean. Next to the pool was an oversized hot tub with a covered eight-seat bar. This was a home designed for entertaining large numbers of people—wealthy people.

After taking a moment to immerse himself in the beauty of this place, Dwyer walked out to the patio and headed toward the real reason he had been summoned to this villa.

Sitting under the patio near a couple of guards was a man who was probably in his early thirties. He was shirtless, sporting white board shorts. The man had shaggy blond hair and a couple of tattoos on his right arm and chest. Dwyer squinted. The man before him looked calm, relaxed even.

Michael Dwyer had seen this type of character before. He didn't believe for a second that the man was there on vacation with a hot local girl. *He's a killer*, he thought. He could tell as he looked in his eyes and observed his demeanor.

Dwyer turned to size up the woman next to him; she was very beautiful. Her skimpy Brazilian thong bikini was barely covering any part of her voluptuous figure. With her perfect olive complexion and long brown hair that ended midway down her back, she could have easily passed as a model. She was the perfect honeypot—the distraction. She also seemed unusually comfortable with what was going on around them, like she had expected it.

I need to rattle them, Dwyer thought.

Dwyer walked over to the lead police inspector and Cardoso, the Brazilian Intelligence Agency rep that was his chaperone. Leaning in and talking so only they could hear him, he asked, "What are my rules for questioning them?"

"I was told do whatever you deem necessary to get the location of Mr. Lamy," Cardoso replied quickly, before the inspector could say anything.

The police inspector's mouth hung open for a second. He looked like he was about to lodge a protest until Cardoso shook his head. The inspector then called out to his police officers, "Time to leave, men!" and they all exited the premises. Clearly he didn't want his officers to be a part of whatever was about to come next. If they didn't see it, he couldn't be held responsible for it.

This left the man and woman at the table, under guard by a couple of Dwyer's men. Dwyer took another look around the estate with Cardoso to try and get a sense of what this place was and who these two people might be.

The estate was large. In addition to the villa and expansive pool and outdoor bar area, there were three outbuildings. One seemed to be some sort of garage or oversized shed, and the second building looked like a large guesthouse of sorts. But it was the third building he found most odd. It appeared to house what must have been two cells or interrogation rooms. There was a small observation room that sat between the two rooms with a one-sided mirror, allowing whoever was inside to observe the interrogation.

What struck Dwyer as truly odd was the differences between these two rooms. One was staged to appear rather dingy and dilapidated while the other room looked very sterile, almost like some sort of surgical room or a midcentury modern office space. There was also a lot of computer equipment, cameras and other stuff that confirmed his suspicions. This was a CIA black site. It was also the most likely place the Americans had stashed Mr. Lamy.

Just outside the building, Cardoso pointed to a chimney that was partially obscured by a tree. A small amount of smoke was still wafting into the air there. Then, as they approached the tree, something seemed off.

It's fake. This isn't real, Dwyer realized. It looked like some of the other trees nearby, but the leaves were a very realistic plastic and fabric hybrid.

As they approached the artificial tree and base of the chimney, they discovered what appeared to be an industrial-grade incinerator. It was well hidden, designed not to stand out. Dwyer put his hand out; it was still hot. There was a low hum to the machine as it continued to run through its burn cycle. Someone had clearly thrown whatever they could into the device before they'd arrived to prevent them from finding something important.

Dwyer ran his hand along the side of the machine and eventually found the panel cover. Lifting it, he observed a timer, slowly counting down. There were three minutes and twenty-seven seconds left.

A few buttons identified the different burn cycles: paper, metals, and organic material. The metal button was the one currently glowing. The contents inside were probably electronics that the CIA wanted to get rid of. His eyes drifted back to the organic material button and lingered.

Damn. They probably dispose of bodies they want to make disappear in this thing, he thought. For half a second, he worried that Mr. Lamy might be inside. Then he realized he was far too valuable.

So where did they go with him? Dwyer wondered. *How are they going to get him out of the country?*

Dwyer walked away from the building at the end of the property and turned to face Cardoso. "Mr. Lamy was here," he asserted. "This place is clearly a CIA black site or safe house of sorts. No one has an interrogation building like that unless they're 'interviewing' people," he insisted, using air quotes around the word *interviewing*.

Cardoso nodded. "I agree. We've known the CIA was operating a site like this in our country, but we had no idea where."

"We need to find out who owns this place and who all works here. Then we need to track down who's been coming and going and when."

Dwyer walked back toward the kitchen with Cardoso. His intelligence analyst, a quasi-IT guy, was getting set up.

"Liam, pull up the drone feed we have of the area. See if you can find this place on it," he directed. "Then see if you can spot any vehicles coming or going from here anytime today."

Liam was an exceptional analyst and an IT savant. If anyone could find their needle in the haystack, it would be him.

When Dwyer's company had been contracted to find Mr. Lamy, one of the first things they had done was establish a handful of surveillance drones over the city. Now that they had a lead, they could rewind the video feed and get to work.

"How do you want to go about questioning them?" Cardoso asked, eyeing their two subjects.

"We'll question her," Dwyer insisted. "She's the weak one…but we'll use the big guy."

"You don't want to start with him?" Cardoso asked skeptically.

Dwyer shook his head. "No. He's a soldier. He's been trained to resist, and we don't have time to break him down. We need answers and we need them fast. She's our best bet."

Dwyer walked around the kitchen island and opened one of the drawers. He found a couple of steak knives and meat tenderizer. He gathered a collection and walked out to the patio.

"Bring the woman over here," he directed. "Tie the tough guy up over here. Restrain his arms, hands, feet, and neck to the chair."

Dwyer's men did as they were told. The man and woman were now sitting opposite each other, looking nervously at each other and wondering what was going to happen next.

Dwyer plopped down in a chair next to the man while keeping his eyes on the woman. "We know Roberto Lamy was here," he said confidently. "We've seen your interrogation room. It's obvious this is a CIA black site, so let's just dispense with your cover story. We're not buying it." His Irish accent seemed especially thick in that moment.

The woman looked a bit nervous when he finished speaking. Her eyes darted between the man Dwyer was sitting next to and the meat tenderizer and steak knives he had placed on the table.

Dwyer smiled. He had her attention.

"Julia, is it?" he asked.

She nodded but didn't say anything.

"We know Roberto Lamy was being held here. What I want to know is how long ago did he leave?" he queried, keeping his tone lighthearted for the moment.

She held her chin up and continued to say nothing.

"Hmm…OK. I get it. You don't want to talk to me," Dwyer responded. "You want to play it tough. Then here's what we're going to do. Each time you fail to answer one of my questions, I'm going to hurt your boyfriend here."

The woman looked at the man with panic in her eyes.

"Don't worry about me, Jules. Stay strong," the mystery man insisted. "They're just going to kill us as soon as you tell them anything."

Dwyer shook his head. "That's not necessarily true. If you cooperate, we'll let you live. If not, well…then this is going to be painful for you both."

He pulled a small pouch out of his cargo pants pocket. Unzipping it, he took out a small spray bottle. He removed the cap and turned to face the American, spraying one shot into the man's ear; his prisoner tried to struggle for a moment before his entire body went limp.

Dwyer returned his gaze back to the woman. "I gave your friend a paralytic drug. It essentially freezes his body for the next couple of hours. While he can't move, he will be able to feel, see, and hear everything."

"You're a sick, pathetic little man!" Julia shouted. Then she spat on him, anger burning in her eyes.

Moving with lightning speed, Dwyer slapped her hard across the face. Julia looked stunned. Then a tear briefly formed in the corner of her left eye. A red mark was already forming on her face.

"Let's try this again. When did Roberto Lamy leave the compound?" Dwyer asked, grit in his voice now.

"Go to hell!" Julia yelled.

"Have it your way."

Dwyer cut the zip tie restraints off the man's left arm and hand. He then placed his hand on the table. Grabbing the meat tenderizer, he hammered the man's pinky finger with one hard, vicious blow. The American grunted as he did his best to stifle a scream. He glared at Dwyer with hatred.

"How long ago did Mr. Lamy leave the compound?" Dwyer asked again. He could see the woman's lower lip quivering.

"I don't know."

"Aha. See? He *was* here. That wasn't so hard to admit," Dwyer said soothingly. "Now, let's dispense with this charade. Your poor American's finger is a bloody mess. How long ago did Mr. Lamy leave the compound?"

"Don't tell him anything," the American managed to muffle out.

Dwyer picked the tenderizer up and this time placed it over the man's left ring finger, right near the middle knuckle. He looked at Julia, who tried to turn away. One of the guards held her head and made her watch.

Bam.

The American let out a guttural scream this time as his next finger was shattered. His two broken fingers were now bleeding from the trauma.

"Julia, I could do this all day, but at some point, your poor friend here is going to run out of fingers. Then I'm going to have to start on his toes. By the time you finally tell me what I want to know, this poor sap won't have any fingers or toes left. You'll be leaving him with four bloody stumps and no toes to walk with. What kind of life are you condemning him to?"

Julia looked so conflicted. Tears ran down her face. Sweat poured down her forehead. Dwyer let her sit in the uncomfortable pause for a moment.

"They left around four p.m.," she finally blurted out.

The man with the battered fingers looked defeated.

Smiling, Dwyer said, "See? That wasn't so hard. James might still keep his fingers and toes. Now, where were they going?"

Julia now began to sob uncontrollably.

"She doesn't know that information. She was never told anything," the American muttered through gritted teeth. It was clear he was doing his best to fight against the throbbing pain.

Dwyer nodded his head. "OK. I can buy that. She's just local help, so you didn't include her in everything. But that means *you* know."

Dwyer got up and walked around the table. He nodded to one of his guards, who held Julia's head while he sprayed the paralytic drug in her ear. A few seconds later, her entire body went limp. Then he sat down next to her, picked up her hand, and placed it on the table.

He saw her eyes grow wide as saucers as she realized what he was about to do. Her American friend had been trained to withstand torture, but Dwyer could tell that she had not.

"No, no, no, please don't do this," she whimpered. "I just work here. I wasn't involved in anything. I don't know anything. Please, God, don't do this to me." Tears streamed down her face.

Dwyer coldly replied, "I'm not doing anything to you, love. Your friend here is. If he doesn't want to answer my questions, well, then you're going to have to learn how to get by without fingers or toes."

The American looked like he wanted to jump out of his chair and rip his head off, but he still couldn't move his body because of the drug.

"Now, we've established that Mr. Lamy was here. We've established that he left at four p.m., nearly ninety minutes ago. I think you've given your friends enough of a head start. So why don't you tell me where they are going so we don't have to mutilate poor Julia here?"

With hate burning in his eyes, the American tried to turn his head but couldn't because of the drug, so he tried to close his eyes.

"No, you don't get to escape watching this, James. Can I call you James?" Dwyer asked. He motioned for the guard behind him to hold the man's eyes open.

He reached down and grabbed the meat tenderizer. With one swift motion, he slammed it down on Julia's pinky finger, shattering the bone and pulverizing it.

Julia didn't even try to hold her emotions in check. She let out a terrible scream of pain and agony. With tears running down her face, she begged, "Please tell them what you know!" After several gasping sobs, she pleaded, "Don't leave me a mutilated mess."

"Damn you," the American muttered. He hung his head low. Finally, he admitted, "They took him to the marina. They're going to smuggle him out of the country by boat."

Smiling, Dwyer put his arm around Julia. "Now that's a keeper," he said, acid dripping through each word. "This guy must really have feelings for you, because he just gave up his friends and comrades for you. That's a big deal."

With his arm still around Julia, he looked back at the American. "What marina did they bring him to, James?"

"That part I don't know. I wasn't going to be part of that plan. My job was to burn the classified material and keep you guys occupied for as long as I could."

"How were you going to get out of the country?"

"I was going to present myself to the US embassy and they would fly me out on a diplomatic flight."

"Is that how the rest of your team is going to get out of the country?"

"There isn't a rest of the team. It was just me and the guys smuggling Lamy out of the marina," the American explained.

Dwyer shook his head. "James, I thought you and I had just reached an understanding," he said in a voice that sounded disappointed, almost hurt. "I ask you questions, you tell me the truth, and Julia here gets to keep her fingers. You just lied to me."

Before any of them could say anything, Dwyer had the meat tenderizer in his hand and smashed Julia's left ring finger. She screamed again before another wave of sobbing overtook her.

"For God's sake, stop hurting her!" the American shouted.

"God has nothing to do with it, James," Dwyer responded. "You do. Now, is that how the rest of your team is going to get out of the country?"

James didn't say anything, but he nodded.

"See? That wasn't so hard."

Dwyer nodded to Cardoso, who walked back into the house as he pulled his smartphone out. He was going to call his masters and alert them that the State Department official meeting with the Prime Minister was just a ruse to get the Americans out of the country. He would also pass along the information about the marina and explain that they could be trying to smuggle Mr. Lamy out that way as well. With any luck, they could close the marinas and stop any boats from leaving the harbor.

Returning his gaze to James, Dwyer asked, "So your American friends are going to put Mr. Lamy into a boat and then take him out to sea?" He shook his head. "I'm not buying it. Who's going to pick them up? How are they really getting him out of the country?"

Sensing the American's hesitation to answer the question, Dwyer grabbed the steak knife and proceeded to cut Julia's pinky finger off. She screamed and wailed and then summarily passed out from the pain.

"Enough! Stop hurting her. I've been telling you everything I know," the American shouted.

Dwyer launched himself out of his chair and leaned over the table, thrusting face within inches of the man before him. "*No*," he insisted. "You haven't. You don't seem to understand something, James. I don't care about you or Julia. I have no interest in killing either of you, but I'm here to find Roberto Lamy, and right now, you're hindering me from doing that. So, you either start cooperating and tell me what I need to know so I can reunite this man with his family, or I'm going to mutilate this beautiful woman."

As Dwyer sat back down, he glared at the American. "I'm not going to kill her, James. I'm going to hurt her, scar her, and make it so she'll never work a normal job again. Then I'm going to leave you alive so you can live with the knowledge of what you did to this woman. All you have to do to prevent that from happening is tell me how they are getting Lamy out of the country."

The American glared back at him for a moment before he finally complied. "There's a destroyer that's going to meet up with them at sea. *That's* how they're going to get him out of the country."

Dwyer smiled. "See? That wasn't so hard. Had you told me that a few minutes ago, Julia would still have her finger. Now, what did Mr. Lamy tell you guys?" he asked.

Dwyer couldn't help but notice James's demeanor suddenly change. A stupid grin spread across his face. "What did he tell us?" he repeated. "He told us everything…"

****

Rio de Janeiro, Brazil
Marina da Gloria

Seth and Smith helped Roberto walk over to the boat Rich had rented for them. Darkness had finally arrived, but the marina was well lit up. From an outside perspective, it would have looked like two people were helping a drunk friend walk to their boat. A couple walked by, and Rich muttered something in Portuguese about their friend who couldn't hold his liquor. Fortunately, no one had recognized Lamy yet, but Seth wasn't confident their luck would hold if they ran into any more people.

As they continued down the dock, they eventually came to a boat named *Lane Spirit Ferretti*, a beautiful thirty-eight-foot speedboat with a twin engine and cabin. They helped get Roberto to lie down while Rich got the engine started and cast off their lines.

"Check the bedroom," Rich said to Seth as he steered them out of the marina.

Seth made his way to the only bedroom on the boat, where he found a note that read *Under the bed*.

He squinted at the note before lifting the bed up and revealing a storage compartment. Seth smiled. He reached down and picked up an FN Minimi MK3 light machine gun, a short-barreled weapon that fired belt-fed 7.62mm rounds. Next to that weapon were three fifty-round pouches of ammo.

Smith walked into the room to join him. "Man, when you Agency guys want firepower, you don't mess around," Seth remarked jovially. "You just go for the best, don't you?"

Smith laughed. "Well, Seth, when money isn't a problem and you have no bureaucratic oversight, you'd be surprised what you can get done. Which one do you want?"

Seth looked back down and pointed to the SCAR-L assault rifle.

"Figured you'd leave me with this pig," Smith replied as Seth handed him the machine gun. Smith grabbed the six loaded thirty-round magazines and the chest rig and carried the ensemble to the cabin. He placed them where they would be out of sight of anyone that might casually pass their boat but ready to be used in a hurry should the need arise.

Ten minutes went by as they continued out of the marina and harbor. They eventually motored right past Ilha de Cotunduba, a small island that used to house a military fort to protect the harbor. As they moved past the island, Rich applied a lot more power to the engines. The boat picked up speed, putting more distance between themselves and the people trying to find them.

As they cleared the edge of the harbor and got past the breakwater, Seth turned around to look behind them. He saw the silhouette of something. A medium-sized ship was sailing toward them, like it was following them. Grabbing the night vision spotter scope from his bag, he looked at the vessel, trying to figure out if it was a threat. The first thing he noticed was a gun mounted to the front of it.

Damn. That doesn't look good.

Turning to find Smith, he called out for him to join him. As Smith walked up to him, he handed him the spotter scope. "Tell me what you see."

As he looked behind them, Smith swore under his breath. He marched up to the flying bridge and handed Rich the spotter scope. "Hey, what do you make of this?" he asked as he pointed to the dark object in the water behind them.

"Damn. It looks like a corvette. Do you think he's after us?" Rich asked.

"Hell if I know. I think you better get us moving a bit faster. I'm going to send another message to headquarters that we need help, right freaking now."

****

Off the Coast of Rio de Janeiro

"We're coming up on the drop zone," the crew chief called out to Lieutenant Calland.

The C-17 Globemaster started leveling out for its descent. The internal bay lights switched over to red. One of the other crew chiefs opened the rear hatch of the plane, allowing the cool air to swirl through the bay. Then they prepped the pallets with the rigid inflatable boats on them, making sure they were ready to be kicked out the back.

The Navy Special Warfare Operators ran through their equipment checks, making sure their parachutes and gear were prepared. Once the RIBs were cut loose, they'd have to run out of the aircraft after them—otherwise, they would end up being dropped a long way from their boats.

Calland looked at each of the boat chiefs who would manage the crews assigned to them. They both gave him a thumbs-up, letting him know they were ready. Then the SEALs brandished a thumbs-up too—they were locked and loaded.

Calland flashed the loadmaster his own thumbs-up—they were a go.

Seconds later, the drag chute for the first RIB was released and thrown out the back of the plane. It quickly caught and filled with air, pulling itself taut. The loadmaster then released the locks holding the pallet with the second RIB on it. It shot out the back swiftly. Within a second of starting their free fall, the three parachutes attached to the RIBs had opened, slowing the boats down on their trip to the water.

As soon as the RIBs cleared the cargo bay, both lines of operators ran after them as they launched themselves right out the back of the plane. They fell for a second or two into the darkness and then deployed their own chutes. It was a short drop since they were jumping from around five hundred feet. The operators did their best to angle themselves to land in the water as close as possible to the RIBs, which were now rising and falling in the waves.

When Lieutenant Calland got closer to the water, he readied himself mentally to release from his parachute. This was the one part of this job he hated—jumping at night, into a dark ocean.

Seeing the water quickly approaching, Calland hit his quick release and fell free of his parachute the remaining twenty or so feet to the dark water below. As his body crashed through the water, he felt himself plummeting into the wet abyss for a moment before his safety vest automatically inflated. The CO_2 cartridge did its job and filled his vest up with air, quickly shooting him and his equipment to the surface. When his face broke through the water, he took a big gasp of air.

Calland immediately looked around for the others and saw a few IR flashing strobe lights, indicating where they were. Then he spotted the flashing IR light that was higher above the water—the RIB. He swam to it. When he reached the edge, he climbed aboard. Seconds later, several others started climbing in.

The crew began the process of preparing for combat. Now that everyone was on board, they turned the strobe light off and started putting on their IBA and combat rigs. The radio and engines were flipped on. Next, they used the GPS to calculate their exact location and destination. They had roughly sixty miles to cover and not a lot of time to do it in.

Twenty minutes into their journey to extract a high-value package, Lieutenant Calland got an urgent call from the *Laboon*. After his conversation, he relayed the news over the crew's internal communication network.

"Listen up, guys. The Agency asset with the package is being pursued by a Brazilian Navy patrol boat. We've been instructed to make best possible speed to retrieve the package and then get the hell out of there. We've been given the green light to engage the patrol boat if necessary, but we are to protect the package at *all* costs. This mission is of foremost importance to the war effort."

The SEALs before him nodded and readied their weapons. One of the RIBs was armed with a Mark 19 40mm grenade gun and an M240 light machine gun mounted in the rear of the boat. The other RIB had the M2 .50-cal in the rear with the M240 mounted in the front. For small RIBs, they packed a lot of firepower. If they had to carry out a hot extraction, they should have more than enough firepower to make that happen.

They raced along at maximum speed to the rendezvous point. It wasn't long before Lieutenant Calland spotted something on the horizon—a bright searchlight was being aimed at something. They steered toward the light and continued toward it like a guiding beacon. Five minutes went by as they watched the Brazilian patrol boat close the distance on its target. It looked like the Agency assets were trying to outrun it in a rather large vessel that was designed more for play than speed.

As they approached the two boats, Calland saw the bow-mounted gun on the Brazilian boat fire a couple of times. The Agency boat slowed down, and someone on the patrol boat started issuing commands in Portuguese.

Pointing to the Brazilians, SB1 Ross yelled, "It looks like they're about to be overtaken and boarded!"

Lieutenant Calland took the night vision binoculars Ross was handing him and surveyed the scene.

Damn! That patrol boat may have damaged their engine, he realized. The Agency assets were dead in the water.

Depressing the talk button on his mic, Calland announced, "Prepare to attack that patrol boat. I'm going to announce our presence and let them know that this boat is under the protection of the US Navy. Be ready, guys!"

SB1 Ross shook his head, and Calland understood why. The whole point had been to do this operation as a stealth mission, but if they didn't announce themselves, it would certainly result in a shoot-out with the Brazilian Navy.

Lieutenant Calland grabbed the microphone handset. "Brazilian Navy, this is the United States Navy," he announced over the loudspeaker. "This civilian craft has US persons traveling on it and is under the protection of the US Navy. Stand down and don't attempt to board or you will be fired upon!"

Two of the Navy SEALs fired off flare guns into the night sky to illuminate the civilian speedboat they were racing toward and help them see what kind of patrol boat they were facing.

The Brazilian boat wasn't particularly large, but it did have a small cannon mounted on the front. There were also half a dozen or so Brazilian Marines near the rear of the vessel that were climbing into their own RIB to head over to the American speedboat.

Lieutenant Calland hailed them one more time as their RIBs pulled up closer to the Agency boat. Calland signaled for his RIB to stay moving, in case they needed to provide covering fire. The other US RIB moved closer to the disabled boat so the SEALs could extract the package.

The patrol boat responded, using their own PA system. "This is the Brazilian Navy. These are criminals who have kidnapped a Brazilian citizen. We are taking them into custody. Stand down or we will be forced to fire on you."

"We got more trouble, LT!" shouted SB1 Ross as he pointed toward the coast some twenty or so miles away. Off in the distance, at least two helicopters were flying toward them.

Calland grabbed for the radio that would connect him to the *Laboon*. He relayed what he saw and requested help ASAP. The officer on the other end replied that they already had their helo on the way to them, but it was still roughly fifty miles out. The *Laboon* itself was moving toward them at flank speed, but it was at least fifteen minutes out.

The other American RIB had reached the speedboat, and two of the SEALs took up position on the Agency boat and trained their weapons on the Brazilians. The other SEAL had gone inside the cabin to retrieve the package. A minute later, he emerged from the cabin with three men. Two of them appeared to be heavily armed, and the third man looked like he needed to be helped; he might have been injured.

The Brazilian Marines pulled up a couple dozen meters short of the American boat in their own RIB. The gunners on the US Navy RIB trained their weapons on them.

"Stand down!" shouted the Brazilians over the PA. "You must allow us to take these kidnappers into custody."

The SEALs ignored the warning and loaded Mr. Lamy into their RIB.

"We will not allow you to leave with the kidnap victim!" the Brazilian officer shouted, this time sounding more determined, even angry. The other Brazilian Marines aboard that boat began shouting at the Americans, but they kept their rifles at the low ready. The Brazilian Marines on the other vessel started shouting at the Americans but also kept their rifles at the low ready.

Then a Brazilian helicopter arrived on the scene. It shined its spotlight on the RIB with Mr. Lamy on it.

Damn, thought Calland. *There goes the last hope of keeping this mission low-profile.*

At this point, the two other men with him had climbed aboard and so had the SEALs. The Americans began to push off from the speedboat when one of the Brazilian Marines raised his rifle to fire at them. The SEALs moved their weapons to the Marine, illuminating him with their rifles' laser designators, but they held their fire. A tense couple of seconds passed as the boat driver of the American vessel applied some power and turned them away from the disabled speedboat.

Bang.

A shot rang out. A bright flash sparked on one of the two outboard engines on the American vessel—the engine had taken a direct hit. In that instant, the rear gunner opened fire on the Brazilian Marines closest to them. The driver of the boat did his best to get them out of there with their remaining good engine.

Ah, hell. Here we go, Calland thought.

"Light 'em up!" he shouted.

****

Seth held on for dear life as the driver of their RIB did his best to speed away from danger. Looking behind him, Seth saw the .50-cal gunner banging away at the helicopter that had just lit up the other RIB. Whoever was in that other boat had decided to turn around and attack the Brazilians head-on. They were doing their best to buy them some more time to get away into the darkness.

"Stop shooting!" called out the boat driver to the rear gunner.

The man stopped firing his weapon and the boat driver made a few course corrections to throw off anyone who might have thought they knew where they were going. Even with a single engine, the RIB was still fast.

But can we outrun the patrol boat? Seth asked himself.

A second later, the RIB behind them blew up.

As the flames and debris rained down on the water, the helicopter turned its light in a different direction as the pilot continued his search for them.

Off in the distance, Seth saw several more helicopters coming out to join in the search. There were also two more patrol boats racing to join the original one. While not yet in danger of sinking, the original Brazilian patrol boat had two small fires their crew was trying to put out. It had stopped speeding toward Seth's RIB—as a matter of fact, it appeared to be dead in the water.

"What do we do now?" Seth asked the driver.

"We continue to race to the *Laboon* and hope like hell those helicopters don't find us," the man replied.

Five minutes went by as the other helicopters searched the area. Two of them must have either spotted them or found them on their FLIR, because they were now heading right for them with their searchlights on.

One of the choppers finally managed to illuminate them with their beam. Both Brazilian boats immediately headed toward them at top speed.

One of the machine-gun operators aboard Seth's RIB started firing at the helicopter. Then the other one joined in. Together, they forced the helicopter to break off and fly to a higher altitude. The Ma Deuce gunner continued to fire some rounds to keep them from getting too close.

"Those two boats are gaining on us!" shouted one of the SEALs to the driver.

"Yeah, I see that. The *Laboon*'s helo is nearly to us. They're going to take care of the patrol boats," he replied.

Just then, two missiles streak through the night sky. They flew right past the Brazilian helicopters and slammed into the patrol boats, unleashing fiery explosions. While neither of the boats was in danger of sinking yet, they quickly discontinued their pursuit of the American RIB. The helicopters also turned away and headed back to the patrol boats.

Seth breathed a deep sigh of relief. For the next fifteen minutes, the American helo stayed with them as it escorted them to the *Laboon*. When they pulled up to the

American warship, a number of crewmen were standing by to help get them aboard and load the RIB up on the ship.

When Smith and Seth climbed aboard, they made sure Mr. Lamy was quickly taken down to sick bay so they could give him a good once-over to make sure he was OK.

Then Seth found a lieutenant who appeared to be in charge near the helicopter bay. He walked up to him. "I'm Lieutenant Colonel Mitchell from JSOC," he said. "I need to speak to the captain."

The lieutenant nodded and led him and Smith through the ship as they made their way to the CIC. Once they entered the ship's nerve center, the lieutenant led them over to the captain. "Sir, the Agency folks wanted to speak with you," he explained.

The captain stood up and guided them out the hatch so they could stand outside and talk away from prying ears.

"I'm Commander Jett. What the hell is going on?" he asked.

"I'm Lieutenant Colonel Mitchell, and this is Smith from the Agency. The man you helped us extract was Roberto Lamy, the Director-General of the World Trade Organization. He's provided us with some invaluable intelligence about who was behind the election rigging and the genesis of the UN peacekeeping mission. We have to get him back to the US at all costs, Captain."

The captain stared at the two of them for a second. He appeared to be trying to figure out if they were serious.

Smith cleared his throat. "Captain, there's a good chance the Brazilians may attack this ship to prevent us from bringing Mr. Lamy to the US. You need to be prepared to deal with whatever they may throw at you," he explained.

Commander Jett shook his head, then cursed a couple of times under his breath before he returned his attention to them. "All right. Thank you for cluing me in on what the hell is going on. All I'd been told is I needed to recover you guys and not allow anything to get in my way. Now I understand why. So, here's what I want you guys to do: go down to sick bay and check on your boy. Get some food, and one of my guys will get you put up in officer country. Let me worry about fighting the ship while you guys protect Mr. Lamy. If you need anything at all, please let me know."

When they returned into the CIC, the radar screen showed half a dozen planes forming up around Rio. They were still more than ninety miles away, but that could change rapidly.

The rest of the evening went by in a blur. The Brazilians appeared at a few points like they were going to attack the *Laboon*, but ultimately, they backed off. The Brazilian Navy hailed the American ship no less than a dozen times, directing them to stand down and return Mr. Lamy. Several Brazilian destroyers and frigates also assembled at a point further north of their position, and it appeared that they might try to intercept the *Laboon* as it headed back to the Caribbean.

For the next twenty-four hours, the *Laboon* played a game of cat and mouse as the captain sought to keep the ship out of reach of the Brazilian Navy's weapon systems. When a group of Brazilian aircraft flew within range of their surface-to-air missiles, the *Laboon* sent a few missiles in their direction, which forced their planes to break off their assault.

It was a tense situation until two more *Arleigh Burke* destroyers linked up with them near French Guiana. At that point, the naval task force was too strong to even consider attacking and the Brazilians called off the efforts. Once the *Laboon* got within helicopter range of Eugene F. Correia International Airport in Guyana, they flew Mr. Lamy to the small airport, where a Gulf Stream would ferry him back to the US. To make sure no attempt would be made to shoot down the plane carrying Mr. Lamy, the Navy sent an EA-18

Growler along with a pair of F-35s to escort them to US airspace.

With Mr. Lamy safely in the US, Seth hoped that the conspiracy to destroy America and foment an internal civil war would finally unravel.

Chapter Two
Final Gasp

San José de las Lajas, Cuba

Staff Sergeant Haverty of India Company, 3rd Battalion, 6th Marines, sat next to the lance corporal's computer as he controlled the small scout drone they were using. The Marine had a virtual reality headset on and a small controller in his right hand that looked something like a Wii game controller. He was moving the scout drone ahead of their position to locate the Russian unit that was currently the last major obstacle between them and moving on Havana.

A smile crept across Gunnery Sergeant Mann's face as he, too, watched the computer screen. He gently leaned down and directed the young Marine to go back to a specific set of houses near the highway.

"See if you can get a bit closer to that section, will you?" he asked.

The little drone headed closer to the cluster of homes. Although the lance corporal kept a little bit of distance so as not to have the drone discovered, they were able to spot several groups of Russian soldiers. Leaning against the wall of one of the buildings were three RPG launchers. A handful of rockets rested nearby.

"Someone write down the grid of this location or as close to it as we can get," Gunny Mann said, speaking to no one in particular.

They did a bit more scouting of the area and wrote down a few more sets of coordinates where the enemy was hiding. Their lieutenant walked up to them.

"How's it going?" he asked. They showed the LT a few of the pictures they had taken with the drone and the exact locations of the trouble in the city.

"Let's get an airstrike to hit those coordinates," the LT finally ordered.

Gunny Mann shook his head. "There are too many civilians in the nearby area to use an airstrike, sir," he explained. "We need to either hit them with the mortars or go root them out ourselves."

The LT frowned but then seemed to realize the gunny was right. "All right, then let's have the mortar platoon try and take them out. After that, we'll advance on foot and clear this last cluster of resistance."

Twenty minutes went by as the platoon and the rest of the company moved into position. They also positioned their LAVs nearby, so they'd be able to lay down some covering fire while the grunts got themselves into the town and did the dirty work of clearing the enemy out.

A day earlier, the battalion had tried to bypass the town using the main highway. However, they'd lost a few tanks when a series of antitank guided missiles had been launched at them from the town. Unless they wanted to conduct a serious detour, they needed to clear this town and then move on.

Staff Sergeant Haverty and his men approached the town from the southeast, moving swiftly through the wild grass and rows of trees and underbrush. They wanted to get close to the Russian soldiers when the LAVs made their move—that would be the signal for them to bum-rush the town.

They all kneeled beside a row of trees that placed them roughly two hundred meters away from the Russian positions. Their company commander radioed to the LAVs. "We're ready for you," he announced.

From somewhere behind them, Haverty heard the thumping sound of the mortar platoon firing their projectiles. He and his fellow Marines waited for the rounds to sail over their heads and explode on the Russians. When the first couple of mortars hit the enemy positions, Haverty heard the whine of the engines of the six LAVs along with clattering of the tracks of their two tanks as they all moved toward the outskirts of the town. A few moments later, he could hear the 25mm gunners open fire.

Gunny Mann stood up. "That's the signal!" he yelled. Mann leapt forward, fearless of the enemy soldiers, and sprinted towards the enemy positions. Everyone in the platoon followed him, running for their lives and trying to cover the wide-open space while they had cover from their armored vehicles.

Fifty meters from the edge of the nearest set of houses, a light machine gun opened fire on them. Bullets hit all around them, a few of them thudding into the chest, arms, and legs of some of the Marines. As Haverty continued charging forward, he heard several men call out for a corpsman.

Slamming himself against the side of a home, Staff Sergeant Haverty did everything in his power to regain control of his breathing. Looking back, he saw six of their Marines had been hit. Two corpsmen were doing their best to render first aid while taking heavy enemy fire.

"You four, with me," Haverty said as he edged forward to look around the side of the house he was using for cover. As he peered around the corner, the area looked clear at the moment. There were five more houses all in a line and a dirt road that connected this cluster of homes to the rest of the town.

Taking a deep breath, Haverty willed himself to leave the safety of this side of the house and head down the alley. The four other Marines with him followed his lead. Before he knew it, another ten Marines had followed them down the alleyway. When they reached the end of it, they spotted two homes filled with Russians who were shooting at them. They had part of India Company pinned down with a couple of their PKP machine guns.

Staff Sergeant Haverty turned to look back at the Marines behind him. Finally, he spotted what he was looking for. "I need you two guys with the SMAWs to hit those buildings with the machine guns in them," he ordered. Eyeing the rest of the Marines nearby, Haverty added, "When they fire their rockets, we need to rush those positions and clear them out."

Everyone nodded. The two guys with the SMAWs unstrapped them from their rucks and got ready to fire. A few moments later, they jumped out from behind their covered position, unleashed the rockets, and immediately jumped back behind the side of the house they were using for cover.

Boom, boom.

Without waiting a second longer, Haverty ran past the edge of the house they had been hiding behind and charged forward. He had his rifle at the ready as he scanned for threats. The other Marines behind him ran to catch up. Less than sixty seconds from the time the SMAWs had hit the building, Haverty and half a dozen other Marines were inside both houses. They shot a couple of Russian soldiers who'd survived the rocket attack and cleared the house. With no more machine-gun fire emanating from the two buildings, the rest of the company swarmed the town.

As the Marines continued to clear the edge of the town near the highway, several of the LAVs and tanks made their way there to provide direct fire support and help them clear the area faster. Meanwhile, the other two battalions of Marines that made up their ground force pushed past the town and continued their drive on Havana. The battle for Cuba was nearly over.

Chapter Three
Unraveled

White House
Washington, D.C.

The Attorney General sat at the table with the heads of the FBI, CIA, NSA, and Homeland Security, waiting to see how the President wanted to proceed. For the last couple of days, the FBI and CIA had been debriefing Roberto Lamy on what had transpired in the Swiss village of St. Moritz several years ago. Mr. Lamy had confirmed to them that a secret plan had been hatched at the meeting to replace the American President with one that was more amenable to the economic wishes of the EU, Russia, and China. Working through their American colleague, Lance Solomon, who was now the head of Goldman Sachs, this secret cabal had been introduced to Senator Marshall Tate.

The secretive Yale society Skull and Bones, which had selected candidates to promote in the past, had set their sights on another one of their members becoming president. Senator Marshall Tate had unknowingly been groomed for most of his life to become a presidential contender one day. However, given the political climate, the international cabal hadn't wanted to take the chance of him not winning, so they'd developed a plan to rig the results and stage a series of domestic terrorist attacks to distract the government and people from finding out about the postal worker scheme.

As video of some of the key interrogations was being played for the President, AG Malcolm Wright declared, "I believe we have enough evidence to convene a grand jury and get them to indict Senator Marshall Tate and his coconspirators. We just need to figure out how we should convey this information to members of Congress and the American people. They need to know what has transpired so we can put an end to this growing civil war and finally have a unified fight against the Chinese."

President Sachs let the statement hang there for a moment. "OK. Let's convene a grand jury and get the indictments," he finally said. "I think after that, we'll need to have Congress hold a public hearing. We have you and Director Polanski testify and explain everything. Show them the same videos and evidence you've shown me. Once you've done that, have Mr. Lamy come in and provide a statement of what his involvement was in this scheme and what his other coconspirators' parts were. We need him to provide some context to this scheme and how it all started."

The President paused. "I'd really like to get Lamy's take on what the heck the Chinese are doing. It would appear they have some ulterior motive beyond what was originally developed."

Leaning forward, the Chairman of the Joint Chiefs explained, "We're working that angle as we speak. Right now, it would appear the Chinese used the delay in launching their invasion to allow them more time to build up their ground force in Mexico. That said, it doesn't make any sense militarily why they would have waited to attack us until three weeks after the UN force in the north did. By the time they launched their invasion, we had largely defeated the bulk of the UN force."

The President's National Security Advisor chimed in. "I don't have proof of this, so this is just me shooting from the hip, but I think the Chinese held off on attacking us because, yes, they wanted to allow for more time—not just to build up their ground forces in Mexico but also to give our forces and the UN more time to bludgeon each other. We've largely destroyed the UN army at this point, and that army represents the bulk of the military combat power in Europe *and* Russia. Who stands to gain from these militaries being largely destroyed? The Chinese."

The room was silent for a moment as everyone digested what NSA Grey had just explained. President Sachs finally asked, "You think there's more to all of this than just rigging our election?"

"I definitely think there's more than we are currently seeing. From my vantage point, the Chinese saw what was happening in our country before the UN force attacked us, and they modified their plans. They saw the popular uprising against you wasn't forming fast enough to allow the UN to ride in and save the day. Once the UN launched their attack on Washington, D.C., the entire base of support Marshall Tate had been building up evaporated almost overnight. Even the media, which has obviously not been a supporter of yours, turned on Tate when they saw images of the Capitol building and Pentagon burning and foreign soldiers crossing into our country and occupying American cities."

CIA Director Marcus Ryerson spoke up. "Then how do you explain the Chinese cruise missile attack during the opening day of the war? They didn't hold back when they attacked us with those merchant raiders. They really hurt us bad with those."

"Simple," Grey responded. "They had the element of surprise on their side, and in that moment, they knew they could hurt both our Air Force and Navy if they unleashed their surprise attack. Had they waited even a day, most of those combat aircraft they blew up would have been shifted north to deal with the UN, and they would have lost the opportunity to hit them while they were still exposed on parking ramps on our southern bases. Furthermore, they knew the carrier strike groups would have been more alert to their actions the longer they waited. I think they saw the opportunity to hurt us and they took it."

"OK, but why nuke Guam, Arizona, and Oklahoma?" Ryerson countered. "Why hit Pine Gap and San Diego with an EMP, and why use nuclear weapons on our carrier strike groups? They had to know we'd retaliate, and last I checked, we've effectively wiped out probably close to eighty or ninety percent of their nuclear weapons capability."

"Director Ryerson, from a military standpoint this was an exceptional exchange for them," NSA Grey asserted. "Although they lost the bulk of their nuclear weapons and missiles, they didn't lose their ability to build more at a later date. Rather, they exchanged a weapons system they know they can't use in this war. They traded the bulk of their existing nuclear weapons capability for removing our naval and air base on Guam, destroying an entire carrier strike group, wiping out one of three army formations we had along the southern border, and crippling our only military force in California that could stop them. To add further insult to injury, that nuke that hit Oklahoma destroyed more than thirty percent of our military's munition reserves. We're also incredibly fortunate the missiles headed to Texas were intercepted, or there's a good likelihood the Chinese would've captured all of our border states and be in position to threaten the entire heartland of our country."

Trying to regain control of the meeting, Attorney General Wright exclaimed, "Mr. President, this is why it's important that we brief Congress and get Mr. Lamy to testify before them! The sooner we can expose this corrupt plot to our own people and the rest of the world, the sooner we'll be able to get control of things in our own country and focus our military's entire attention on the Chinese. I'm pretty confident that once the people of Europe learn they were lied to, they will turn on their leaders for leading them into this war. They will demand an end to the fighting. When that happens, we can have those forces moved to fight the Chinese."

The President nodded.

By the end of the meeting, there were plans to impanel a grand jury as soon as the next morning. Then they'd seek to get the indictments issued. After that, they'd brief both houses of Congress on what they had learned up to that point and bring to light the entire scheme to defraud the world.

Chapter Four
Consequences

Geneva, Switzerland
United Nations Headquarters

Johann Behr couldn't believe what he was reading. It didn't seem possible that the Brazilians had really let the Americans escape with Roberto. But the thought that continued to plague him the most was *How could Roberto have betrayed us like this?*

His secretary popped in the door. "Sir, General McKenzie is on the secured video teleconference," she announced.

Johann looked up at the beautiful woman before him and wondered where her loyalties were now—were they with him, or the German BND and her host nation government?

Hell, I'm German, too, he realized. Although since taking charge of the UN, he had viewed himself more as a global citizen.

"Thank you," he finally said. Then Johann got up and walked over to the side conference room with the video monitors.

When he entered the room, he saw his military commander. "General McKenzie, how are things going on your end?" Johann asked, hoping the alliance wasn't unraveling on him just yet.

McKenzie shook his head. "Not good, sir. It pains me to report this, but several of my coalition partners have just informed me that their nations have ordered them home. They are either to extract themselves from the fighting or surrender in place to the Americans."

Johann sat in stunned silence for a moment. *This is happening faster than I thought it would.*

"Which members are throwing in the towel?" he grumbled.

"Let's just say it'd be easier to list who's still willing to fight," General McKenzie replied with a grunt. "Right now, I'm left with the Norwegians, Russians, French, and Germans—but to be honest, I don't know that they'll all be willing to fight much longer."

Johann sighed. "General McKenzie, if your own government is withdrawing from the peacekeeping mission, how does that impact our operations—in particular, *you*?"

"I've made my bed, sir. I'm in this for the long haul," McKenzie answered. "However, the Canadian government is now demanding that the UN take its military force and leave. They are no longer going to provide any support to us. In fact, they've ordered the entire Canadian Armed Forces to surrender to the Americans. A handful of key military officers and I have refused that order."

Johann shook his head in dismay. He couldn't believe things were imploding around him so hastily. The Americans had made a very public spectacle of Roberto's testimony before their legislature. Roberto had sung like a canary begging not to be eaten by a cat. He'd revealed their entire plan: how they were going to rig the election, who they had selected to be their candidate, and how they had planned on returning America and the world to the old order of being managed and ruled by the global oligarchy.

The calls for Johann's own resignation were ringing louder and louder each day. He wasn't even sure how long he'd be able to remain the UN Secretary-General if something didn't change soon.

Johann looked back at his general, who sat dutifully awaiting his next set of orders. "What are our options at this point, General?" he asked. "Can the mission continue?"

McKenzie quietly took a minute to think. Finally, he replied, "Sir, I'm a soldier. If you tell me to fight on, I'll do my best to fight on." He paused for a second, as if contemplating whether he should say something else or not.

"Sir, as the commander of the UN peacekeeping force, I'm also responsible for tens of thousands of lives. I'd be derelict in my duties if I didn't make you aware of some critical problems we're going to face. Will you allow me the opportunity to explain?"

Johann could see the conflicting feelings in the man's face, even through the computer screen. He nodded for him to go ahead.

"My force is demoralized," McKenzie admitted. "Several of my key military groups have withdrawn from the war or are in the process of surrendering. This is going to have the effect of a rapidly spreading contagion on my remaining force. I can direct what forces I have to continue to fight, but we can't win. We'll be sacrificing the lives of our men and women in a war they have no hope of winning. Many of my soldiers know that, which means they won't fight as hard as they would have when they thought victory was on the horizon. As more of them learn of Mr. Lamy's betrayal and what he told the world, many more will either surrender outright, or they'll refuse to fight. My advice as your military commander, sir, is that you order us to surrender. Save the lives of our remaining forces so they can return home to see their families."

Lifting his head up to look at the ceiling, Johann let out a long sigh. Returning his gaze to his general, he asked, "What about the insurgency that is finally taking root in America? The American militia forces are getting themselves mobilized and seizing power. What will happen to them if we just up and surrender?"

General McKenzie nodded. "I have thought about that as well, sir," he replied. "Our surrender will hurt them, but it won't cripple them. What I propose is we hand over the vast majority of our weapons and munitions to these militia forces. They can use the equipment we'll be abandoning to carry on the fight without us. America is a big country—we've started the fire of civil war, and we've fanned the flames for nearly six months—now we can sit back and let it burn the country to the ground."

"What about China? They've effectively pulled out of our peacekeeping mission, but they're continuing to fight. How will this impact them?"

McKenzie shrugged his shoulders. "Frankly, I don't care. We're in this situation because the Chinese were apparently playing their own angle in this war. I'm not sure what kind of plans or agenda they had, but it certainly wasn't to coordinate and work with us. They essentially left us high and dry right when we needed them the most. At this point, I hope the Americans crush them."

"I think you're right about them having an ulterior agenda," Johann agreed. He popped the knuckles on his right hand. "But what exactly is going to happen to President Tate?"

"I have no idea," McKenzie replied, shrugging. "I know my government has withdrawn their support of him. They've also said he's not welcome in Canada—no one from his exiled government is. I hear they've set up a temporary capital in Boston." He sighed again. "Sir, I recommend we surrender. Do you accept my recommendation?"

Johann sat back in his chair for a moment. *I wonder if this is how Hitler felt at the end*, he thought. He asked himself how he could have ended up in the same position as that monster; it felt as though the Russians were at the gates of Berlin and the Allies were closing in from the west. *But Jonathan Sachs is the monster...he's Hitler, not me.*

"General, part of me obviously wants you to fight on, but I also recognize that we can't win and that course of action will only cost us more lives. So, here's what I want you to do. Before you surrender your force, do your best to distribute your weapons and what munitions and supplies you have to the Civil Defense Forces. If we can't carry on the fight, then I want to make sure we do whatever we can to make sure they can."

The two of them talked for another five minutes before Johann ended the call. He wasn't sure if or when he'd be able to speak with General McKenzie again, but he was eternally grateful for all he'd done.

Johann got up from his chair and made his way to his office in the next room, where his secretary, Monika, stood waiting for him, a grim expression on her face. "Sir, I just received a message from President Gloria Uribe," Monika announced. "She said to inform you that an emergency meeting of the General Assembly was being called. Tomorrow morning, she's going to introduce a resolution to have the UN peacekeeping mission disbanded and have you removed from office."

Johann felt like he had been punched in the gut, and then he started to feel a little lightheaded. Seeing him get a little wobbly, Monika moved over to help him. She gently guided him over to the couch, where he sat down.

"Let me get you a drink, sir," she said. She made her way over to his desk, and grabbed the glass decanter of Zwetchgenwasse, Johann's favorite plum brandy. She filled one of the matching glass tumblers, then turned around to hand it to him. When she handed him the drink, she leaned over a bit, and Johann couldn't help but notice her cleavage practically spilling out above the neckline of her V-neck sweater. He forced himself to look up to her eyeline, and she smiled at him coyly.

"Here you go, sir. Drink this," she said. "It'll help settle your stomach. We'll sort this out together."

My God, is she really flirting with me? Johann thought, wondering if his hidden desires were about to be fulfilled. He nodded and reached for the tumbler.

"Thank you, Monika. I'm a bit of a sucker for a good plum brandy," he told her, as if she hadn't already heard this story. "My grandfather used to drink this when he had to think on a tough decision." He sighed again, thinking of all that was transpiring around him. His entire world was falling apart—well, everything except his drink, and his gorgeous secretary, who was sitting next to him.

"Oh my, where are my manners?" he asked aloud. "Please, pour yourself one and let's talk, Monika."

She smiled again. "That's very nice of you, sir. Let me do that."

She stood up and walked back to his desk.

Oh my God, is she shaking her hips more than usual? Johann wondered. His face flushed.

As she sat down to pour herself a glass, he lifted the tumbler to his lips and downed the whole glass. She laughed. "How about I just bring the whole decanter and we finish it off?" she asked flirtatiously.

Johann chuckled. "That sounds grea—"

Before he could finish his sentence, a strange expression washed over his face. Then the tumbler fell from his hands and he sank down into the couch.

****

Monika walked over to him. She sat down next to him as his eyes drifted off into space, his expression almost blank. She pulled out the eyedropper she'd used in her boss's drink, then squeezed a few more drops into his now-open mouth.

She walked back to the desk, where she'd left the decanter and tumbler. She filled a glass and downed it, then filled it up again and downed a second drink.

She could see Johann's lips turning blue, which was followed by a gurgling sound as he struggled to breathe. She knew his body was overdosing on the Fentanyl she had given him. It wouldn't be long until he was dead.

Johann seemed to have a seizure, and then his body went stiff. She waited a minute, then checked his pulse. Once she confirmed that he was gone, she sent a message back to her handlers in Berlin. They had been adamant that he had to be taken out.

The Chancellor had felt betrayed by Johann, and her own party was ready to crucify her. She needed to extricate Germany from this disastrous war and do her best to eat humble pie. The best way to do that was to place all the blame on the UN Secretary-General, who, according to the news reports that went out later that day, had chosen to take his own life rather than be arrested.

Chapter Five
Q Project

Naval Air Station Coronado
San Diego, California

General Han Lei sat in an office that used to be occupied by a US naval admiral, before he'd abandoned it along with the rest of the naval bases. Across the table from him was Vice Admiral Hu Zhanshu, who appeared to be reveling in the fact that he was sitting in a most coveted US naval position. The office had a beautiful view of the surrounding area. With the windows opened, a nice breeze wafted in, carrying the smell of saltwater air, and they could hear the sounds of the seagulls outside.

General Han, however, was not impressed. He preferred a more utilitarian office, one that was devoid of such niceties. He believed these luxuries made a person soft. Unlike some of his fellow generals and admirals, he didn't view command as a job that should come with special perks and privileges but as one that should be held in high regard and should focus on how one could better serve the state.

Han looked pointedly at his naval counterpart. "Admiral, is your force going to be able to keep the sea lanes open so my army can stay supplied?" he asked.

Hu narrowed his eyes at the possible accusation. "China has suffered greatly to ensure your army will be able to stay supplied," he answered icily. "I have every advantage to make sure it stays supplied and will be able to achieve victory. The bigger question I have is how will your forces hold up against the Americans now that the UN peacekeeping mission in the north has collapsed?"

General Han smiled at the probing inquiry. He had anticipated this line of questioning and had come prepared. "I would not be worried about the Americans, Admiral," he explained. "Our plan to have the Europeans and Americans bash each other's armies apart has worked better than we thought possible. Their Army and Air Force has been seriously degraded. They've also lost a significant portion of their industrial capability in the Midwest and the Northeast. It is going to take them time to rebuild—time they do not have."

Han crossed his arms. "When will the 16th, 26th, and 39th Army Groups arrive?" he grilled.

Han needed those other three army groups *now*. He had achieved a temporary breakthrough here in California, but his offensive in Arizona and New Mexico had stalled. The Americans had also halted his attack in Texas. Those three additional army groups would more than double his current force and should be enough for him to finish capturing California, Oregon, Arizona, and Nevada. If he ended up losing Texas and New Mexico but was able to hold on to those other four states, that would still constitute a win in his eyes, and in President Chen's.

"The 16th will arrive in San Diego tomorrow; the 26th, and 39th will arrive in LA over the next five days," Admiral Hu answered. "Are you sure you want me to still use the ports in LA? It's going to put my ships pretty close to the front lines."

"Are you afraid your sailors might have to see some combat, Admiral?" Han asked, a mischievous smile curling on the left side of his face.

Hu shook his head. "No. I'm afraid I may lose some valuable ships that I can't afford to lose because *you* want to place them in unneeded danger," he responded.

"I'm having you offload them in LA because it puts them closer to the front lines so I can throw them into the battle sooner," General Han explained, speaking as if instructing a schoolchild. "The Marines and a small contingent of California Army National Guardsman are all that stands between us capturing the entire lower half of California. I have a finite amount of time to secure the state before the Americans are able to reposition their forces from the East Coast to the West Coast. *That's* why I'm having you offload them in LA." Han was annoyed at the questioning of his tactics.

"Let's change topics, General," said Admiral Hu. "Once my ships are offloaded in LA, do you want the cargo and troop ships to be brought back down here to San Diego to be loaded up with people for the Q program?"

Han nodded. Although he didn't particularly care for this part of the job, he was doing his part for the Q program just as his political officer had demanded. "Yes. We have thirty thousand women who need to be transported back to China for the program."

"Why not fly them back?" Admiral Hu asked. "It would take less time and then my men wouldn't be distracted by having them on our ships."

General Han sighed at the question. He'd asked it himself many times before. "If I could fly them all out, I would. As it stands, I've only been allocated ten aircraft a day for the program. That means I can only transport 3,230 people a day. As it stands, the political officers are identifying nearly twice that number a day. I can't support and feed that many extra mouths and my army at the same time."

Admiral Hu shook his head. Leaning forward and speaking in a hushed tone, he said, "This entire program is wrong, Han. When word gets out about what's going on, it's not only going to turn the locals on us, it's going to turn the rest of the world against us as well."

General Han also leaned in before he replied, "I have no say in this, Admiral. The political officers have been given the task by the President and he's directed me to cooperate. The sad part is, this is only the first step. Phase Two is supposed to start next month."

Hu's left eyebrow rose. "Phase Two? What's that?"

Han felt his expression sour. "Something I nearly lost my command over when I voiced my opposition," he answered. "Let's just say this won't bode well for any of us if we don't win this war, Admiral."

Admiral Hu snorted at the vague response. "Then we best not lose, General Han."

※ ※ ※ ※ ※ ※ ※

Mandeville Canyon Park
Just North of Los Angeles

Staff Sergeant Mack of Regimental Combat Team One held his hand up and closed his fist into a ball. Then he lowered his arm. Turning briefly to look behind him, he saw his squad had taken a knee, ready for whatever may come their way.

Returning his gaze to his front, Mack breathed slowly and quietly as he tried to use all of his senses to hear for something in front of him. A few seconds ago, he thought he'd heard a tree branch snap. His eyes darted from one clump of trees and bushes to another as he looked for the source of the noise. It was now nearly summer, and the forest had returned to life; branches were full of leaves and flowers, and animals roamed the woods.

Was it just a squirrel? he wondered.

Lieutenant Ray Ambrose stealthily moved up a few feet behind him. In a barely audible whisper, he asked, "What did you hear?"

Mack turned slightly to his side. "I think I heard a twig or branch break," he murmured.

The lieutenant turned around to face the rest of the squad and used a hand signal to tell them to spread out to form a line formation abreast of him and Mack. The squad spread out quietly, rifles at the ready, waiting for a possible ambush.

The squad behind them also spread out as they moved forward to reinforce First Squad. Third and Fourth Squads would stay in reserve until they figured out what they were facing in the dark.

It was nearly dawn. They had sent a drone over the area the day before and it had found a sizable element of Chinese infantry moving into Mandeville Park, just west of the Los Angeles neighborhoods of Westwood and Brentwood Heights. The PLA was aggressively expanding their perimeter beyond the city of LA as they sought to press home their numerical advantage over the Marines and the lone California Army National Guard brigade fighting alongside them.

While the sun hadn't crested the ridgeline and canyon yet, the predawn light was slowly pushing away the darkness. However, as he glanced up, Staff Sergeant Mack could still make out some of the brighter stars in the sky above. Then he noticed that the birds had stopped chirping their morning melody.

When did they stop singing? he wondered. He didn't know how long they'd been silent, and he asked himself how badly he was messing up.

Seconds after he noticed the absence of the birds, Sergeant Mack spotted a flare as it shot up through the trees.

It burst open and began its slow journey back to the ground, illuminating the forest around them in an eerie artificial light that danced off the trees and vegetation. Then Mack heard the unmistakable loud shriek of a PLA officer's whistle, ordering his soldiers forward.

"Contact front!" he screamed instinctively. Then he fired into a group of bushes where he saw movement.

Mack fired off maybe three or four rounds before he dove behind a depression next to the hiking trail. A string of tracer rounds and bullets hit right where he'd just been, ripping apart several smaller trees and bushes.

Lieutenant Ambrose, who had also dived for cover only in the opposite direction, shouted into his radio headset. "Move forward!" he directed the rest of the platoon. "We need your help!"

Mack looked to his left and right. His squad reacted just as they had trained. They were all seeking out good cover, firing a handful of shots, and then moving to a different position.

Explosions started happening around their positions as several mortar rounds landed nearby, throwing more shrapnel into the air and shredding some of the new undergrowth.

"I'm hit. Corpsman, corpsman!" shouted one of his Marines.

"First squad, grenades!" Staff Sergeant Mack yelled.

Crump, crump, crump.

A handful of grenades exploded to their front as his squad followed his orders and lobbed them at the wall of enemy soldiers charging towards them.

"Alpha Team, advance. Bravo Team, covering fire!" Mack screamed. He always felt that the best way out of an ambush was to charge it—it was the last thing an enemy would be expecting.

Sergeant Mack jumped up, raised his rifle to his shoulder and dashed forward with his Alpha Team. As he raced through the trees, he spotted several Chinese soldiers who appeared completely surprised and caught off guard by the Marines' sudden charge and their screams like men possessed.

Before Bravo Team even had a chance to charge forward, Mack and Alpha Team were already on top of the PLA soldiers. Sergeant Mack spotted a group of four Chinese soldiers manning a Type 80 general-purpose machine gun, or MG for short. Leveling his rifle at the shocked soldiers, Mack fired relentlessly at them until he saw all four of them dead or incapacitated.

Jumping down into the enemy fighting position, he dropped his empty magazine, grabbed a fresh mag and slapped it in place. Then he hit the bolt release, ramming a fresh round into the chamber.

Looking around him, Mack realized he was the only Marine on this side of the enemy line. He heard a lot of shouting, screaming, and shooting coming from further down the line, and Bravo Team was advancing forward now.

Mack ran toward the loudest screaming and yelling and found one of his Marines rolling on the ground, fighting with a Chinese soldier who was doing his best to drive his knife into the young Marine's chest.

Mack swooped in and kicked the Chinese soldier in the side of ribs and followed that blow with a swift kick to the side of his head. The blunt force caused the enemy soldier to lose his grip on his Marine, and his brother-in-arms was able to throw the Chinese soldier off himself. Once the enemy soldier was clear of his Marine, Mack fired three rounds into the man's chest and face, killing him.

The Marine looked simultaneously relieved that Mack had helped him out and terrified that he'd nearly died. "Grab your rifle and keep shooting!" Mack shouted.

Sergeant Mack heard the sound of another machine gun banging away at the rest of their platoon, and more cries for a corpsman. He advanced along the top of the ridgeline and spotted a cluster of four PLA soldiers: two of them were manning another MG while a third guy fired his QBZ-95 assault rifle. The fourth guy was talking on a radio, presumably calling either for reinforcements or for some artillery or air support. In either case, he needed to be taken out.

Mack dropped down to a knee as he settled in against the side of a tree. He aimed at the officer first and fired several rounds at the man. He saw one of his rounds hit the side of the man's face and the radio receiver he'd been using. The soldier grabbed at his face with his one good hand as he fell to the ground.

The PLA soldier nearest him tried to render first aid, pulling a bandage from the wounded officer's body armor. Mack almost felt bad about killing the soldier trying to render aid, but he swiftly pushed those thoughts out of his mind. He fired a single round, hitting the man in the head and killing him instantly.

Mack was only about thirty or forty meters away now. He zeroed in on the two soldiers firing the MG next. After flicking the switch from semi to three-round burst, Mack squeezed the trigger. He adjusted his aim a fraction of a degree to the left and squeezed the trigger again. With just two pulls of his trigger, he'd taken out a second machine-gun position.

"Don't shoot! We're coming up on your six," shouted one of the Marines from Bravo Team.

Mack turned around as several Marines ran past him and took up positions on the top of the ridgeline. The lieutenant came up next, with Second Squad right behind him. Some of the Marines had already turned the enemy machine gun around to face the Chinese lines as they prepared it for the next attack.

Lieutenant Ambrose walked up to him as more Marines ran past them to secure the enemy position. "Staff Sergeant, that was outstanding. I don't think I've ever seen a counter-ambush like that. Now, see if you can get the rest of your squad fanned out along that position over there," he said as he pointed to a position higher up on a nearby hill. That location would provide them with a better vantage point to help cover the ridgeline.

Sergeant Mack nodded. He couldn't help but think that the PLA soldiers should have positioned one of the MG teams up there. It would have been a lot harder taking this ridgeline had they done it.

Mack called out to his squad and pointed at the hilltop. They trudged up toward that position, trading shots with a few PLA soldiers along the way as the enemy had fallen back to another position further away. As they continued to move, Mack heard the sound of incoming artillery.

Boom, boom, boom.

Trees, dirt, and rocks were thrown into the air as the 152mm artillery rounds began to land along the ridgeline his squad had just captured. For the next five minutes, the area was hit with a variety of artillery and mortar rounds.

Mack kept pushing his squad to get to the top of the hill and get their own light machine guns set up on the high ground. He knew that when the barrage lifted, another wave of infantry would charge forward and attempt to throw them back.

As soon as they crested the hill, Mack's eyes went wide as saucers. Thirty or forty PLA soldiers were there, attempting to capture the position for themselves so they could lay waste to the Marines below.

Bringing his rifle to his shoulder, Mack fired practically point-blank into the attackers. One of the soldiers following behind him opened fire with his M240, cutting down enemy soldiers like a scythe. Another Marine opened fire with his M27 while a third Marine fired his M203 grenade gun into a cluster of Chinese soldiers.

Bullets flew right back at the Marines as the enemy reacted to the sudden appearance of the eleven leathernecks that had beaten them to the top of the hill.

Mack felt something hit him in the chest, and it threw him against a tree trunk behind him. Before he could move, he felt several more jackhammers slam into his chest. His knees went weak and he slumped down on the tree until he was sitting against it, stunned and unsure of what had just happened to him. All he knew for certain was that his lungs were on fire, screaming for oxygen.

Finally, his body stopped spasming and he was able to take a deep breath. He gasped for air a second time when his brain snapped him out of whatever fog he had been in.

I have to keep firing at the enemy or I'm dead, he determined.

Reaching down, Mack grabbed the rifle, which he'd involuntarily dropped. He noticed the bolt was in the open position, letting him know his magazine was empty. Before he could replace the mag, several Chinese soldiers saw him slumped against a tree and started running right toward him. Sergeant Mack reached down and grabbed for his Sig Sauer. Pulling the pistol up, he fired several rounds at the enemy soldiers charging towards him.

To his surprise, he dropped both attackers with his first couple of shots. Holstering his pistol, he slapped another magazine in his rifle and got up. He moved to the opposite side of the crest of the hill, where several of his Marines were shooting at enemy soldiers. Another group of Chinese soldiers was doing their best to fire and cover each other as they advanced.

"Take those guys out!" Mack yelled to the nearby Marines.

Several of them turned their machine gun on the attackers, and the M240 gunner fired several controlled bursts at the enemy soldiers.

"Incoming!" screamed a nearby Marine. The young man grabbed the live grenade that had just landed right next to him and lobbed it right back at the enemy.

Bang.

Unfortunately, the grenade went off in the air maybe a few feet away from the Marine, blowing most of the man's arm off and hitting his face and upper torso with shrapnel. The young man fell backwards, screaming in agony and pain as he saw the now-bloody stump of what was left of his arm. With each heartbeat, a large volume of blood shot out of his body.

Mack ran to the young Marine and placed his rifle down next to him as he grabbed for the guy's tourniquet. He placed it a couple inches above the wound. Looking the man in the eye, he explained, "This is going to hurt, but I have to tie this bleeder off or you're going to die."

The young man just nodded through gritted teeth.

Mack tightened the tourniquet on his arm. As he tied it tighter, the man let out a few shouts in pain, but eventually, Mack saw the blood stop squirting out with each heartbeat. Once it was sufficiently tight, Mack helped to prop the Marine up against a tree and handed him his Sig Sauer. "Keep shooting at anyone that you think you can hit. Don't lose my pistol, or I'll have your ass. Here's my other two mags in case you need them."

With nothing more he could do for the wounded man, Sergeant Mack grabbed his rifle and went back to killing the attackers that were trying to dislodge them from the top of the hill.

Mack looked to his right. Two of his Marines lay on the ground, motionless. Three others were still shooting at the enemy. To his left, he saw another Marine sprawled on the ground and two more who appeared to be wounded but were doing their best to stay in the fight. Behind them, the PLA was still hammering the ridgeline with artillery fire.

One by one, the ground and air burst artillery rounds tore the area apart.

How the hell are any of our guys going to survive this maelstrom? Mack wondered.

He grabbed one of his grenades, pulled the pin and threw it down into a group of three enemy soldiers who were trying to sneak around a boulder to get a better angle at his men.

Crump.

The grenade went off, killing one of the soldiers and wounding the other two. Aiming his rifle at them, Mack fired several rounds, killing the wounded men before they could return fire at him.

Then he heard the best sound he'd heard all day—artillery landing amongst the attackers. Half a dozen friendly 105mm rounds landed amongst the enemy positions, wiping out the next wave of Chinese soldiers.

"Staff Sergeant Mack, if you can hear me, you need to get your squad off that hill," Lieutenant Ambrose said over the radio. "The company is being pulled back before we're outflanked and cut off. Do you hear me, Mack?"

Hitting his talk button on his platoon radio, Mack responded, "Copy that, sir. I've got several wounded guys up here. Please provide us with some covering fire while we get down from here."

Mack called out to his remaining squad members to pull back. Several of them grabbed their wounded comrades as they began the trek down the hill. Seeing that he was still pretty close to the Marine who had lost his arm, Mack crept back over to him.

"I'm going to help you get out of here. We've been ordered to pull out," he announced. Sergeant Mack reached down and picked the Marine up, throwing the man's good arm over his shoulder. He did his best to help guide them down the hill to the rest of their platoon.

For the next twenty minutes, friendly artillery pounded the enemy position with high-explosive rounds intermixed with smoke rounds to help cover their retreat. It took them nearly an hour to get out of the area.

When they finally came back to the parking lot where several of their vehicles were located, Mack was able to get a corpsman to take a look at his wounded Marine. In less than a minute, the injured young man had been given a shot of morphine and an IV had been started for him. Sergeant Mack and the corpsman loaded him into one of the vehicles. Two other wounded comrades were placed into vehicles by the rest of the squad, and then they all climbed aboard to ferry them back to the next defensive position.

Over the next couple of days, the area would be fought over relentlessly as the Chinese sought to break out of the Los Angeles basin. The outcome was certainly not clear-cut.

****

Nogales, Arizona

Chad looked at the two guys before him with a scrutinizing stare. The man on the right, José, looked to be in his early twenties; the other guy, Todd, had to be pushing fifty. They'd both been recommended to him by a trusted friend in the Arizona Minutemen group.

After motioning for the two of them to take a seat, Chad asked, "Why do you want to fight the Chinese?"

The younger guy, José, had a quizzical look on his face. He glanced at the older man to his left. "Is that some sort of trick question?"

"Just answer the question, José," Chad responded. He put his pen down and crossed his arms, waiting for his answer.

A smirk spread across the young man's face. "To kill Chinese. Why else?"

Chad smiled at the answer, then reached for his glass of water. He took a couple of sips before placing it back on the table.

"OK, José. Thank you for the honest answer," he replied. Then he turned to Todd. "Same question—why do you want to fight the Chinese?"

Without missing a beat, Todd explained, "Because they killed my wife and son. Now my daughter is missing, and I'm afraid they may have either snatched her or killed her, too."

He's the one I'm going to train, Chad thought.

"Thank you both for your honesty. Unfortunately, I can only train one of you," Chad said. "So, I have one last question. Have either of you ever worked with explosives or had any electrical training?"

José answered first. "I used to work at Best Buy. I was part of the Geek Squad, so I used to do a lot of work on computers and things like that."

Todd added, "I did a stint in the Rangers during the first Gulf War. Got out in '95 as a staff sergeant. Before the war, I worked as an OTR driver for a trucking company here in Arizona. I know just about every road there is around here."

"What did you do in the Rangers?" asked Chad, his interest piqued.

"I was a demo guy."

Furrowing his brow, Chad followed up. "Why did you leave the Army and become a truck driver? Nothing personal, just trying to figure you out."

"I saw a few too many of my buddies get killed in Somalia. I liked driving trucks, and frankly, it's not bad pay. Especially when your wife is pretty frugal with money."

"Fair enough," Chad replied. "OK, I wasn't expecting to have two guys who I could reasonably train. So, here's what I'm gonna do—I'm gonna make an exception and train you both. From now on, you guys belong to me. You go where I tell you to go, and you do what I tell you to do. Over the next couple of weeks, I'm going to teach you guys how to build IEDs. I'm going to teach you how to build car bombs, and more importantly, I'm going to teach you how to not get caught.

"You both come highly recommended, so don't screw that up by proving them wrong. And don't make me look bad for choosing you," Chad explained. He wanted them to understand that people had put their reputations on the line for them and he was taking a risk by agreeing to teach them his trade.

José raised his hand to ask a question.

"Go ahead, José."

"If you don't mind me asking, what's *your* background? How'd you learn how to build IEDs?"

Chad pulled his Grunt Style T-shirt sleeve up and showed them a tattoo on his right upper arm. It was a tattoo of a Trident and a frog's bones. "Twenty years in the Teams."

José quickly replied, "I was told you worked for Customs and Border Patrol."

Chad laughed. "I did. I retired from the Navy four years ago. I double-dip now. I'm working on that second government pension."

For the rest of the day, Chad's plan of action was mostly to get to know his new apprentices. He needed to make sure his gut reaction was correct and that these two men would have the right mindset to handle something so deadly. One day this war would end, and bomb making wasn't exactly a marketable skill. He wanted to make sure he wasn't training future Unabombers or something.

The following morning, Chad woke them both up at 0600 hours. They did some morning PT, which consisted of fifty reps of front-back-goes. They each did five pushups, then rolled over to their back, did thirty seconds of flutter kicks, then jumped to their feet and held their hands out in front of them and ran in place for thirty seconds. Then they repeated the entire process forty-nine more times. Chad didn't have a lot of space to exercise, so he had to make do.

When the Chinese had nuked Yuma at the outset of the war, they'd wiped out the bulk of the military force in the state. With that gaping power vacuum and a heavy cruise missile attack that devastated Fort Huachuca and David-Monthan Air Force Base, there wasn't much left to slow the Chinese advance. They captured most of Arizona in one fell swoop. However, some of the remaining US Army units stayed behind enemy lines to work with the local militia units.

When it became clear they'd be running an insurgency operation, the local militia and Army units opted to take advantage of all the vacant mines around the Huachuca Mountains. Chad, being one of the most important guys in the militia for his bomb-making skills, had been given a nice cave to work his magic. It was a deep cave, deeper than Chad had explored or cared to explore for the time being.

He'd set up his little bomb-making shop probably about half a mile inside—far enough away that he could detect if someone entered the cave and was approaching him, but close enough that it wouldn't take him half a day to get out. The only drawback to working this deep in a cave was carrying the IED materials in and out, along with food and other resources he needed.

He was fortunate, though—toward the end of the little space he'd taken over was an opening in the mountain above. It wasn't very big, maybe two inches wide, but it provided some natural light, and when it rained, which wasn't often, it allowed water in. But more importantly, it created a steady flow of air that moved through the cave.

Chad didn't live alone. Four militiamen had been assigned to protect him, and he already had one bomb-making assistant before he'd added these two new trainees. Once in a blue moon, his cave would be used as a shelter for one of the militia's roving patrols, but they mostly stayed near the entrance.

Once Chad exited the cave, he had to hike about a quarter mile down a trail until he came to a dirt road that cut through the mountain. It was an improvised road the Customs and Border Patrol would use from time to time when they needed to travel through parts of the mountain range during their patrols. That was where Chad's assistant would bring the IEDs to be picked up by one of the militia units. They'd pick them up in a truck, by horseback, or sometimes on foot, and take them to either Nogales or Sierra Vista, where they'd use them against the Chinese. So far, they'd done quite a bit to make things as difficult for the Chinese soldiers as possible.

****

"OK, for today's lesson, I'm going to teach you how to make a heat-sensitive infrared triggering device," Chad announced as he held one up in his hand. "Can you tell me what's different about a heat-sensitive IR device versus just a regular IR device?"

"The sensitive one allows you to set what temperature you want it to activate at," Todd replied confidently.

Chad smiled. "Exactly. You see, José, we don't want this bad boy to go off when it detects a person walking by, or even when a car or truck drives past it. We want it to go off when one of those heavy diesel engines the PLA use in their vehicles passes by. This is essentially the same thing that was done to us in Iraq and Afghanistan. A car or truck could drive past it all day long, but once the IR sensor detected something that went above its temperature threshold, it went off. That's what I'm going to teach you guys to build. Once we crank out a couple dozen of them, I'll show you how we construct the actual IEDs," Chad concluded before beginning his demonstration.

If all went well, then in two or three weeks, he'd have two more competent bomb-making assistants. In a couple of months, he'd graduate these guys and they'd go start another bomb-making cell somewhere else in the occupied zones. Until then, they'd help him crank our IEDs as fast as they safely could. Interstate 19 was about to get a lot more dangerous for the Chinese and their allies.

Chapter Six
Occupation

Washington, D.C.

White House

"So, what's the plan with the UN and Canada?" asked National Security Advisor Robert Grey.

General Tibbets, who was joining them via video teleconference from the Cheyenne Mountain complex, responded. "Right now, we're moving the 10th Mountain Division, the 38th Infantry Division, and the 28th Infantry Division into the country to establish an occupation force for the time being. That'll essentially give us roughly thirty-four thousand soldiers to administer the occupation and continue to handle the insurgency and military forces that have not surrendered. Two of the divisions are National Guard divisions, but they've performed quite well, so I'm confident they'll be able to handle the job. I've also tasked 5th Special Forces Group and SEAL Team One and Two to support them as well.

"This entire force is responsible for the occupation of Canada and the continued hunting down of the remaining CDF forces in our northern states that tried to defect. I've largely given the task of dealing with the CDF to Special Forces. They have the intelligence, aerial support, and capability to move around the area rapidly. But before I conclude, I'd also like to recommend that we set up a plan to bring in some private military contractors. My soldiers can't be everywhere, and frankly, I'd rather leave the security work to the PMCs while we shift my soldiers down to face the Chinese."

The President thought about that for a moment. He wasn't particularly fond of using contractors like that, but he also understood the need to get more of their divisions shifted south to deal with the Chinese.

Finally, Sachs nodded in agreement. "OK, General. You may start incorporating some security contractors, but I want them kept on a tight leash and given proper oversight. Now, what's going on out west in Washington State, Oregon and the western part of Canada?"

"The divisions and Special Forces I mentioned earlier will also cover the western Canadian provinces as well," Tibbets responded. "This is why I proposed bringing in some security contractors. Right now, we've divided Canada up into Occupation Zone East and Occupation Zone West, or as we're now calling them, OZE or OZW. Once we get the security situation sorted with the right PMCs, I'll shift two of the three divisions out of Canada south to join our forces fighting the Chinese. We'll still leave the same number of Special Forces up there, but it'll free up more than twenty thousand soldiers to fight the PLA."

Patty Hogan from DHS added, "I'd also like to say that, at this point, we've now grown the Federal Protective Service to a little over one hundred eight thousand personnel. We've moved around thirty thousand of them to the upper East Coast and another fifteen thousand to Illinois and Wisconsin. I believe the FPS can now help out with more of the occupation duties if you'd like to incorporate them into your planning, General Tibbets."

"Yes. What about that, General?" asked NSA Grey. "We've spent four full months training this force to essentially handle the law enforcement functions where the local and state governments haven't been able to act independently. Can we perhaps use them to help with the occupation in Canada to help free up more of your men?"

General Tibbets shook his head and frowned. "No, I don't think it would be wise to bring them into Canada," he answered emphatically. "Director Hogan's group is a US law enforcement entity. We should focus on using them in the liberated zones to continue to help put down the CDF groups wherever we find them. I'd feel much more comfortable with the PMCs working with our soldiers on foreign soil."

The President leaned forward in his chair. "That makes good sense to me, General," he responded. "We'll stick with the PMCs in Canada and have Patty's group stay focused in the US. Now, let's move on to the situation with China and the Pacific. What are we doing to regain control of the Pacific and cut off their supply lines?"

The Chief of Naval Operations, Admiral Chester Smith, took his cue. "Now that the conflict in Canada and the Atlantic is largely over with, we're shifting a large percentage of our naval forces from the Atlantic to the Pacific. Even now, our Atlantic subs are transiting under the northern polar caps and will enter the Pacific near Alaska. Then they'll travel closer to Chinese waters and interdict some of their convoys as they head to the US. I'm also ordering several additional submarines to join our flotilla around Hawaii. The island's still a mess since the EMP and cruise missile attack—I want to make sure the Chinese don't get the idea that they can just waltz in there and try and take it from us."

"What about our two carriers in the Atlantic: how do you plan on using them?" asked the President.

"I'm going to have them take up positions in the Gulf," Admiral Smith explained. "They'll be able to provide support to our ground units fighting in Texas."

"When will we be ready to recapture Panama and the Canal?" asked Sachs, eager to get that passageway reopened to the US.

The admiral grimaced at the question. "I'm afraid not for some time, Mr. President. We're in the process of moving the 29th Infantry Division to join our Marine force on Cuba so they can finish liberating the island. Next, they'll move to liberate the Dominican Republic and Puerto Rico. That force will then continue to conduct a series of island-hopping campaigns to take back the rest of the Caribbean. Our plan right now is to hold off on liberating Panama until we're ready to launch Operation Odin."

General Markus held a hand up. "We can talk more about Odin later if you want, Mr. President, but not everyone in this room has been cleared to know about that yet."

The President quickly nodded. "Thank you, General." He took a swig of coffee, then continued. "Someone please tell me what is going on in Texas, New Mexico, and Arizona."

General Tibbets spoke up. "We're holding the enemy in Texas, but just barely. I'll be frank—if it wasn't for thousands of Texas militia members carrying out all sorts of hit-and-run attacks on the PLA, I think the Chinese might have captured the bulk of the state. As it is, the Chinese have had to keep a substantial number of troops stationed in a lot of the cities and surrounding areas to try and tamp down the insurgent attacks. It's a bloody mess all across Texas right now.

"As to New Mexico, we just don't have enough forces to keep them from capturing more of the state. We're looking to try and hold them along the Colorado border. Arizona is pretty much the same. The nuclear attack on Yuma wiped out an armor brigade that would have held the enemy at bay. That hit really hurt us. The PLA has pushed our remaining forces to just south of Phoenix. Again, if it wasn't for the local militia units joining in, I think we would have lost the state a few weeks ago. As it stands, we're doing our best to evacuate our assets out of Luke Air Force Base and establish a new line of defense near Fort Mohave. This'll allow us to block them from breaking out into Nevada and threatening our assets in that area."

The President blew some air out his lips forcefully, as if trying to create a smoke ring. "Are we going to be able to keep the Chinese contained in the Southern states? I'm concerned that if they break out, there might not be anything to stop them for hundreds of miles."

"We're doing our best, Mr. President," General Markus insisted. "That's all the more reason we need as much of the security work in Canada handed off to some competent PMCs so we can shift at least two of those divisions down to the Arizona and New Mexico fronts."

"How many soldiers and Marines are we graduating from training each week?" Sachs inquired.

General Markus took the question. "The Marines are graduating two thousand new Marines a week. It'd be more, but they've lost all of their training facilities on the West Coast, so they're only able to rely on the East Coast facilities for training. The Army, on the other hand, is cranking out eight thousand soldiers a week. That number will double in four weeks and it'll double again eight weeks after that. By the end of the summer, we'll be graduating thirty-two thousand soldiers a week. That'll be our max we can effectively train—"

"Pending we don't lose Fort Sill in Oklahoma or Fort Polk in Louisiana," NSA Grey interrupted to add.

The President sat there for a moment, digesting what everyone had just said. He wanted to make sure he had all the angles covered. Finally, he requested, "OK, before I clear the room out so we can talk further about Operation Odin, what have we heard from the UN and Britain?"

Secretary Haley Kagel jumped in. "I've spoken with the President of the UN General Assembly. They have disbanded the UN peacekeeping force and ordered all units currently in North America to cooperate with us and fully surrender. They are also stopping any material or advisory support to the CDF militias per the terms of surrender. The general assembly leader also asked that we try to work out some sort of end to the war with the member states that participated in the UN peacekeeping operation. They want to put this ugly disaster behind them and allow everyone to return to normal."

Sachs shook his head angrily. "I'll bet they *do* want to put an end to their ugly disaster. The problem is, we're still stuck having to deal with the death, destruction, and invasion by the Chinese that have happened as a result of their actions. I'll be damned if we're going to let them get off the hook that easily. I want you to work out some sort of reparations they'll have to fork over to help us recover from this foolish endeavor." The President paused for a second before adding, "I really wish Johann Behr hadn't taken his life. I would have loved to have tried him here in the US.

What about the other coconspirators Mr. Lamy told us about? Have we made any progress on their extraditions?"

Secretary Kagel explained, "I know the Attorney General isn't here, but I will do my best to handle that question," she replied as she opened her binder. "The Norwegians and Germans are thus far unwilling to hand over their people who were involved in this conspiracy. Their argument is that we still have the death penalty and they know there is a good likelihood that if their citizens are convicted in a court of law for their actions, they'd be put to death."

Sachs slammed his hand down hard on the table, startling everyone present. "How many people have they killed because of this plan they hatched to steal our election? Our country was viciously attacked and then invaded. Hell, it was German and Russian Special Forces that nearly killed me on the first day of the war. No, you tell them they have forty-eight hours to hand them over to us or we'll resume attacking their nations."

Secretary Kagel nodded sheepishly. "I'll convey the message," she muttered, clearly a bit unhappy about the task she'd just been assigned. Then she straightened herself up in her chair. "If I may, I do have good news on some other fronts," she offered. "The Italians, Spanish, French,

Russians, and the Netherlands have agreed to our terms of surrender. They ask that we not launch any attacks against their countries."

NSA Grey's left eyebrow rose in surprise. "They agreed to the punitive financial terms we gave them as well?" he asked. The US had requested that each of the member states that had participated in this military action compensate the families of the civilians who had been killed during the war with one million dollars per family member killed. The US also billed the group of nations collectively for one trillion dollars in damages. While that amount wouldn't cover the damage that had been caused, it would go a long way toward helping to rebuild what had been destroyed, and President Sachs had made it abundantly clear that if the offending countries didn't pony up the money, the US would begin systematically attacking their infrastructure.

Secretary Kagel lifted her chin as she proudly reported, "They are working out the details, but I think an agreement is going to be achieved. Obviously, some of the richer nations—in particular Norway, France, and Germany—are going to pay the bulk of this fine we're levying. But I don't think they have a choice."

"OK. What about our allies?" asked the President. "Are any of them going to join our cause and help us out?"

He desperately wanted the former NATO members to step up and come to their defense.

"Yes. Poland and Romania have agreed to send ground and air forces to the US. To my surprise, the British are also going to come to our aid. They're still facing some domestic blowback from the Labour Party, whose members convinced Great Britain to join the UN force at the outset of the war, but now that they knew it was a farce, they're coming to our aid."

Sachs let out an audible sigh of relief. "I'll call the PM later to personally thank him for his support. We need to get their forces moved to the US ASAP. The Chinese are tearing us up out west." The President paused for a moment. "OK, people, I think this has gotten us up to speed for the moment. I'm going to ask that we clear the room so I can talk with Secretary Howell, Admiral Smith, General Markus, and NSA Grey. We'll resume our war updates in two days during our next NSC meeting."

****

With only the five of them in the Situation Room, NSA Grey asked, "Can you bring us up to speed on Operation Odin? Where does it stand and when will it be ready?"

The President leaned forward in his chair, his crossed arms resting on the table as he waited for the status update of this extremely secretive program. It had been sucking an immense amount of resources out of other critical projects, and he wasn't convinced it was worth it yet.

Admiral Smith sighed. "It's been a rough go of it. We've been hindered at nearly every possible turn in getting the two ships ready for operations. At this point, even with twenty-four-hour shifts working seven days a week, I think we may be delayed by as much as three or four months from starting the ships' sea trials, let alone sending them into combat."

Sachs shook his head in frustration. "That's not acceptable, Admiral. What's been the holdup? Do I need to get personally involved in unscrewing this situation?"

Clearly frustrated, the admiral explained, "With all the damage sustained by our naval ships in the Pacific and Atlantic, we've lost more than half of our work crews to get those other ships repaired and turned back around. We've also had to divert nearly all of our nuclear technicians and reactor fuel to getting our two carriers in their maintenance cycle rushed out of their repairs and ready for combat. The *Nimitz* also sustained a lot more damage to the internal workings of the ship than we had first thought when we seized control of her again. We're just spread too thin without enough resources to make it all happen, sir."

"How do we increase your workforce so you can meet the increase demand?" asked NSA Grey, a look of concern on his face.

Admiral Smith huffed some air threw his teeth. "I could use an executive order waiving some of the security requirements; we're bogged down with on hiring new people. Specifically, we need to hire twelve thousand electricians, nine thousand plumbers, fifteen thousand welders, and some six thousand HVAC personnel. I also need another eighteen thousand computer programmers to help us sort through the software codes, along with roughly three hundred nuclear technicians to get the reactors up and running. We're currently offering twice what they can make on the outside plus unlimited overtime. These positions are essentially paying between $160,000 to as much as $450,000 a year with overtime. We've been inundated with more than two hundred thousand applications, but the problem is getting them security clearances to work on the project."

"OK, so how can I fix that problem for you?" the President asked, eager to get the project back on track by any and all means necessary.

"If you can waive the rule that says they have to have a finalized clearance in order to start work, this would allow me to hire everyone we need next week. We can give them an interim Top-Secret clearance so they can start while their clearance is adjudicated. Until it's finalized, I'd have them work on our damaged destroyers, cruisers, and carriers, and shift our currently cleared workforce to Operation Odin. That would help me out immensely and still keep that project under wraps."

The President turned to look at Secretary Howell. "Have the DoD draft up whatever I need to sign to make this happen. We need this enacted tomorrow, the day after by the latest. It's imperative that we get this project back on schedule."

Howell nodded his head and scribbled some notes down on his paper.

"Are these new weapon systems still going to work?" Grey asked skeptically.

Admiral Smith nodded. "Yes. We've been testing them at the Aberdeen proving grounds and the Nevada test range for the past two years since we initiated the program. We've finally got the direct energy weapons working the way they're supposed to, and the railgun technology has been proven to be effective now for more than a decade."

NSA Grey crossed his arms. "So those media reports about the various weapon systems not working properly or still being years away are selective leaks?" he asked.

"Exactly. Now that we've solved the problem of safely constructing micro-nuclear reactors, we've finally got a power generation source that can make these weapons a reality. We're going to use one of the reactors to power the day-to-day ship functions while the other three reactors are going to be used solely to power and operate the weapons platforms. This was the last missing link in solving our power consumption problem for a weapons platform on a ship like this."

The President snickered. "Oh, how Congress is going to crow when they find out what we've done to the hulls of the two new *Ford*-class carriers."

"I don't think they'll give us much trouble once they find out how effective these weapons are going to be," replied NSA Grey. "We just have to make sure we don't lose the entire West Coast and Hawaii to the Chinese before they're able to make a difference."

****

Milwaukee, Wisconsin
General Mitchell International Airport

Captain Regan found Colonel Beasley standing with his hands on his hips, looking at the long line of heavy equipment transporters that were loading the brigade's tanks up for the long trip down to Colorado Springs.

Sensing someone had walked up near him, Colonel Beasley turned to find Captain Regan. Beasley smiled and pointed to three C-17 Globemasters down near the Air National Guard side of the base. "You see those planes?" he asked.

"I do. Is that our ride to Colorado?" Regan asked, hoping they weren't going to have to drive down with their tanks. The crews were exhausted from months of fighting. They needed some time to recover.

"Yes," Colonel Beasley confirmed. "The Stryker vehicles and other nontracked vehicles will provide security—not that we need it. Seems like the entire UN force has collapsed at this point. But anyway, all the tank crews and the nonessential folks that don't need to drive down with the JLTVs and Strykers will fly down with us.

"When we land in Colorado. I'm giving everyone two weeks R&R. You all have earned it, and I know many of you would like to see your families. We've been deployed for nearly six months now. The men need a break. I was told by the division CO that our brigade will receive new replacements and equipment during that two-week hiatus. He wants us fresh and ready to go back into battle when we return from R&R."

Regan smiled at the thought of being able to go back home for a couple of weeks. "That's the best news I've heard all day, sir," he replied. "When do we load up, and how soon after we land do we start our R&R?"

"Once we land at Colorado Springs International Airport, we'll drive over to Fort Carson. They've set up some temporary lodging facilities for all the units transiting to the base. From what I've been told, there are a handful of nearby hotels that are also being used for the officers and senior NCOs to help ease the overcrowding. The next day, Major General Walker is going to hold an awards ceremony for our brigade at Pershing Field. So that we're not all standing around baking in the sun, he's going to hold several of them throughout the day—each one will be broken down by battalions."

Regan raised an eyebrow at the thought of a daylong dog-and-pony show right before two weeks of R&R.

Seeing his reaction, Colonel Beasley smirked. "Don't worry, Captain. I know what you're thinking, and this won't be a whole-day affair. He's only sticking around to award Silver Stars and above. The battalion commanders will finish awarding the rest of the medals. As soon as they are concluded, everyone's being cut loose to start their R&R.

"Each soldier will be given a round-trip ticket to wherever their home of record is to go see their families. It's going to be imperative that you company COs make sure your people know when they have to return by. We won't have a lot of time after everyone gets back to get our units ready to deploy. They're gearing up for a major offensive to try and block the Chinese from breaking out of New Mexico. It's imperative that we keep them bottled up in the Southwest. If they break out into the heartland of the country, they could tear us apart."

Regan nodded. That was a major concern among a lot of his own soldiers. The Chinese had been bulldozing through the Americans. At some point, they needed to stop them.

Returning his thoughts to the awards ceremony, Captain Regan cleared his throat. "If I can, sir, I put a lot of guys in for Purple Hearts and Bronze Stars with Lieutenant Colonel Short—"

Colonel Beasley interrupted him. "You also recommended half a dozen Silver Stars and two guys for the Distinguished Service Cross."

Regan nodded. "I did. I thought they more than earned them."

The colonel paused for a second before he turned to look at Regan. "I think so too, Captain. Based on my recommendation to the general, they are all receiving the awards you put them in for. Your battalion commander has a lot of promotions he's handing out during the award ceremony as well."

Captain Regan smiled with satisfaction.

"Now, as for you, Captain—your battalion commander put you in for a Silver Star. I wanted to be the one to tell you that I approved that award, but I also put you in for a Distinguished Service Cross as well. You fought bravely, and more importantly, you saved a lot of lives when we broke out of southern Illinois." He put his hand on Regan's shoulder. "I'm also going to be promoting you to major. I hate to take you away from your command, but I need your smarts with me for this coming battle. This next fight against the Chinese is going to be a lot tougher than our fight against those UN losers. I'm going to have you take over the brigade S3 shop for the time being."

"Wow. Thank you for the decorations and promotion, but what happened to Lieutenant Colonel Rodgers, the current S3? Is he OK?"

Beasley lowered his head briefly before he responded. "Rodgers needed to be transferred to a noncombat job for a little while. We found out two days ago that his family had been killed in a freak car accident. He lost his wife and three sons. He's in no situation to continue fighting with us, so he'll be sent back to the brigade armory and given light duty for a month or so to get his affairs in order. We'll reassess if he'll be able to rejoin the unit or if we're going to have to keep him back at the armory permanently."

Regan let out a low whistle. "Oh, man. That's terrible news, sir. I can't even imagine what he must be going through right now. Did he already fly home?"

"Yeah. He left yesterday. That's why you didn't see him today at the commander's call. Look, I need to get going, Captain. Make sure your men know what's coming down and make sure they know they only have two weeks at home. They must report back to the unit when the time comes." With that, Colonel Beasley walked away to go talk with one of his battalion commanders.

Chapter Seven
On the Run

New York

Lake Placid

President Marshall Tate sat in the theater room of the massive home, where he'd been hiding out for most of the last month. His beautiful bride and some of his closest advisors, the ones that hadn't jumped ship, were all there too, and they seemed to be thoroughly enjoying the film that was playing. However, Tate couldn't help but mull over the current situation.

What do I do now? How did it all come down to this?

Tate glanced behind him. Two of his bodyguards were standing there stoically. Ten more guarded the rest of the property. Although any president would need security, it felt a bit more like they were holding him hostage than protecting him at this point.

He'd been hunkered down in this beautiful home on Lake Placid for a month. The house was owned by one of Tate's most staunch supporters and financial backers, who'd agreed to let Tate hide out in his vacation home until they could find a safe country for him to seek sanctuary and establish a government in exile.

Marshall Tate already knew the gig was up with the Europeans and even with most of his own countrymen. As much as he hated to admit it, the only way he was going to stay President was if the Chinese won the war or agreed to let him take over as President of the occupied territories. He'd already reached out to the Chinese several times during the last couple of weeks to try and get that in the works. They had agreed to allow him to flee to China until they could set up a more permanent solution for him in America.

The challenge Tate's security team was dealing with now was figuring out how to move him to China. When the UN force had collapsed and surrendered en masse, Tate had suddenly found himself in a precarious position. With no military support or help from the UN, he'd been cut off from his safe passage out of North America.

Sure, some of the CDF militia forces were still fighting on in New York and the Northeast, but they wouldn't last much longer. Now that the secret was out about how the election had been rigged to allow him to win, his popular support among the people was rapidly evaporating. The people who had once rallied to join the militia to fight and retake their government had suddenly realized they had been duped. That had swiftly ended their will to fight and die for his cause.

I wonder how Lance is doing in all of this, he thought.

Lance Solomon, like Marshall, was among the most wanted men in the world right now. Lance had somehow managed to flee the country prior to everything collapsing. That said, there was a worldwide manhunt underway to find him.

Suddenly the movie ended. Tate hadn't even noticed until someone turned the lights on and his wife brushed his arm.

"Honey, are you going to stay up for a little while longer or come to bed?" she asked. Her eyes betrayed how tired she was.

Looking up at her, Tate smiled. "I'll be up soon. I just need to talk with Jerome and Page first."

She smiled and kissed him on the forehead. "Don't be too long, darling. You need to rest more."

He nodded and then got up to go find his two senior aides. A moment later, he walked into the study and found Jerome and Page sitting there with Retired Admiral David Hill, his Secretary of Defense.

The trio stopped talking when he walked in. Hill quickly got up and poured him a glass of some of the finest Scotch whiskey Tate had ever tasted. They both took their seats, and then there was an awkward pause, as if everyone knew they were about to talk about something difficult.

Tate took a sip of the alcohol and allowed it to seep all the way into his gut. There wasn't a drink in the world strong enough to dull this awful situation. Finally, he decided to rip the Band-Aid off. "What are our options at this point?" he asked bluntly. "Is there any way to take the Chinese up on their latest offer and get out of the country?"

Page leaned forward. "We'd like to just get you on a plane and fly you directly to Russia and then China, but obviously that can't happen, so we're working on an alternate way of getting you out of the country."

"OK. This sounds promising. But I take it there's a hitch to this plan?"

Admiral Hill nodded. "There sure is. Right now, there isn't any direct air travel between the US and Russia, or between Canada and Russia, so we're trying to figure out how we can get you out surreptitiously without being spotted."

"There is one way we can get you out, but it's a lot longer, and frankly, I don't think you're going to like it," Page said as she took a sip of the whiskey.

"All right, Page. Well, let me be the judge of what I won't like," Tate countered. "It can't be any worse than being cooped up here, unable to even leave the house for fear of being spotted." He was growing stir-crazy. The only time he was allowed to venture outside was at night, when even a neighbor couldn't see him to recognize who he was.

Admiral Hill grunted. "We've got a small aircraft that's going to pick you up at the airport in town. It'll fly you to the Canadian island of St. Johns. From there, you'll catch a ride on a freighter that'll be sailing back to Europe. Once the ship is at sea, there's a Russian billionaire who'll meet up with the freighter, and you'll board his mega-yacht. They'll cruise the rest of the way to Russia, where you'll be able to catch a private jet that'll take you to Beijing."

Tate leaned back in his chair. *It's crazy, but it just might work*, he thought.

"I see two issues," said Tate. "How is the plane going to make it there without getting caught? And I wasn't aware there were freighters being allowed through the American blockade yet."

"The plane will make it through fine," Page countered. "We're reconfiguring the plane's transponder to make it appear like one of the Air Force's Skytruck planes. It's a small troop transport craft used for small rugged landings on remote outposts. It'll easily carry you and your wife along with a handful of your security personnel out of here."

Furrowing his brow, Tate clarified, "You guys are coming with, right?"

Admiral Hill shook his head. "No. We're going to stay here and try to keep the insurgency going while you get a government in exile set up in China."

Marshall Tate didn't say anything right away. He couldn't help but wonder if it might be better to just let the insurgency die out while they try and play their cards with the Chinese and hope for a better outcome. Looking at his closest advisors, though, he saw they were not going to be swayed. They'd stay and fight and put their trust in him being able to work out a better deal for them with the Chinese in a postwar world.

Finally, Tate nodded his head in approval. "OK. I'll do what I can for us from China. We'll figure out how they can provide support to the insurgency and your efforts. So, when do I leave?"

****

Trondheim, Norway

Lance Solomon pulled his fedora a little lower on his head to help hide his eyes and face as he left the bakery. With his goods in his bag, he walked down to where he had locked his bike up. After retrieving his bicycle and placing his groceries in the back, he pedaled toward the Airbnb he had rented. While Lance had never thought he'd need to escape America, here he was, hiding in plain sight in Norway, hoping with everything in him that he would one day be able to return to his home country and not face treason charges.

When he'd developed his bug-out plan several years ago, Lance had had a very good forger create a new US passport and a Norwegian passport for him. After his fake identity had been created in Norway, he'd stashed away a few million dollars in multiple different banks for just this type of scenario. Lance knew if he had to go to this extreme and flee his country, he'd need credit and debit cards ready in advance so he could legitimately live out the rest of his life in obscurity in another country.

Then his whole world had come crashing down when he'd received an urgent message, alerting him that Roberto had gone missing. Fearing the worst, Lance took it upon himself to fly to Brussels for an impromptu meeting with some of his EU banking counterparts. He hoped the activity wouldn't draw suspicion. It was a normal thing he'd do as the head of Goldman Sachs, especially as his bank was doing its best to help the Sachs administration put the financial sector back together once New York had been liberated from the UN.

When Lance had completed his business for the firm, he'd told Goldman Sachs that he'd decided to stay for an additional week to meet with some additional bank executives from the UK. It was during this period that he vanished. While a body double he'd hired was using his electronic devices in London, Lance had gone to ground. He'd had his hair dyed and used specially designed contact lenses that caused his eye color to change depending on the ambient light outside.

Next, he'd made a trip to a plastic surgeon who could do discreet work. He'd had his nose changed, added some collagen implants to change the dimensions of his cheeks, and then utilized some Botox in his forehead for good measure. When the surgeon was done with him, he truly did look like a completely different person.

Two days later, the forger Lance had been put in touch with had changed the image on his Norwegian passport to match his new look. Then he was off. That had been nearly a month ago. As he continued to read the headlines online, he realized he'd gotten out at just the right time.

Within a day of him pulling off his disappearing act, his face had been plastered all across the news along with photos of his coconspirators. His heart had sunk when he'd listened to the news reports and heard what was being said about him. He'd spent a lifetime getting to the position he had achieved. Once Marshall Tate had taken power, he had been slated to be designated as the new Treasury Secretary. He'd finally be in a position to influence the course of the US economy. But now he was a hunted man. He wasn't sure how long he'd have to live in hiding, but if this was to be his new life, then he was determined to make the most of it.

For the time being, he spent nearly every waking hour learning how to speak Norwegian. He watched endless hours of Norwegian TV and news channels to help speed up his learning. He had known a little bit of the language before he'd chosen this place to hide out in, but he now needed to make himself appear as if he'd lived there his whole life. He didn't want the Norwegian government or the Americans to somehow figure out who he was and hunt him down.

****

Oslo, Norway

Erik Jahn looked around the table at the Prime Minister, the Finance Minister, the Minister of Justice, and the Minister of Foreign Affairs. They were deciding what to do with him now that all the cards had been laid on the table by the Americans. The evidence of his involvement in this plot to rig the American election was pretty overwhelming.

"You've put us, and the entire Norwegian Sovereign Wealth Fund, in great jeopardy, Erik," said the Prime Minister as she studied him.

"You've done more than that. You've endangered every citizen in this country," insisted the Finance Minister. "Our nation, our people, and our entire financial system depended on the success of the fund you managed. The Americans are threatening to seize any US assets the fund currently owns, including stocks, along with blocking the fund from doing any business with the American banking system. We're talking about more than one trillion dollars,

Erik." His face conveyed the sheer panic that was just below the surface of everyone in the room.

Sitting as straight as he could, Erik exclaimed, "You can't hand me over to the Americans. They will surely put me to death."

"You should have thought about that before you financed this entire scheme," scolded the Prime Minister. "What were you thinking? Financing a coup d'état inside America—my God, Erik. Do you realize what you have done to Norway? To the world?" The look of disappointment on her face belied the anger that was burning in her eyes. Erik had been a key reason why she'd become Prime Minister, but he had put her in an untenable position.

The Minister of Justice looked at Erik briefly with a sad expression before he turned his full attention to the Prime Minister. "Madam Prime Minister, Erik's right. They will put him to death for this. Under our current laws and EU treaties, they can't extradite a Norwegian citizen to a nation that has the death penalty if we know that country will pursue that charge."

The Minister of Justice was one of the few allies Erik currently had left. They had a long history together.

Erik knew he needed to say something. "You could try me here, Madam Prime Minister," he offered. "Under our laws. I could be convicted and spared the death sentence."

The Prime Minister silently thought for a moment. She reached over, grabbed her coffee cup and took a sip, not saying anything as the others waited for her response. Eventually, she leaned in and in a soft tone replied, "Erik, I think you should wait outside for the moment. We need to discuss what would be best for Norway."

Erik grimaced. What would be best for the country might not coincide with what would be best for him, and he knew it. Nodding, he got up and made his way to the door and the chairs outside the office. He hoped his society brother would be able to persuade them to agree to charge him in Norway. If his friend failed, then his time would be up.

****

Once Erik had left the room, the Foreign Minister jumped into the conversation for the first time. "We have to hand him over, Madam Prime Minister," he insisted. "If we do not, the Americans have said they will attack our country with their stealth bombers. They can and would do considerable damage to our country."

The Minister of Justice shook his head. "No," he countered forcefully. "If we do that, they'll condemn him to death. It goes against every law we have and our treaties with the EU. We cannot hand him over. We must try him here in Norway."

The Foreign Minister slammed his hand down hard on the table, startling them all as he raised his voice, "He deserves to be put to death! Look at America. More than one million people have been killed in that country in the last four months. What Erik and his fellow cronies did has forever changed the course of history. The UN as an organization may never recover from this, and our relationship with America is going to be affected by this for generations, Madam Prime Minister."

He paused for a moment as he shook his head. Then he added, "We need to be strong and show the Americans that our government had no idea Erik was doing this—that he had somehow gone rogue. We need to make amends with the Americans and do it publicly and swiftly so we can regain control of the situation in the eyes of our people and the Americans."

The Prime Minister raised her hand to silence the arguing between her senior advisors. She looked out the window, where she could see thousands of protesters holding signs and yelling some sort of chant. They were angry. They were confused. They were looking for a scapegoat.

Turning around to face her three advisors, she announced, "Here's what we're going to do. We're going to tell the Americans where Erik is and a specific time he'll be in that particular location. We'll let them apprehend him so we're not breaking any of our own laws or EU treaties. The Americans are demanding that the member states that participated in this now-illegal UN war be held financially liable for the damage they've caused. I propose that we take all of the US-held assets and stocks in our sovereign wealth fund and liquidate them. Then we should contribute the funds to the trusts the Americans have set up to compensate the victims of this terrible war. It isn't going to make everything right, but it will show the Americans and the rest of the world that we are serious about accepting responsibility for what we've done and that we are trying to make amends."

The Foreign Minister visibly breathed a sigh of relief. "I'll work something out with the Americans," he said.

"I'll make the appropriate arrangements," echoed the Finance Minister.

With that, Erik Jahn's fate was sealed.

Chapter Eight
The Camps

Metcalfe, Mississippi
DHS Detention Camp 14

Captain Quinn stood inside an air-conditioned terminal of Mid Delta Regional Airport with George Thomas, watching the first Air Force C-5 Galaxy land and taxi over toward them. Just outside the terminal were roughly one hundred private contractors and fifteen yellow school buses, ready to greet the passengers of the giant Air Force transport planes.

As the first Galaxy moved off the runway and taxied towards them, a second aircraft landed. Each plane carried roughly 350 prisoners from the UN force that had surrendered. Each day, a total of four of these aircraft would make two trips—one in the morning, then a second in the evening. It was a grueling task having to move this many prisoners a day, but they had to do it.

"Do you think we're going to have enough camps for all these prisoners they keep sending us?" asked Captain Quinn as he finished downing his coffee. He crumpled up the disposable cup and tossed it in the nearby wastebasket.

George shrugged his shoulders. "I think so. We have sixteen camps with a capacity of six thousand prisoners apiece. Then again, I could log back into my email when we get back to the office and find out I've been tasked with getting any more camps set up."

Quinn snickered. "You know, my battalion commander is happy as hell with this gig," he said with a smile. "He hopes we have to build more because it means we'll have plenty of work here, so we won't have to deploy to go fight the Chinese."

George eyed Captain Quinn. "And you?" he asked. "Would you rather be running a prison camp or fighting the Chinese?"

Quinn paused, watching the Galaxy taxi to the buses. Finally, he turned back to George.

"My wife's happy I'm here," he replied. "So are my kids, because we can see each other throughout the month. But our country's been invaded. I'd like to be doing what I can to free America."

George nodded. "I'm with you there. But look at it this way—your battalion is freeing up other active duty units to go fight instead of babysitting a bunch of POWs. You're doing your part in this war. Don't let anyone tell you otherwise. You're a damn good company commander,

Quinn. Your camp is run so much better than many of the others."

"Thanks for the compliment," Quinn said nonchalantly. "But I'm only as good as my soldiers. I'm fortunate to have eight of my guys who just so happen to work in the prison system in their regular day jobs. They've helped me get things squared away faster than I think I could have otherwise."

"Really? Which ones. What do they do?" asked George, his interest clearly piqued.

"Ah. I see what you're doing. You want to poach them from me. Well, I'm not telling you," Quinn replied jovially. They both laughed. "Actually, four my guys are sheriff's deputies who work for the county jail in Jackson, another guy works at a federal prison, and another three work at the state penitentiary," he explained.

"You know, that is the one thing I love about you National Guardsmen; you guys have soldiers from all types of civilian jobs in your units," George commented. "Your guys really know what they're doing—in some ways, more so than the active duty guys."

The Galaxy had now stopped in front of the prison guards and the school buses. Slowly, the nose of the plane opened up to reveal 350 prisoners wearing bright neon green jumpsuits with a POW emblem printed on both the front and rear. Each jumpsuit had the prisoner's name, home nation and military rank on it as well.

Intermixed with the prisoners being offloaded was a rare sight—roughly fifty or so prisoners wearing the bright pink jumpsuits. These prisoners, unlike the POWs, had hand and leg shackles, and the word *traitor* was printed on the front and back of their uniforms, along with their name and their home state. These were the captured Civilian Defense Force militia members.

Each camp had roughly ten percent of its population made up from these former CDF soldiers. These prisoners would be given a public defender and a court date when they'd be prosecuted. If they were found guilty, then depending on their charges, they'd either serve a sentence in a federal prison or they'd face a firing squad shortly after their conviction.

As the first aircraft emptied its human cargo, the second Galaxy taxied over to the parking spot next to the first one. A fuel truck came out to attach the fuel lines to the ground pumps to get the first C-5 fueled back up and ready to go pick up its next load.

"Well, George, I need to get out there and make sure things are running smoothly," said Captain Quinn. "It was good talking to you. Let me know when you're going to pay us visit. I'll make sure we have some fresh sweet tea ready for you." He then waved farewell and headed out into the heat.

I think we're going to need more camps if they keep bringing us planeloads of prisoners like this every day, Quinn thought as he walked to his next task.

****

Martin sat near the front of the school bus next to a couple of military contractors as they drove from the airport to wherever it was they were taking him. As they traveled through the countryside, Martin had to admit he liked what he was seeing. The large magnolia and oak trees were beautiful, and the famous Spanish moss that hung from so many of the trees down south seemed mysterious and inviting. What he didn't like, however, was the oppressive heat and the thick humidity. They were barely into May, and the hot sticky air was already becoming unbearable.

Fifteen minutes into their drive, Martin finally saw the edges of the large sprawling camp that would become his home. As they drew closer, he could see that the fifteen-foot-tall outer fence was lined with multiple layers of razor-sharp concertina wire. He quickly noticed there was probably about a fifteen-foot gap between the outer fence and the next fence. The inner fence was probably around twelve feet in height and was also duel wrapped in concertina wire. In between the two fences, pairs of German shepherds roamed the no-man's-land accompanied by guards.

Wow. They sure mean business at this camp, thought Martin.

The bus finally came to a halt in front of a long, narrow building. The bus ahead of them was in the process of unloading its prisoners, filing into one end of the building and out the other end. It was what was happening at the other end that concerned him. In his pink jumpsuit, he stood out from the rest of the crowd—there were only a handful of prisoners on his bus wearing the same color as he was.

"Everyone off the bus," ordered one of the guards. "Form two lines behind the groups ahead of you. Those of you wearing a pink jumpsuit, you'll line up against the wall over there by those other four." Martin stood at the front of the bus and got off along with the other guards and the driver as they stood guard at the entrance, ready to guide the new arrivals to where they needed to go.

People started exiting the bus and getting in line, just as they had been told. Martin made his way over to the line with half a dozen others in pink jumpsuits.

"You guys have any idea what's coming next?" he asked.

"Nothing good, I'm sure," one of them replied glumly.

After standing around in the heat for five hours watching busload after busload of POWs move through the building, their group was eventually processed into the camps.

"Put your right hand on the screen in front of you," ordered one of the guards. "Now your left. And look into this camera. Chin up."

There was a pause. "State your name," another guard ordered.

"Martin Brown," stated Martin matter-of-factly.

After another pause, the first guard announced, "Biometrics check out."

"Move along to that table against the wall to provide your home of record and your emergency contact, if you have one," ordered a third guard.

Martin followed the instructions. After that, he was organized into a group of twenty prisoners and marched to a shower room.

"Strip down naked," ordered one of the guards. "You will each be deloused, and then you will be allowed three minutes to shower and wash up."

Dear God, please let that be all that happens in here, Martin thought, horrified by a million scenarios in which his situation could go sideways.

Several minutes later, he was done cleaning up, and a guard told him to put his jumpsuit back on. When they were all dressed again, they were moved as a group to the next room.

At the next station, they were bought in ten at a time to a barber chair, where their hair was summarily buzzed off, leaving them bald. The guards explained that this would cut down on the chance of them getting any lice and would help with the heat as they were starting the hot summer season.

Following that joyous experience, they were each handed a laundry bag. Inside each bag was a prison-issued toothbrush, deodorant, towel, two changes of pink jumpsuits, and a pair of Crocs they'd use for shoes. At the next station, their names and home state were stenciled onto their jumpsuits. Once they had gone through all that, they walked into another room to see several nurses or medics standing there with what appeared to be medical air guns with small vials attached to them.

"Walk through the line one at a time," ordered the guard at the door.

As they passed each person, they were given two shots, one in each arm. After receiving a total of six shots, the guard announced, "Now pull down your pants a bit. You'll be given a penicillin shot in your gluteus maximus."

When the entire process was completed, Martin and the others were moved into a large room with rows of bench seats. The room was about half-full when Martin arrived, and one of the guards gruffly ordered, "Take a seat and don't say a word to anyone."

A couple of prisoners tried to comment quietly to each other, but a guard walked over and shouted at them, "Shut up! What part of 'don't talk to anyone' didn't you understand?" A few expletives were shouted, and the men visibly shrank back. An uncomfortable silence followed, which felt like an hour to Martin.

Once the room was full, an Army officer walked in with several armed guards. The captain moved to the podium at the front. He took a moment to look them over before he spoke. "My name is Captain Quinn," he began. "You are now at a joint DHS-DoD prisoner camp. This is Camp 14. For the duration of your stay here, you will listen to the guards and do as you are told. We will for the most part leave you alone, but if you choose to not listen or be rebellious, then we'll make your life incredibly hard.

"For the time being, you will be treated just like the other POWs in accordance with the Geneva Convention. However, the moment you start a fight, the moment you try to break out, you'll experience a world of hurt you didn't know was possible. Right now, you are classified as unlawful enemy combatants. You will be tried for your crimes by a federal judge within thirty days.

"Tomorrow, you will meet with your public defender. If you're wealthy enough to afford a private lawyer, you may discuss that with your PD. Your PD will work with you to go over the evidence against you and advise you of what your options are. Depending upon what you are convicted of, you will either be cut loose, serve a prison term given to you by the judge and jury, or be put to death by firing squad."

Martin heard some murmurs amongst the prisoners before a guard shouted at the crowd to shut up.

I sure hope they aren't going to give me the death penalty, Martin thought, horrified.

Captain Quinn continued. "If you are convicted of a crime that results in the death penalty, you will be executed the following Friday. Every Friday, all prisoners in pink jumpsuits are required to attend the public executions."

Martin shuddered.

"Court dates are Monday through Wednesday of every week," announced Quinn. "Your lawyer time with your assigned PD or private lawyer will be on Thursdays and Sundays, depending on when your lawyer wants to meet with you.

"You are not allowed any visitors. You will be allowed to make one five-minute phone call on Thursday and one call on Sundays. If you are given the death penalty, you will be given a final meal the night before and allowed to talk to whomever you want for up to sixty minutes to say your final farewells. You will also be afforded four hours of time with a legal professional to get your will in order, if needed. If you have any questions, you may direct your questions to your barracks representative. They will bring those questions up to the barracks guard in the morning after breakfast and in the evening directly after dinner."

Captain Quinn paused for a second before he continued. "Now, listen very closely to what I'm about to tell you. *If* you attack one of my guards or any of the contractors in the camp, you will be summarily executed on the spot. If you kill one of your fellow prisoners, you will be executed on the spot. I run a tight ship here. Your stay can either be pleasant or it can be miserable—that decision is entirely yours.

"Breakfast is served between 0600 and 0800 daily; your barracks rep will let you know what time slot your barracks may enter the chow hall. Lunch and dinner work the same way. If you are hurt or sick, there is an infirmary in the center of the camp. Sick call starts at 0600 and runs until 1400 daily. Lights out is promptly at 2200 hours. Reveille is at 0500. What you do during the day is up to you, but do *not* cause trouble or fight. I won't tolerate it, and neither will the other prisoners. That is all." Then Captain Quinn promptly turned and walked out of the room.

One of the guards then shouted, "All right, everyone up. Time to get your barracks designation. Call out your last name when you reach the door, and I'll tell you what barracks you've been assigned to. Once you have that information, proceed to your barracks and report in to your rep. He'll give you the rundown from there."

One of the other guards moved over to the door near the front of the building and propped it open. The prisoners then lined up in front of the guard with the clipboard.

Martin had to marvel at how smooth this entire process had been. Aside from being the last group to process into the camp, they had moved them along like they were on some sort of assembly line.

As the line in front of Martin got smaller, he readied himself. Finally, it was his turn.

"Brown," he announced.

"First name?" asked the guard. Apparently, there was more than one person with the same last name.

"Martin."

The guard looked at him. "You're in Barracks 6C. Next."

And just like that, it was over. All that waiting in line, moving from one station to another had finally ended.

Martin walked out the door so the next guy could get his assignment.

Barracks 6C...where the hell is that? he wondered.

Then he saw a large map of the camp a few feet away, where a handful of other prisoners had gathered. As Martin approached, he could see that there were ten lines of tents with six tents to a line. He found 6C and headed that direction.

As he walked through the camp, Martin saw several people playing chess or checkers. Some were reading books, and others were just talking. He heard people speaking other languages. More than a few of the prisoners must have been Chinese.

Eventually, he found the tent he was looking for and opened the outer door. He took a deep breath and let it out, walking into an uncertain future.

Chapter Nine
Project Odin

Newport News, Virginia

Vice Admiral Ingalls was stressed beyond belief. His pet project of developing a truly revolutionary weapon platform for the twenty-first century was both a dream and a nightmare. The challenge of creating a new technology and weapon system was an enormous undertaking—trying to create it to save his country from certain doom, however, was almost too much. The US Navy had suffered some horrific losses these past five months. They had to find a way to regain their naval advantage and supremacy if they were to have any hope of stopping this endless Chinese onslaught.

The Chinese had caught them all off guard with how rapidly they had been able to negate their forces in Hawaii. These new battleships could prove to be the needed game changer to return the balance of power in the Pacific back to America. Ingalls constantly wondered, though, if they could build out the weapons systems fast enough.

He sat in his chair, gazing out the window of his office for a moment at the two massive domed structures outside.

America's newest superweapon, he thought. *Will it be ready in time, though?* he asked himself as he ran his fingers through his hair.

He swiveled back around to face the four men sitting in front of his desk. "Mr. Lake, it's been two months since the President signed an executive order giving the new hires an interim TS clearance so they could get hired and start work. What's the holdup? Our two ships out there are still falling behind schedule," Admiral Ingalls said as he waved his arm toward the domes outside. "We need these ships to start their weapons testing in a few months so we can get them ready to deploy by the end of the year." He felt incredibly annoyed at the continued delays in the project, and his voice betrayed it.

The CEO and the COO of the Newport News Shipbuilding Company glanced at each other for a moment before reaching a silent agreement that the COO would respond. "Admiral, this is an incredibly complex weapons platform we're building. You've asked us to speed the construction of this ship up by nearly three years. That's a tall order, even during peacetime. During the middle of war, it's nearly impossible."

Ingalls paused for a moment to take a deep breath and collect his thoughts so he wouldn't explode with all the anger and frustration he felt. Finally, he let it rip. "During World War II, it took US shipbuilders between thirteen and fifteen months to build a carrier. It took our shipbuilders five *days* to build a liberty troop transport ship. This was with 1940s technology and without automation, 3-D printing, and many other advanced construction tools and advancements."

He stopped for a moment to let that sink in before he leaned forward in his chair. "Our country has been invaded. We are in the fight of our lives right now. We've lost three carriers in this war and have another five more in the shipyards for repairs or complex overhaul. Our naval presence in the Pacific has been devastated, and as a consequence, the Chinese have invaded us. I don't care what you have to do, you get these ships back on schedule!" he insisted, smacking an open hand on the table.

The men before him sat there silently, seemingly stunned.

"I don't care what other projects you have to strip workers from to make this happen, but this is your number one priority for the US Navy," Admiral Ingalls continued. "If I have to, I'll have the President call you directly to get this project back on track. Hell or high water, these ships had better be ready to test their weapons by the end of summer and ready for their shakedown cruise in November. Do you understand?"

The CEO of the company leaned forward. "Yes, Admiral," he responded quietly. "We'll do our best to get the ships back on track—"

Ingalls interrupted him. "No. Not your best. These ships *have* to deploy. If we don't stop the endless flood of Chinese forces landing in California and Mexico, we may lose half the country by this time next year. I need you to understand how critical it is that these ships be made ready for war."

The project manager, Mr. Lake, finally broke into the conversation. "Admiral, if you'll allow me to strip the repair crews from the *Stennis* and *Nimitz* and move them from the West Coast to here, we should be ready to begin testing the weapons system by August fifteenth."

Ingalls smiled. "See? That wasn't so hard."

"But what about getting those two ships ready?" stammered Mr. Bullard, the company's lead project manager, who oversaw all of the construction projects. "We're maybe five months away from completing their repairs."

Ingalls shook his head. "This is far more important than getting those ships fixed. As your workers finish repairs on the damaged destroyers and cruisers, you can move them out to Washington State to finish the overhaul of those two carriers. But in the meantime, this has to happen."

The CEO nodded. "Admiral, we'll shift the workers around today," he asserted. "We'll do whatever is necessary to get this project back on schedule. With the adjustment to the security clearances, we now have fifty thousand new workers currently in orientation and completing their thirty-day assessments. In a month, we'll be able to get most of these projects back on track."

"Excellent, gentlemen. Now, if you all could please excuse yourselves so Mr. Lake, Mr. Bullard and I can discuss the specifics of the ship, that would be greatly appreciated."

"Um. Yes, of course," replied the CEO, standing up. "Thank you, Admiral, for allowing us to shift some folks around and for helping us get through the security clearance logjam."

The CEO and COO both left the room, leaving Mr. Lake and Bullard alone with Ingalls. Despite the other two men being the leaders of their company, they had not been read on to the program and therefore did not know the nitty-gritty specifics of the ships or what they were truly capable of. The only reason Admiral Ingalls had wanted to speak with them was to make sure they understood that their five-billion-dollar completion bonus was on the line if they didn't meet the year-end delivery date.

I think they got the message, Ingalls thought to himself as he smiled.

"OK. Now that we have your bosses backing you guys again, let's get started."

Mr. Lake smiled and opened the folder he had with him. He cleared his throat. "Admiral, as of two weeks ago, we got the reactors in both ships fueled. We initiated the reactor start-up two days ago, and thus far, they are performing normally. Over the next few days, we'll be increasing the reactor load to make sure everything is fine before we seal up that portion of the ship. This is the last major obstacle we needed to overcome before the ship could be fully closed up. In another month, we'll officially be ready to launch her into the water, if you so desire."

Admiral Ingalls held a hand up to pause him. "We're going to hold off on launching the ships until we're a lot closer to conducting their weapons testing," he insisted. "Once we bring them out of their cover, the secret's going to be out."

Mr. Lake nodded. "I think that's a good idea as well, sir. As to the weapon systems, tomorrow we'll be installing the last of the VLS pods. We're going to begin testing the firing circuits before we move to the next platform."

Mr. Bullard interjected, "I still have some reservations about the direct energy weapon. We're not quite ready for it. The Nevada test range has not been able to demonstrate its effectiveness beyond sixty miles."

"Whoa, wait a second," exclaimed Ingalls. "That's not what I read last week from them."

"Yes and no, Admiral," Mr. Lake calmly insisted. "What you read, sir, was that the direct energy weapon was able to successfully hit the target at two hundred and ten miles. However, it was not able to hit the target with enough energy to destroy it at that range. The effective destructive range is currently around the sixty or so miles."

Ingalls let out a huge huff of air at the thought of another possible delay. "Look," he said. "You guys have to get this sorted out. Power isn't going to be a problem with this ship. If you need more help from DARPA or some egghead groups at a university, then let me know and we'll make it happen. Keep testing it at the Nevada range. We also need to make sure the gun crews who'll be working this system are continually trained. The gunners and the technicians need to know how to effectively work and repair the system before we deploy it."

Mr. Bullard jotted a few notes down, then muttered, "I'll get with DARPA and see if they have any ideas on how to increase its lethality range."

"On that note, I'm proud to report the railgun tests have been completed and were successful," announced Mr. Lake. "We'll be able to mount both caliber railguns. With the added height and using an arc when it fires, we'll effectively be able to hit sea or land objectives as far as three hundred and sixty miles away with more than enough destructive power to pulverize whatever it targets. The smaller-caliber point-defense guns will have an effective range of one hundred and twenty miles—more than enough range to take on enemy missiles or projectiles fired at them or the battlegroup."

Ingalls nodded. He was excited about this new weapons system. After the debacle with the *Zumwalt*-class ships, they needed to prove that a railgun system was not some futuristic toy to dream about. This gun system would provide the new super ships an unparalleled amount of firepower. It could save them from having to use cruise missiles or aircraft to hit other ships or land targets.

"What about the projectiles themselves? Did we get that piece sorted?" asked Admiral Ingalls.

Mr. Lake smiled. "Yes. At the Nevada range, we're now using 3-D-printed projectiles to fire the railguns. They work. We've move from theory to fact in less than six months. DARPA also completed their test on the various types of warheads. We can use a solid projectile that'll rely solely on its velocity and density to hammer its targets, and we still have the proximity high-explosive rounds."

The Navy had struggled with projectile costs in the past. Then a young officer at the naval research lab had suggested they use industrial-grade 3-D printers to just make the rounds on the ship. Now that the tests had proved successful, it would be a game changer for Navy logistics going forward. No longer would they have to maintain a large stockpile of projectiles on each ship.

Ingalls smiled. He stood but motioned for them to stay seated. He walked over to the window and looked at the two massive bubbles that were shielding his two babies from prying eyes. Then he turned around. "What about the EMP projectiles?" he asked.

Mr. Lake shrugged. "Still a work in progress. It's not that the EMP can't be fitted into the projectile; the challenge is making it still function after it's been fired. Right now, the electronic innards of the warhead get fried when they're shot through the railgun. The magnetic field that runs through it currently fries the trigger device and wipes out its software code."

Admiral Ingalls crinkled his eyebrows. "Wasn't there talk about encasing the EMP equipment inside some sort of magnetic shield?"

"Yes," Mr. Bullard answered, "but in order to make the shield work so the EMP can still detonate and the projectile still work with the magnetic system that shoots it, the shell size would need to be increased beyond what our current barrels have been designed for."

Ingalls sighed audibly. "How much larger does the new barrel need to be to make it work? And if we adjusted the barrel size, how much would that throw a wrench into everything else?"

Looking at his notes again, Mr. Lake replied, "There are several variants DARPA's been working on. One included a projectile skin that would fall off once it was fired, kind of like what happens with a tank's sabot round— but even that variant is still going to require a larger barrel. Right now, to make this thing work it's going to require us to change the barrel dimensions from a twelve-inch slug to a sixteen-inch."

Ingalls shook his head in frustration. "OK, so if we moved to sixteen-inch barrels and projectiles, would the EMP round still work?"

"Technically, yes," Mr. Bullard replied. "It should be able to generate an EMP field of roughly one kilometer from detonation. The more difficult question DARPA is still trying to grapple with is whether the EMP field generated would be strong enough to disable some of the more hardened electrical systems of a military target."

"OK, then here's what we're going to do," said Ingalls. "Develop a short-barreled sixteen-inch gun so DARPA can begin their tests. *If*, and I emphasize *if* it works, then we can retrofit the ships with the new gun barrels. We can hold off on installing the main guns and the turret for as long as possible, but time is running out. Once the system is proven to work, then we can make the necessary modifications at a later date."

"OK. We'll get on this right away," Mr. Lake offered. "It may delay our ability to field the railgun system for the weapons test on August fifteenth, but if this works, I think you'll agree it'll be worth the delay." He wrote a few more notes down on his paper.

"Agreed. Let's move to the next platform," Ingalls said.

Mr. Bullard raised his hand. "I have a concern that I believe we need to address before it becomes a major problem, Admiral. Will Lockheed be able to deliver the LRASMs we need for both ships?" he asked. "It's a lot of missiles, and we're still burning through a ton of cruise and standard missiles right now."

Admiral Ingalls sighed. This was one of his biggest concerns aside from getting these two ships completed. Delivering four thousand LRASMs by the end of the year was a tall order, considering the company was still trying to ramp up production of their existing weapon platforms and aircraft. The restart of the F-22 program was probably the biggest challenge Lockheed was facing—especially considering their aircraft production facility in Fort Worth had already come under attack several times.

"It's on my radar," Ingalls said. "Let me deal with it. In the meantime, do what you can to keep things on track. I hate to cut our meeting short, but I've got to handle a few other fires aside from this one." With that, he concluded the discussion.

Chapter Ten
Operation Viking

Haldon, Norway
Haldon Prison

Erik Jahn blinked a couple of times as he used his hand to shield his eyes from the bright glare of the sun. As his vision adjusted, he saw two guards motion for him to get in the back of the prison van. He trudged over to the rear door and climbed in. When he sat down, one of the guards placed a set of handcuffs on him and strapped him into the seat. Then the guard closed the door and locked it before opening the front passenger door and getting in.

Looking around the van, Erik just sighed. For the time being, he was being held in Haldon Prison while he awaited trial in Oslo. Thus far, his friend at the Ministry of Justice had prevailed in preventing him from being handed over to the Americans, but how much longer that would last was anyone's guess.

Once the two guards got settled in the vehicle, Erik asked, "Where are we headed?" They hadn't told him where they were taking him when they'd told him to be ready to leave the prison a couple of hours ago.

The driver looked at Erik in the rearview mirror. "You're being moved back to Oslo so you can meet with the Ministry of Justice—that's all they told us," one of the guards replied. He then closed the screen that separated him from them, giving him some privacy to think.

The van drove for thirty minutes before one of the guards opened the screen. "We're stopping in Sarpsborg along the way for a coffee," he announced. "Would you like one as well?"

Erik smiled at the kindness of the guard. "Yes. That would be lovely. Thank you for asking."

They drove for another fifteen minutes and eventually stopped at an Esso station just off the highway. "I'll be back in a moment," said the kind guard as he got out to go inside the deli that was inside the petrol station. The driver of the vehicle stayed with Erik.

Ten minutes later, the guard returned with a cupholder containing three coffees. He used his free hand to open the back door and proceeded to give Erik a hot cup of morning java.

"Thank you. I appreciate it." Erik took the cup and managed to take a sip despite his hands being cuffed.

The guard climbed into the passenger seat and handed the third coffee to his partner.

Erik took several more sips and felt the caffeine immediately hit his body. Seconds later, he suddenly felt woozy. He placed his drink in a nearby cupholder as he sought to try and steady himself. Erik leaned his head back briefly, then slipped into the black abyss.

****

Seth stared at the man before him: Erik Jahn, one of the most influential financial figures in the world. To be honest, he'd never heard of Erik prior to his interrogation of Roberto Lamy. Then again, he wasn't really a part of the financial circles Mr. Jahn ran in, either.

They'd strapped the prisoner into a chair, and one of the guards had made sure the sensory deprivation devices were attached to Mr. Jahn. Now he was ready to be woken up. Seth snapped the smelling salt packet open, placed it near the man's nose and waited a second. A moment later, Erik woke with a start. He tried unsuccessfully to look around the room to see where he was—the device on his head flooded his vision with flashing lights. Then, suddenly, Erik seemed to realize his hands and legs were firmly tied to the chair he was sitting in. Unable to hear or see anything, he called out for the guards in Norwegian.

Seth reached over and pulled the noise-canceling headphones off his prisoner's ears. He didn't speak a lick of Norwegian, but Seth knew he would be understood perfectly well if he spoke in English. "Erik. Calm yourself. There are no guards to call. It's just us now," he said.

Erik's mouth gaped open in surprise for a moment. "You can't treat me like this!" he shouted, sounding deathly terrified. "I demand to be let go. I am a prisoner within the Norwegian justice system. You can't just kidnap me with impunity."

Seth smiled at the statement. While Erik couldn't see him shaking his head, he had to try hard to stifle a laugh. "Erik. It's over. Your government has given you over to us. You're going to come back to America with me. The only question that remains to be seen is if you'll be going to America as a man who is cooperating with our investigation or as someone who is still trying to protect his coconspirators."

Seth watched the man think that over for a minute before he asked, "So, are you saying there is room to cut a deal?"

Seth smiled and motioned for the guard to take the rest of the sensory deprivation equipment off the prisoner. A moment later, the entire headset was removed from Mr. Jahn, revealing a man who looked tired but determined.

A true businessman—always angling for a slice of the pie, Seth thought.

He leaned in toward Erik, lowering his voice. "A deal could be had, but you'd have to have something worthwhile. What is the bargaining chip you'd like to place on the table?" he inquired.

"How about you tell me what kind of deal I can strike, and I'll tell you what kind of chip I have," Erik swiftly countered.

Seth steepled his fingers as he thought about this for a moment. He hadn't fully thought about a deal. He figured he'd extract the information they needed through their tried and tested method, but if he could obtain a cooperating source without having to go that route, it was certainly worth considering.

Finally, Seth nodded. "I'm going to need to check with some folks back in Washington, obviously," he began. "Depending on what you're willing to give up, I am certain I can get the death penalty taken off the table. As to prison, that's going to be hard. You're going to have to serve some time. I might be able to work that down to twenty years, but

I doubt I could get it any lower. Not after all that has transpired with this little scheme of yours."

"Fair enough," Erik replied. "If you can get it in writing, signed by your President, that I will serve no more than twenty years in one of your minimum-security prisons, I can tell you where Lance Solomon is currently hiding."

Seth's left eyebrow rose, and he sat back in his chair for a moment. That would be a big get if he could deliver.

We'd only need to find Tate and the Peng then, he thought.

Seth stood up. "I need to make a call about this. If I can secure a deal for you, you'd better not screw me over on it or the deal will get shredded and I'll extract the information I need from you in a way you'll regret for the rest of your life." Seth turned to leave the room, but he could tell from the look on Erik's face that he wasn't lying about the information he had.

Seth made his way over to the living room of the safe house they were using. Once there, he grabbed the secured satellite phone and placed a call to Major General Lancaster.

"This is Lancaster," the gruff voice on the other side responded.

"General, it's Mitchell. I just began talking with our friend here in Norway."

"Ah, good. Has he given you anything useful yet?" Lancaster asked.

"Actually, that's why I'm calling you. Just before I began my usual routine, he told me he can give us the location of Lance Solomon if the President would agree in writing to a sentence of no more than twenty years in a minimum-security facility."

Seth heard Lancaster laughing. "Is that all?" the general asked. "So he wants the Club Med treatment and in exchange he'll give us Solomon, eh?" A pause ensued for a moment before he asked, "Do you think you can still extract the information from him with your bag of tricks, or are you telling me this is the best route for us to take?"

Seth took in a deep breath before he replied, "I'm pretty confident I can get the information we need now that he's hinted at knowing where Solomon is. However, the reason I'm interested in taking him up on his deal is that I think we can find out a lot more about how this whole scheme started and who else was involved. Mr. Jahn here was the money guy, after all. He knows where the funds are, who's donated to them...shoot, he may even know where Marshall Tate is. As good as my bag of tricks is, a cooperating source who has an incentive to spill the beans is always better than trying to get a man to cooperate while under the influence of pharmaceuticals."

Seth heard an audible sigh on the other end. "All right, Mitchell. I'll run this up the flagpole. Give me at least a day to get you a decision." Then the call ended, leaving Seth wondering what to do next.

Under normal circumstances, he would put the sensory deprivation equipment back on his prisoner and leave him alone and gagged until he had a decision. But if he did that, he might destroy a working relationship he needed to establish with the man. He drummed his fingers on the desk.

After a few minutes, an idea occurred to him. *This just might work*, he thought.

****

Thirty minutes later, Seth, two other American security guards dressed in civilian attire, along with four members of the Norwegian FSK climbed into the pair of SUVs parked outside the home. The FSK men were a part of Norway's version of the Special Forces. Many of their members had been killed in the war in America, so there was a bit of distrust in having to keep them around the CIA's little operation, but it was a requirement of the Norwegian government if they were going to operate openly in their country.

One of the Norwegians sat in the driver's side of the lead SUV, while one of Seth's guys got in the passenger seat. One of the other US guys climbed into the rear third-row bench while Seth and Erik sat in the two captains' chairs in the center of the vehicle. The other three FSK members piled into the chase vehicle behind them. Everyone was well armed but keeping their weapons out of sight.

"Where are we going?" asked Erik, nervous that they were moving locations.

"I presented your offer to my superiors; however, I may not get a response back until tomorrow. In the meantime, I thought we'd take a short hike at a nearby park one of the FSK members mentioned. I know you're an avid hiker, and this may be the last chance for you to walk amongst the trails of your native Norway."

"That…is actually very considerate of you," Erik replied, clearly not sure how to react to the kind gesture.

"It's a beautiful day, why spend it stuck indoors when we can be out amongst nature and enjoy it?" asked Seth. "Besides, I'm tired, Erik. I want a break from all this cloak-and-dagger stuff as much as I'm sure you do."

The vehicle drove to the rear of the park and found a parking spot for both vehicles. The FSK members got out and immediately began to survey the area. All six members of the security detail had translucent earpieces in so they could communicate with Seth should they need to.

When Seth placed his sunglasses on, he gently depressed a button near the right side of the frame and the lens. It activated a camera and recording device on the glasses and would transmit whatever Seth said or saw to a handful of analysts back at the safehouse. Seth had also placed a small microphone and tracking device on Erik's clothes so they could listen to whatever he might say. They weren't taking any chances with him.

****

As the group left to head down one of the trails, one of Seth's guys stayed back at the vehicle for a moment. He pulled a small case out of the back and opened it up. One of the FSK guys stood nearby and raised an eyebrow when he saw the small compact surveillance drones. Seth's security guy turned both drones on and threw them up into the air. Their little quadcopters activated, and the drones rose rapidly above the trees and then chased after Seth and Erik.

With the drones launched, the CIA man began to walk after their charge.

The FSK soldier walked briskly to catch up. "How are you controlling them?" he asked, mystified.

With a smirk on his face, the CIA man replied, "Magic, my friend. Magic."

****

The group walked for thirty minutes into the woods. The trail took them along several beautiful spots along the way, with picturesque views of the surrounding area. Erik breathed in his last moments of freedom.

They eventually stopped and took a seat, just the two of them, while their security minders fanned out and turned away to make sure no one came near them.

Just as the American seemed to be ready to speak, his smartphone buzzed, letting him know he had a message. He pulled it out and read, then placed his phone back in his pocket. Erik studied the man's facial expressions carefully.

His new friend pointed to one of the drones loitering above. "My eye in the sky was telling me they're observing us."

Erik grunted. "We were foolish to think we could remove President Sachs," he muttered.

The American took a deep breath. "Why *did* you guys try to remove him?" he asked. "Why not just either let him lose in the election fairly or wait him out?"

He really is naïve, thought Erik.

He cocked his head to one side as he sized up the man he assumed must be part of the CIA. He decided to answer the question with one of his own. "Why do you think?"

"It can't be about money," the man responded. "At least, that can't be the only reason."

Erik smiled. *Perhaps he's not as clueless as I thought. Maybe I can work with this guy.*

"You're right; it's not entirely about money. While that was a major driver, it was about more than that." He paused for a moment as he thought about how much he should tell this outsider. Looking out at the scenery before him, Erik asked, "Did you get the response from your superiors about my offer?"

Lifting his chin, the CIA man replied. "I did." He produced his smartphone and then showed him a text message he had received. "Deal is a go. There will be an official letter signed by the President when you return to the safe house. Get us the information."

Excellent. They are willing to deal, Erik thought. Maybe he could even get them to lower his sentence further if he gave them another big fish.

"Money is pointless unless you have power, and power is useless unless you have control," Erik said.

"Can't money buy power? And can't it also give you control?" asked the CIA man.

Erik shook his head. "There is much I can teach you about how the world truly works," he explained, sounding very much like a disappointed professor. "First off, even if you have money, you don't have real power. Look at the CEOs of Tesla or Amazon—both of those men are worth a fortune, but they don't control your country or world affairs. Then you have senators and governors—they may have some political power and maybe some money, but even they are subject to the whims of their political donors. The minute they stop doing as they are told, the spigot of money is turned off and they get primaried out of their position."

Erik paused to unscrew his water bottle and took a couple of gulps. He saw that the American was paying very close attention to him. He didn't appear to be eating out of his hand, but he could tell he was hungry for what he was hearing.

"You still haven't answered my question, though. Why not wait out Sachs or let him get unseated through our normal political process?" the man pressed.

"Sachs is a wild card. He's out of control. Our world order relies on precise control of things and he threw a wrench in that plan," Erik expounded. "He had to be removed. We couldn't take a chance that that buffoon would somehow be reelected by a bunch of disgruntled voters."

"Why was it so important for you to replace him, though? He can't be that dangerous to the global order," countered the CIA man.

Erik let out a long, loud sigh. "You still don't see it."

"See what? Enlighten me."

"Fine. If you need to be spoon-fed the facts, then that's what I'll do," countered Erik condescendingly. "Sachs is dangerous because he represents far more than just rewriting some trade deals to better America. Sachs represents an idea: a belief that is far more dangerous to the global order than just trying to get America a better trade deal. Sachs has made many other leaders around the world and the people of those nations believe that they can have a true voice—that if they stick together, they can overcome globalization, nationalism, and every other form of servitude or bondage."

The American's face wrinkled up. "Hasn't the argument since he's been elected that Sachs is a nationalist or fascist?"

Erik snickered. "Sachs is no more a nationalist or fascist than his predecessor. Titles and names are thrown around because they incite people; they rile them up. It was a means we used to try and neuter the man. It clearly didn't work, which is why we had to replace him with someone of our choosing."

"So, the thought was that if you didn't remove him now, then what he represents that you feel is a threat to you will somehow spread and you'll lose more control around the world?" asked the CIA man skeptically.

"In a nutshell, yes. Exactly." Erik held a hand up. "First, what is your name?" he asked. "I hate not knowing who I'm addressing."

A smile spread across the American's face. "Joshua. But you can call me Josh."

Erik knew that wasn't his real name, but he went along with it for the time being. "OK, Josh. If you say so." He looked off into the horizon again for a moment before he continued. "Josh, it wouldn't have mattered if Sachs was a Democrat or a Republican. We don't care what political party the President belongs to. We only care that he doesn't upset the apple cart. As long as he doesn't stray too far, he's pretty much allowed to do what he wants."

Josh, or whoever he was, placed a hand on Erik's arm to pause him before he could go on. "You keep saying 'us' and 'we.' Who are you referring to?"

Now he's using his noodle, thought Erik.

"I'll share that with you later," he responded. "Suffice it to say, we only care about being left alone to do our business. To be honest with you, we never thought Sachs would find out about the postal worker scheme. We certainly didn't think he'd be able to link the Islamic terrorists to China and Germany. What really led us to believe we had miscalculated the situation, however, was when he opted to fight the UN and not leave office. He'd been offered a handsome amount of money to leave, but he wouldn't. That's when I, at least, knew the jig was up. We had overplayed our hand."

"So how does Lance Solomon play into all of this? Was he just the face of the money operation in America?" asked Josh.

Erik tilted his head to the right. "I'm sure at this point you know Lance is a member of the Skull and Bones society," he stated.

The CIA man nodded.

"We've always worked with the Bones to help pick presidents. There are a few other groups from time to time as well. But it was their turn to have a member in the White House. Lance picked Tate and told us who to throw our weight behind. He also set up the SuperPACs we were supposed to plus up with cash. Lance was also responsible for buying off many of the people in government who could have found out about our plot earlier on. If it hadn't been for Lance, I doubt this entire thing would have even taken off the ground."

"So where is he now?" Josh prodded.

"He's here. In Norway."

The CIA man pursed his lips but didn't say anything. He seemed skeptical.

"He's here," Erik insisted. "He's undergone some plastic surgery to change his looks and he's living under a new identity. I helped him get his finances and new identity established. He's currently staying in a house in Trondheim, Norway. Give me a piece of paper and I'll write down his address for you."

Josh handed him a small notepad he had in one of his pockets and a pen. Erik proceeded to write down the details.

"We're going to check this address out," the CIA man announced. "If it pans out, then your deal is still good.

If you're lying to us, then I will extract the information from you in another manner, and I'm sure you won't find it enjoyable."

Erik studied the man; he saw a glint of something in his eyes. He didn't doubt for a second that this "Josh" was more than capable of getting the information he wanted from him. He wondered why he had been allowed to cut a deal if he was a skilled extractor.

There's more to this man's strategy than I first thought.

"He's there," Erik maintained. "Do you mind if we stay in Norway until you verify he's there? If something does go wrong, I'll have more ways of finding him if I can stay here than if I'm in America."

The CIA man nodded and then signaled their security detail that they were heading back to the safe house.

****

Oslo, Norway

The surveillance team had been sitting on the address Erik Jahn had provided for two days now. In that time, they had spotted Mr. Solomon leave his home at least six times. Each morning, he'd purchase some bread and croissants from the bakery just down the road. Around lunchtime, he'd go for a four-mile run and then return home. Then at dinnertime, he'd meander into town and eat at a local restaurant.

Seth was sure if they kept watching him, they wouldn't see much deviation in Lance Solomon's daily routine. The discussion among his colleagues centered on how much longer they should wait until they snatched him. Seth decided to leave the room with the monitors, walk down the hall and fill in the information gaps.

Seth spotted the man with the information and walked toward him. "Commander, can you give me an update on when our ship arrives?"

The naval attaché to the embassy turned to look at Seth. He placed his coffee cup down on the table and made a quick call. He relayed a request to his assistant and waited for the response. Smiling, he looked back at Seth. "The USS *Jason Dunham* is still about eighteen hours away."

"Thank you," Seth replied as he nodded. He walked back down to the monitoring room.

"Are we taking this guy down soon?" asked one the team members from TF Avenger.

Seth grinned. "Yes," he responded. "Let's get our FSK guys over here. It's time to talk about the takedown."

"We're still going to let the Norwegians take him into custody?" the same team member asked. "This would really be better done by us."

"I agree, and I'd love for us to be the ones to raid the home, but we're guests of the Norwegian government," Seth responded. "Thus far, they've given us everything we've wanted or needed. Tell Joe to go with them, though. I want him on scene to take Solomon into custody once the FSK has secured the home."

****

Four hours later, the eight members of Task Force Avenger in Oslo were on a video call with the Minister of Justice, the Prime Minister, and the Minister of Defense. Seth briefed them on Mr. Solomon and asked for final approval of the plan to take the American hiding in their midst into custody.

The Norwegian leaders agreed unanimously without any hesitation. Then the video call transitioned to a conversation with the Minister of Defense, the head of the Norwegian military, and the head of the FSK.

Seth went over how he'd like to see the raid go down, and the leaders were generally amiable to his suggestions. "Now, while the FSK will be the ones to breach the home and capture Mr. Solomon, I'd like to request that two of my counterparts that are currently in Trondheim be allowed to advise the team on the raid," Seth requested.

"What are their backgrounds?" asked the FSK leader. "Can they handle being a part of a raid like this?"

"The two men are active members of the US Army's Delta Force," Seth answered bluntly.

The FSK chief smiled and nodded his consent.

****

Trondheim, Norway

Master Sergeant Bruce "Deuce" Wilder and Sergeant First Class "Larry" Flint walked around the back of the police station. They kept their heads low and eyes sharp as they made their way to the back entrance of the police station.

Deuce rapped his knuckles on the back door and waited. A few seconds later, the door opened, and a uniformed police officer came into view. The man lifted an eyebrow when he saw Deuce and Larry but held the door open for them to come in.

"Good evening," he said, sounding rather formal. "Follow me to the briefing room. The others are waiting there."

Deuce couldn't help but notice a lot of odd looks from the police officers and staff as he and Larry walked through their facility with their large black hockey bags slung over their shoulders. Deuce smiled; he knew he and his compatriot didn't exactly look like the kind of guys you'd want to pick a fight with—to the Norwegians, they probably didn't look like they belonged in a police station without handcuffs on.

Larry wasn't a particularly big man. He stood around six foot one, but under his loose-fitting shirt, he was built like a brick house. He was a deadly jiujitsu master and one hell of an operator.

Deuce had a similar background. He had a fourth-degree black belt in Krav Maga. Like Larry, he'd spent some time in Rangers before moving to selection with the Unit. Deuce was only five foot ten, so he was shorter and not nearly as built at his friend. However, he liked to think he was much better looking, especially when he had his goatee braided into a pair of two-inch Viking braids.

The police officer then opened the briefing room door and said something in Norwegian to the group. One of the men waved for them to come in and sit in the back row.

Deuce and Larry took their cue and walked over to a couple of empty chairs and a table. The other FSK men were suiting up while their leader appeared to be talking to them about some aspect of the raid. Neither Larry nor Deuce could speak a word of Norwegian, so they went to work on getting their own gear set up.

Deuce unzipped one of the large bags he'd brought with him and pulled out his FN SCAR-SC along with all the gear he liked to have on it for a mission like this. Next, he grabbed his tier-one body armor with the newest-in liquid gel inner shell. He placed his helmet on the table and then proceeded to do an equipment check of his rifle while Larry did the same.

Pausing for a moment, Deuce noticed that the police officer who had brought them to the room was standing near the door, still eyeing them suspiciously. Ignoring the stares, Deuce pulled his chest rig over his head and cinched the side straps, tightening it against his chiseled body. His O-neg blood type patch showed on the front of his rig, along with his Punisher patch and a few others he'd added for fun.

At this point, the ten other FSK men in the room had stopped talking and watched Deuce and Larry as they fastened their helmets in place and attached their weapons to the single-point sling. Continuing with their task, Deuce and Larry began to do a quick rattle check by jumping in place a couple of times. They tightened up a few items before they took their equipment off.

The man in front of the room, who appeared to be in charge, announced in English, "I'm Major Sunde. You are our two American observers. What exactly is your background, and why are you suiting up like you are going with us?"

Looking at the major, Deuce replied, "We're from the Unit. We're here to help you guys take Mr. Solomon into custody."

The major lifted his chin up a bit. "I wasn't aware we were being sent two…Delta Force operators, yes?"

"Yes, Major. We're both from Delta," Deuce confirmed. "We were told your men will conduct the breach; our job is to take Mr. Solomon into custody."

Major Sunde nodded in approval. "OK, you can come with us. I still need you to let us lead the raid, but if you have ideas on how to do it better, we'll certainly listen."

195

For the next hour, Deuce and Larry went over the plan again. They made a lot of recommendations on how to breach the home better in order to ensure Mr. Solomon wasn't injured. This was, after all, a grab mission, not a kill mission.

When they felt like they had everything reasonably in order, they all headed down the hallway to the two vans that that would take them to the target's home. They piled in. Moments later, they headed into the city.

Deuce sent a quick text message to the American contingent monitoring the raid, letting them know they were on their way to the target. They also made sure the wireless connections on their body and helmet cameras were working correctly. This would allow the team in Oslo to see what they were seeing.

The two vans moved through the sleepy city with ease. There was no traffic—virtually no vehicles or buses moving about. There wasn't even an early-morning jogger at 0400 hours. It was all but silent as they stealthily moved towards their objective.

As the vans approached the target's home, the FSK operators switched back to their native language. When the van stopped in front of the house, the doors were silently opened as the operators spilled out of the two vehicles, weapons at the ready as they moved.

Five of the FSK men and Larry ran around to the back of the home. Deuce, along with the team leader and four other FSK operators, advanced to the front door.

The breacher placed a specially designed breaching tool against the seam of the front door and the frame. Deuce smiled when he noticed it was the same tool the US military used—crowbar on the front, mallet on the other end, with a collapsible handle that could extend to give them more leverage.

Once he'd placed the pry bar gently into the frame where the door lock was located, the breacher applied just enough force to separate the door from the frame enough to allow them to open it. With the front door unlocked, the soldier gently pushed it open and the operators began to rapidly search the first floor. As they came around to the rear of the house, one of the operators turned the lock on the back door and quietly let in the team that had been waiting just outside.

Major Sunde pointed to the staircase, indicating to Deuce that he should follow him up. The two of them crept up to the next story in the house. The rest of the team followed behind. The group of men fanned out behind Deuce and Sunde to place themselves near the closed door of the master bedroom.

Turning the handle slowly, Sunde opened the door to reveal a single figure sprawled out on the bed. He had a blanket covering half his body, with the other half exposed to the cool air that was circulating in the room due to a ceiling fan. Sunde motioned for Deuce to make the arrest.

Deuce nodded and pulled a pair of flex cuffs off his chest rig. Silently, he approached Mr. Solomon. Before he placed the cuffs on the man that would be his prisoner, Deuce pulled a small syringe from one of his front pouches. In one seamless move, he injected the man with the drug as he held his hand over his mouth, watching until his body went limp. Once he'd put the syringe away, Deuce grabbed Mr. Solomon's hands and zip-tied them.

Major Sunde flicked the lights on and called out that they had secured the target. He then stormed up to Deuce. "Is he still alive?" he asked angrily.

"Of course he's alive," Deuce insisted. "A dead man can't tell tales. We need this guy to sing. I only knocked him out so that when he wakes up, he's in new surroundings with no idea how he got there."

Major Sunde's expression softened. "OK. Good. I was told it was imperative that this man be caught alive. I didn't want to discover you guys killed him when we clearly could have captured him."

Deuce smiled. "No worries, boss. He's alive. You can check his pulse. This is how we like to perform our grabs if we can. It leaves very little to chance if he's knocked out when we capture him."

The team carried Mr. Solomon out of the house to the vans waiting out front. It was now 0406 hours. The neighborhood was still asleep and completely oblivious to what had just happened.

Thirty minutes later, the group sat waiting in their vehicles in the parking lot near the Hurtigruten Port along the waterfront of Trondheim. Eventually they heard what they'd been expecting, the thudding rotor blades of a V-22 Osprey as it headed toward them.

Deuce got out of the vehicle and cracked a couple of extra-large chem sticks, throwing them into the center of the empty parking lot. Larry already had Mr. Solomon thrown over his shoulder.

Major Sunde extended his hand to Deuce. "Thank you for your help," Deuce said as he shook the major's hand.

When the Osprey had settled on the ground, Larry ran toward the rear ramp with the package. A couple of Marines came out to greet them and helped Larry get Mr.

Solomon on board. Deuce then trotted off to climb aboard himself. He stood near the ramp exit as the Osprey lifted off and gave a quick salute to the FSK operators below.

A second later, the tilt-rotor speeded towards their mothership, the USS *America*, which was stationed no more than twenty miles away and flanked by three *Arleigh Burke* destroyers.

****

USS *America*

"How long has he been awake?" Seth asked of one of the CIA men who had been keeping an eye on Mr. Solomon.

"Once he got here, we put the devices on as you requested and woke him up. He's been awake with the equipment running for six hours."

Seth smiled and nodded. "Good. He's going to be thoroughly exhausted and disoriented by now." Then he headed out of their observation room and walked down the silent corridor to the room where they were holding Mr. Solomon. This part of the ship had been cleared of any personnel besides the couple of TF Avenger team members that were standing guard at both ends of the hallway.

Seth entered the small room that would be used for questioning and sat down opposite Mr. Solomon. He nodded for the guard to remove the equipment from his prisoner's eyes and ears and cut the man's zip ties.

It took Mr. Solomon a good thirty seconds of blinking and rubbing his eyes before he was able to focus on his new surroundings. Although he wouldn't know exactly where he was, he would probably be able to tell they were on some kind of ship. The amphibious assault ship didn't rock too much in the water, but it still swayed a bit with the waves.

Mr. Solomon blinked several times and rubbed his eyes. Then, noticing Seth for the first time, he whispered, "Where am I?"

"You are aboard a US warship," Seth explained.

Lance Solomon's facial expressions remained stoic. Seth had to hand it to him—for a man who'd been captured in the middle of the night and drugged, he didn't seem in the least bit surprised.

"Can I have some water?" Mr. Solomon asked.

Seth smiled warmly. "Of course you can." Then he handed him the bottle of water he'd brought with him. Seth had already mixed the happy drug into the beverage; he didn't want to wait around and see if his prisoner would cooperate. He needed to find out quickly if Mr. Solomon knew where Marshall Tate was or who else was involved in this conspiracy. He still had Mr. Jahn providing him information willingly for the time being, and he didn't want the man to have a sudden change of heart.

Mr. Solomon gulped half the bottle down. "If we're going to talk with each other, what is your name?" he inquired. It was clear that his wits were steadily coming back to him. He seemed like he was gearing up for a tough negotiation for Goldman Sachs.

"You can call me Josh. At least, that's what my friends call me," Seth replied.

"I don't think you and I are going to be friends, but you can call me Lance."

Seth noticed the man's eyes glazing over as the drug took effect.

"OK, Lance. I have an urgent question I need to ask you. We believe President Marshall Tate is in grave danger. Our warship has been sent to rescue him before the forces loyal to Sachs are able to capture him, but right now, we believe you are the only man who can provide us with his exact location."

Giving him a quizzical look, Lance asked, "If you aren't on Sachs's side, then why did you kidnap me and bring me here?"

Seth leaned in closer. "We had to make it appear like we're working for Sachs," he replied in a hushed tone. "National Security Advisor Page Larson sent us here at great risk to our ongoing operations to locate Marshall before he's captured. Once we know where he is, we'll be able to use our position on board this ship to help him stay at least one or two steps ahead of the military that's hunting him. Are you able to help or was Page wrong to have sent us?"

At this point, Lance looked really confused. The drugs were wreaking havoc on his ability to think clearly. Sensing that Lance might not be buying his ruse, Seth whispered, "Erik Jahn told us you were Marshall's American money guy. He said if anyone knew where Marshall was right now, it would be you because you handled the finances for him."

Lance nodded like a person who's had one too many alcoholic beverages. "OK. If Page and Erik told you to get in touch with me, then I believe you," he responded. "I don't know the specific location where President Tate currently is, but I do know the bank account that's being used to pay for his security detail and his lodgings. Every seven days, they change to a new bank account so they can stay ahead of the Treasury Department. Do you have a pen and paper? I'll write it down for you. Once you look at the most recent payment history, you should be able to figure out where he is. You need to move quickly, though, if we are to get Tate moved to China. It won't take Sachs's people long to find him now that the UN force collapsed."

"OK. Yes, that makes sense," Seth answered reassuringly. "Is it possible that we can help get him moved to China? Maybe we can steer the Navy in the wrong direction."

"Um. I'm not totally sure on that part. I believe they were going to move him to Russia and then fly him to China," Lance explained.

"I don't think there are any commercial flights between the US or Canada and Russia right now, so do you know what ship he's on?"

Lance shrugged his shoulders. Then his eyes grew wider. "Petr. I'll bet they are going to use Petr's yacht."

Seth fought to control his facial expressions. "Which Petr? There are like a million people in Russia named that."

"Petr Maslov. He's a Russian oligarch. He's also a member of the Thule Society."

"Aren't *you* a high-ranking member of the Thule Society?" Seth asked, trying to piece together this new information with what Erik Jahn had already told him.

Lance shook his head. "No, not at all. Even though I'm the head of Goldman Sachs, I'm only a midlevel member. Roberto, Erik, Peng An, and Johann are senior members. They're involved in the key decisions of the group."

Seth nodded. "OK. That makes sense, Lance. Was the organization itself behind the rigging of the election, or was it some rogue elements within it?"

Lance Solomon shrugged. "Does it matter?" he asked flippantly. "I mean, I think key leaders in the organization may have been involved, but I don't know who all the members are or what their involvement has been. I was just supposed to set up the money funnels needed for Tate to win. When that failed, I helped to redirect that money so it could be spent supporting the CDF militias and fund some of the private military contractors that were being flown in to help stir up more trouble inside the country."

"Ah yes. The PMCs. Do you know which specific ones were going to be used and where? They aren't going to try and actually use American ones, are they?"

Lance broke out in laughter. "Most certainly not. No. They're going to use several different ones for different functions. For instance, Defion International is a Peruvian PMC. These PMCs primarily speak Spanish, so they're going to be used in Texas and California; they'll help the Chinese to pacify the captured cities while their army stays focused on capturing the country. The Senaca Group is responsible for providing a lot of the ground intelligence and counterinsurgency operations in the captured states to support the Chinese forces. They also supported the UN mission prior to it dissolving. I'm not sure what happened to their northern operation once the UN fell apart—they most likely tried to make their way closer to the Chinese positions to help stir up trouble and eventually link back in with their other groups down there."

Lance paused for a moment, clearly struggling to remember details. This was one of the few drawbacks Seth saw in the drugs—when his subjects suddenly became chatty and cooperative, they were often hindered in how much deep knowledge they could provide.

"Ah, yes. Sorry. I lost my train of thought there for a moment," Lance said as he seemed to shake off his mental fog. "The Wagner Group was just contracted to send in their force to join the Chinese in their attempt to finish capturing Texas.

"Before Johann killed himself, he had also succeeded in getting the German Chancellor to turn a blind eye to the Asgaard security group to assist the Chinese in capturing the West Coast. Then there are also a couple of Chinese PMCs that were contracted to help augment their operations in California, but I honestly can't tell you what their names are. I'm sadly not very good at pronouncing their Chinese names." Lance blushed a bit.

"So, you mean to tell me all these private military companies have already been paid to go assist the Chinese in the Southwest?" Seth asked. "I mean, what has all this cost the Thule Society?"

"They were expensive. I was against spending the money once I saw the writing on the wall after that German division surrendered in Chicago. That's why I started making my plans to disappear in Norway. But Johann was insistent that these groups be hired and sent to try and help the Chinese.

"Then Johann had to go and take the easy route when things started falling apart," Lance said with a snort. "The bastard should have stuck around to help us continue the fight." He let out a long sigh before he looked back at Seth.

"You have to understand, it wasn't supposed to turn out like this. We hadn't developed a plan for what to do if Sachs opted to actually fight the UN peacekeepers. Had we known he was going to do that, we would have had these PMCs in place at the outset of the mission and we would have had them infiltrate the country much sooner."

"Everything we've been doing has largely been on the fly with less than reliable partners. I mean, look at the Chinese—they screwed this whole thing up by waiting nearly a month to start military operations. Had they hit the Southwest when we hit the Northeast, there's a good chance Sachs would not still be in power right now. But that didn't happen.

"Personally, I think Peng must have convinced someone in the organization to change plans or he used his knowledge to change the plans for his benefit. But that's my theory. I think Erik would be able to give you a better read on that than I can. He and Peng have known each for a very long time."

Seth nodded. They talked for another hour or so about the finer details of the Thule Society and the private military contractors. Lance wrote down all of the important banking information. At that point, it was only a matter of time until the drug wore off.

Seth spent a few more minutes talking with Lance, giving him some additional details about how he needed to play things out while he was on the ship. Seth told Lance he should trust only him and only talk to him unless he confirmed that the person was safe. Lance nodded his head in agreement, and then Seth slid an Ambien pill across the table.

Lance stared at the white pill with a quizzical look. "I need you to take this so you'll fall into a nice, long, deep sleep," Seth explained. "I'll convince them to leave the sensory deprivation devices off you because you've been cooperative," he said with a wink, "but this will make you collapse into sleep. No one else will be able to question you if you're passed out, OK?"

Lance nodded happily.

"I'll come back and talk to you some more at a later date, but for the time being, I'm going to try and do what I can to make sure Sachs and his cronies don't capture President Tate, OK?"

Lance nodded vigorously. "OK, Josh. I'll do my best to play stupid and only talk with you. I'm sure glad Page and Erik sent you for me. I wasn't sure how much longer I was going to make it before Sachs's people found me."

Leaning in, Seth whispered, "Remember, right now, Sachs and his people think they've captured you. Everyone on board this ship thinks they've captured you. What they don't know is that I'm on *your* side and not theirs. We have to keep that a secret between us so I can get you and Marshall out of this mess, OK?"

Lance smiled a devilish smile. He popped the pill Seth had given him and then walked over to the small cot in the room and lay down.

With nothing more to discuss, Seth got up and headed out the door. He briefly looked at the footage from one of the two hidden cameras that were in the room before he left to go over what they'd just uncovered. They needed to get this information run up the flagpole immediately so it could be disseminated to the appropriate forces.

Chapter Eleven
California Dreaming

California
Fort Tejon State Historic Park

Staff Sergeant Mack jumped a bit when he heard the series of explosions. The morning had otherwise been silent, so it caught him off guard. The engineers were dropping both of the overpasses along the edges of the state park and Interstate 5. The entire 1st Marine Division had been beaten out of LA County. Following their tactical withdrawal, the division had been split up into two forces. Regimental Combat Team 5 was fighting the PLA as they moved up the coastal part of the state, doing what they could to slow or delay the enemy. RCT 7, on the other hand, had the task of trying to keep the PLA from breaking out of southeastern California into Nevada and northern Arizona.

Mack's group, RCT 1, had the unenviable job of trying to keep the Chinese bottled up on this side of the valley before Bakersfield. If the Chinese broke through their lines here, they'd have a straight shot all the way up to Sacramento. The valley, of course, was the prized possession the Chinese were really after—it was the bread bowl of the entire state. It represented more agricultural output than nearly any region in China. Properly managed, the valley could meet a substantial portion of China's agricultural needs for generations to come.

"You think dropping those bridges is going to slow them down?" asked Lieutenant Ambrose as he sat down next to Mack. The two of them could easily see the valley leading toward their positions from their perch.

Staff Sergeant Mack shrugged. "Probably not. But it'll make people feel better. If you ask me, they'll just move infantry around the interstate and secure the area from the rear. Then they'll bring in construction equipment and move the rubble so their tanks and other vehicles can make it through."

Ambrose snorted at the dreary assessment. "Aren't you full of optimism, Staff Sergeant?" he asked sarcastically.

"I'm just being realistic, sir. It's what I'd do if I was in their shoes, and you would too." Mack paused for a minute, contemplating. "I know this is our last line in the sand, so to speak, but we don't have enough combat power to slow these guys down, sir. That National Guard brigade took a brutal mauling covering our retreat back to this position. Did you see how few of their vehicles and men made it back to our lines yesterday? They're spent, LT, just like most of RCT 1."

"That may be so, Staff Sergeant, but we have to stay positive for the men," Ambrose countered. "They're going to need your help more than ever in the coming days. Things are going to get rough when they decide to push us off this perch." The LT waved his hand around at the land around them.

"It'd be a lot easier if we had the state and the people on our side, then. At least half the population out here hates our guts. Heck, we got shot at by a farmer the other day while out on patrol. We even yelled out that we were US Marines. He just yelled for us to 'go back to Sachs country' and continued to shoot at us."

With a look of concern on his face, the LT asked, "What did you guys do with the farmer?"

"We shot him. He wouldn't stop shooting at us, and I wasn't about to lose any of my Marines to some turncoat, so we shot him dead. He didn't cause us any more problems after that," Mack replied angrily as he kicked some dirt with his boot.

"We have to do our best to hold the state or at least slow the Chinese until reinforcements from other parts of the country can arrive and help us out," Ambrose insisted. The young Marine officer was having a hard time dealing with the civilians attacking them too. No one was happy about it, but those were the cards they'd been dealt.

"I wonder how the rest of the division and III MEF is doing along the coast," Mack said. "Part of me wishes we were the ones fighting along the coast. There's a lot more vegetation to hide and fight in than out here. We're pretty out in the open if you think about it."

Lieutenant Ambrose let out a frustrated huff. "I heard from the CO that half of III MEF ended up getting diverted to Hawaii, so we don't even have most of their combat power here to help us like we were supposed to."

"What? When did that happen? I thought that was the whole reason we took the Port of LA."

"It was," Ambrose confirmed. "But half of the division was sent to Hawaii to beef up their positions. They ended up having to recapture the Johnston Atoll, Wake Island, and Midway from the Chinese who had seized them all and were looking to add them to their unsinkable missile platforms in the Pacific. I heard we only have one carrier strike group in the Pacific, so there's some real concern the Chinese might capture Hawaii." The LT paused for a moment as he took a drag on his cigarette. "As it is, Staff Sergeant, we can't really get a lot of supplies flown into the island from the States, and certainly there's no resupply coming from California or even Oregon. The entire Pacific and the West Coast is a bloody mess."

As the two of them were talking, they heard the sound of aircraft flying overhead. Every now and then they'd hear an aerial battle taking place in the skies above them. Sometimes they'd even see a parachute descend to the ground below. If the pilot appeared to be reasonably close to their positions, they'd send a team out to go fetch them. Sometimes they'd end up returning with a Chinese prisoner, other times they'd come back with an American Air Force or Marine pilot.

Just as they were about to resume their conversation, the pitch of the noise coming from the fighters changed, and Mack realized whatever was above them, it was suddenly coming down to attack them. Staff Sergeant Mack looked up and pointed. "I think that's one of those Flounders again!" he exclaimed. "You know, the JH-7s they told us to be leery of."

"Time to hit the deck!" Lieutenant Ambrose yelled. The two of them dove for some cover and watched as the aircraft continued their attack runs.

Ambrose grabbed his radio. "Incoming aircraft, incoming aircraft. Take cover, over!" he shouted, alerting the units below.

A second later, they saw several missiles streak away from one of the aircraft as it turned hard and lit up its afterburners. Moments later, they heard several loud explosions but couldn't quite see what had been destroyed. Then the planes circled back around. They appeared to be lining up for an attack run on the troops scattered about in the hills and woods of the state park.

As the fighter bombers got closer to their positions, they cut loose a swarm of rockets into the valley and hills where the Marines had taken refuge. Then the warplanes pulled up hard and sped away. Two Stinger missiles shot up through the underbrush and immediately gave chase to the retreating fighters.

The Chinese planes spat out flares to distract the heat-seeking warheads. One of the Stingers went for the flares, while the other one detonated just behind the engines of one of the Chinese planes.

"I think one of the engines blew up," Sergeant Mack told Ambrose. "Check out all that flame and smoke."

The pilot ejected as his plane lost control. The aircraft blew up shortly after that. The pilot's parachute filled with air, and he began his slow descent to the earth below.

For the next thirty minutes, Chinese warplanes showed up in larger numbers as they sought to attack the Marine position. However, shortly after the Chinese aircraft began arriving in larger groups, US fighters joined the fray.

While the knights of the air fought it out, the King of Battle made his presence known. A rolling crescendo of artillery fire rained down on the valley and the ridgelines where the Marines held their positions. Explosion after explosion rocked the area, sending debris and shrapnel in all directions.

At one point, the artillery barrage on the state park had gotten so bad, Staff Sergeant Mack wasn't sure there would be anyone left alive.

They must have moved an entire brigade's worth of artillery, he thought. *This is insane.*

The attack lasted for nearly two hours. Once it had finally let up, Mack stood up and looked around for his Marines. Fortunately, everyone had dug a fighting hole for this very reason. The one thing they'd been forced to learn rapidly when fighting the Chinese was that they loved artillery. They'd hammer an area for an hour, or three or four, and *then* launch their ground assault.

Staff Sergeant Mack knew their strategy. He was concerned that the Chinese had been using the hours-long barrage to move their infantry into place.

Sure enough, within the first few minutes of the barrage finally letting up, he heard the unmistakable shriek of a PLA officer's whistle.

"Everyone up!" Mack screamed to his squad. "Man the trench line *now!*"

The other squad leaders began yelling the same thing at their men. In an effort not to give away their positions, the Marines had dug several trench lines just below the top of the ridge. They'd also built a secondary line that was directly on top of the ridge, in case they needed to fall back.

On the reverse slope, the Marines had dug another set of positions where they'd ridden out the bombardments. The logic was that if they gave the enemy something to shoot at, they'd focus their attention there and not where the Marines were actually hiding.

As Mack reached the top of the ridge and looked down at their two defense lines, he smiled. Those positions looked like a moonscape. The PLA had pounded them relentlessly, but no one was there. Their strategy had worked. Despite hours of artillery attacks, very few of their men had been injured or killed.

Seeing his predesignated position, Mack jumped into one of the six-man trenches. His M240 gunner soon joined him. Mack had also swapped out his M16A2 for one of the newer M27 IARs; this significantly upgraded his squad's firepower and gave them a real boost.

While everyone was filtering into the positions, bullets started to crack and snap all around them. Looking down the ridge, Mack saw a veritable wall of humanity attempting to race up to them. It was almost like a tsunami wave steadily rising towards them, threatening to overwhelm and envelop them—only this wave was not made of water but of angry Chinese soldiers hell-bent on killing them.

The sight sent a chill down his spine. Turning his emotions off, Mack fell back into his training, just as he had done so many times before.

"Open fire! Give 'em hell, men," Mack screamed. He raised his M27 to his shoulder and began firing single-shot rounds at the incoming horde as accurately as possible. The enemy was three hundred meters away, but they were steadily gaining ground.

Several of the M240 gunners opened fire, sending sheets of hot lead down the ridge, cutting down huge swaths of enemy soldiers. The two other M27 gunners also joined the fray, and then the rest of the company began to place well-aimed shots at the enemy.

At this range, killing the enemy required a lot more skill and technique than what the Chinese soldiers were showing. The PLA soldiers were just aiming their QBZ-95s up the ridge and firing a few shots indiscriminately in between running forward and pausing long enough to catch their breath. Every now and then, Mack would spot a handful of soldiers sporting the newer LR17 battle rifles, which were very much like the Army's M4, tricked out with Agoc sights, forward handlebars and other convenient attachments that made killing one's enemy easier.

Mack and his squad had only been in the trench line firing for maybe two or three minutes when he heard the familiar sound of mortars flying over their heads towards the enemy. The mortar rounds landed directly on the ranks of the charging infantry, throwing metal fragments everywhere.

Sergeant Mack allowed himself to breathe for just a moment. The mortars were effectively blunting the enemy's relentless assault of the hill. He flipped the unlock lever for his machine gunner, who swiftly changed out the barrel before it overheated.

Unfortunately, the reprieve was short-lived. While the mortars were decimating the enemy ranks, six Chinese C-10 attack helicopters fired a barrage of antimaterial rockets right at the Marine positions. Then the choppers raked their lines with their chin-mounted 14.5mm Gatling guns.

"Take those damn choppers out!" someone yelled to the Stinger operators.

Seconds later, a pair of Stingers flew out towards the killing machines. The appearance of the missiles caused the C-10s to break off their attack run and take evasive maneuvers. Fortunately for the Marines, both missiles found their marks and two of the helicopters crashed to the ground in a fiery mess.

An American F-15E swooped in low over the Marine positions and fired off four air-to-air missiles, which summarily obliterating the remaining enemy helicopters. When the F-15E banked hard to the left to get back over friendly lines and gain more altitude, dozens of strings of enemy tracer rounds flew out from every which direction after the American warplane. While the Eagle pilot managed to evade what looked like a carpet of anti-aircraft fire, a missile streaked down from higher altitude and blew the plane apart. Mack didn't see a parachute, so he figured both pilots must have been killed.

They saved our lives and it cost them theirs, he thought.

He shook his shoulders out and returned his attention to what was directly in front of him. The enemy had recovered from the mortar attack and was once again charging up toward them. They were now just under 150 meters away.

Mack aimed his M27 at a small cluster of enemy soldiers and squeezed the trigger once, hitting the man he was aiming at in his right shoulder. Adjusting his aim slightly to the left, Mack fired another round, hitting a second guy. Then he dropped below the lip of the trench to reload his rifle. A string of rounds hit the sandbags right where he had just been.

One of the guys in his squad that was standing next to him grunted as he clutched his chest and then fell backwards into the trench. Mack saw he had been hit just above his body armor. Blood was pulsing between the man's fingers as he tried to slow the bleeding. Then he coughed. Blood spewed out of his mouth. Sergeant Mack knew immediately that his squadmate was dying. He'd been hit in the lungs, and they were already filling with blood. The young man didn't have much time, maybe a minute or so before he'd be gone.

Mack saw fear in the young man's eyes. He'd probably put two and two together just like Mack had done. He knew he was going to die.

Despite all the shooting, screaming, and death going on around them, Mack placed his rifle against the side of the trench wall and reached for the man's free hand. Looking him in the eye, he said, "Don't be afraid, Pinkman. I'm here with you. You aren't alone. You did a great job. You did everything you could to help your brothers, and I couldn't be prouder of you than I am right now."

Tears streamed down the young man's face. Then he let go of the bullet wound and reached into his cargo pocket. Blood was still leaking out of the wound, but it wasn't gushing like it was before. His body was starting to fail, but he held out long enough to place a bloody envelope into Mack's hand. With his dying breath, he said, "Give this to my parents. I want them to know that I'm no longer angry at them, that I still love them."

The man's grip suddenly loosened, and his hand fell to the ground. His head drooped down to his chest and he was gone.

Wiping away his own tears, Mack shoved the bloodied letter into his pocket and grabbed his rifle. It was as if the world around him had come to a complete halt as he spent the last minute of Pinkman's life with him, holding him and reassuring him that he was loved and his brothers were proud of him. A second later, though, the sounds of war rushed right back into his head and reverberated throughout his body. Each explosion felt like a body blow as the sound waves hammered his senses.

Looking around him, Mack could see that maybe a quarter of their platoon was dead, while at least another quarter had been wounded in some fashion but was continuing to fight. They all knew if the enemy broke through their positions, they'd be killed for sure and the rest of the valley would be at the mercy of this marauding army invading their country.

Gripping his rifle handle tight, Mack looked down at the charging soldiers. They were now within a hundred meters. They were getting close—close enough that Mack could see the raw emotions of fear, anger, hatred, and determination written on their faces.

Mack flicked the selector switch on his M27 from semi to full auto and squeezed off controlled bursts of automatic fire into their ranks. He knew this would burn through his ammo, but he had to slow the Chinese down and do what he could to stop them from overrunning his position.

Soon after, Sergeant Mack dropped his second magazine of the battle; he slapped the next one in place and hit the bolt release. He changed positions slightly and proceeded to fire another set of controlled bursts into the enemy ranks. As soon as he'd cut down three or four enemy soldiers, the gap would fill up with more soldiers charging from the next row below. It was pure murder what Mack and his platoon were doing to these men, but if they didn't keep killing them, they'd be wiped out themselves.

Over the constant roar of machine guns and rifles firing at each other, Mack heard an F/A-18 Super Hornet, flying low along the valley. As the aircraft flew over the enemy positions, a series of cluster munitions released across their positions. Intermixed with the cluster bombs were a handful of Mk 82 Snake Eye bombs. Between the cluster munitions and the 500-pound dumb bombs, the enemy was severely hammered.

The attack started to falter and lose steam, but the enemy officers continued to blow their whistles, urging their soldiers onward. Just then, nearly a dozen smoke rounds exploded over the tops of the enemy positions. The smoke rounds threw dozens of little smoke canisters down into the

PLA soldiers' positions, which immediately began to blot out the Marines' ability to see them.

Oh, this isn't good, Mack realized. If he and his men couldn't see the Chinese soldiers, they'd be able to charge right up to their positions.

Then dozens of smoke rounds dispersed right over the Marine positions. At this point, Mack knew he and the rest of the Marines were in trouble. The enemy was going to smoke the entire area out and force everyone to fight practically at point-blank range, which would favor the attackers, not the defenders.

Mack heard their platoon leader, Lieutenant Ray Ambrose, yell out. "Everyone, fall back to your secondary positions!"

Sergeant Mack grunted. He couldn't see squat—maybe moving to a new position might help.

Before leaving, Mack grabbed Pinkman's remaining rifle magazines. He knew he'd need them. Then he reached over to set off the series of claymores they still had out there.

The first claymore he tried to detonate didn't go off. *Damn it, the artillery must have severed the detonator cord.*

He grabbed for the second clicker and depressed it several times in rapid succession, just like he had done many times before. This one blew up immediately. Mack couldn't see if he had hit anything, but he wasn't waiting around to find out either. He repeated the process with the remaining two clickers and then ran to their fallback positions.

While they waited for the next wave, the M240 gunners swapped out their barrels and attached additional belts to the ones they already had in the weapons. The Marines knew they wouldn't have time to do these tasks when the enemy emerged from the smokescreen. By the time the Chinese reached their first defensive line, it would place the enemy soldiers no more than fifty meters from them.

The one blessing Sergeant Mack could perceive, however, was a shift in the wind. It was now blowing over the ridge top and moving down the slope, pushing the smokescreen further down into the valley and exposing the PLA infantrymen a lot earlier.

The Marines wasted no time in taking advantage of the change in situation. As soon as the Chinese soldiers emerged from the smoke, the Marines resumed firing, killing as many of the enemy soldiers as they could as they continued their relentless charge up the hill.

"Staff Sergeant Mack!" shouted Lieutenant Ambrose.

Mack spotted the LT waving for him. He jumped up and ran over to him. "What do you need, LT?" he asked as he plopped down next to the lieutenant.

"Gunny Crockett is dead. Staff Sergeant Matz was also killed. You're my new platoon sergeant. We have to hold this position until our rides show up."

Staff Sergeant Mack felt his jaw hang open from surprise. "What do you mean until our rides show up? Are we leaving?"

Ambrose nodded, his disapproval evident. "Yeah. The entire RCT is going to try and pull back to Camp Nelson in the Mountain Home State Forest. No idea what the plan is once we get there, but we're supposed to get ready to move in twenty mikes."

Mack fired off a couple of short bursts at an attacking group of enemy soldiers, then turned back to the LT. "They *do* realize we're in the process of trying not to get overrun right now, don't they?" he asked. The enemy was already at their first line of defense.

"I know, Staff Sergeant. The captain is over there trying to repulse this attack as well. We have some fast movers inbound. When they plaster the enemy positions, that's when we're supposed to beat feet down to our rides." He pointed further down the road behind them, where there were several long lines of LAVs, JLTVs, and a few amphibs. "Just make sure the rest of the platoon is ready to move. I'm going to go tell Third and Fourth Squad; I need you to make sure First and Second Squads are ready."

The LT didn't wait for any further comments. Despite incoming enemy fire, he dashed off to Third and Fourth Squads' positions so he could tell them to be ready to move.

Mack made his own way back down the line and passed the information along to his Marines, firing a burst from his M27 every time he stopped moving. The enemy was now less than forty meters from their positions.

At that point, Mack yelled, "Start blowing the claymores!"

Seconds later, one by one exploded all along the line. Swaths of enemy soldiers turned into a bright red mist of pulverized flesh from the barrage of tiny steel ball bearings. The antipersonnel mines acted like giant scythes, cutting down nearly everything in their paths for a solid ten to twenty meters. Further back, they were still hitting soldiers—the small metal balls that would often break bones or blow tiny holes through their bodies. The claymores were brutal but incredibly effective for the type of fighting they were doing.

Four F/A-18 Super Hornets swooped over their positions, releasing more cluster munitions and 500-pound bombs on the enemy charging their positions. When the fighters made a second pass, they used their cannons to strafe the Chinese soldiers that were practically right on top of the Marines.

"First and Second Squad, fall back!" Sergeant Mack yelled.

It was controlled chaos. The Marines stopped firing at the enemy, and under the cover of the air attack, they ran like hell down the ridge to get in the waiting vehicles. The gunners on top of the vehicles and the LAV turrets were all aimed up at the Marines who were running toward them. They were ready to cover their retreat should the enemy manage to crest the ridge.

Mack made sure to pull up the rear of the position. He wanted to make sure none of their guys got left behind. He helped a couple of the wounded guys maneuver down the trail and got them seated inside the vehicles. As soon as the last Marine was loaded up, the vehicles peeled out. They headed down the road that would lead them through a series of ridges in the park to the other side of Interstate 5, where the engineers hadn't destroyed or blocked the road yet. It was a race against time to put as much distance as possible between themselves and the enemy they were retreating from.

Once inside the relative safety of the vehicles, a couple of the soldiers broke down and shed a few tears for their dead comrades. No one said a thing about them crying. The guys just needed to let those emotions out so they could go back to killing the enemy when the time came.

As they moved back onto the Interstate and picked up speed, Mack ordered, "Start reloading your magazines! There's a stash of ammo in this LAV."

Corporal Phillips dropped a few f-bombs. "I can't believe we're retreating again, Staff Sergeant. We've been leaving one position after another now for nearly two months. I'm tired of retreating."

Many of the others nodded their heads in agreement. The troops were getting frustrated by defeat after defeat. It was demoralizing to be constantly losing friends fighting on a hill, only to have to fall back and give that hill up to the enemy.

Although Mack agreed with their frustrations, he decided to try and lighten the mood a bit and remind them all of the bigger picture. "Corporal, first of all, we are not retreating. Don't ever let anyone tell you that, and don't you ever believe it. We're merely fighting in the opposite direction and making sure the enemy doesn't capture the land to our rear." A handful of Marines laughed. It was kind of an old cliché, but it got the message across.

"Second, we are bloodying them immensely with each of these battles we fight. Did you not see how the entire ground before us was covered like fall leaves with their dead? The enemy can't continue to sustain casualties like that. Besides, our next location we're going to secure is a hundred times better than what we just left."

Corporal Phillips smiled as he shook his head. "OK, Captain America. Where are we headed to now?" he asked.

Mack grinned. He was glad to see Phillips snap out of the doom-and-gloom mood he'd just been in. "We're headed to the Mountain Home State Forest," he explained. "It's a densely packed wooded forest with some good hills and some low-lying mountain ranges. It's the type of covered terrain that will allow us to thoroughly destroy these Chinese soldiers."

The rest of the guys in the vehicle nodded and smiled. They clearly liked the idea of that. Mack knew they'd just suffered a tough loss and that they'd all lost some friends, but they still had a war to fight and there'd be plenty more battles that needed to be fought; he had to get their minds back in the game or they could end up falling apart as a platoon.

For the next three hours, the remnants of RCT 1 drove like madmen trying to get away from the Chinese force. They were fortunate in that a squadron of Air Force F-35s had been assigned to provide them with air cover. The Lightnings did a hell of a job keeping the Chinese Air Force off their backs.

When the Marines reached Bakersfield, it was almost like they'd reached a "Welcome Home" party. Well-wishers gathered outside, waving flags and displaying signs that thanked the Marines for liberating them. Sadly, the Marine vehicles couldn't stop. The residents' initial cheerful reaction soon soured when they noticed the dilapidated states of the vehicles and saw that they were only passing through—they had to know that the men weren't there to liberate them from the California state government and that they were fleeing from the Chinese Army.

As they continued along the road, Mack and his men saw several citizens follow behind them in their own vehicles. The people must have figured they'd have a better chance where the Marines were than as sitting ducks waiting in their homes.

****

Long Beach, California
Bluff Park

Xander and Trojan, both a part of SEAL Team 7, had been hiding out in one of Trojan's family homes in Long Beach. They kept observing and sending a microburst transmission of their data every eight hours.

Their platoon had been told to disperse and disappear within the population of LA and the surrounding area and await further orders just before the Marines pulled out. Some of the platoons, like theirs, had been broken down into small observation teams. Their goal was to provide a variety of surveillance and intelligence of what was going on in the city and the ports back to SOCOM and the Pentagon.

Each day, they'd send up two high-altitude signals intelligence drones, which were roughly twelve inches in diameter and hard to detect unless someone knew to look for them. Once the drones reached about fifteen hundred feet in the air, a small set of wings would unfold and allow the devices to largely glide on the wind. Interwoven on the wings were a series of solar panels that allowed the batteries to continue to charge, which kept the drones flying for a solid eight to twelve hours. When the batteries were getting low, the wings would retract and the drones would descend to the rooftop, where Xander or Trojan would retrieve them so they could recharge them in the house.

Mounted on the bottom of each drone was a small electronic device that was specifically tuned to listen to and copy radio traffic on the bands the PLA were using. When one of the drones needed to land due to a low battery, Xander or Trojan would download the copied radio traffic and include it in their next burst transmission. They'd wipe the memory card clean and then load it back into the drone before they launched it again later. This allowed them to continually scoop up the radio traffic in the occupied zones for further analysis by the NSA, DIA, and CIA.

"I still can't believe your family owns this place," Xander commented. It was probably the hundredth time he'd made the same remark since they'd set up shop here more than a month ago.

"You keep saying that. Why are you so surprised?" asked Trojan, the lieutenant in charge of this particular intelligence operation.

"I don't know. I grew up in a poor neighborhood in Chicago. I used to walk along Michigan Avenue as a kid, looking at all the fancy apartments and condos along Lake Michigan. I mean, I knew there were rich neighborhoods and people lived in those fancy places, but I never knew anyone who lived there. I guess I was surprised when you said we could bunk out in one of your family homes, that's all."

Trojan sighed. *And this is why I never talked about my background or where my family lives*, he thought.

"My dad has always been smart with money," Trojan explained. "He knew the market was going to crash in 2006, so he started liquidating all of his rental properties. He made a mint doing it. Then he dumped everything into gold when it was still cheap. When the market tanked, he tripled his money with the gold he'd bought. Then in 2013, when the market started to stabilize, he sold all his gold and dumped it all back into real estate again. I saw him snatching up properties left and right for half of what they'd sold for just five years earlier. By the time I graduated college in 2014, the family business owned fourteen houses in Long Beach.

"When I graduated SEAL training, my dad sold two of his properties to me dirt cheap so I could build my own equity in them. That way, I'd have something to fall back on when I got out of the SEALs. I kept them rented, and here we are, staying in my house that I rented to my aunt. It's the perfect cover, Xander."

"Tell you what, Trojan, when this war is over with, you need to sit down and show me how to get into this business," said Xander. "Clearly it's paying off for you. I've spent eighteen years in the Navy, I've never been married, and I save like a packrat. At this point, I've got about five hundred grand in my investment account. Maybe you can help me figure out the best way how to use it to set myself up for life after the SEALs."

Trojan nodded. "I like that idea. We'll definitely do it. When this war is over, the whole of San Diego and LA is going to be ripe for buying and flipping. We'll make a fortune if we time it right."

Trojan returned his gaze to the spotting scope they had set up in one of the bedrooms. It provided them with an exceptional view of the port and all the ships docked there. Spying something unusual, he tried to angle the spotting scope to get a better look, but he just couldn't get the right angle. "Look at that, Xander," he remarked. "That must be the fourth freighter I've seen pull up to the cruise terminal this week. Something seems odd about it. You never see them offload any troops or equipment, so what are they doing?"

Xander walked up to the scope and looked at the terminal for himself. From their vantage point, they couldn't really see what was going on. The angle was wrong, and they couldn't see what all was going on in the nearby parking lot with the floating museum in their way.

Xander shrugged. "I don't know what's going on at the cruise terminal, sir. What I *do* know is there's a long gravy train of transports and supply ships offloading at the port. That's what we need to keep our eye on."

"Yeah, but don't you think we should turn one of the surveillance drones to head over in that direction and at least see what they're doing?" Trojan asked. "I mean, you've heard the rumors about people turning up missing all over LA. This could have something to do with it."

Xander snorted. "Look, I get it. I know you want to believe your nephew and all, but we can't risk losing one of our surveillance drones to check out a rumor," he insisted. "I mean, at the end of the day, sir, you're in charge, but my advice is we don't risk one of our few surveillance drones by attracting any unwanted attention. We need to keep feeding the guys at SOCOM and the Pentagon with a steady report of what's being offloaded and the radio traffic. If we attract the PLA's attention because they spot a surveillance drone, they might trace it back to us and then the jig is up. We've been lucky they haven't already found us. I don't know if we want to push the envelope any further than we already have."

Trojan nodded grudgingly, but he still couldn't shake the feeling that something was off about those transports.

****

Later that evening, after dark, Trojan opened a small case that held some of their microdrones. These little drones were the size of his hand. They didn't have a long battery life, but they were outfitted with night vision and thermal sensors that could allow them to see what was going on no matter what the conditions were like outside.

Walking into the room, Xander saw him looking longingly at the little drones. "You want to use one of them to go check it out, don't you?" he asked.

Trojan nodded but didn't say anything.

Xander shrugged. "Well, these are more of a throwaway drone, and you'll probably have a better chance of seeing what's going on over there now than if we try to do this during the day. Let me get the laptop up and running so we can record what we're seeing."

A smile crept across Trojan's face. He hurried to set up one of the drones and synced it with the laptop so they could see what it saw. They walked out to the patio and he set it on the ground. Then he put on the virtual reality goggles he'd need to fly the drone and grabbed the hand controller.

Once the system check had been completed, he initiated flight. After the drone had reached about three hundred feet, Trojan aimed it toward the cruise ship terminal and sped off to go investigate. As he neared the terminal, he moved the drone up to around eight hundred feet. They could finally see past the transport ship and into the nearby parking lot.

There were dozens upon dozens of buses. Some were leaving the parking lot, while many others appeared to have just arrived. Using the zoom on the camera, Trojan saw a lot of people getting off the buses. Still not sure exactly what was going on, he lowered the drone five hundred feet.

"Oh my God," Xander remarked. "Why the hell are they loading a bunch of women into the transport ship?"

"There have to be some men in the group," Trojan responded. But a moment later, he hadn't seen any either. "Xander, *both* of these transport ships are being loaded up with nothing but women." He could feel his mouth hanging open at the horror of it.

"What are they doing with all of them?" asked Xander, concern in his voice.

"I don't know," Trojan replied. He turned the drone around to help provide them with a clearer picture of the cruise terminal and the ships in port. He made sure to get a good look at the ship number and name for the analyst they'd be sending this data back to.

With the VR headset still on, Trojan asked, "Don't these microdrones have a tracking device on them?"

"Um, yeah," said Xander. "Why are you asking?"

"I'm looking at the battery life and right now we're showing roughly twenty-one percent. I'm not sure it'll make it back home before it cuts out, but I could try and find a nice spot to set it down on one of these transports. If it has a tracking device, we can have the NSA track the ship and find out where it's heading."

"You know, if you find a nice little spot for it to land, you can deploy the little solar panel wings. They're slow as hell when charging, but if it's going across the Pacific, it'll have plenty of time to recharge. When it arrives in China, the NSA could probably remote access it and see where they are taking the women. It might help shed some light on what's going on," Xander explained.

Trojan smiled at the idea and looked for a nice quiet little spot where he could set the drone down. He found a small ledge near the top of one of the smokestacks. It had just enough of a lip that it looked like it would keep the drone from getting swept off the ship by the wind or a rainstorm during the journey across the ocean, so he opted to set it down there. With only six percent left on the battery life, Trojan extended the little rechargeable solar wings and shut the drone down. It would now trickle charge for a few weeks as it journeyed to wherever it was going.

Later that evening, they both wrote up what they'd seen and included the file of the video they'd taken. They provided the serial number of the drone along with its unit identifier number—that would allow the NSA or CIA to remotely access it once it reached China, assuming they had a satellite nearby that hadn't been shot down that could take control of the drone.

With their work for the day done, they prepared the information packet to be sent off along with the other data they had collected during the day. In twenty minutes, it would all be transmitted back to SOCOM and the Pentagon for further analysis.

Chapter Twelve
Texas Discovery

Ciudad Juárez, Mexico

Diaz lay on the ground under a desert camouflage IR-resistant netting, looking through his spotting scope. Under the cover of darkness, they'd found this spot, just far enough away from people not to be spotted but just close enough to provide them a good view of what the locals were telling them was a mass grave site. He and Perez had dug a shallow fighting position and then set up their camouflage over top of it to help ward off the heat and provide them with enough room to move a bit underneath and not get spotted.

It had taken them nearly four days to reach this position undetected. They had been fortunate to have found a local that hated the Chinese as much as the Americans and had been willing to show them where to look.

Perez and Diaz were members of the 7th Special Forces Group out of Eglin Air Force Base. They were both Latino Americans and native speakers of Spanish, which meant they had an easier time infiltrating into Mexico and being passed off as locals instead of Americans. Their ODA team had been tasked with crossing the Mexican side of the border and investigating some claims being made by American refugees that had escaped from the Chinese occupied zones.

There are had been rumors of mass killings. Thousands of women were supposedly disappearing. No one really knew what was going on and satellite intelligence and even drone surveillance over the battlefield raging across the southern border was sketchy at best. A pair of human eyes needed to investigate it further.

By the middle of the first day of them observing the abandoned stretch of desert, all they had seen was what appeared to be a random bulldozer and two large Caterpillar front-end loaders. Then, around 1600 hours, a PLA Mengshi, the Chinese version of the American Humvee, showed up. Four soldiers got out.

Two of the soldiers started marking out something on the ground while what appeared to be an officer pointed at a few areas. Each time he pointed somewhere new, the soldiers ran to where he was pointing and sprayed something on the ground, then they moved to the next area and repeated the process. This went on for maybe thirty minutes before one of the soldiers climbed into the bulldozer and started up the metal beast. As the diesel engine got warmed up, it belched thick black smoke into the air.

The soldier driving the vehicle maneuvered it over to one of the marks where they'd sprayed the ground. He dropped the front blade and then began to dig a long trench. He made three passes over the same stretch of dirt, creating a four- or five-foot-deep trench with large mounds of dirt on either end.

Once the trench had been dug, two other PLA soldiers hopped into large front-end loaders and started digging the ditch a little deeper in the center portion. It took the guys who were working the construction equipment maybe an hour to get whatever it was they were doing completed. Then the officer appeared to place a call, which didn't last long, and he and the three other soldiers made their way back to the Mengshi and began eating some food.

"What do you think they're doing?" Perez asked quizzically.

"Not sure yet," said Diaz. "But if you look further behind the trench they just made, there appear to be several long mounds of dirt—almost like they've done this before. The mounds don't stick up much above the ground, but you can see they're still fresh, like they've just been created in the past few days."

Perez grunted. "If I didn't know any better, I'd say these are mass grave sites, kind of like what we've seen down in Colombia, Iraq, or Syria."

Diaz shivered at the thought. "If they are, then it'd confirm some of the stories those refugees have been telling."

When the soldiers appeared to be done eating, Diaz turned to Perez. "I think you should set up the transmitter," he said in a low voice. "We won't have a lot of time once whoever it is that's coming shows up."

Nodding, Perez pulled out a small directional communications antenna and angled it toward the Gulf of Mexico. The Air Force had a couple of UAVs that'd be operating in the area to relay whatever they transmitted and make sure it was passed along to SOCOM.

While Perez was setting up his part of the operation, Diaz grabbed a SOCOM version of the Swarovski 20-60x80 spotting scope, which had a specially designed video recorder and transmitter fitted to the back of it. After setting the $5,000 optical masterpiece up next to their other spotting scope, Diaz snapped his fingers for Perez to toss him the coax cable for the transmitter. Diaz attached it to a USB-coax converter and placed the USB device into the small Toughbook laptop he'd set up next to the scope. He then attached another USB cord from the Toughbook to the spotting scope and started running through a quick systems check.

Next, Diaz grabbed the small roll-out solar pack and tossed it to Perez. Barely sticking his hand outside their IR protective netting, Perez unrolled the camouflage solar panels and then attached the power cable from the panel back to the computer. This DARPA-designed rollable solar panel was just large enough to power a Toughbook and their directional communication antenna. It was also painted in a color pattern that would make it very hard to spot with the naked eye and impossible to see from the sky. For their operations, it was absolutely critical that the sun not glint off it, giving away their position.

Next, Perez pulled out a small Israeli-made surveillance drone, about one foot in diameter. It could reach a maximum altitude of about three thousand feet. If it wasn't moving aggressively, it could stay aloft for upwards of two hours, providing nearly constant real-time video of whatever they placed the drone over. The video feed could either be transmitted back to them or be stored on a memory card for later download.

Once the drone was ready, Perez placed it just outside their protective netting and grabbed the VR headset and the handset. All he had to do at this point was turn it on and start transmitting the video.

Diaz made sure the secured Wi-Fi was in stealth mode and synced to the drone. This would allow them to see the video feed was working correctly before they launched it. Diaz set up the computer screen so that the drone feed would display on half of the screen while the view from the spotting scope would be on the other side. At the bottom, he had the communication control panel opened so he could monitor the communication status of the data.

"I'm sending the code to the Navy to get their relay system set up," Perez announced. It was time to get ready for whatever was coming next.

Nearly an hour went by before they saw their first sign of activity. It was now 1900 hours, and they probably had about another hour or so of sunlight. Perez suddenly pointed down the road; there were dozens of trucks and buses heading towards them. "I think this is it—what we've been sent out here to see." He sent a text message via their Thuraya phone to their HQ, letting them know they would start transmitting data soon.

Up in the air, two Air Force RQ-170 Sentinel UAVs waited to receive their data. One loitered a hundred miles away, and the other was flying eight hundred miles away.

These stealth surveillance UAVs would hover above the battlespace and act like radio receivers, grabbing data and then parsing that data out into small data packets that would be transmitted in microbursts. The Sentinels were an excellent tool because they could transmit data while drastically reducing the electronic signature. The Air Force couldn't use the drone for constant real-time surveillance or it's stealth features wouldn't work, but for short one-off missions like this, they were the perfect tool, despite the risk that they might get detected.

When the trucks and buses stopped near the Mengshi, Perez quietly commented, "Hey, check out all the passengers. They're all slumped over like they fell asleep during the drive or something."

"Get the drone up. We need to start getting more angles to this," Diaz whispered. "Try to make sure the drone has a good view of what's going on over that trench."

Perez nodded and began to fly the drone. Diaz activated the video recorder on the spotting scope and recorded what he could. He started his video feed by showing how many vehicles were there. Then he zoomed in on one of the truck bays with the bodies all slouching on each other. Using the zoom magnification, he was able to make out that the passengers in the back of the truck appeared to be older. He didn't spot many people under the age of seventy. There were a few younger-looking folks, but not many.

Moving the scope to one of the trucks a bunch of soldiers were near, Diaz saw the two large Caterpillar front-end loaders line up at the end of the truck. The equipment drivers then raised the front bucket up a little bit to place them more level with the back of the truck. When the first front-end loader moved up the edge of the truck, a couple of soldiers in the back bay grabbed some of the slouching bodies and started throwing them into the large bucket of the front-end loader.

"Perez, those slouching people weren't asleep," Diaz moaned. "That wasn't a sedative they were using, either—they're all dead." Instinctively, Diaz grabbed his pen and started making a tick mark for each person he saw being dumped into the front bucket of the loader.

Each time the bucket appeared full, which was usually when eight or nine bodies had been tossed into it, the loader would back up and head towards the trench while the other loader took its place.

Using the spotting scope to follow the loader, Diaz made sure they got a good image of it dropping bodies into the trench. He followed the loader back to the truck, where the process was repeated.

By the time the loader made its third trip, the sun had gone down. Some of the soldiers had set up portable lights near the truck that was being emptied and had placed a couple along the trench to help light it up.

The whole process went on for probably six hours as they emptied all the trucks and buses of their human cargo. When all of the vehicles were empty, they left as a group to return to where they'd come from.

Once the buses and trucks were gone, the soldiers who were driving the loaders and the bulldozer began to cover up all the bodies with the dirt piles they had created. It took them close to sixty minutes to fill in the mass grave and level out the dirt. When they were done, a small mound remained, just like the ones behind it.

Finally, the soldiers then parked the construction equipment nearby, hopped back into their Mengshi truck and headed into town.

A couple of hours into the whole ordeal, Perez had to bring their drone back to base. He immediately swapped out the spent battery with a new one but held off on launching it until after the enemy soldiers had left the area. They had seen what they needed to see. Now that they were certain each of those mounds represented a mass grave, all that remained was to count how many of them were already out there.

Twenty minutes after the soldiers had left, they sent their drone back up to investigate. They spent the next thirty minutes counting and investigating every possible mound they thought might have been a mass grave. In short order, they'd counted forty-seven of them.

Turning to look at his partner, Perez asked, "Roughly how many people would you say were buried in each mound?"

Diaz looked down at his pad of paper and then did some quick math. "There were around five hundred bodies in the mound we just saw them cover up. If all of those mounds hold roughly the same number of dead, then that'd add up to something like twenty-three thousand bodies."

Perez shook his head. "We should snatch one of these guys and try to find out how these people died. They were clearly dead when they showed up. Are they being executed and then brought out here or what's the deal?"

Diaz nodded. "I agree. Let me see if HQ will let us do that or what they want us to do next. Otherwise, I don't think we need to stay out here now that we've seen what we needed to."

****

Brownwood, Texas

Sergeant Matt Higgins of the 2nd Armored Brigade Combat Team looked at the Sergeant First Class Velcro insignia he was holding in his hand. He knew he should be elated that he was being promoted two full grades. Instead, he just felt sorrow and anger. He hadn't earned this rank. It wasn't being given to him because he was qualified to hold it or because he was a model soldier.

Hell, two weeks before the war, they gave me an Article 15, he remembered. He'd been demoted from staff sergeant to sergeant after he'd gotten tangled up in a bar fight at a strip club with some guys from his platoon and had unknowingly struck an officer who'd gotten into a heated argument with one of the soldiers in his squad.

Then the war had broken out, and it had been nonstop fighting ever since. Looking down at the new rank insignia again, he knew why he'd been given this promotion: he was one of the few remaining sergeants left alive in his platoon. They'd already lost two lieutenants since the fighting had started, as well as a company CO. The unit was running on fumes, and it didn't look like they were going to slow down anytime soon.

For the time being, their company had taken over a small budget inn not far from US-67. It was on one of the main roads that connected San Angelo to Dallas-Fort Worth to the west, and Junction City to the south along Interstate 10. It wasn't a very large city, but it did straddle a couple of key four-lane highways that led to the Dallas area.

Most of the brigade was scattered around the area. The infantry units acted as the stationary fixed force and the armor and cav units were the mobile force that would shift around, depending on where the enemy was hitting the line the hardest. It was a tough position for the infantry battalions to be in since they would largely be on their own with only helicopters and minimal air support until a battalion of tanks could show up. At best, they had their Strykers, JLTVs, and armored cars for immediate support, but that was about it.

Higgins ripped the sergeant patch off the front of his uniform and placed the new rank in its place. He grabbed his patrol hat and took the old rank off. Next, he pulled the pocket sewing kit out of his ruck to stitch his new one in place. He knew the job he'd just done wouldn't pass a close inspection, but it would get the job done for the time being. He placed the patrol cap back in his right trouser leg, got up and walked over to check on his guys.

After exiting his hotel room, Higgins walked around to the swimming pool. The location of the pool, in the middle of the hotel, was convenient in that it let his soldiers get a little wild and cut loose a bit without making fools of themselves in front of members of the general public who might happen to wander by. While this place wasn't a permanent lodging solution, it was working out well for their company.

As he neared the pool, Higgins heard the voices of men and what sounded like a number of women laughing and goofing off. When he rounded the corner, he saw a sight that brought a big smile to his face—dozens of women wearing bikinis and attractive one-piece swimsuits all around the pool.

Some of them were doing chicken fights, sitting on top of his soldiers' shoulders and trying to see who could knock the other girl off their perch first. Others were floating in the water, chatting with his men, while others lounged around in the chairs nearby. Higgins hadn't seen a scantily dressed woman since that evening at the strip club around six months ago. He really wanted to take a minute and chat one of them up, but then he was drawn back down to harsh reality by the sight of his company commander waving to get his attention.

He slumped his shoulders and sighed audibly, but he made his way over to see the captain. *Here we go again*, he thought.

As Higgins walked toward his CO, Captain Peavler, he saw him talking with a new officer he hadn't met yet.

Peavler smiled at him. "Ah, there you are, Sergeant Higgins," he said happily. "The lieutenant here is from division. He said he has some new replacements for us. I'd like you to go greet them and figure out how many should go to each platoon. Top's still at battalion trying to look into getting us some additional supplies and he has Sergeant Morris with him. Sergeant Riker is checking on our guys at the hospital—so I'm afraid you're the senior guy for the time being."

He pulled a paper out of his pocket and handed it to Higgins. "Top put this together last night when we were told we were getting replacements. It says how many guys each platoon is short. Do your best to get the platoons leveled out if you can."

Higgins nodded.

"Oh, before you go, at 1700 hours we're going to have a company formation. I've got a number of promotions we need to hand down, and we've got a lot of awards to give."

"Awards?" Higgins asked drearily.

Captain Peavler held his hands up in mock surrender. "I know, Higgins. Now that we aren't in constant combat, the freaking battalion and brigade CO are all over me to get our paperwork sorted and up to date. Starting tomorrow, I'm going to need you to work with Top and figure out what NCOers need to get done and what career counseling statements are due."

Sergeant Higgins shook his head in disgust. "Damn Army and their paperwork."

Peavler laughed. "You should try being an officer. It's far worse on our end," he teased. "OK, take the lieutenant here and go 'round back and get them sorted. We've got evening formation in four hours—plenty of time for these guys to get moved into whatever platoon they're assigned to."

Higgins nodded. "Not a problem, sir." He turned to face the lieutenant. "Sir, if you could drive the vehicle around to the rear of the hotel, I'll take it from there."

The lieutenant smiled and walked off to retrieve his vehicle.

As Sergeant Higgins walked toward the rear parking lot, he saw all of the soldiers hanging around by the pool again. He envied the position of being a lower sergeant, when he could just chill in the pool with a girl and let the higher-ups deal with all this crap. Now he was the higher-up and he was stuck with running the platoon on his own, at least until a new officer was assigned.

As he walked around the corner to the rear of the hotel, Higgins wondered how many replacements they were getting and if they were going to be National Guardsmen or raw troops fresh from basic training. He almost stopped dead in his tracks when he saw two Greyhound buses. Soldiers started getting out of the buses and falling into a formation.

The lieutenant spotted him and walked towards him. "Sergeant, this is the roster of the replacements being assigned to your company. I'll have them get their gear off the buses and we'll be on our way. I have a few more trips I need to make to Fort Worth to pick up more guys."

Before the LT could leave, Higgins asked, "Are we actually starting to get a lot of replacements?"

The lieutenant smiled. "Yes. All those draftees and volunteers are finally starting to graduate from training. When I left the airport a few hours ago, there had to be three or four thousand new replacements waiting to be sent to their units. It's quite the gaggle."

With that, the LT yelled for everyone to get their gear off the bus.

Higgins watched the gaggle of raw, green soldiers for a moment. He didn't know if he should laugh or cry at the sight of them. They desperately needed replacements, but the thought of so many brand-new soldiers joining them also concerned him. Five minutes later, the buses left, and Higgins was left staring at fifty-two new, wild-eyed replacements.

While they were standing in formation in front of him, he pulled out the paper the captain had handed him and started figuring out how many replacements they actually needed. As it turned out, they needed forty-six replacements, but they'd been given fifty-two. Higgins smiled as he realized they'd have a few extra for each platoon.

He looked the new guys up and down before he addressed them. "Listen up, I'm Sergeant First Class Higgins. Welcome to the 1st Battalion, 6th Infantry Regiment. I've been with this unit for six years. It's a good unit with solid people in it."

He paused for a second before he added, "In the last four months, we fought inside Mexico just after we nuked the Chinese. Then we fought a brutal battle along the Texas-New Mexico border that turned into a bloody street fight in El Paso for three weeks. Next, we battled through a series of delaying actions for another two months across much of

Texas. In that time, our company suffered thirty-six KIAs and another twenty-two wounded.

"I'm not going to sugarcoat things. We're in the fight of our lives against these Chinese bastards. They don't take prisoners, and neither do we. If they catch you, they will torture and kill you, so don't surrender. You fight to the bitter end with your squad and platoon mates. You understand?"

A resounding "Yes, Sergeant" echoed from the new soldiers, though many of them suddenly looked nervous.

Sergeant Higgins cleared his throat. "I'm going to call out some names. When I do, I want you guys to stand over near that area. That first group will be going to First Platoon. When I call out the next group, you all will be going to Second Platoon."

He explained that they'd stay in their groups until he got their platoon sergeants to show them to their rooms. Then it would be the platoon sergeants that would go over further information on what would come next and what to expect.

The next fifteen minutes went by expediently as he broke them all down into four groups. Then Higgins told them to sit tight while he rounded up their platoon sergeants.

He pounded on Sergeant Simmons's door for a couple of minutes. "What the hell, Simmons?" he called, trying not to disrupt the entire floor of the hotel but hoping to get the sergeant's attention.

When Simmons finally opened the door, he was sporting a pair of gym shorts and nothing else. Higgins saw a naked girl lying in the bed, covering herself with the sheets. Simmons didn't say a word but shot him a very irritated look.

Sergeant Higgins smiled and tried to keep himself from laughing. "You've got five minutes," he announced. "I've got the replacements for your platoon and I need you to get them squared away."

Simmons nodded. "I'll be out there in five minutes," he replied gratefully.

Once Higgins had the four senior sergeants for each platoon in the parking lot, he told them about the evening formation and made sure they knew they had to have their guys ready. They'd be cut loose after the formation to enjoy the rest of the evening. By and large, they had only been having one formation a day, usually around 1700 hours, just to make sure everyone was still alive. The rest of the time, they either slept most of the day or got thoroughly drunk at the bar attached to the motel.

When 1700 hours rolled around, Higgins was standing in front of his platoon at attention as their captain called out the various soldiers being promoted, beginning with E-3s and going through E-6s. It took a little while to get through all the promotions, but Higgins realized that it was important for the men to get them. The increase in pay and rank was helpful for the ones that were married, which was close to half the company.

Next came the awards. They started with the guys getting Army Commendation medals with V devices, denoting it as a valor award. That included everyone in the company who wasn't getting awarded a higher-level medal. Next came the Purple Hearts. Again, nearly all of the original guys in the company received one of these medals for one injury or another. Then came the Bronze Stars with V device.

As he stood through the awards, Higgins was actually getting kind of angry. *Maybe I ticked off one of our COs or Top when they were writing these things up*, he thought. Aside from the two Purple Hearts he'd gotten, his name hadn't been called.

Then, the captain called Higgins forward, along with three other soldiers. He presented them with Silver Stars. Higgins was a bit taken aback. As the captain read off the citation, Higgins thought back to that horrible day when he had lost his entire fireteam in that battle at the elementary school near El Paso. It was the single worst day of his life. His platoon had fought like hell and had nearly been wiped out in the process. Yet, somehow, he'd survived.

An hour later, Higgins was sitting at the hibachi grill of the SAWA Japanese Steak House next to the hotel. He still had his Purple Hearts and Silver Star medal attached to his uniform and he wore them proudly.

This might be the last time I get to wear them if the war continues to go the way it's been going, he thought. He wasn't sure any of them would survive more than a month or two at the current rate.

Higgins spotted a gorgeous-looking woman who had to be in her late twenties or early thirties. That probably made her about five to eight years older than him, but he didn't care. She was looking hot and he was horny as hell. He motioned for her to take a seat next to him and she did. The two them talked for an hour over dinner and drinks. He probably had four or five shots of sake, and she had a couple herself.

The next thing he knew, they were having a wild romp in his room. When he woke up the next day, she was still there, lying naked in the bed next to him. He got up and used the bathroom and brushed his teeth. She did the same

263

and used the mouthwash he left out for her. They went a couple more rounds that morning before she said her goodbyes. She made sure to give him her cell number and address in case he wanted to call her or write.

"If you have any family or anywhere else to go, you should get out of town," he warned.

She seemed concerned by his comment but nodded at the advice. They agreed to try and see each other again, but he told her when the Chinese did eventually arrive, she needed to get out of Texas. He hated telling her to leave because he knew he wouldn't be able to see her again, but he didn't want anything to happen to her either.

"If I leave, I'll write you and give you my new address," she said with a wink. They shared a long passionate kiss before she finally left.

Feeling like a million dollars, Higgins spent the rest of the day just chilling next to the pool. He felt invigorated and ready for whatever was going to come next.

****

San Antonio, Texas
JBSA-Kelly Field Annex

Igor Radchenko stood up and stretch his legs now that the plane had stopped moving. The aircraft had finally landed and come to a halt next to the main terminal on what had been the US Air Force's primary training facility. Now, it was the central logistical hub for the PLA Air Force and Army, along with the flood of military contractors that were now arriving by the hundreds per day.

When the door to the aircraft opened, Igor immediately felt the humid heat of June in Texas smack him in the face. He breathed in deep and savored the rich smells of the Texas air intermixed with the scent of aviation jet fuel.

Smiling, he led the way off the plane, followed by roughly two hundred and twenty of his men. They were the first members of the Wagner Group to arrive on American soil.

Looking off into the distance, Igor saw rows and rows of planes being offloaded. Hundreds, maybe thousands of Chinese soldiers quickly fell into formations in front of the aircraft as they awaited their next set of orders.

Beneath the planes, baggage-handling equipment and K-loaders unloaded the soldiers' weapons and gear from below. But then Igor saw something that caused him to pause. He pulled out a pair of pocket binoculars out of his breast pocket and surveyed the gaggle of people who were waiting to board one of the many aircraft the soldiers had just exited.

Why would they be loading the planes full of women? he wondered. It seemed a bit odd.

A Chinese military walked up to him with his hand extended. "I'm Major General Zhu. You are Igor Radchenko?" he asked.

Igor nodded and shook the man's hand. "Yes, I am," he replied. "Thank you for meeting me here. Where would you like my men to set up our headquarters?"

General Zhu smiled. "We've assigned two of the buildings that used to house the Air Force trainees to your group. They can accommodate up to six hundred people comfortably. As requested, we acquired eighty Chevy Suburbans along with forty-five Chevy quad-cab pickup trucks. They are parked in front of your buildings, ready for use."

Igor grunted and nodded his approval. A week before leaving Russia, the head of the Wagner Group had put in the request for the vehicles. "Were your men able to find the police BearCat vehicles we had requested?" Igor asked. "Also, do you have the fifty linguists on hand to help my men interact with yours?"

"Yes. The police SWAT vehicles are parked near your buildings," General Zhu confirmed. "I've assigned fifty of my officers who speak fluent Russian and English to your group. They have the necessary gear with them so your forces can communicate with our army groups."

"Excellent, General Zhu. Thank you for making this a smooth transition. Most of my men will arrive today and tomorrow. We're going to spend a couple of weeks familiarizing ourselves with the city of San Antonio, and then we'll spend some time on the rifle ranges before we set out to join your forces. Do you have a particular area where you are wanting to deploy my men?"

"Yes. I have a colonel assigned to be the liaison between my office and yours. He'll go over where we're going to assign you."

The two talked for a few more minutes as the plane finished emptying. Then a slew of buses started to show up, ready to take them over to their new living quarters and base of operation.

****

When their bus pulled up to the massive four-block building, Igor's Chinese LNO pointed out the two blocks of the building that were assigned to the Wagner Group. There were rows and rows of vehicles parked in the parade field next to the buildings. They looked to be either brand-new from a local car dealership or newly acquired vehicles from the local population. In either case, they appeared to be in perfect working order, which was a good thing.

As the buses pulled up to the buildings, everyone started to get out. They grabbed their gear, moved into the buildings, and immediately went about assigning rooms to everyone. A handful of the men did a quick once-over of the vehicles, turning them on so they could check their fuel gauges and make sure everything was working. As any problems were detected, they wrote down the issues so they could be addressed.

After each inspection, Igor's men painted the letters "WG" and a vehicle number on the front and rear bumpers of the vehicles. That way they'd be able to identify them within the group. Next, they used a placard to paint "WG" on the front doors so their Chinese counterparts would easily be able to identify them as friendlies.

The next ten days went by in a blur. They broke themselves down into small fifty-man units and spent several days driving around the various neighborhoods and parts of the city as well as doing some foot patrols through the area. They needed to familiarize themselves with their new surroundings and get used to being inside an American city. They also spent several hours a day at the various rifle ranges on the base. They redid their qualifications on their rifles, pistols, and any other weapons they'd brought with them. They also made sure everyone was familiar with how to use a myriad of American rifles and pistols, since there might come a time when they'd have to use them.

Once Igor had determined they were operationally ready, they'd start infiltrating the front lines just ahead of the Chinese forces to cause as much havoc as possible. The PLA was gearing up for another major offensive to finish capturing the state of Texas. Once they captured Houston and Dallas, they'd be able to cripple the American defense aerospace industry and put a major dent in their petroleum manufacturing capability.

Two more weeks, then we'll be unleashed on the Americans, Igor thought with a devilish smile.

Chapter Thirteen
No Good Decisions

Washington, D.C.
White House

The President sat fuming in his chair, almost numbed by what he'd just watched. General Markus, the Chairman of the Joint Chiefs was furious as well, and so were all of the other generals and senior advisors in the room.

The National Security Advisor, Robert Grey, spoke up first. "This needs to be made public," he demanded. "The rest of the country needs to see this. They need to know what these bastards are doing to our country. We also need the rest of the world to see this and finally get off the sidelines."

The Secretary of State quickly chimed in. "I agree. This just might finally be the spark we need on our side to convince our hesitant allies that now is the time to join us, to come to our aid. Furthermore, I think this just might be the nail in the coffin to get the Indians to finally act and open up a second front against the Chinese."

Admiral Smith shook his head. "The Indians won't open a second front—not now that our last carrier in the

Pacific has been destroyed. The Chinese have fully mobilized their population for all-out war against us. The last human intelligence report we got from the Japanese three days ago said the PLA has gone from one hundred and eighteen divisions to nearly two hundred divisions over the last six months. Their militia force of nearly three million members has also been fully mobilized. Worse, the Japanese said the Chinese have already sent nearly two hundred thousand People's Armed Police Force to administer the occupied zones. They're even creating massive penal battalions from their prisons, promising freedom after they complete their military service in the Americas."

CIA Director Ryerson asked, "Have you seen some of the recruiting videos they are creating to get people to join their army? All they run is footage of the dead and dying from our bombing raid on Beijing at the outset of the war and the devastation caused by destroying the Three Gorges Dam. I'd have to say it's pretty damn effective, if you ask me."

The President shook his head in anger and disgust. "This can't be happening," he said in a voice just above a whisper. "Someone, tell me this is some sort of sick joke—that what we just saw isn't happening to American citizens?"

He searched the faces of his advisors for any glint of hope that this was all just some elaborate prank.

Vice President Powers let some air blow out past his lips. "I wish this was some sort of bad dream, Mr. President," he said glumly. "I wish I had been able to do more during the first week of the war when you were trapped in the tunnel."

Turning to look at his Vice President, Sachs replied, "You did everything you could, Luke. Don't beat yourself up over it—it's not your fault. I'm just frustrated with this situation and I feel powerless to stop it. I can't believe we're seeing American citizens being buried in mass graves in Mexico."

He turned to Secretary Kagel. "What do the Mexicans have to say for themselves?" he demanded.

She sat a little more erect in her chair. "Sadly, not much," she replied. "I think the government may be having some buyer's remorse for allowing the Chinese to set up shop in their country, but there's not much they can do now."

Secretary Kagel shuffled her papers. "On a good note, the Colombians are mobilizing their country for war. They're going to attempt to attack Panama and seize it back from the Chinese. Chile, Brazil, and Argentina will join the fight as well. None of them like what the Chinese have been doing.

"Heck, even though the Brazilians are still upset with us about the whole Lamy incident, they're saying they want to get involved in removing the Chinese from the hemisphere. Once they heard Lamy's public testimony and his private interrogation, they were appalled at what he had done. They said he'd brought real shame to their country. Not all has been forgiven between them and our military, but they do agree that China is a threat to the region that needs to be dealt with."

President Sachs nodded in approval. "This *is* good news, but make sure they're coordinating everything with General Markus and Admiral Smith here. This needs to be a well-planned joint operation if it's going to succeed. I don't think our Navy is quite ready to support an operation like this yet, but that will hopefully change soon."

Turning to look at Admiral Smith, the President asked, "Speaking of the Navy, what the hell happened in Hawaii? How did we lose another carrier?"

Smith sighed and turned red with embarrassment. "It was two carriers, Mr. President," he admitted bashfully.

Sachs slammed his hand down on the table and let loose a string of obscenities before he calmed down enough to say, "Explain to us what happened."

Admiral Smith took a gulp of the glass of water in front of him. "During the first day of the war, sir, the Chinese used their new stealth bombers on us," he began. "That's what hit us at Raven Rock, the H-20. We weren't sure how many of them they had, although we know we successfully destroyed two of them—one during the first day of the war, and a second one a few days later."

Smith tugged at the collar of his shirt as if it were suddenly choking him. "As you know, we've had the *Stennis* and *Vinson* in the repair yard at Pearl since the first few weeks of the war. We were going to move them to Bremerton in Washington to finish their repairs. We held off on doing that because we didn't have a real way of protecting them during the transit. Nearly all of the ships in their previous strike groups had been redeployed elsewhere to support the Marines retaking the Johnston Atoll, Midway and Wake Island. That meant the Hawaiian area was only being protected by the Roosevelt and her strike group."

The President cut him off. "Enough with the lead-up. What the hell happened? How did the Chinese manage to get enough forces close enough to Hawaii to hit us like this?"

Admiral Smith sighed. "We believe the Chinese seizure of Wake and Midway Islands was a diversion, an attempt to draw more of our naval forces away from Hawaii to support the Marines landing on the island. When they saw our forces hit those two islands, they launched their *real* attack on Hawaii. With much of the islands' electronics still fried, they were able to deliver a knockout punch to our forces there.

"Last night, a group of H-20 stealth bombers paid Pearl and the surrounding area a visit. The *Stennis* was hit with a couple of two-thousand-pounders that wrecked her flight deck again and caused considerable damage to the hangar decks below. She's still afloat and the fires are finally out, but she'll need months of repairs before she'll be back in the fight.

"The *Vinson* took twelve hits across her flight deck and control tower. She's a burning mess right now. Even if they can get the fires under control, we have no idea how bad the rest of the damage is yet. She isn't taking on water but she's completely ablaze, so it may only be a matter of time.

"As to the *Roosevelt*, this was a much more complex and organized attack. The Chinese Navy engaged the strike group with two of their own carriers along with four of their merchant raider ships. They threw a missile swarm at the strike group. They also had a handful of submarines join the fray. It was a huge, multidimensional attack: the first real naval multiforce style attack we've seen the Chinese carry out. While all that was going on, some of their H-20s got within range to drop a dozen JDAMs, which hit the carrier. She ended up going under about six hours ago."

Admiral Smith held a hand up to forestall the likely barrage of questions. "I'd like everyone to know we also sunk one of three Chinese carriers and half of her escort ships. It wasn't a completely one-sided affair; we hurt their navy bad."

General Vance Pruitt blurted out several f-bombs very loudly before popping all of his knuckles. "How are we supposed to keep the damn Chinese from capturing half the country if we can't stem the flood of reinforcements they are getting from the Mainland?" he shouted.

"Project Odin is going to put an end to that," Admiral Smith insisted.

"Yeah, if it ever gets completed," Pruitt replied hotly. "By the time it does, if it still stays on schedule, the Chinese will have moved more than five million, maybe even ten million soldiers to our country. I don't know that we'll be able to defeat them when that happens. Plus, we're still putting down domestic uprisings all over the country." Then he let loose a torrent of obscenities.

The President held a hand up to stop the bickering. "Hey, Vance, let's try and tamp down the cursing. I'm the only one allowed to blow my lid in the meeting," he said jokingly, trying to lighten the mood.

Sighing, General Pruitt nodded. "You're right, Mr. President. Sorry, Admiral. I know your guys are doing their best. I think we're all just a bit frustrated with these setbacks."

"Agreed. But let's not go after each other, all right?" asked General Markus.

The Attorney General, who had been invited to this meeting because of the new video SOCOM had acquired, had been silently sitting there watching everything play out. Patty Hogan from DHS had done the same. In the break in the arguments, the President suddenly noticed them sitting there with shocked expressions on their faces. They didn't normally attend war briefings, so their knowledge of the broader military situation was not as deep as many would have thought.

The AG raised his hand like a college student waiting to ask the professor a question.

"Go ahead, Malcolm," said Sachs. "What do you have for us?"

AG Malcolm Wright leaned forward in his chair. "First, I wanted to agree with Mr. Grey about releasing this information to the public. Second, I wanted to address the domestic issue General Pruitt brought up, which is a very valid argument."

The President nodded for him to continue.

"OK, I'll start with the video first. Right now, the wounds of the UN occupation and the discovery of this grand foreign conspiracy to rip our country apart is still fresh in people's minds. Both sides feel betrayed, and no one really knows who to trust.

"The only thing that has held us together up to this point was the UN invasion and then this brutal nuclear attack and invasion by the Chinese. I think we need to use that to our advantage. We need to show the American people that not only did this global cabal conspire to steal our election and divide us, the Chinese are now using our weakened position to commit mass murder of our people. We can use this video to rally the country to defeat this dastardly enemy. We have to convince the people in the states that are currently still in open rebellion against us that we are not the enemy—that the Chinese army, which was part of the UN force, is not on their way to liberate them from us."

"And what do we do if they won't come around?" asked General Pruitt angrily. "Do we just pull our forces out of those states and let the Chinese have their way with them?"

"I'm not a military man, so I can't speak to that," Wright countered. "But I think it's safe to say that our forces in California are getting wiped out. Between the non-support we're getting from the state and the fact that we can't effectively reinforce those units, we may need to abandon the state for the time being until we can make a concerted effort to retake the state."

General Markus shook his head. "We can't just give up California," he insisted. "Especially if we know what the Chinese are doing to people in the occupied zones."

"If we can't keep our forces in California supplied and able to fight, we won't have a choice," Pruitt argued. "I've shared with you the reports of some of our Marines and soldiers having to fight the California Civil Defense Force militias in addition to the Chinese." He glared at General Markus.

Sachs understood the animosity. Between the Army and Marines, the two services had been getting hammered with losses. They had constantly been on defense since the war started some six months ago.

"We're not giving up California," the President announced. He pointedly looked at General Pruitt. "That's final," he stated flatly.

Sachs then turned to look at Patty. "What's going on with your security force?" he asked. "Are they having any luck at restoring order across the country?"

"In some states, yes, but not out west," she replied, shaking her head. "We're sending a flood of people out to Washington State to get it back under control, but it's slow going. We've also been sending a huge number of our people to the East Coast to help free up the military so they can be sent south. We're still cranking out six thousand recruits a week, but it'll be another five or six months before we have the numbers to handle all the current needs."

"OK, Patty. Keep us apprised of the situation. You know, I was skeptical about your security force in the beginning, but I think they're proving to be exactly what we needed."

Sachs turned back to his Army and Marine leaders. "How's the training program going? Are we getting enough people run through basic and boot camp to keep up with our losses and expand the size of the military?"

The Commandant of the Marine Corps, General Miles Harris, replied first. "Yes and no. With the loss of our West Coast facilities, we've effectively lost half of our training capacity. However, we've tripled the size of our facility at Paris Island, and we've also opened up new training bases at Quantico and Camp Lejeune. We shortened their training to just the initial thirteen weeks of boot camp. Presently, half of the recruits are sent directly to the lines units that need replacements. The other half of the recruits are forming up the nucleus of the new divisions we're reactivating. As each new division becomes fully staffed, we move them to front lines. For the Marines, we're fighting primarily out west in California and the Caribbean."

"Thank you for the update, General Harris," Sachs said with a nod. He turned to the Army chief. "Same question for you, General Pruitt. How are things coming along for the Army?"

"Like the Marines, we've shorted some of our advanced initial training. Two-thirds of the new recruits are going directly into the infantry. For soldiers going into the infantry, we've simply expanded their basic combat training from ten weeks to thirteen. Right now, we're using Fort Jackson and Camp Shelby for all non-infantry training. Nearly every Army base in the south has been turned into a basic training base. We're graduating approximately twenty thousand new recruits a week now that we're fully up and running. Roughly one-third of them will go on for a condensed advanced training.

"Like the Marines, we're sending half of the newly graduated recruits directly to units at the front that need them. The rest of the recruits are being thrown in with the new soldiers as they form up a lot of newly reconstituted divisions. We've reactivated the old V Corps and VI Corps. At current pace, they'll be ready to fight as independent Corps elements in a couple of months."

"What about the PMCs?" asked the President. "I've been getting a lot of calls about integrating them in with our forces. Thoughts?"

A couple of the generals looked uncomfortably at each other, and an awkward silence followed. While many of their soldiers would go on to work for PMCs after getting out, Sachs had heard concerns from them in the past about how to integrate the private military contractors into the main fighting.

Patty Hogan from DHS raised her hand. Sachs nodded for her to speak.

"Mr. President, while integrating them into the military may be problematic, I'd like to incorporate as many of them as possible into my security force. They bring a wealth of experience that our present security force doesn't have. If you'll let me, I'll work with the DOJ to figure out how best to integrate them into our organization. This could be the force we need to get some of these Western states back under control."

The President smiled and said, "Get it going, Patty."

The meeting went on for another hour as the various individuals got the President up to speed on their particular areas. While there were still disagreements about how to proceed, the thing that everyone agreed on was that they needed to get the country solely focused on defeating the Chinese or they were toast.

Chapter Fourteen
High Seas Abduction

Greenland-Iceland Gap
USS *America*

Seth stood on the bridge of the warship, along with the captain of the ship, Drake Connor, and the Marine colonel in charge of the contingent of Marines on board, Tony Del Monte. The three of them watched as several CH-53 Super Stallions loaded up a Marine FAST team to go after the yacht the analytical team at Camp Perry had identified as the ship most likely carrying Marshall Tate. Accompanying the Super Stallions were two attack helicopters, which would provide them with additional support should they need it, and which carried the two Delta operators that had been accompanying Seth.

The *America* and her contingent of four other naval ships were now less than seventy miles from the yacht. Once the helicopters left, the ships would move to flank speed as they tried to further close the distance between them and the target.

Colonel Del Monte turned to look at Seth, who was still dressed in his 5.11 clothes. "I hope your intel is good," he said dryly. "I don't want my Marines to get jammed up on a dry hole."

"It's as good as we're going to get, sir," Seth insisted.

Captain Connor turned to him. "You going to level with me and the colonel here and tell us who the hell you're holding on my ship and why two Delta operators are going with our Marines on a mission they should be able to handle?" he asked in a low voice, glancing around to make sure no one could hear him.

"Yeah, that's a good question," echoed Colonel Del Monte. "I think this is the first time in my Marine career that I've seen two Delta guys accompany my men and not a couple of SEALs. What gives?"

Seth motioned with his head for them to walk out of the bridge, away from prying ears. He knew the two of them really wanted to know who'd been brought aboard their ship. All they had seen was two men wrapped in black hoods being escorted by a couple of JSOC operators. They'd been told explicitly by the CNO, Admiral Smith, to honor any requests made by Seth Mitchell and his team and not to ask any questions.

However, seeing that they were about to capture Marshall Tate, Seth figured he might as well as tell them what was going on. There wasn't a reason to keep things secret at this point.

Seth surveyed the area to make sure no one else could hear them, then he explained, "The first guy we brought aboard was Lance Solomon."

Captain Connor just shook his head and let out a soft whistle. "The head of Goldman Sachs and the second-most-wanted man in America? Wow." He uttered a few curse words under his breath. "You guys actually tracked him down to Norway?"

"Yeah, well, it wasn't easy. We had to cut a deal with the second guy we brought aboard to get him to snitch on him."

"OK. Then who's the second guy?" asked Del Monte, his curiosity obviously piqued.

"You know who Erik Jahn is?"

"You mean the Norwegian money guy who funded this entire charade?" asked Captain Connor.

Seth nodded. "He's the second guy we're holding."

"Hot damn. You guys are good," said Colonel Del Monte excitedly. "They only announced who these traitors were a few weeks ago and you guys already found them."

"Eh. It wasn't that easy," Seth replied. "We basically told the Norwegians they either hand Solomon over to us or we'd start bombing Oslo. They gave him up. But convincing him to talk required a lot of horse trading. He still may end up walking if he can give up a few more people." He still wasn't sure if that was a good thing or a bad thing.

"Hey, whatever you have to do to get all the people involved in this, do it," said the captain, conviction in his voice. "If he has to walk so we get everyone else, it's a fair swap, you hear me?"

Seth nodded his head. "I suppose we should go down to the CIC to monitor the raid?"

"Nah. We have at least thirty minutes before they're close to the target," remarked Captain Connor with a flip of his hand. "Let's just enjoy the fresh air for a few minutes before we're stuck in that cold, poorly lit room."

The three of them chuckled.

****

Forty minutes later, the trio watched the raid on one of the video monitors in the CIC while it was happening. They had several surveillance drones up at this point, providing them with multiple angles.

The Cobra attack helicopters hovered on either side of the superyacht, making sure the people on the ship knew not to try any funny business. Next, one of the two Super

Stallions hovered over the rear of the ship, and a string of Marines slid down the ropes onto the yacht. The other Super Stallion did the same, only it hovered at the front of the ship. In the span of less than sixty seconds, they had dropped twenty-four Marines and two JSOC operators onto the ship.

The JSOC operators made a beeline for the interior of the ship with the Marines covering their six and clearly everything else. Once the Americans were on the ship, two of the video screens in the CIC switched over to the team leader in the rear of the ship, and the team leader in the front of the ship. They watched the boarding party swept through the yacht and secured it. Sure enough, within minutes of landing on the ship, the JSOC operators had found Senator Marshall Tate hiding in one of the staterooms with his wife.

The Marines disarmed the half dozen security guards, along with the crew. They lined the crew all up on the front deck of the ship while they waited for the *America* and its strike group to catch up to them.

It took nearly two more hours for the squadron of ships to rendezvous with the mega-yacht, but once they did, a number of small boats disembarked from the *America* and the destroyers to surround the yacht. Marshall Tate was brought over to the *America* and handed over to Seth and his team for further questioning.

Once the Americans had what they had come for, they released the Russian crew and security personnel to continue on with their journey. The entire incident took less than three hours to resolve without a single life lost in the process.

****

Seth watched Senator Marshall Tate sitting in the interrogation room and wondered what was going through the man's head. Tate had to realize the futility of his situation, but Seth tried to calculate the best approach to get him to disclose any further participants of the plot. More importantly, Seth wondered if there was a way to get him to speak with his supporters and tell them that the fight was over and that they should shift their concerns to the real fight—the one against the Chinese.

"You going to show him the video?" asked Ashley Bonhauf as she stared at Tate. Since she was FBI, General Lancaster had thought that she might be able to add some additional leverage should Seth be unable to break Tate.

Seth nodded. "I think it might be enough to get him to make an appeal to his followers."

Ashley placed a hand on his shoulder. "You can do this, Seth," she insisted. "I've seen you work your magic;

you can do it one more time." She stared into his eyes a little longer than she probably should have.

Smiling at the encouragement, Seth noticed her lingering glance. He'd spent a lot of time with her over the past two months, and it had been nearly four months since he'd seen his own family. He brushed off the thoughts that were suddenly trying to break through to his mind and returned to the task at hand.

Grabbing the Toughbook on the table next to him, he got up and walked out the door. He made his way down the corridor to the room where they were holding Tate. The guard unlocked the door and held it open for him to enter, which he did.

Senator Tate scrutinized Seth and his plain clothes as he walked into the room and sat down at the opposite side of the table.

Seth glared at the man who had so divided his nation. He tried not to let how he felt about his prisoner rise to the surface, but he had to admit, of all the people he had interrogated up to this point, Marshall Tate had pushed him to the edge.

"What are you going to do with me?" asked the Senator, concern and fear written on his face.

Turning his head slightly to the left, Seth replied, "That largely depends on how willing you are to talk with me."

"And if I choose to not talk, to wait until my lawyer arrives?" asked Tate.

Seth laughed at the ludicrous nature of the question. "Senator, where exactly do you think you are?" he asked.

"I'm on a US warship, which means I'm on US soil," Tate replied smugly. "The Constitution still applies to me, and I still have rights."

"I'm not sure if you remember, but the President and the Congress labeled you and the members of your cabinet enemy combatants. You betrayed your oath of office and led an attempt to overthrow the federal government. You may be on a US warship, but you have no rights," Seth replied with a certain amount of satisfaction.

"I'm not saying another word until I speak with my lawyer," Tate insisted.

Seth felt his jaw tighten. "You have two choices, Senator. You can either cooperate and answer my questions truthfully, in which case the DOJ may decide to show you some leniency, or I can pull out my bag of tricks and make you talk. But keep in mind, Senator, I'm *very* good at my job, and I *will* make you tell me everything I want to know."

Marshall Tate recoiled a bit in his chair. "You mean torturing me for the information?" he inquired. "You know that's against the Geneva Convention."

"Senator, you threw out any protection you had under international law or our own Constitution when you led a civil war against our country. You knowingly participated in the theft of our election. You can deny it all you want, but we have sworn statements from Roberto Lamy, Lance Solomon, and Erik Jahn attesting to that fact."

Leaning in, Seth added, "The jig is up. It's time to come clean and hope leniency will be granted to you. If not, then I will have no choice but to extract the information I need from you through any and all means necessary."

Seth watched Tate's facial expressions. The smug, arrogant look he'd worn so proudly a moment before had faded. His body suddenly slumped in the chair, and in that moment, he looked deflated. Seth had seen that look hundreds of times before.

Time to press in, he thought.

"Senator, as you know, the UN peacekeeping force has collapsed. Nearly all the nations that were part of it have either surrendered or are in the process of making peace with the US. The two countries that have not come to the table are Russia and China. I'm going to go with the position that you didn't fully know what was happening—that you may not have fully understood this grand scheme that was using you as its pawn. But right now, you do have some power to help end this civil war."

Tate looked up at Seth with an expression that seemed like a sad puppy. "How?" he asked defeatedly. "How can I help to end this civil war? Everything has been proven to be a charade, a sham. Even *I* didn't know how big this thing was until the wheels of war had already been set into motion. I was just told to shut up, to play along and do my part and I'd be president for eight years. I honestly had no idea the level of duplicity that was going on. I'm not sure there is anything more I can do to help."

Seth watched as any semblance of strength Tate had portrayed moments before collapsed. Seeing that his subject was sufficiently prepped, Seth walked over to the DVD player in the room and started up the video. As Marshall Tate watched the footage of the mass graves in Mexico and of the women being loaded into the Chinese ships, he started crying. Soon he was sobbing uncontrollably at the weight of it all.

With tears streaming down his face, Marshall pleaded, "What can I possibly do to help? How will anyone ever believe what I say after all that's happened?"

Seth leaned forward. "First, you need to disclose everything you know about this plot to remove Sachs. Next, you need to come clean about your part in all of this—what they promised you and what they wanted you to do in exchange. Third, we need you to make a desperate appeal to your supporters and to the governors of the states that were backing you. We need you to help us convince them that the Chinese aren't coming to liberate them but rather to occupy and kill them. Most importantly, we need your help to reunite the country so we can focus on fighting the Chinese as a cohesive force, instead of fighting amongst ourselves while dealing with the Chinese. Do you think you can handle that?"

Tate didn't say anything for a moment. Then he wiped a few tears from his cheeks and nodded. "Enough people have died because of me," he said, his voice still a bit shaky and emotional. "This bloodshed needs to end. I'll do it. Tell me what you guys need from me and I'll do it."

Seth nodded, then got up, but before he left, he turned back to Tate. "Senator, thank you," he uttered. "I'm going to send in a woman by the name of Ashley Bonhauf. She's a deputy assistant director with the FBI. She'll go over what we need you to say and who we specifically need you to reach out to. We'll create a video and then we'll provide you with a sat phone. There's probably about two dozen people we need you to personally plead with for peace."

Seth then undogged the hatch and walked out of the room. He walked over to where Ashley had been monitoring the interrogation and signaled it was now her turn. She stood and winked at him. She grabbed her pad of paper and the portable camcorder she had already mounted on a table tripod for this very purpose.

When she left the room, Seth made a quick call to Camp Perry to bring them up to speed on what had transpired, and to let them know that Senator Tate had agreed to make the necessary phone calls. Seth felt a wave of relief—this just might be enough to stop the civil war.

Chapter Fifteen
Operation Spartacus

Albuquerque, New Mexico

Robert Lucas looked at the two Special Forces soldiers dressed in regular civilian clothes sitting on his couch with skepticism. He wasn't sure if these guys were being genuine or if they were simply trying to test him and see how committed his little crew of like-minded people were.

Leaning forward in his La-Z-Boy rocking chair, Robert asked, "Are you serious about this plan?"

The leader, a man who only went by the call sign "Punisher," answered, "Deadly. Is your band of patriots willing to work with us?"

Robert sighed at the thought of carrying out a mission like this; he just wasn't sure. This is the kind of stuff that would bring a lot of heat down on them by the occupational authorities. He leaned back in his chair and rocked slowly as he thought about it. He'd served in the Army himself, during the first Gulf War, but he'd been out of the Army for fifteen years. While he'd managed to rally close to twenty like-minded patriots, he wasn't sure if this was a mission they could reasonably take on and survive.

"So, if I understand this right, one of your guys is going to give us IEDs and locations of where and when you want them placed around town and the highways?"

"Exactly," replied the soldier. "We'll build them so you don't have to worry about them accidentally going off. We've also scouted out all the locations we'd like you to place them and will provide instructions about when and how to do so."

Robert squinted. "How do you know when to place them and what's so special about these specific locations?" he inquired.

A smile crept across the soldier's face. "Let's just say complacency and a sense of security makes people do stupid things." The soldier paused for a second as he surveyed Robert's face. "Look, I know this is dangerous work, but your group knows the area well. You've been providing good intelligence of what's been going on in the city for more than a month. We aren't locals and we can only be in so many places at once. With your help, we'll be able to do a lot more a lot faster. It's imperative that we do our best to tie down Chinese resources here in Albuquerque. It's that many less soldiers our guys have to face up in Colorado. It'll also inspire other patriots in the area to take up arms and make a stand."

"We're already carrying out sniper operations along I-25 just south of the city," Robert countered. "We've managed to hit several of them already."

"We know. That's why we believe you guys could be used for this operation as well. This'll really get you into the action where you can do a lot more damage."

Robert paused, then nodded. "OK. We'll do it. Let's talk about how you're going to get the IEDs to us and how you want this to go down."

The next hour was spent going over those specific details. They also gave Robert several sets of wireless communication devices so they could effectively communicate before and during each attack.

****

Albuquerque, New Mexico

José arrived at the dilapidated building Robert had told him about. The structure was a dingy old auto repair shop—a simple three-car garage that used to be a gas station at one point in its life.

As he hopped out of his truck, José saw a man smoking a cigarette in the shadows near the entrance to the office and waiting room. José approached him. "I was told you are able to fix CV joints for a good price," he said.

The man in the shadows flicked his cigarette to the ground as he emerged from the darkness. "I can. We're running a special on them for $49.99 per joint. How many do you need?"

The man from the shadows walked towards José, who felt his pulse quickening as the stranger approached.

"I need three," he answered.

As the man came into view from one of the nearby streetlights, José saw a slight smile creep across his face. He then extended his hand. "Sounds like we have a deal. My name is Janus. Why don't you come inside? I have a loaner car I can let you borrow."

"Thank you. My name is José."

José followed the man inside the shop. They made their way into one of the rooms in the back. A light was on there and a map of the city was taped to the wall. José scrutinized Janus as he walked up to the map; the guy looked like one of those people he might cross the street to avoid walking past him at night. José couldn't say for sure, but this guy looked like a convict to him.

Robert sure knows how to find some interesting people, he thought.

"OK, José, you're going to drive the vehicle I'm going to lend you to this location here," Janus instructed, pointing to a bus parking lot on the corner of Louisiana and Gibson. "Once you've dropped the vehicle, I need you to walk down the block on Louisiana Boulevard and catch the bus. I want you to stay on the bus and get off at the third stop. Another man in a beat-up-looking Ford Escort is going to pick you up and bring you back here. Then I'll have the next vehicle ready for you with your new assignment."

The man paused for a moment before asking, "Do you have any questions?"

José just shook his head. It seemed simple enough.

Janus nodded and walked them into the three-car garage connected to the little office, where he showed José a 2015 BMW 3 series vehicle.

Suddenly, Janus grabbed José by the arm and leaned in. "Do not deviate from the plan," he hissed, in a manner that was half warning and half threat. "Bring the vehicle to the bus parking lot and park it with the rear of the vehicle facing Gibson Boulevard. Put the sunshade in the front just like every other driver does." Then he repeated his previous instructions. "Walk to the bus stop a block further down

Louisiana Boulevard. Catch the next bus and get off on the third stop. I'll see you back here when you're done."

José listened intently and nodded at each step in the instructions. Then the man let go of his arm and handed him the keys to the car. José got in the vehicle, started it and then drove out of the garage to exactly where he'd been told.

He parked it exactly as he'd been instructed, locked it, then walked further down the street to the bus stop and patiently waited. It was only six in the morning, and the street was quiet.

I guess there won't really be a rush hour here anymore, José realized. Ever since the Chinese had taken the base over, there were no service members, contractors, or government workers to staff it.

When José got off on the third stop, he spotted a man in a dirty, banged-up Ford Escort. Without saying a word, José got into the Ford and they drove away. Fifteen minutes of silence went by as they drove back to the garage.

Once there, Janus handed him a maintenance coverall. "Put this on," he instructed. When he'd finished that task, Janus walked him over to what appeared to be a Burlington Northern Santa Fe utility truck, with a bright orange BNSF painted on the side.

"You're going to drive this to the main trainyard and park it near the railroad turntable," Janus directed. "Once you've parked, make up an excuse to go to the convenience store across the street and exit through the back door. The man who drove you here earlier will meet you out back and take you back here."

José nodded and took off. Thirty minutes later, he was about to pull into the trainyard when he was greeted by a couple of armed private security guards and two BNSF workers that were manning a checkpoint to the facility.

Crap! No one told me there would be guards, he thought.

He could feel his pulse rate increasing and his palms turned sweaty.

"Please step out while we search your vehicle," ordered one of the guards.

José was almost frozen. His mind panicked. *How the hell do I get out of this?* he wondered.

Then he heard a voice say, "You know he was cleared yesterday, right?"

There were a couple of comments back and forth between the railyard worker and the hired guns, but then they waved José on in without any further trouble. As he drove the truck through the gate, the railyard worker winked at José as if telling him, "I have your back."

When the truck was completely out of view of the security guards, José breathed a huge sigh of relief. *That was way too close.*

He parked the truck where he'd been told, which was oddly nowhere near the locomotives. He got out, steeled his nerves and walked back to the security checkpoint.

José had noticed on the way in that one of the guard's name tags read "Phil," so as he approached the gaggle of armed men, he called out, "Hey, Phil!" in a friendly voice.

The man popped his head out of the guard shack. "Yeah?" he asked.

"I need to use the bathroom and grab another pack of cigarettes before work starts. I'm just going to walk over to the 7-Eleven real quick. Do you guys want me to bring anything back for you?"

"Thanks for the offer man, but we're good," Phil replied.

And just like that, José was through the checkpoint again with no issues. He walked into the store, all the way through to the back and then exited the back door. The same man from the garage was there to drive him back.

The two of them drove back to the shop, where José grabbed a third vehicle. Thirty minutes later, he had driven to the overpass just north of Tramway Boulevard and Interstate 25. Following the instructions Janus had given him, when José reached a specific landmark, he hit a small button that caused his car to start smoking. His vehicle rolled to a stop just in front of the overpass.

José got out of the vehicle and lifted the hood, which allowed even more smoke to escape. A soldier had rigged up a little device that spilled a bunch of oil on the hot engine, making it appear that this car had overheated.

José looked around. A taxicab pulled up nearby and stopped. Sure enough, the same guy from the garage was sitting in the driver seat. José hopped in and then two of them drove back to the garage.

This time, Janus handed him back the keys to his truck. "Go home," he ordered. "Stay out of sight for a few days and just play it cool. If anyone finds out you were the guy who had delivered the vehicles, then we'll tell you when and where to go next."

******

Albuquerque, New Mexico
Safe House

"Are the VBIEDs in place?" asked Punisher.

His explosives expert, who went by the call sign "Bang-Bang," nodded. "Our guy drove them to the various locations. Janus radioed in every time one was delivered."

"OK. Then let's detonate the one at the railyard," Punisher ordered. "That's the one that's most likely to get discovered the longer it sits there."

Bang-Bang smiled and grabbed his burner phone. He placed a call to the phone in the BNSF truck that would act as a trigger device.

"Well?" asked Punisher impatiently.

"Rang once and disconnected, just like it's supposed to," Bang-Bang replied with a devilish grin. "One down, two to go."

Twenty minutes went by before Janus, who had been observing the defunct American Air Force base from nearby, radioed in. "That convoy of buses is leaving. They're nearly to the site."

"The next flight of new soldiers must have arrived," another one of the SF soldiers said in a jovial manner.

Punisher chuckled. "Well, let's make sure to give them a warm welcome to America, shall we?"

Bang-Bang nodded, and they all watched the remote surveillance camera they had placed nearby. Sure enough, a column of fifteen buses was driving away from the defunct American air base and heading into the city. They all knew most of these soldiers would travel to the BNSF railroad vehicle storage lot—the PLA had been making heavy use of the American and Mexican railroad networks to move their armored vehicles and tanks to the front lines, and they needed the soldiers who could operate the equipment.

They watched in anticipation as the vehicles drove along the most expected path. When the fifth bus traveled into the kill zone, Bang-Bang depressed the call button to the second burner phone, which would activate the next car bomb. To make this particular VBIED more deadly, there were three layers of ball bearings glued to the inner shell of the trunk, and it had been packed with block after block of C-4 with a piece of metal welded behind it. Bang-Bang had basically turned the car into a gigantic claymore mine that would devastate whatever it was aimed at.

In a fraction of a second, the boulevard was thrown into utter chaos as one of the PLA buses was blown completely apart, throwing huge chunks of shrapnel into the buses in front of it and behind it. Both of those buses were so damaged that they careened off the road. Several of the other buses in the convoy were also hit by ball bearings, but nothing like the first three. In the blink of an eye, three buses and over one hundred PLA soldiers had been wiped out.

"Damn, Bang-Bang," said one of the SF soldiers. "You're going to have to write up how you build those VBIEDs so we can spread that around to the other groups and partisans we're building up."

Bang-Bang laughed. "Sure thing."

Punisher stood up and stretched. "Now we sit and wait until either a PLA unit investigates our third VBIED or we see a military convoy drive near it," he announced.

"What's the plan for tomorrow, boss? You have more of these we're going to place?" asked Crispy, their other demolition guy. While Bang-Bang had been building VBIEDs for the resistance to use, Crispy had been constructing a variety of IEDs. He'd been super clever with how he was camouflaging them so they could hide in plain sight.

Punisher looked back and forth between Bang-Bang and Crispy. "How many VBIEDs and IEDs do we have ready to go?" he asked.

Bang-Bang replied first. "I have two more VBIEDs just like the ones we saw today, ready to go. I'm working on getting five more, but I'm at least three or four days from having them ready."

Crispy added, "I have twelve IEDs ready to go. I can probably crank out more, but we're starting to run out of C-4. Any idea on when we'll get another supply drop?"

Punisher smiled mischievously. "As a matter of fact, yes. In two days, we're supposed to head out to the dead drop."

"Excellent," said Crispy. "Then do you want my crew to start placing the IEDs or Bang-Bang's crew?"

"I think it's your group's turn, Crispy," answered Punisher. "Bang-Bang, get working on more of your car bombs. We'll look to introduce more of them around town next week once the PLA is sufficiently scared of Crispy's IEDs. But in the meantime, I want you guys to make sure that wherever we end up placing these devices, we do our absolute best to minimize the risk of civilian casualties. I know we can't rule them out entirely, but it's our job to make sure we aren't placing these devices in heavily populated areas where a lot of people will be present. We want to hurt the PLA, but we don't want to turn the public against us. Got it, guys?"

"We know, boss. We're doing our best to make sure that doesn't happen."

****

Albuquerque, New Mexico
Johnson Field

Mikhail Lazarev stood next to Colonel Commandant Song Puxuan as they watched the last bus unload its human contents. For the last three hours, some two thousand civilians had been rounded up and brought to the University of New Mexico to bear witness to the consequences of supporting an insurgency against their benevolent liberators.

Colonel Commandant Song turned to look at the Russian standing next to him. Speaking just loud enough so only the two of them would hear, he asked, "You really believe this is going to work and not cause us further problems?"

Mikhail shrugged his shoulders. "Does it matter? The hostages will either give up the names of the people working with the resistance or they won't. In either case, this execution will serve as a warning to anyone else who might want to take up arms."

Song nodded at the callousness of the Russian. If these Russian mercenaries could end this growing insurgency in his city, it would go a long way towards pacifying the city.

Just then, Mayor Delgado, the mayor of Albuquerque, walked up to them.

"Excuse me, Colonel. I am asking that you please don't do this," he begged. "Please allow me to talk with my citizens and try to talk some sense into them."

Mikhail smirked at the American. "Your lovely citizens killed one hundred and thirty peacekeepers. Many more were maimed and injured, Mr. Mayor. We need to show your renegade citizens that this type of behavior is unacceptable."

Undeterred by the Russian's comments, Major Delgado pressed, "Colonel, please. If you want to convey the message that you're here to liberate our state from the Sachs regime, then you can't just kill our people like this. It'll only fuel this insurgency."

Colonel Song sighed. "Mr. Mayor, you may speak with the hostages, but unless they tell us who is working with the insurgency, they are going to be made into examples."

Delgado smiled and bowed slightly. "Thank you, Colonel."

****

The mayor headed over to the gymnasium nearby to try and speak with his residents. Some 260 men, women, and teenagers were in the building.

For ten minutes, the mayor pleaded with them to provide any information they could to the Chinese. Several took him up on the offer, but many more called him a collaborator and traitor for working with the enemy.

Those who agreed to talk were brought to a side room where they were questioned. Everyone else, however, was marched out to the open field.

When Mayor Delgado left the auditorium, he tried to walk towards the bleachers where the citizens of Albuquerque were sitting. He had nearly made it there when one of the Russian mercenaries walked up to him.

"You're wanted by Colonel Song," the man said gruffly.

Delgado approached the Chinese commander again. "Please, Colonel, the ones who know something are already talking to your people."

"Enough!" barked the Chinese officer. "You've made your case. I gave you an opportunity to talk some sense into them. It is now time to render judgment."

As the group of Americans who'd waited in the gym stood at one end of the athletic field, a loudspeaker blared at the thousands of citizens who had been dragged from their homes and places of work to witness the public execution. "This is what will happen to you if you attack our forces. Watch!"

Some of the Russian mercenaries pointed guns at the crowd, to make sure they would see what was about to unfold. Another group of twenty Russians moved into position between the hostages and the people in the bleachers. They set up a couple of light machine guns on their tripods and readied them to fire.

"Ready, aim, fire!" someone shouted.

While the mayor and a few other city officials stood there, the Russians opened fire on the hostages. The machine gunners were swift and ruthless as they fired into the crowd of unarmed people.

When the shooting had stopped, the people in the bleachers wailed and cried. None of them could believe what they'd just witnessed. A few desperate souls amongst the hostages who'd been shot but remained alive cried out for help.

Before the mayor could say or do anything, the leader of the Russian mercenary group grabbed him by the collar and dragged him to the pile of bodies. He eventually found a wounded person lying on the ground—a woman who'd been shot several times. She reached her hand out to the mayor.

"Help me, please!" she pleaded.

Mikhail pulled a small pistol out of one of his cargo pockets and handed it to the mayor. "Put her out of her misery, Mr. Mayor," he instructed with a sickeningly sweet voice. "End her suffering."

Delgado looked at the Russian in horror. He dropped the pistol to the ground. "*You* put her out of her misery."

"How about we do this?" asked Mikhail, grinning sadistically. "You either pick up the pistol and shoot the wounded, or my men will turn their machine guns around and begin shooting all the people in the bleachers. Which would you rather do?"

"You're sick."

Mikhail yelled something in Russian and a second later his guys had turned the four machine guns around to face the civilians in the bleachers. The people shrieked with fear. Then the sobbing, screams of horror and profanity started up again.

"Pick up the weapon *now* and finish off the wounded or I'll order my men to fire," Mikhail ordered. "Five, four, three—"

Delgado picked up the pistol from the ground and aimed it at the woman. He pulled the trigger once, hitting her in the face. Her body fell backwards to the ground, dead.

"Good. Now walk with me. You're going to finish off the rest of them. If you try to shoot me or any of my men, they will kill everyone in the bleachers. So, think about them before you try something stupid," Mikhail instructed.

The next five minutes were the worst moments of the mayor's life. When he had finished killing the last of the wounded hostages off, the people in the bleachers were permitted to leave and go home.

The story of what happened that day spread like wildfire.

When twenty-eight members of the resistance were turned in to the Russians two days later, a weeklong spat between residents of the city erupted as resistance members began killing anyone and everyone they knew that was working as a collaborator with the Chinese. More than six hundred civilians had been killed that week, and the infighting had only just started.

Chapter Sixteen
US Northern Command

October 2021
Cheyenne Mountain

General Tibbets yawned and stretched his back a bit. He was tired. The war had been sucking the life out of him. Somehow, he'd managed to hold the military together up to this point and he'd successfully discovered ways to beat the Chinese back in some areas and contain them in others. With the war in the north officially over, he was finally able to shift the bulk of those forces to the southern front, where they were desperately needed. He just hoped they weren't too late.

Tibbets looked at his watch; he had about forty minutes until his next major briefing. Given the time frame, he opted to head over to the briefing room and spend a few extra minutes looking over the maps. He liked maps. They allowed him to see the big picture, to really know what was going on and where the action was most likely going to be.

In a way, he was fortunate that the country was as big as it was. He'd been able to trade space for time when necessary. Those sacrifices had also meant many millions of

Americans had suddenly found themselves trapped behind enemy lines. It had pained him to have to abandon many of these great cities of the Southwest, but he didn't really have a choice. He needed time for General Markus back in D.C. to train up an army large enough actually to win this fight, and time for America's manufacturers to crank out the tools and weapons needed to win it.

As General Tibbets walked through the hallway on his way to the briefing room, he passed by many workspaces. Hundreds of people continued to work tirelessly, tracking the multitude of aerial contacts and monitoring the movements of friendly and hostile units. It was a daunting task, but it was necessary to help paint the broad picture of what was going on around them.

They'd been steadily launching more satellites to replace the ones they had lost. For the time being, the Chinese had agreed to a global detente of sorts when it came to the world's satellite infrastructure. Britain and India had threatened the Chinese with military action if they shot down any more of their satellites, and the strategy seemed to be working.

Tibbets finally made his way into the briefing room and walked right up to the digital map display on the wall of the conference room. He now had twenty-eight minutes until the meeting with the various Corps commanders and the service chiefs back at the Pentagon. They had some hard decisions to make that would have a profound impact on the war.

The PLA had been sending nearly all of their reinforcements into New Mexico as they sought to capture Colorado. Thus far, the US had been able to hold the PLA just south of Pueblo in a small town called Colorado City, but no one knew if the Army would be able to hold that position for much longer. That was why Tibbets had called this emergency meeting.

The 4th Infantry Division and two other National Guard divisions were spread too thin across the front lines. The enemy had continued to probe around the edges of their lines, looking for a weak spot they could exploit and use as a breakout point. This kept forcing the Americans to have to extend their lines or move units further away from the main front to protect their flanks. It was a strategy Tibbets quickly recognized as a means of weakening his center so the PLA could punch a hole through them and drive their tanks toward the very installation where he now stood reviewing maps.

Tibbets had to make sure the Chinese didn't find that weak point. The enemy was less than ninety-three kilometers as the crow flew from NORAD. They were getting dangerously close to the central nerve center running the war. If Tibbets didn't find a way to turn things around soon, they'd have to relocate the command. As it was, they had already started evacuating all the family members and nonessential personnel to Offutt Air Force Base in Omaha, Nebraska. Normally they'd relocate to the Pentagon, but the building had already been bombed once and Raven Rock was thoroughly destroyed. The President had been very explicit that he didn't want to have all the military leadership in one location.

Major General Brian Sims walked into the briefing room and joined Tibbets at the map. With a wry smile, he sarcastically stated, "We're pretty well screwed right now, aren't we?"

Tibbets chuckled at the blunt assessment from his long-time friend. "Well, you always said you liked a decent fight," Tibbets countered with a wink. "I'm about to give you one hell of a good one."

"I do like a good fight, but I don't like being surrounded in a sea of hostiles."

General Tibbets slapped his friend on the shoulder. "Come on, Sims. You get the chance to shoot in all directions and still hit the enemy."

The two laughed, and then for a few minutes they caught each other up on their families and what they'd been up to for the past month or so. It was like the war paused for those few moments while they stopped being military commanders and reverted to being old friends.

Brian Sims had been a platoon commander in the 75th Rangers when he'd finished OCS and Tibbets had been his battalion commander. Tibbets had really taken a liking to Sims. In fact, for the next couple of years, Tibbets had helped mentor the up-and-coming officer until Sims had been promoted to O-6 and taken over command of a brigade that was gearing up to deploy to Iraq. They'd kept in touch throughout the years and when Tibbets had made brigadier, he'd selected Sims to be his one of his aides at the Pentagon. It had allowed Sims to meet some of the right players, and that had helped him to make colonel ahead of most of his peers. As Tibbets's career moved up, he'd done his best to take Sims with him.

Now, Major General Sims was the Commander of the 101st Airborne Division. The division had seen a ton of action in the Midwest before being shifted to the East Coast when the UN forces there had collapsed. Now, the 101st had been transferred to the Southwest to try and slow the enemy down.

After their little catch-up, the conversation took a more serious turn. "Are you serious about dropping us that far behind enemy lines?" Sims asked, prodding his mentor. "Is there a legitimate chance of us actually surviving the heliborne assault?"

"Under any other circumstances than what you're about to hear in a few minutes, I'd say no. However, the situation has changed and it's about to transform for the better. I don't want to spoil the surprise, but let's just say we now have some allies coming to our aid at long last."

Sims smiled and nodded, and then he walked over to the seat reserved for him. Right behind his seat, two spots were reserved for his aides. They were his official scribes, and they'd also pass him questions to ask if they felt something needed to be clarified.

As it neared the time for the brief, the room suddenly filled up. General Tibbets moved over to a seat at the center of the conference table. He cleared his throat. "Gentlemen, ladies, before we start this meeting, I want to make you all aware of some new reinforcements that are arriving to help us out," he announced. "As of 2000 hours yesterday, the British have agreed to join the war and come to our defense. Even as we speak, the British 16 Air Assault Brigade is arriving at Peterson Air Force Base just down the road from us. Most of their equipment will begin to arrive via rail in the next thirty-six hours."

Almost everyone at the table smiled. A few quietly commented to one another. Many of the soldiers in the military had figured their European allies had abandoned them in favor of this UN peacekeeping force. It appeared their luck was changing, at least amongst the European allies who hadn't participated in the UN force.

General Tibbets held a hand up to calm everyone down. "The Polish 11th Armored Cavalry Division is also going to be arriving at Fort Carson. In the next couple of days, we're going to receive twenty-two thousand additional soldiers, plus General Sims's 101st Airborne Division. We're finally going to stop the Chinese at Colorado City and push them out of the state."

"Yes, sir!" they answered in unison.

"Now, in forty-eight hours, the British paratroopers and our own 101st Airborne are going to get dropped behind the enemy lines. They'll air assault into Walsenburg while the British paratroopers will land approximately twenty-five kilometers south of them at a small city called Aguilar. Both drops place our forces along Interstate 25 and the main supply routes the PLA are using to keep their front lines operational.

"While this is happening, the 1st and 4th Infantry Divisions will launch a ground assault of the front lines with the 1st Cavalry Division and the Polish 11th Armored Cavalry Division. This will force the PLA to either engage our forces in front of them or withdraw to deal with the paratroopers in their rear area. In either case, we're going to make the enemy react to *us* instead of the other way around."

The division commanders spent the next hour going over some of the broader strategic goals and the units that would be involved before they broke to go figure out some of the finer details with their own brigade commanders.

While the rest of the military leaders filtered out of the meeting to work on their plans, the III Corps commander and the two Marine Corps division commanders stayed on the secured video teleconference with the service branch chiefs.

Now it's time to make some tough decisions, thought Tibbets.

General Markus, who was talking to them from the White House, started the conversation. "General Tibbets, what's the plan with California?" he asked. "We've lost nearly the entire state to the PLA, and it appears they're bringing more and more troops into the state via the ports and airports."

Tibbets had known the question was coming, so he had a ready answer. "Sir, the Marines have largely kept the PLA from capturing Las Vegas, which is a good thing. Losing Nellis and Creech Air Force Bases would have had a huge impact on our ability to support our efforts out west. That said, we can't keep our forces in northern and central California properly supplied or supported. We're just spread too thin right now."

"What about I Corps in Washington?" General Markus suggested. "They've pretty much mopped things up in Washington State and British Columbia. Why don't we shift them south into Northern California?"

"We've looked at that option. The issue is they're so spread out with occupation duty they don't have enough forces to head down into California," Tibbets countered. "Plus, Oregon is still a mess right now. We'd need at least one or two combat brigades to clear out the resistance in Oregon before we could do anything."

"OK, then what do you suggest we do?" asked General Markus, clearly frustrated by the lack of progress on the West Coast.

"I hate to say this, but I propose we have what's left of our two Marine divisions pull back to the Oregon-California border and establish a new defensive line. At the same time, I propose we send the newly reactivated 4th and 5th Marine Divisions to Boise, Idaho. From there, they can use Interstate 84 and take it all the way to Portland. They can put down the uprising in the state and then move south to reinforce the 1st and 3rd Marine Divisions. I'd also like to plus up Regimental Combat Team 1 that's been fighting it out from Yosemite National Park all the way up to Tahoe National Forest. It's a huge piece of rugged terrain that we need to hold if we're to keep the PLA out of upper Nevada."

General Miles Harris, the Commandant of the Marine Corps, jumped in. "I agree. I think we should also plus up RCT 1 with the 6th Marine Division. I know we had originally slated them for deployment to the Caribbean, but the fact is we need to hold the line in California. If the PLA is able to break out of the California pocket that we've kept them stuck in, it'll shift our entire line of defense."

A lot of the generals at the table nodded, agreeing with his assessment.

"OK. I can see the merits in that plan," Tibbets conceded. "We'll move forward with that if General Markus doesn't have any objections."

Markus tipped his head, deferring to the group.

"What's the status of V and VI Corps?" asked General Tibbets. "When am I going to have them released to my command?" He really wanted those two new corps that had been training up for the past six months. The vast majority of the new recruits were being filtered into these units to get them ready for combat.

"In two weeks, I'll be able to release V Corps," General Markus answered. "You'll also be getting the Polish 12th Mechanized Division and the British 3rd Division at the same time. We're going to marry them up with V Corps to give them some added armor punch. As to VI Corps, it's going to be another two months before they're staffed up. We had initially wanted to use them in the Caribbean as we get closer to retaking the Panama Canal Zone. I'll have them released to you if you absolutely need them, but I'd have to take them away in November to get them ready for the next phase of the war."

Tibbets nodded. "Let's wait and see what kind of difference the new Marine divisions and V Corps will make. If we can stop the Chinese from capturing Texas, hold the line here, and keep the PLA bottled up in California, then I think we have a chance of defeating them as we move into 2022."

"OK, then that's the plan," agreed General Markus. "Now it's my turn to bring you all up to speed on some recent intelligence we've gotten from Japan and the UK," he announced, effectively taking over control of the meeting.

"The Chinese have dispatched one point three million militia men to reinforce the regular PLA Army," Markus continued. "That number is expected to grow by nearly one hundred thousand soldiers a month. On top of that, they've sent some six hundred thousand Chinese People's Armed Police Force or PAPs to Mexico and the occupied territories. Right now, a large percentage of that force is actually in Panama and the rest of Central America—but make no mistake, they're using them more and more in the American-occupied territories."

General Markus paused for a moment, seemingly calculating how to approach the next topic. "I have some rather disturbing news that's going to be made public," he said. "I wanted you guys to hear it from me first."

Many of the officers in the room looked confused. Markus continued. "Two of our Special Forces units uncovered some incredible news about horrific atrocities being committed in the occupied zones. The Chinese, for whatever reason, seem to be culling the population of the sick and elderly and essentially leaving only the young and healthy alive. We're not sure how they're killing off their marks, but teams on the ground have captured video of them dumping the bodies into mass graves just across the US-Mexico border."

A few quiet expletives rumbled through the room.

"In California, one of our SEAL teams uncovered something that may be even worse," General Markus pressed. "The Chinese appear to be rounding up young women and loading them onto transport ships. We believe the women are being sent back to Mainland China, but we don't have any definitive proof of that yet. What we've learned our operators, who are still hiding out in the major cities and providing us this intel, is that there's beginning to be a noticeable absence of women between the ages of sixteen and thirty-five. That demographic of women are apparently disappearing from the cities all over the occupied territories."

General Tibbets shook his head in disgust and anger. It made him want to fight that much harder to make sure the PLA didn't capture any more of the country than they already had.

"If we know this is happening, are we going to start releasing it to the media and the people?" Tibbets inquired. "This could help us turn those states that are still rebelling against the country back to the fold. If nothing else, it'll make our soldiers fight a hell of a lot harder if they know what's happening."

General Markus nodded. "Yes. That's why I wanted to be the one to tell you about this first. I wanted you to hear it from me before it's released. The President has directed the military, DOJ, and CIA to put this information out to the public in a coherent way so it won't go out through selective leaks. They want to use it to rally the nation together. For now, I'll leave it up to your discretion how to disseminate that information to your subordinate commands."

The group talked for a little bit longer about military production levels, recruitment progress, and some of the other minutia involved in rapidly growing and equipping a multimillion-man army before the meeting was ended. It was time to get ready for one of the largest military operations since the invasion of Iraq in 2003.

Chapter Seventeen
Operation Spartan

Fort Carson, Colorado
Butts Army Airfield

For over an hour, all Staff Sergeant Riker had heard was the constant takeoff and landing of attack helicopters and the sonic booms of fighters overhead. It was 0230 hours and his squad of soldiers sat in a line outside the hangar in the morning darkness, their rucks next to their bodies. His men had their faces painted, their equipment double-checked, rifles clean and ready to roll. Now it was time to do what the Army did best—hurry up and wait.

Riker's unit, the 1st Battalion, 506th Infantry Regiment, was going to assault the Walsenburg golf course, just west of their primary objective. The small town of Walsenburg would place them thirty-two kilometers behind the front lines and was being used as a headquarters and logistical hub for many of the PLA brigades and divisions that were fighting it out with the Americans near Colorado City.

Riker's battalion had been given the task of capturing the various headquarters units. If possible, they were also directed to seize the city before the PLA could send reinforcements. His platoon had been tasked with securing the landing zones on the golf course for the battalion. His group would be the first ones to land, which was an honor but also scary as hell since they'd be on their own until more units arrived.

While 1st Battalion assaulted the city, their sister battalions in their brigade would be ferried in to help reinforce their positions. The other two brigades would be dropped into the mountain ridges to the southwest of the city to further secure Interstate 25, a critical logistical lifeline for the PLA.

In preparation for this assault, the Air Force had dispatched two full squadrons of F-16 Vipers to specifically go after and eliminate any air-defense systems near the landing zones. While the Vipers went to work on suppressing the enemy SAM sites, two squadrons of RAF Eurofighter Typhoons, a squadron of A-10 Thunderbolts, and two squadrons of F-15Es had been assigned to provide them with close air support for the duration of the operation. If all went according to plan, in two days they'd link up with the main body of the III Corps as they punched their way through the Chinese positions.

Staff Sergeant Riker looked toward their chariots in time to watch a string of the Army's newest airmobile weapon, the V-280 Valor tiltrotor helicopter, start their engines. The crew chiefs stood outside the tiltrotors as the pilots got them powered up. Steadily, the blades picked up speed until the crew chiefs gave the pilots and the troops waiting to load them a thumbs-up.

Riker stood up, threw his ruck on his back and attached his rifle to his single-point sling. The CO approached him. "It's time to load up!" he ordered. Then he made his way down to the next platoon's position.

Riker turned to look back at his men. "All right, everyone, mount up!" he yelled to be heard over the noise of the flight line. "The mission's a go and our aircraft are ready."

Riker walked over to the soldier sitting on the ground right behind him and extended a hand, helping him to his feet. Everyone assisted each other to get their gear loaded up, saying words of encouragement as they completed their tasks. The soldiers were pumped for this mission—a real mission behind enemy lines. No more fighting off militiamen on the East Coast or in Canada. This was the real deal against a massive Chinese army.

Everyone lined up in single-file lines and they walked the parking ramps to where their chariots awaited them. As they approached the V-280s, the rotor wash whipped the warm morning air into their faces.

The crew chief, who was still wearing his aviator helmet, walked toward them. "Get on!" he directed.

Fireteam Alpha climbed into the seats facing rearward while Fireteam Bravo loaded on the opposite side. Staff Sergeant Riker made sure to position himself next to the door facing forward. This would allow him to be among the first off the Valor. He knew he'd need to get a read on the situation on the ground ASAP.

A few moments after they'd boarded the Army's newest tiltrotor, it taxied toward the runway, along with 110 Valors, Blackhawks, and Chinooks that would ferry the brigade to its objective.

These helicopters are going to be busy today, thought Riker. They had four full brigades of the division to drop behind enemy lines.

The pitch of the engines changed, and Riker felt the Valor lift off. Then they were in the air, joining up with the other helicopters in this once-in-a-lifetime massive air armada. The platoons in the V-280s would zip ahead of the

Chinooks and Blackhawks to secure the various landing zones for the follow-on helicopters.

The Valors were swift. In their airplane mode, they could reach speeds of 322 miles per hour. They were also very nimble and could maneuver on a dime, which made them perfect for slicing through contested airspace.

Twenty minutes into their high-speed race south, the Valor that Riker was riding in swooped into one of the valleys, hugging the terrain as much as possible to avoid enemy aircraft and radar stations. Their main fear was surface-to-air missiles. The PLA had been building the area up with SAMs as they'd moved their front lines forward, obviously aware that this was their one weapon system that continued to give the American Air Force fits.

Every now and then, Staff Sergeant Riker would spot a missile—or sometimes two or three—streaking down from the sky to slam into some unknown object on the ground. Occasionally, he'd see a missile fly up to the sky above in search of a target. It was an incredibly nerve-wracking experience for Riker, knowing he could be blown from the sky and he'd never see it coming.

As the air swirled around inside the bay of the tiltrotor, Sergeant Riker looked back at the painted faces of his squad. He saw both excitement and fear. They were flying into the jaws of the enemy; they'd either succeed and live to fight another battle or they'd get smoked and be forgotten among the other casualties of the day.

Near the end of their flight, the Valor exited the valley and suddenly appeared just north of their objective. The tiltrotor changed positions, shifting from flying like an airplane back to its helicopter mode, steadily bleeding off speed in preparation for landing.

Looking out the side doors, Riker saw the unwelcome sight of tracer fire. Long strings of it reached out into the early-morning sky in an effort to swat them down to the ground. The Valor's pilot immediately took evasive maneuvers as he sought a safe path through the treacherous sky.

They soon angled to land. Several large trees swept past them until they settled down on the ninth hole of the golf course. Once on the ground, the soldiers undid their six-point harnesses and were on the ground in no time flat.

With its human cargo delivered, the tiltrotor increased speed and was once again airborne, turning for home. It was time to grab the next load of soldiers.

Bang, bang, bang!

The sudden sound of a large-caliber machine gun shook them, eradicating any sense of safety Riker had in thinking that maybe the enemy wasn't nearby. The soldiers scanned their sectors to find where the shooting was coming from.

"Over there!" shouted Staff Sergeant Riker.

He spotted several GDF-002 anti-aircraft gun positions at the far end of the golf course, rapidly firing their twin 35mm cannons at the remaining helicopters in the area. One of the Valors took a string of rounds to its engines and crew compartment and exploded seconds later. It fell to the ground, a burning hunk of useless metal and parts.

"We got more AA guns over there, Staff Sergeant!" yelled one of Riker's soldiers.

Turning to see what his soldiers had found, Riker saw two PGZ-95 self-propelled AA gun trucks moving towards their landing zone and four SX2190 transport trucks packed with soldiers.

Oh, this is going to be trouble, he realized.

Their lieutenant shouted to be heard over the chaos. "Staff Sergeant Riker, take your squad and put those AA guns out of commission!" Then the LT dashed off to get the rest of the platoon focused on taking out the PGZs and the incoming troop trucks.

Riker turned to his guys. "Second Squad, on me!" he bellowed.

He jumped up and sprinted toward the AA guns at the end of the golf course, his men not far behind. When they got closer to the enemy positions, Riker spotted what appeared to be three of the AA guns anchored on what was probably the highest point on the golf course. The position was protected by a couple of machine guns.

Once Riker's squad had gotten within one hundred yards of the position, Riker halted their advance. He looked at his second fireteam leader. "Sergeant Black, your team is going to charge the enemy positions with me," he ordered. "We need to clear that position out before the next wave of helicopters show up." Riker paused for a second as he looked down at his watch. "We have roughly ten minutes until the next wave arrives, so that doesn't leave us much time."

Riker turned to his next fireteam leader. "Sergeant Lighthorse, I want your fireteam to hit those two machine-gun positions with your AT4s once I give you the signal. I want to see how close Bravo Team and I can get to them before they spot us. Once you've taken those positions out with the rockets, I want your M240 gunner to lay down suppressive fire on the remaining machine-gun position. You need to keep their heads down while we charge forward."

The two fireteam leaders quickly told their guys what they were going to do. The first group of guys got their two AT4s ready to fire while the M240G gunner got his bipod set up and his assistant gunner unslung several additional belts of ammo.

In a low crouch, Staff Sergeant Riker led the way with Bravo Team toward the enemy positions. Using their night vision goggles, Riker and his team advanced stealthily through the golf course entirely unnoticed. With the NVGs, night appeared like day as they crept up on the enemy, who probably had no idea they were about to be attacked.

When they had reached the halfway point to the anti-aircraft positions, the AA guns opened fire on some unseen aircraft overhead. The loud banging of their heavy-caliber guns was unmistakable, and the bright flashes from their muzzles temporarily made it harder for Riker and his men to see.

Riker continued to move forward undeterred. Then he heard the loud scream of jet engines flying overhead. The AA guns did their best to fire on the jets, but so far they were unsuccessful.

Seeing that they were practically on top of the enemy positions, Riker motioned for his guys to find a covered position and get ready. Once he saw them take a knee behind something, he depressed the talk button on his communication system.

"Now, Sergeant Black," Riker said in a voice barely above a whisper.

Pop...swoosh...boom.

The AT4 rockets flew fast and true, slamming into the two machine-gun positions overlooking the golf course. Then the M240G gunner opened fire on the enemy positions. His bright red tracers looked like lasers as they reached out and hit the Chinese positions.

"Follow me!" Riker shouted over the roar of the machine guns.

Riker and the six soldiers with him were less than twenty meters from the enemy positions when they charged the remaining distance. As they got closer, their heavy machine gunner to their rear stopped firing so he wouldn't inadvertently hit them.

When Sergeant Riker reached the nearest enemy position, he saw it was empty—there wasn't anyone in it. He didn't stop, continuing to charge into the center of the enemy position. Riker found around ten guys manning the GDF-002 AA guns.

By the time the Chinese soldiers realized Riker and several other soldiers were inside their position, it was too late. Riker fired off several three-round bursts from his M4 into the enemy soldiers. The other soldiers that had charged with Sergeant Riker unloaded on the remaining Chinese soldiers. The rest of Riker's fireteam then cleared out the enemy position and then went work on turning the position into a fortified stronghold for the Americans to use.

One of the first things Riker noticed about the enemy soldiers they'd just killed was that they didn't appear to be frontline PLA soldiers. They were older and less physically fit than the Chinese soldiers they'd encountered in the past. Riker figured they might have been militia soldiers or reservists.

Looking at the AA guns, Riker saw a couple of his soldiers were already trying to figure out how to use them. One of their guys radioed the lieutenant. "Sir, we've secured the position. If we can figure out how to use these guns, do you want us to try and use them to support you?" he asked.

As Riker's gaze went further down the road that led to the golf course, he saw that the two PGZ-95 anti-aircraft trucks had been reduced to burning wrecks, but the other four SX2190 troop transport trucks had stopped and dismounted their infantry. It looked like at least fifty or sixty enemy soldiers were now on foot, exchanging shots with his platoon.

"See if you can lower the AA gun and aim it at those enemy soldiers," Riker directed. "Let's see if we can't take some of them out." A couple of his soldiers finally figured out how to traverse and lower the gun. Once they'd managed to reposition the first one, they promptly got the other two ready.

Seconds later, their first captured AA gun sent a slew of rounds at the PLA soldiers, cutting many of them down. They kept firing short bursts at the cluster of enemy soldiers wherever they found them as the company continued to secure the rest of the golf course for the incoming wave.

The next set of helicopters to land was the CH-47 Chinooks. They offloaded more soldiers, along with additional crates of ammo and five-gallon jerry cans of water.

Staff Sergeant Riker and his men continued to hold the AA gun position, and the rest of their platoon eventually made it over to join them. Their position was at the front of the golf course closest to town, so it would be one of the first positions assaulted by the Chinese once they sent a substantial force to the golf course. Knowing this, Riker and the rest of the platoon did their best to prepare the position to repel the inevitable enemy attack.

An hour went by. The dawn slowly began to fight back the darkness. Meanwhile, down in the city of Walsenburg, the fighting was intense. There was a near-constant crescendo of gunfire and explosions. Illumination flares were constantly being fired over the city in the direction of the golf course.

The third set of helicopters to arrive was a string of CH-47s that had sling-loaded a dozen M119 Howitzers and brought in their crews. The 105mm cannons would help provide the ground pounders some fire support as they made their move to capture the city and the interstate that ran parallel to it.

Following the Chinooks was another wave of Blackhawks, which offloaded more soldiers. While these new units were getting themselves sorted out, the artillerymen got their guns positioned the way they wanted so they'd be ready to action calls for fire support.
****

Colorado Spring, Colorado
Peterson Air Force Base

Major John Zamboni, who went by the call sign "Zombie," held his hand against the wall above the urinal while he emptied his bladder. When he finished his business, he zipped up and walked over to the sink. As he washed his hands, Zombie looked at himself in the mirror. What he saw looking back at him was an exhausted hollowed-out shell of a man—a man who hadn't had more than six consecutive hours of sleep in three weeks. He hadn't seen his family in two months, and he wondered if they were even still alive.

Zombie's family had unfortunately been caught behind enemy lines when the PLA had broken through the Marine positions in Yuma, Arizona, and the Army's position around Fort Huachuca, Arizona. When that had happened, the PLA had been able to cut off Tucson before anyone had a chance to get out. His squadron had barely made it out of Davis-Monthan Air Force Base when Chinese tanks were spotted heading down the interstate.

Since that fateful day, many people in the 354th Fighter Squadron hadn't heard from their families at all. All they knew was what they were being told by the media and the occasional tidbits of information they'd glean from the command. News of what was happening in the occupied zones was hard to come by and not particularly reliable.

When Zombie walked back into the squadron room, their flight surgeon walked up to him. "Take two of these," he ordered. "They'll help you get through the next couple of hours. When you guys get back from this next mission, we're going to put the squadron on twelve hours of mandatory crew rest. You guys are getting too burned out, and we need you sharp and ready to fight in the coming days."

Nodding, Zombie swallowed the two uppers and chased them with a glass of water. He took a seat in the squadron room and waited for the briefer to come in and give them their next assignment. He looked around him; the other pilots seemed just as tired as he felt.

A few minutes later, a captain walked in and went right to the front of the room. She cleared her throat. "The main offensive officially starts today," she announced. "As you know, the last couple of days have largely been spent preparing the front lines for the armored assault today. Your main objective is to support our armored forces as they look to break through the enemy lines.

"This'll be a tank-busting mission," the captain continued. "You'll be loaded up with Mavericks. Once the squadron is airborne, you'll head to Sector F and look for targets of opportunity. Your operational zone is going to be Sectors E, F, and G. Do *not* stray outside your operational sectors. There are a lot of other aircraft operating in the AO, and we don't want any of you guys to accidentally get hit by any friendly aircraft."

One of the pilots raised his hand, and the captain nodded for him to speak. "Is there any possibility of enemy aircraft showing up?" he asked.

"I don't think so," the briefer responded, "but if they do, your aircraft still have two Sidewinder missiles and there's a flight of F-22 Raptors loitering above you for assistance."

A few of the other pilots had questions, but once those were answered, the briefing dismissed, and everyone headed out to their aircraft.

Zombie began his preflight checklist and walked around the aircraft. He looked over each of the missiles, making sure everything looked correct. When he was satisfied with what he saw, he moved around to the front of the aircraft and climbed up the ladder to get in.

As he was sitting down, the quiet night sky suddenly filled with the noise of aircraft engines and helicopters. This was gearing up to be a massive air operation. Squadrons from all over the country had been arriving throughout the past week in preparation for this major push. If they were successful, the ground pounders might be able to break through the PLA lines and hopefully drive them back into New Mexico.

With his body strapped to his ejection seat and his helmet hooked up to his communications and oxygen system, Zombie lowered his canopy and ran through the rest of his checklist. One of the airmen disconnected the aerospace ground equipment that had provided his aircraft with external power until he got his engines going.

"Bulldogs, Bulldog-Action," called his squadron CO over the radio. "Let's get airborne and go blow up some tanks."

Zombie gave the engines a bit of throttle, and his A-10 fell in position with the rest of the squadron. They'd take off in pairs and then rush toward their objectives, hunting for targets.

Zombie lined his aircraft up on the right side of the runway. His turn finally arrived and he applied more power to his engines. By the time he'd reached about two-thirds of the way down the runway, his plane had enough speed built up for him to lift off the ground. Steadily, he pulled back on the flight controls and the plane clawed its way into the sky.

"Hey, Zombie. You ready to go kill us some Chinks?" his wingman Joker asked with a laugh.

"You know I don't like that name," Zombie said angrily. "But, yes, I'm ready to go blow up some enemy tanks."

Zombie and his wife had adopted two kids from Asia, so he didn't particularly care for his wingman's choice of words. But Joker being Joker, he liked to use whatever pejorative was relevant to the enemy they were attacking. In the Middle East it was ragheads; in Afghanistan it was dirt farmers. In this war, it was either Krauts, Canucks, Frogs, Ivans, or Chinks.

Joker sighed over the radio, clearly a bit irritated by his partner's sense of morality. "All right, Zombie. I'll follow your lead."

The two flew in silence for another ten minutes as they approached the front lines. As they got closer, below them there were lines and lines of American main battle tanks and other armored vehicles, all lining up for the main attack against the Chinese positions.

In the lead of these massive armored columns were two distinctive vehicles. One was a tank with a specially designed thrasher system attached to the front. This piece of equipment would spin in a circle, whipping close to a dozen metal chains in front of it as it drove forward. It would essentially clear a path for the tanks behind it through any PLA minefields they had sown.

The second vehicle was another specialized mine-clearing vehicle. This truck would fire out a string of explosives several hundred meters in front of it, and then the controller would detonate those explosives, creating a massive hole through any existing minefield. The two vehicles would work in tandem, clearing a path for the armored force behind them.

As Zombie and Joker got closer to the front lines, they saw strings of enemy tracer fire rising from the ground, almost like a laser show in the sky. The enemy gunners were searching for the F-15Es and Vipers that were hunting them. These were the aircraft performing the critically important Wild Weasel missions for the A-10s. They'd largely clear the battlespace of enemy SAMs and aircraft, allowing the much slower Warthogs the opportunity to swoop in and wipe out the enemy's tanks and armored vehicles for the ground element.

Looking briefly at his clock, Zombie saw it was now 0215 hours. *Right on time.*

"All Bulldogs, good hunting and good luck," called out their squadron CO. "See you guys in Valhalla or the squadron room."

Zombie looked down at his ground targeting radar, searching for targets of opportunity. He depressed his talk button to speak to Joker. "If you find a target before I do, call it out," he said. "Let's figure out what we have down here before we engage. I want to take out as many of these bastards as possible in one pass. How copy?"

Joker just clicked his radio talk button twice, acknowledging the order. Zombie knew he was hard at work, trying to find the enemy armor as well. While flying at night had its advantages, it also made it hard to find some targets. Granted, a tank would usually illuminate pretty easily on their IR scope. However, it was nearly impossible to tell if the column of enemy vehicles was being protected by AA guns since those systems were typically fixed to a spot and didn't have a running engine to give away their location via heat signature.

Watching the battlefield before them was almost surreal. Never in his fourteen years in the Air Force had Zombie seen so much anti-aircraft ground fire or friendly aircraft attacking an enemy position.

"Makes you kind of glad we're still loitering on the edge of the battlespace as opposed to flying in that soup," Joker said over their radio net.

"Yeah, you're not kidding. I say we let the Vipers and Eagles clean up some of that ground fire for us before we go into that mess."

"All Bulldogs, be advised. We have inbound J-7s and J-11s," announced their CO. "We're going to move to Sector

A while the Raptors clear them out for us. Continue to stay frosty and keep an eye out for enemy targets."

"Oh, damn," Joker said. "I'm glad they warned us about those J-11s. Those are nasty fighters."

Zombie snorted. "Joker, *any* fighter coming at us is a nasty fighter," he quipped with a chuckle. "A-10s aren't exactly fast planes."

As they flew a bit further from the front lines, Zombie observed some of the Vipers and Eagle drivers continue to pound the AA guns and SAMs. Steadily, some of the enemy fire did begin to dissipate. Either the Wild Weasels were silencing them, or the gunners had gotten wise and turned their radars off, waiting for them to leave.

Switching his radio over to the frequency the Raptors were operating on, Zombie listened in on the aerial fight taking place above them. From his perspective, it sounded like a one-sided turkey shoot. The Raptors were absolute beasts in the air, and this current war was proving exactly how deadly they could be. Heck, they had a better combat record than the F-35, and that was saying something.

Five minutes went by before Zombie switched back to his own squadron's net. Joker finally got through to him. "What happened to you? You weren't responding to my calls."

"Sorry about that. I jumped on the Raptors' frequency."

"Well, while you were checked out of what's going on here, Bulldog told us a flight of B-1s is going to hit the enemy lines. Once they're done, we're supposed to swoop in and pick off any stragglers that survive the whoop-ass that's about to be unleashed on them," Joker explained, a bit of sarcasm in his voice.

Zombie chided himself for not staying on his own squadron's frequency; he knew he'd probably get scolded about it later. He sighed and then depressed his talk button. "Sorry about that, Joker. Thanks for covering for me. I owe you another beer."

"No worries, Zombie, but seriously—get your head back in the game. We're about to fly into a hornet's nest. I'm the wingman here, not you, so man up."

Zombie nodded, even though no one else could see him. He knew Joker was right. His mind wasn't in the fight like it needed to be. He needed to push his family concerns out of his mind.

They're either alive or they're dead. Either way, I can't do anything about it, he realized. He needed to do his part in creating a hole for the American tanks to bust through.

"Thanks, Joker. Let's move to six thousand feet and see if we can get a better picture of what we're about to fly into."

As their aircraft descended below ten thousand feet, the flight of four B-1 bombers flew in across the Chinese front lines. The four planes released 336 five-hundred-pound unguided bombs across a three-mile stretch of the front lines. It was almost like watching a string of M80 fireworks going off during the Fourth of July, only these weren't firecrackers—they were five-hundred-pound behemoths meant to kill hundreds if not thousands of enemy soldiers.

"OK, Bulldogs, that's our cue," announced their CO. "Let's go." Together, the Warthogs moved from their holding pattern into an attack pattern.

All around the battlespace, the Air Force had layers of different squadrons loitering, waiting to be sent in. The air battle managers would either send in a squadron to suppress enemy SAMs and AA guns or they'd send in a ground-attack squadron. This process of sending in different types of squadrons would largely continue unabated throughout the day as they attempted to break through the enemy lines.

"OK, Joker, follow me in," directed Zombie. "I found a string of tanks moving towards the front line.

They're in Sector G heading toward us. Do you see them yet?"

A second later, Joker clicked twice on his radio, letting him know he spotted them. The two of them increased their speed a bit as they leveled out at three thousand feet and began their attack run. Zombie placed a targeting reticle on three of the targets his computer had determined were tanks. That information was instantaneously shared with his wingman to ensure Joker didn't target the same three tanks.

When they got within eight kilometers of the tanks, Zombie and Joker fired off their first barrage of air-to-surface missiles. Once the missiles left their wing pilons, Zombie scanned for the next batch of armored vehicles.

All around them, Maverick missiles flew into the dark night sky and raced towards their intended targets. As Zombie and Joker flew closer to the actual front lines, the warning lights popped on, letting them know that enemy ground radars nearby had been turned on.

"Two o'clock. Looks like at least eight enemy tanks," Joker called out.

Zombie turned his aircraft in the direction of the enemy tanks and began to paint them with his targeting radar. He had three missiles left and he planned on scoring three more tank kills. Then they'd gain some more altitude and swoop in to carry out a gun run on the remaining enemy armor.

"Firing," Zombie announced.

His three missiles flew out from under his wings and were on their way to their targets. Joker's missiles had also joined the fray as well.

Before Zombie could say or do anything else, his warning alarms blared. His aircraft had been painted by an enemy ground radar. His plane's countermeasure system took over, firing off some flares. Zombie gave the aircraft more power and turned hard to the right as he sought to gain some altitude and put some distance between himself and the AA guns below.

While he was taking evasive maneuvers, strings of red and green tracer fire flew past his plane. Some flew over his wings, some under. Then a stream of bullets made a direct hit on one of his wings, tearing holes in it.

Five seconds later, Zombie and Joker had made it to ten thousand feet—out of range of the remaining AA guns below. Zombie still radioed the air battle manager in the JSTARS plane further back to let him know what had happened; some F-16s were dispatched to go deal with the antiaircraft guns.

Now that they were clear of the imminent threat, Zombie checked on his wingman. "You all right, Joker?"

"Yeah. I don't think they hit me, or if they did, I'm not showing anything serious. How about you, Zombie?"

"Ah, I took a couple of hits on my right wing, but it's still operable. Let's get ourselves in position to finish off that armored column."

"Roger that. You lead the way."

The two Warthogs leveled out at eleven thousand feet. Zombie and Joker positioned themselves to strafe the enemy column from the rear. They'd now flown some twenty kilometers behind the front lines and found themselves in a target-rich environment. The PLA was moving a lot of their armored vehicles to the front to meet the American armor head-on.

This armored battle's been brewing for months, thought Zombie.

Zombie would swoop in first to around three thousand feet and strafe the armored vehicles with his infamous 30mm chain gun. Joker would follow right behind him to finish off whatever he'd missed. Then they'd both climb back up out of range of the enemy AA guns before looking for another column to attack. They'd continue the process until they eventually ran out of ammo and had to fly back home.

"Hot damn. That's a lot of AA fire," Joker grumbled.

Zombie looked to the right and saw one of the other flights of A-10s swooping in to strafe the enemy. He knew in a few seconds that would be him and Joker. He wasn't relishing what he was about to have to fly through. It was terrifying, all those bullets being fired at his plane, and he knew if he got hit in the wrong spot, his plane would go down and he'd end up trapped behind enemy lines.

"Let's get this over with, Joker," Zombie muttered. "Follow me in." He increased his throttle and dipped the nose of his plane into a dive.

When this whole crazy war had started, Zombie had had one of his ground crew members attach a shrieking siren on the undercarriage of his plane; he knew it was against regulations, but he didn't care. They'd found a way to rig it so that it would only work when he dove at a specific angle, but whenever he hit it just right, his A-10 sounded like a German Stuka dive bomber. As the siren screamed, Zombie could see the terrified defenders below him scurry every which way, trying to get away from him. It was an exhilarating feeling.

He lined up his gun sights on the rear of the column and depressed the trigger. His 30mm chain gun made its sinister tearing sound as hundreds of depleted uranium rounds tore through the enemy column. Zombie's first set of rounds hammered several infantry fighting vehicles, blowing three of them up easily. His next string of rounds ripped through three ZTZ-96 tanks.

As soon as Zombie saw the three tanks explode, he pulled up hard on his flight control and applied more power to his engines. A lot of guns were flashing in his direction, and Zombie knew a lot of hot lead was doing its best to shoot his plane down.

While his Warthog climbed back into the sky, strings of red and green tracers flew up after him. The enemy ground fire crisscrossed the sky in front of him. Zombie knew his best way out of this was to climb out of the area as fast as he could. He fired off some flares to draw off some of the radar-controlled AA guns and keep any MANPADS from zeroing in on him. A couple of explosions disrupted the air behind his A-10, causing some turbulence. The flares had worked.

His warning lights were flashing in an assaulting way, and his alarms blared in his ears. The missile warning systems had been activated, radar warning lights were on, and critical equipment on his plane had been hit. But Zombie couldn't react to any of these alarms until his Warthog was out of range of the ground fire.

While he continued his climb, Zombie decided to check on his wingman. "How are you holding out, Joker?"

Joker let out a few f-bombs. "I took a few hits on my way in," he finally responded. "I got a handful of vehicles, but my left engine is shot to hell, and so is my right wing." Zombie could hear the tension and fear in his partner's voice, and he worried about his wingman.

Joker was a junior captain and he'd only been with the squadron for two years. While he'd served a tour in Afghanistan in 2019, he hadn't really seen much action during that deployment, so this war was proving to be his first real test. Thus far, he'd been a stellar pilot. He'd held strong when many other pilots had cracked, unable to handle the stress. Zombie knew if the hotshot pilot lived long enough, he'd make a good squadron commander.

"How are you holding out, boss?" asked Joker.

Now that he wasn't actively evading AA fire anymore, Zombie looked more closely at his gauges and then did his best to turn around and look at his wings and tail section. One of his alarms was alerting him that he was losing hydraulic pressure in his main system. Zombie used the manual switch and moved the aircraft over to the alternate system. Unless the backup system was shot up as well, he should be fine.

Next, he looked at his engine warning sign. The plane was riding a little rough, and it sounded like he had something grinding in the left engine. Zombie dialed down the throttle on the left engine, and that reduced the noise and the shaking. The engine appeared to stabilize, although he wasn't going to get a lot of thrust from it.

Zombie depressed his talk button, finally responding to Joker. "My primary hydraulic system is down. I'm on the backup system for right now. My left engine also took some hits, so I've had to throttle it back. Both my wings are shot, but somehow, I'm still airborne. Let's fly up to eleven thousand feet and get back across to our side of the line in case either of us has to bail."

"Bulldog-Actual to all Bulldog elements. Sound off," ordered their CO over the squadron net. It was time to get a count of how many of them had made it.

One by one, the pilots reported in. Zombie and Joker were Bulldogs Nine and Ten. When they called in, only one pilot appeared to have been shot down. Then they got to Bulldogs Fifteen and Sixteen. They were radio silent. No one saw them, so it was assumed they had been shot down. It'd be up to the AWACS and JSTARS to figure out where they had gone down. They'd determine if a search and rescue mission could be launched to try and retrieve them.

Zombie and Joker were just about to cross the main part of the front lines when a J-7 swooped in out of nowhere, guns ablaze. All Zombie saw was a string of bright objects slamming into his canopy, shattering it. The exposed part of his face was suddenly buffeted with cold air, which startled him half to death.

Zombie wasn't sure if it was just a reaction to his past training or if his mind was on autopilot, but he had somehow switched his targeting computer from air-to-ground mode to air-to-air mode, which activated his two Sidewinder missiles. He banked his aircraft to the left as he sought to get a bead on the bastard that had just shot them up. Seconds later, he heard the warbly tone in his headset that told him the Sidewinder had a solid lock. He depressed his firing button and the missile leapt from its rail and flew after the Chinese interceptor.

The missile streaked after the attacker, detonating just behind the rear of the plane. The back half of the J-7 exploded in flames. The pilot ejected out of the stricken aircraft just before the plane spiraled a trail of smoke on its descent to the ground.

Zombie pulled up on his flight control. The wind assaulted his body hard. His body was shaking from the shock of everything. Suddenly, he realized that his left leg was wet. It was only then that he noticed he had a piece of metal sticking out of his left thigh. Blood was oozing out around the wound, but it didn't increase with his pulses.

Oh, thank God, he thought. It didn't look like he'd nicked an artery or anything serious.

"Who got that enemy plane?" asked their CO.

"That was Zombie. He smoked that guy," Joker called out for him.

"Nice shooting, Zombie. Are you OK?"

It took Zombie a moment to reply. His mind was still racing, and he was trying to get the plane leveled out and apply a pressure bandage to his leg. "Negative, sir," he finally said. "My canopy got shot up. Some sort of metal object hit me in the leg too. It's sticking out of my left thigh. I'm attempting to put a pressure bandage on it to help slow the bleeding, but I'm going to need to land ASAP."

"Copy that, Bulldog Nine," his CO answered. "You land first. I'll radio ahead that we need EMS to meet you on the ground. Hang in there, Zombie. You can make it."

The next thirty minutes were the toughest thirty minutes of Zombie's life. His plane could only fly so fast with one good engine, and he was fighting to keep the plane from shaking itself into pieces from all the holes in his wings and fuselage. Then he started feeling lightheaded. Zombie had to keep shaking his head as he fought off the desire to just close his eyes. Several times he thought he'd just eject and let a SAR team come get him, but he knew the fastest way to get help was to fight through the blackness that was beckoning him and land at the air base.

The sun had finally pushed the darkness away. It was a beautiful day, not a cloud in the sky—just lots of contrails from the hundreds of aircraft flying back and forth between Peterson Air Base and the front lines. Zombie finally spotted the city of Colorado Springs and started guiding his plane to the runway on Peterson. The control tower hailed him, saying they'd cleared the runway for him to land and that EMS was standing by.

As he approached the runway, Zombie saw a string of fire trucks and ambulances with their lights on, ready to render him aid once he landed. He also saw rows of F-15s and F-16s waiting on the taxiway. They were loaded down with more bombs and missiles to go pummel the Chinese.

Zombie reached over to lower his landing gear. He held his breath for a second as he pulled the lever to lower the wheels. He let out a sigh of relief when he saw the green light come on, indicating they'd locked in place.

Zombie reduced his throttle. The altimeter continued to drop. The runway appeared much larger as he continued to lose altitude and speed. Then Zombie saw he was about to slam into it, so he pulled up on the stick a bit. His engines were almost ready to stall when his rear wheels finally touched down. He leveled the nose, allowing the front wheels to grab the runway. Once he had the aircraft firmly on land, he tried to use his air brakes but quickly discovered they'd been shot to hell and weren't worth a damn. He swiftly applied the wheel brakes as he throttled the engines back to an idle position.

He was fortunate that he had landed at such a slow speed or he might have run out of runway. It was a real challenge to slow the plane enough without his airbrakes or the ability to reverse the engines. His plane was so shot up, it was a veritable miracle that he'd even made it back to the base.

As his plane finally came to a halt, Zombie guided it off the main runway to the side of the taxiway. He then shut down the engines and finally pulled off his face mask. He took in a couple of deep breaths and then disconnected his helmet from the aircraft. He started to unstrap himself, but then the first rescue vehicles began to arrive. A ladder was thrown up against the side of his plane and a paramedic climbed up to him.

"Where are you hurt, sir?" the man asked.

Barely able to keep his head up straight, Zombie pointed to his left leg, which was now soaked in blood. The medic checked to see if his leg was pinned to the chair or if they could move him. Once he determined that Zombie wasn't attached to the plane, he tied a tourniquet around Zombie's leg to stem any possible gushes of blood once they started to move him. As the medic tightened the fabric, Zombie winced with pain and fought to suppress a scream. It hurt like hell, but he knew they needed to do it.

A few minutes went by. A stair truck pulled up the A-10 and a second rescue worker was able to climb up there with the paramedic. Then the two of them did their best to gingerly pull him out of the cockpit. By this point, there was a pretty big crowd of people coming over to look at Zombie's plane and to check on him, and most of his squadron had already landed.

As he was being carried down the stair truck, Zombie turned his head to look at his plane. He was shocked to see how much damage it had sustained. He could see holes through numerous parts of the fuselage, the wings, and the tail end of the plane.

A moment later, he was sitting in an ambulance, which sped off to the base hospital. For the time being, Zombie knew his part in the war was over. His only goal now was to recover and see if he could get another plane and rejoin the fight.

The following day, Major John Zamboni "Zombie" was flown to Walter Reed, along with several hundred other wounded soldiers and airmen. A month later, he'd be awarded the Purple Heart and the Air Force Cross, the second-highest medal in the Air Force.

****

Crowley, Colorado

The Mississippi Army National Guard's 155th Armor Brigade Combat Team had been assigned as the lead element to bust through the enemy lines south of Crowley. The attack would allow them to press the enemy's right flank. Their ultimate objective was to link up with the 101st Airborne Unit at Walsenburg some 120 kilometers to the southwest of their position. It was a lot of ground to cover in a couple of days. They'd be facing down the PLA 4th

Armored Brigade, the 46th Motorized Infantry Division, and the 68th Mechanized Infantry Brigade. It was a sizable enemy force standing between them and their objective.

Fortunately, they weren't the only ones assigned this task. They had the 2nd Armored Brigade Combat Team from the 1st Infantry Division saddled up with them to help punch a hole in the lines. Once they broke through, the rest of the 1st ID would follow through as they looked to make a mad dash on Walsenburg. Hopefully, they'd encircle several enemy divisions and force them to surrender. If everything worked according to plan, they could potentially collapse the enemy lines—at least, that was the stated goal the division commander had told everyone during last night's commander's brief.

As the battalion S3, Captain Regan, who had just been promoted to major, was stuck having to attend such meetings. Truth be told, he'd rather be in a tank, but until a more senior major came along or a slot opened up in one of the brigade's battalions, he was stuck being the operations officer for the battalion. It frustrated him since he'd developed a real skill at being a tank commander. Luckily, he was dual-hatted as the battalion XO should the commander get taken out. In the meantime, he'd ride along into battle in the back of their new armored multipurpose vehicle.

Looking at his watch, Major Regan saw it was now 0445 hours. In another fifteen minutes, they'd initiate their attack. In another five minutes, the battalion's vehicles would all turn on at the same time. They synchronized the engine starts so if enemy scouts were in the area, they'd have a hard time identifying how many vehicle engines had just fired up.

Regan heard the sounds of jets above them and instinctively looked up. It was pitch black. The only light came from the millions of stars. Every now and then, he'd hear an explosion somewhere above them. Sometimes he might even catch something blowing up in the sky. All Regan knew was that the Air Force was launching one of the largest air attacks since the beginning of the war. They had moved nearly all of their combat aircraft from the East Coast and Midwest to the Southwest for this operation.

While Regan was looked off into the night sky, wondering how the air campaign was going, one of the sergeants came up to him. "It's nearly time to roll out, sir," he announced.

Regan was about to climb back into the track when one of the young soldiers asked him, "Do you think we'll break through?"

Regan paused for a moment, then looked at the young man. "I do," he responded. "Of all the battles I've fought in, I'm most confident about this one. You hear all those explosions going off in the distance?"

The soldier nodded.

"That's the Air Force bombing the crap out of them. Next is going to come the rolling artillery barrage. Those Chinese soldiers are about to feel the full combined weight of the American Air Force and the US Army's armored fist. We're going to punch through their lines, and we're going to push them all the way back to Mexico."

The soldier smiled. He finished his cigarette off and climbed in the track with Regan. The young man's job was to work the radios and make sure they didn't have any malfunctions during the heat of battle.

Regan took his seat and looked at the blue force tracker. He saw all the units of the battalion. Their drone operator had just launched several of their scout drones to fly out ahead of them; as the drones identified enemy vehicles, they'd relay that information to their integrated friendly-and-foe tracking system on their digital map. Regan would have a bird's-eye view of the entire battle as it unfolded, allowing him to better relay the information to the battalion commander and better direct their artillery fire and units.

Regan turned to find his FIST LNO. "Captain Gillum, make sure your gun bunnies are ready," he directed. "We're moving out in a few minutes. The drones should start to identify some targets for us shortly—I'd like to get some steel-on-steel before our tanks get in range, if possible."

Captain Gillum was their artillery LNO from the 2nd Battalion, 114th Field Artillery Regiment. They were a self-propelled 155mm Paladin unit and their sole artillery support for this offensive.

"Copy that, sir," Gillum replied. "I've already relayed that we'll be sending a number of fire missions through in the near future."

Regan nodded. He felt about as ready as possible for the coming battle. He had a lot on his plate as the S3 and XO, and while he'd still rather be in a tank fighting, he also knew this type of experience he was gaining was going to make him an exceptional battalion commander when the time was right.

Their vehicle lurched forward, and they were officially on the move. Five minutes into their drive, the drones that had flown ahead of them began to relay targets. Regan's digital battle map was getting populated with enemy tanks, infantry fighting vehicles, air-defense vehicles and a ton of foot mobiles. Major Regan knew that infantrymen were the death knell to tanks. They could pop up out of a fighting position and fire a simple rocket that could blow out a track or disable a tank. They had to be dealt with swiftly.

Regan turned to his FIST LNO and ordered in some artillery strikes. He specifically wanted airburst rounds— that would shower the enemy infantrymen with more shrapnel than standard ground bursts.

For the next ten minutes, the battalion steadily moved in closer as their artillery battalion pounded the enemy positions. Then the tanks were in range to exchange fire, adding their own carnage to the landscape.

One of their scout drones had moved further behind the enemy lines, giving them a glimpse of what lay ahead. Roughly ten kilometers behind the front, columns of enemy tanks and infantry fighting vehicles were forming up. It looked like the PLA was waiting to see where the Americans were going to throw the bulk of their force and then hit them with a counterattack.

Major Regan reached for the radio that would connect him to their Air Force LNO at brigade and relayed what their drone was seeing. He asked if they could get an airstrike on those units. The airman on the other end said they had a number of aircraft on standby for a mission just like this.

The battle along the front lines continued, with the American and Chinese tanks exchanging fire from their maximum range. Then four American aircraft swooped into the enemy's rear area, where they found the waiting units. They hit the PLA tanks with dozens of five-hundred-pound bombs, destroying many of the infantry fighting vehicles.

While the battle raged, Regan watched a fair bit of it happening from the couple of scout UAVs they had launched at the outset of the battle. They'd already swapped out one of the UAVs when its battery had been running low. Another one of their UAVs had been shot down about thirty minutes into the fight.

Watching the battle unfold like this from the sky above was amazing and gave Regan a perspective on battle he hadn't had before. The UAV was able to help him better track where each of the battalion's and brigade's vehicles was in relation to the enemy, which was proving helpful. Regan was easily able to relay what he was seeing to the battalion and company commanders so they could respond better.

Regan remembered something he'd read in college about how the Germans were the first to incorporate radios into their tanks at the outset of World War II. It was such a revolutionary concept at the time and had allowed the Germans to coordinate their air and ground attacks so effectively that a much smaller German unit could outmaneuver and defeat a much larger British or French force. Major Regan couldn't help but see what they were doing with the integration of UAVs into their unit tracking system as a similar advancement—he was spotting gaps in the enemy positions in real-time, allowing him to relay that information directly to the units that could exploit it.

When the sun had finally brushed the darkness aside, it revealed an even greater level of destruction than what the UAVs had been able to relay in the darkness. After a couple of hours of relentless combat, Regan witnessed the true toll the battle had taken on the men fighting it and the machines they used to wage it.

Major Regan saw a mass grave site of American and Chinese armored vehicles strewn around a moonlike landscape where there had once been a beautiful tract of land. Looking at the digital map of the battlefield, Regan watched his old company push past the original enemy lines.

They were quickly followed by the rest of the battalion and eventually Regan's own track.

He missed his old unit. It pained him not to be the one leading them through this battle. He just hoped his guys were doing OK in his absence. Then, knowing his track was driving through the original Chinese lines, Regan had an overwhelming urge to see the situation with his own eyes, not on some digital feed from a UAV. Major Regan swapped positions with their turret gunner for a minute, and his eyes were assaulted with the sight of burning vehicles, upturned military equipment, and blown-apart bunkers intermixed with the twisted and torn bodies. The stench of diesel fuel, feces, and burning flesh was almost overwhelming.

The fighting for this particular piece of land had been brutal. His headquarters track had been positioned near the rear of the battalion, so he hadn't experienced any of the fighting directly—seeing this as they passed through was unnerving.

Regan turned to look behind them. The next battalion of tanks was moving through the hole in the enemy lines they had created. Further behind them were the mechanized infantry units. The Bradleys and Stryker vehicles ferried in a lot of their infantry support units.

It was a chaotic scene of death and destruction his track was driving through. He felt an overwhelming sorrow when he realized that this was just one part of the lines. As the two massive armies came to blows, this same scene was unfolding at multiple different points, and the destruction probably stretched for miles.

Chapter Eighteen
The Camps

Metcalfe, Mississippi
DHS Detention Camp 14

Martin stood before the federal judge as he awaited his sentence.

For the past two weeks, he had watched and listened as the prosecutor had laid out the evidence against him. The NSA had provided copies of his social media posts on Facebook and Instagram as evidence of his intent to fight against the federal government.

Then they'd showed multiple blog posts Martin had written about wanting to do more than just stand up against the corrupt regime of the Sachs administration. The prosecutor then played the most damning evidence—the video statement he'd created on his computer but had not sent, explaining his reasoning for joining the resistance and how he felt it his duty to fight against what he viewed as an evil dictatorship.

The prosecutor played several different UAV videos for the jury that showed him lying on the roof of the building in Three Rivers, Michigan, the day he'd been detained. They played radio intercepts where he was relaying targeting information to the Dutch commandos and his fellow militiamen working the mortar tubes. Next, the prosecutors played the footage showing him using his hunting rifle to shoot at two helicopters, killing three of the pilots. The jury watched as the helicopters crashed, killing several more soldiers.

Martin hadn't expected to see all this evidence. The weight of it hung over him like a giant stone, and a wave of guilt washed over him when he realized how many people had been killed as a result of his actions.

Martin's case had lasted a lot longer than the trials of the other prisoners who'd been labeled traitors. It had taken nearly three full months before everything had been compiled and the proceedings had started. His defense attorney had tried to rush the case and begin the trial with the evidence authorities had when he arrived, which wasn't much. But the prosecutor had convinced the judge to let them collect and then present their facts all at once.

For better or worse, Martin's trial was also being televised. The government prosecutors had requested that his case be shown to the rest of the country so it could be used as a deterrent against future militia attacks.

The government was doing their best to show the country and the world how this sinister scheme to supplant the American government with a proxy government chosen by foreigners had fomented a bloody civil war. Martin's case was also being used as evidence of how foreign actors had manipulated people's grievances for political gain.

When he had arrived at the camp, Martin had been viewed as a hero by the prisoners wearing the pink jumpsuits. He was seen as a man who'd stood up to the government and killed many soldiers. Then, as more evidence was shown and the foreign aspect was brought into play, that perception changed. It changed for Martin; it changed for everyone. The sudden realization of how they had all been played by foreign countries was overwhelming for many.

Support for antigovernment militias eroded across the country, leading many of them to throw down their arms. They did their best to fade away into obscurity. Steadily, as the war progressed with China, many of the state governments that had rebelled against the federal government came back into the fold. The governors and legislators realized that they, too, had been deceived. While many people had deep political disagreements, they still believed in the idea of a free America.

When the horrors of what the Chinese military was doing in the occupied territories came to light, many people didn't want to believe something like this could happen. The thought of the sick and elderly being systematically killed off and the outright kidnapping of young women only added further resentment toward these foreign invaders. The idea that the Chinese had cloaked themselves as liberators now only further infuriated the country.

As Martin sat in his chair, waiting to hear the verdict, he resigned himself to his fate. He knew he was guilty. He'd been used, but now he was the one who would have to pay. Still, it frustrated him that things had turned out like they had. It wasn't supposed to be like this. But there he was—in a pink jumpsuit with shackles on, awaiting his fate.

Then the judge walked into the room. "All rise for the Honorable Jessica Lake," ordered the bailiff.

Martin stood up with his public defender, as did everyone else in the room. When the judge took her seat, everyone else followed suit.

Judge Lake turned to face the jurors, asking the inevitable question. "Have you reached a decision?"

The lead juror stood up, replying for them, "We have, Your Honor."

The juror then handed the bailiff an envelope. Everyone in the courtroom waited with bated breath for the judge to say or do something. They all watched her facial expressions when she opened the envelope, hoping they might be able to glean something from how she reacted. The judge did not betray any emotion at all.

After reading the paper, the judge turned back to the lead juror. "On the first count of knowingly colluding with a foreign power to overthrow the government of the United States of America, how do you find the defendant?"

The lead juror, a woman in her midfifties, looked at Martin as she replied, "We find the defendant, Martin Brown, guilty."

"On the second count of actively taking up arms to aid in the violent overthrow of the government of the United States of America, how do you find the defendant?"

"We find the defendant, Martin Brown, guilty."

"On the third count of committing treason against the government of the United States of America, how do you find the defendant?"

"We find the defendant, Martin Brown, guilty."

"On the fourth count of premeditated murder of fourteen US military service members, how do you find the defendant?"

"We find the defendant, Martin Brown, guilty."

As Martin sat there listening to one count after another being read off, the jury came back with guilty verdict after guilty verdict. *I'm toast*, he realized. It was obvious he was going to get the death penalty. What frustrated him most wasn't that he was going to have to answer for his crimes but that the men and women who were behind this sinister plot would probably get away with it.

Martin was in a daze. His mind and body were numb as he stood there listening to everything. Then the judge asked him a question. He had to have her repeat it because he hadn't heard it the first time. The continued guilty verdicts were like blows to his gut, knocking the wind out of him with each one.

"Mr. Martin Brown, do you have anything to say before I issue my sentencing?" asked Judge Lake.

He didn't want to look weak, but he knew there wasn't anything he could say or do to save his own life. Still, he felt compelled to say *something*. "I was an unwitting pawn in what we have all come to see was a global conspiracy," he explained. "I do not disagree with the verdicts—I did those things. I did those things believing I was doing the right thing for my country. I did those things because I truly felt the President was an illegitimate dictator and needed to be stopped. For years, that had been pounded into my brain. While I'm not dismissing my own crimes, I do hope that the individuals who started this and the other groups that perpetuated it will one day also be held accountable."

The judge nodded. "Mr. Martin Brown, while I do not hold you accountable for the actions that led our country into this second civil war and subsequent invasion, I *do* hold you accountable for your own actions in it. You knowingly committed treason and took up arms against your country. Worse, you killed at least fourteen US soldiers—people who are sworn to protect our country from this very type of threat."

She paused for a moment, collecting her own thoughts before she continued. "Taking all of these things into consideration, you are hereby sentenced to death by firing squad. You will be executed in four days. You will be afforded some time to work with your lawyer to sort your affairs, such as they are. Phone privileges will be granted to you to allow you to say your final goodbyes to your family, which is something the soldiers you killed were not afforded. I hope this public trial and your public execution will serve as a deterrent to others who may consider taking up arms against our country. It will not be tolerated."

Chapter Nineteen
Finally, Some Allies

December 2021

Washington, D.C.

White House

Sitting at the table in the Treaty Room of the White House were the leaders of Poland, Romania, the United Kingdom, Australia, and India. This gathering of world leaders had taken some time to arrange; many of these once-staunch allies of America had been taking a wait-and-see approach to observe how the internal conflict in the US played out. The leaders hadn't wanted to pick a side only to find out later they had backed the wrong horse. The EU and other world leaders who had sided with the UN and then Senator Tate had found out the hard way what happens when you pick the wrong side.

"Ladies and gentlemen, thank you all for coming and agreeing to meet with me," said President Sachs as he started the meeting.

The White House steward brought in a couple pots of fresh coffee and a pot of hot water for tea should anyone want some. Sachs made some small talk until the steward left and they were once again alone in the room.

When he'd had a few sips of coffee himself, the President set his drink down on the table. "The last year has been a dark chapter in my nation's history," he began. "There was a point when I wasn't sure America would survive. But we have, thanks to the hard work of our intelligence and law enforcement agencies who uncovered this conspiracy. Putting all of that aside, now it's time to discuss how we are going to right some of these wrongs and deal with China."

The Prime Minister of Australia quickly chimed in. "You can count on us, President Sachs. While we haven't sustained the same level of destruction your country has, the Chinese hit my country hard with that EMP. It caused considerable damage to nearly half of our country. We are only just now getting power restored to parts of the country. My people have been clamoring for payback."

The President smiled. "Thank you for your support."

"Poland is also ready to support your nation in any manner we can," confirmed the Polish leader. "The Russians lost a substantial part of their western European army fighting you, and it's left them in a very weakened state. With the threat on our own borders significantly reduced, I feel confident that my country can commit a large portion of our military to your country, to help you defeat the Chinese."

Poland had already contributed sixteen thousand soldiers to fight along the American southwest border. They had played a pivotal role in Operation Spartan's success.

The Romanian Prime Minister also offered up her nation's support. She informed the group she'd authorize the deployment of more than twenty-five thousand troops in addition to the fourteen thousand they had already sent.

The British Prime Minister added, "Mr. President, the United Kingdom will continue to do its part to help. I've asked for our regular Army to be doubled in size, and I believe Parliament will approve that request given what has transpired at the UN. China is a global menace. What they are doing in the Southwest of your country is abhorrent. They need to be defeated before they are able to grow into a larger force than we are able to collectively handle."

All eyes then turned to the leader of India, the one nation that shared a border with China and had an army that could threaten them. Prime Minister Bhamre hadn't said anything during the meeting thus far.

Clearing his throat, Bhamre finally spoke. "I agree that China is a menace and that what they have been doing with the kidnapping of your women and the extermination of your sick and elderly is appalling. The question I am grappling with is exactly how India should respond to this threat. Unlike your nations, we have a very long, shared border with China. We have billions of dollars a year in trade between our countries, but more importantly, China has allies near us.

"The President of Pakistan has already made overtures to us that if we were to get involved in this war and attack China, they would honor their defense pact and declare war on us. While India could certainly handle a war against China now that most of their nuclear forces have been destroyed, a simultaneous war with Pakistan, whose nuclear weapons are still very much in play, could prove to be disastrous for my nation."

The PM paused for a moment and looked around. Sachs could see that the other world leaders were just as disappointed by Bhamre's statement as he felt. After an awkward pause, the Prime Minister cleared his throat. "However, I believe my nation could provide substantial material support to your war efforts against the Chinese," he offered. "In the case of Australia, we can send in thousands of technical experts to help you recover faster from the EMP attacks. We can send large quantities of war stocks and other materials to your nations as you build up your forces to fight the Chinese. We can also offer substantial intelligence reporting on what the Chinese are doing and what is going on inside their country."

President Sachs had feared the Indians would back out of a military confrontation with the Chinese. It had been a long shot trying to get them to join the war, and he understood the predicament they were in. They had a nuclear-armed enemy on their other border they had to think about.

"Mr. Prime Minister, I recognize that India is being placed in a tough position," Sachs acknowledged. "My government cannot offer any direct military assistance to you as of right now. However, I could speak with the President of Pakistan, or at least his ambassador, and make it clear to them that any nuclear attack on India by their forces would result in a nuclear retaliation by the United States," he offered. "And I can have a ballistic missile submarine positioned off their coast to ensure their compliance. If a war were to erupt between India and China, and potentially Pakistan, we could issue that ultimatum that the fighting has to stay conventional. I've already demonstrated to the world that I will not only use nuclear weapons, I will use them in a fashion that will destroy our enemies."

President Sachs paused for a moment as he weighed what he was about to say next. "If an overt threat won't work, I have another option."

PM Bhamre appeared more than a little uncomfortable with the discussion of nuclear weapons. He shifted back and forth in his seat. "I am open to hearing your alternate plan, Mr. President, especially if it does not involve nuclear weapons."

Sachs smiled and leaned in. "My country has been concerned about Pakistan's nuclear weapons for some time. We've gone to great lengths to identify where they are located. We've also gone to great lengths to infiltrate their power grid, in case we needed to remove their nuclear weapons. If India were to join the war against China, we could provide you with the location of their nuclear weapons so they could be attacked. Furthermore, we could also turn the lights out in the country prior to your attack to ensure your mission's success. With their electrical grid down, and their nuclear weapons largely removed, Pakistan would not pose the same threat to you that they presently do."

The three other world leaders looked at Sachs and shivered. Everyone knew that the American leader had changed after being stuck in a tunnel for nearly a week, but it clearly made them uncomfortable how he cavalierly spoke about inflicting damage on a country that could lead to the deaths of millions.

Sachs saw the Indian PM hesitate, so he moved in to try and convince him. "Bhamre, this war needs to end. We cannot allow it to drag on for years. I have no intention of invading China, but we need to get them to stop sending more people to my country. I've already conveyed to you a preferential trade agreement ensuring India would have a fixed price for oil and natural gas for the next ten years. That deal is not for you to sit on the sidelines and play wait-and-see. We need India's help now to bring this war to an end."

"It's not that easy, Mr. President," Bhamre insisted. "You're asking me to gamble the lives of my own people. This puts me in a terrible position. Of course my country would like this trade deal, but you are asking me to seal it with the blood of my citizens and the people of Pakistan. I'm just not sure I can do that."

Sachs sighed. He was doing his best to not lose his patience, but he was getting mad with how many once-strong allies had turned their backs on him at the outset of this war.

"Mr. Prime Minister, are you essentially telling me that you want to wait another three or four months to see who it looks like is going to win this war before you pick a side or choose to get involved?" he asked.

The British PM sat back in his chair and lifted his cup of tea to his lips, as if he were watching an entertaining boxing match on the television.

PM Bhamre paused for a moment, carefully weighing his response. "My apologies, Mr. President. That is not what I meant to imply. My concern is the Pakistani nuclear weapons. If they were able to initiate an attack before their weapons were taken offline, they could devastate my nation. If India is to invade China, then I need some help from you in ensuring Pakistani missiles won't rain death on our cities. If you could perhaps send some of your ballistic missile interceptors and convey your threat to them, then I will work out with my generals the best time to open a second front with China."

Sachs grinned and sat forward in his chair. "Excellent. We'll begin transferring a couple of THAAD batteries immediately. They did incredibly well for us."

"The Chinese did still manage to get a few through, though," commented the Polish PM, who seemed to immediately realize that he'd made a huge gaffe.

Sachs shot the Polish President a dirty look. "A lot *more* would have gotten through without them," he countered, practically hissing. "I've made my point clear to China. If they attempt to use nuclear weapons against

American again, I will turn their entire country to radioactive dust. They won't use nukes again. As to Pakistan—their missiles are crap. The THAAD will more than handle them. Besides, when we turn the lights off, they'll have more pressing concerns to deal with."

The British PM loudly exclaimed, "Excellent! Then I think we all have a deal. Let's drink another round of tea and work out the details."

Sachs smiled, glad the Brit had spoken up. His relationship with Bhamre was tenuous at best. He felt betrayed by the Indians for not coming to his aid earlier, but now he had to rely on them to open a second front against China, something he knew they didn't want to do.

****

Situation Room

Eight Hours Later

General Adrian Markus felt like he had aged ten years in the span of six months. Since taking over as the Chairman of the Joint Chiefs, he hadn't slept more than four hours a night or taken a single day off. While he was grateful to have been chosen to replace General Peterson, he felt incredibly overwhelmed in the position.

He had enjoyed being the head of the Air Force. Before he'd taken over that position, he'd met with the CEOs of several major corporations, learning what they were doing to minimize waste and increase productivity and how they were incorporating AI. General Markus had wanted to use these lessons to make the military more efficient. After seeing the driverless cars, he'd promoted an initiative to create a new series of pilotless fighters that could help handle the never-ending increase demand for Air Force assets. That had all been three years ago; now all his energies were focused on trying to build up the necessary fighting force to defeat the foreign invaders on American soil and prepare the military to bring the fight to China.

General Markus looked down at his watch. He had about twenty minutes until the President, the National Security Advisor and the President's Chief of Staff would arrive. Truth be told, he just wanted to take a nap, but that was entirely out of the question.

Reaching for his coffee cup, Markus downed the rest of its contents before signaling for one of the majors in the room to get him a refill. Then he turned to his briefer. "Do we have the latest updates from General Tibbets and Operation Spartacus?" he asked.

The officer nodded. "We do. I just got their six slides a few minutes ago and updated them in the master deck. We're good to go."

Looking at his notes again, General Markus tried to figure out if he should start with the military updates of the battles going on or the production status of the war stocks and troop training. He remembered how one of his mentors had said, "Amateurs talk tactics, experts talk logistics." It never failed to amaze him how a single kink in the production of a weapon system could have a profound impact on the entire fielding of a tank brigade, or how a shortage of ammunition could delay the graduation of five thousand recruits from basic training.

Suddenly, the room began to fill up as everyone that needed to be at the meeting started showing up. Then the President walked in with his two senior advisors, and everyone stood. He promptly motioned for them to take their seats and signaled for General Markus to get the ball rolling.

General Markus nodded to his briefer. Major Brian Schultz depressed the button on his pointer to bring up the first slide, which showed a large-scale map of southern Colorado sprinkled with a lot of different unit icons.

"Mr. President, the next couple of slides will go over the results of Operation Spartacus," announced Major Schultz.

The President nodded and signaled for him to continue.

"To start the campaign, the US Air Force along with the British Royal Air Force, carried out a series of missions, suppressing the enemy air defenses along the front lines and as deep as seventy kilometers behind their lines. These missions were quickly followed up by more than three hundred multirole fighters and ground-attack aircraft from the US and RAF going after specific enemy strongpoints and high-value targets. Next, two squadrons of B-52 bombers carried out a massive carpet-bombing mission of the enemy front lines and their fortified positions. Our B-1 bombers swooped in next and went after the rear-echelon troops and the units that were being held in reserve and plastered them pretty good.

"Following the multi-hour-long aerial attack, the 101st Airborne Division and the British 16 Air Assault Brigade were successfully deployed behind the enemy lines here and here." Major Schultz used the laser pointer to show on the map where these units had been dropped, sixty kilometers behind enemy lines.

"Next, the 4th Infantry Division and the British 3rd Division conducted a frontal assault on the enemy's main lines here, here, and here," Schultz explained as he again used his laser pointer.

"While this was happening, an armor brigade from the Mississippi National Guard broke through the enemy's right flank here. This breakthrough was exploited by the 1st Infantry Division, which we had been holding in reserve for just this type of situation. Once they were through the gap in their lines, they were able to make a mad dash and cut some ninety kilometers behind the enemy's lines and secured the city of El Moro along Interstate 25. This put them roughly twenty kilometers from the New Mexico border, but more importantly, it completely encircled the PLA's 16th and 26th Army Groups or Corps-level units—"

The President interrupted. "How many enemy soldiers are now trapped in this pocket?"

General Markus jumped in to answer this question. "Roughly speaking, Mr. President, one hundred and thirty thousand to one hundred and sixty thousand troops. So it's a sizable force. More importantly, these are combat units, not rear-echelon or support troops."

"Are they going to surrender?" asked Sachs. "I have to imagine the Chinese will do their best to bust them out of that pocket if you aren't able to get them to capitulate."

Markus nodded. "We're working on that as we speak. They've been trapped now for forty-eight hours. That's after roughly two days of heavy fighting to get them surrounded. They've been expending a lot of ammunition, fuel, and other consumables that aren't getting replaced. Right now, we're tightening our grip on them with additional forces moving into the area. Tomorrow, most of V Corps arrives in Colorado Springs. They'll give us another seventy thousand fresh soldiers. We are also using the Air Force to really pound them hard. If I had to guess how long they'll hold out, I'd say probably a week at best."

Seemingly happy with the response, the President signaled for Major Schultz to continue.

"Out west, the Marines have reached Portland. They have met some resistance from the locals, but they've largely put down any civil disturbances. DHS's Federal Protective Service officers are moving into the city and the surrounding area to take control of it from the Marines. They'll move to join up with II MEF and elements of III MEF. We should be able to keep the Chinese contained in California with their added force."

Next, Schultz brought up a slide of the Pacific. "The Chinese do appear to be moving forces in and around Hawaii. With the sinking of two more of our carriers and the third one having to retreat back to Washington State for repairs, we don't have a lot of forces left to protect the island. Our cruisers and destroyers in conjunction with our land-based aircraft are doing a good job of keeping them from getting too close, but that'll only last so long. Although we've secured Johnston Atoll, Midway and Wake Islands, so that did put a dent in their ambitions."

"Is Hawaii in danger of being invaded?" asked the President, clearly concerned that they might lose the American stronghold.

Schultz shook his head. "No, sir. At least not yet. The Chinese Navy would need to finish off our surface fleet we have protecting it. Even if they managed to do that, they have yet to clear the area of our subs. We have about half of our available subs protecting the Alaskan coast and the upper West Coast around Oregon and Washington State, about a quarter running interdiction operations along the California and Mexican and South American coasts, and the remaining quarter protecting Hawaii and going after the Chinese supply lines. It's tough going as we have an enormous area to patrol and protect, but we're keeping the Chinese at bay."

The briefing went on for another hour as Major Schultz got the President and his advisors up to speed on the war and where things stood. When he was done, Sachs turned to General Markus and asked, "How are we doing on training and equipping our new army? Are we still on track?"

Nodding, Markus replied, "We are, in most areas. A few areas still having some trouble, but we'll get there."

"OK. How about you tell me where the problems are?" asked the President. "Perhaps I can place a call and help get things moving if that's all it takes." Sometimes a call from the President of the United States to a CEO of a company would be enough to light a fire under someone's butt. The strategy did work, but it was seldom used.

"Right now it's ammunition production," General Markus responded. "With the war going on and civil disturbances still taking place in many parts of the country, the civilian ammunition consumption rate is huge. People are basically buying out whatever is available. The manufacturers can make four times as much money selling to the civilian marketplace than they can to the government, so while they aren't *not* fulfilling our orders, they are taking a lot longer than they should. This is having a knock-on effect—we're not getting all the new recruits qualified with their rifles, so we're either delaying their graduations or cutting down the number of training rounds."

Sachs was visibly frustrated. He turned to one of his aides. "Get me the names of the CEOs who own those companies, and I'll call them after this meeting is over," he directed. Then he turned back to General Markus. "What's the next problem?" the President asked.

"We're burning through tanks and other armored vehicles. Same with aircraft. We're just taking a lot of combat losses. Nothing like the Chinese are—but our stuff is a bit more complex to make than theirs. The factory in Lima, Ohio, is cranking out main battle tanks as fast as they can. But we're having issues with General Motors and Ford. As you know, a lot of their manufacturing plants are in Ohio, Michigan, Indiana, Illinois, and Wisconsin. Well, those areas got pretty trashed during the UN invasion and then by the militia units. They're taking a bit longer to get repaired than some of our engineers believe they should have."

Sachs held a hand up to stop him. "Are you saying they're *intentionally* delaying the production of critical armored vehicles?" he asked, visibly upset.

"No, no. I'm not saying that. I'm saying they're prioritizing work at their other facilities to keep producing civilian vehicles and trucks over getting those other factories up and running and retooled to produce armored vehicles and other equipment we need."

"So if GM and Ford switched their factories in the South to producing war stocks while they rebuilt their factories in the North to produce civilian vehicles, would that solve the problem?" asked the President.

Markus nodded. "It would."

General Pruitt, the head of the Army, sighed. He had largely stayed silent during the meeting, but he clearly felt the issue was important enough for him to chime in. "Mr. President, during World War II, the American auto manufacturers took several years off from producing new vehicles and focused solely on producing the tools needed to win the war. Maybe the reason our current manufacturers haven't come to that same conclusion yet is that they don't realize how desperate the war really is. For nearly eighty years, our country hasn't been directly threatened to a point where our entire economy became solely focused on producing weapons and ammunition. We need to make it clear to these companies that we are presently in that same level of crisis and they need to get on board with helping us defeat the Chinese."

The generals and advisors discussed what General Pruitt had said for half an hour as they sought to figure out how to incentivize and, if necessary, strong-arm the thousands of manufacturers across the country to produce the tools of war needed to defeat the Chinese.

****

At the end of the military briefing, everyone left the room except the President and his National Security Advisor. Then the Secretary of Homeland Security, the Attorney General, and the Director of the FBI walked in with a few of their aides in tow.

When everyone had gone through their initial greetings and taken a seat, Sachs asked, "Secretary Hogan, how is the task of bringing law and order back to the rest of the country coming along?"

Patty Hogan leaned forward in her chair before she responded, "Steady, Mr. President. We are graduating some twenty-five thousand, eight hundred federal police officers from training each month. I've been ordering most of these graduates to the East Coast and the Pacific Northwest as requested. We still have roughly seventy thousand federal officers operating in the south and east part of the country, putting out fires in some of the hotspots the FBI has been identifying for us. As more of those areas return to normal, we'll transfer them to the hot zones in the Pacific Northwest and the upper East Coast. I must say, Mr. President, partnering our federal police officers with the local sheriffs across the country has been a big help. It's taken time, but we are steadily putting down this internal civil war and keeping it from spreading."

When DHS had first started graduating large numbers of federal police officers, they had run into the problem of where and how to deploy them. Then the head of the US Sheriff Association had come up with the idea of partnering the federal police officers with the sheriff departments across the country. Each county sheriff would identify roughly how many additional federal police officers they needed to restore order to their city centers and the rural areas where a lot of the militia units had been forming and or training. It had become a perfect pairing of local and federal law enforcement.

Sachs smiled at the positive prognosis and heaped some praises on her for a job well done. Then he turned to his AG. "How did things go with the Brown trial? Has it had the intended results we wanted?"

"It has," Malcolm replied. "I was actually impressed with the number of people who tuned in and watched the proceedings. We conducted a series of polls during and after the trial. As the evidence was laid out and the drone footage was shown, public opinion really flipped. Now the vast majority of people, even in the hot zones, no longer support the civil war. Support for your administration has also risen dramatically. I think people are looking forward to the day that we return to the old order of settling our disagreements at the ballot box."

The President motioned for one of his Secret Service agents to come over to him. The agent leaned down to listen to Sachs. "Tell the kitchen crew I'm going to have ten for dinner. Let the First Lady know she may join us if she'd like, but I'm going to have to take a rain check on our private dinner."

"Yes, Mr. President," the agent responded. Then he walked off to let the staff of the White House know of the change.

The President returned his attention to his cabinet members. "Not a lot has been going right for our country in this war. However, you three and your staff have done an outstanding job. I'm supposed to have a private dinner with the First Lady; however, I want to treat you all to a dinner here at the White House with us. Let's take a few minutes and head upstairs. We can talk more over some food."

Everyone at the table smiled and the conversation turned into friendly banter.

From time to time, Sachs liked to change up his schedule. He couldn't always do something nice for the department heads and cabinet secretaries, but one thing he certainly could do was invite them to stay for a fancy breakfast, lunch, or dinner to break bread, talk, and spend some time getting know the people who were responsible for so much of the managing of the country. It was a way for him to develop deep, meaningful relationships with key people. It also allowed him to get a better sense of what was going on outside the White House.

Chapter Twenty
Battle in the Redwoods

Kernville, California
Sequoia National Forest

Despite the higher elevation in the National Forest, the temperatures had moved from the low seventies to the upper eighties. For an everyday hiker, that wouldn't have been all that bad, but for a Marine lugging 110 pounds of combat gear up and down valleys and ridges, it made for some sweat-soaked patrols.

After the defeat at Bakersville, Regimental Combat Team One had been ordered to take up a series of positions throughout the Sequoia National Forest and keep the PLA from breaking out of California and into the Nevada desert on the other side. Steadily, the Marines had been reinforced and brought back up to strength, but they were still lacking in armored vehicles, helicopters, and artillery. Not that they could move a lot of armor through the winding roads of the park—still, it was comforting to know they could call in a Super Cobra or an Abrams battle tank to blow something up when needed.

Staff Sergeant Mack, now Gunnery Sergeant Mack, was preparing to inspect the replacement Marines that had been assigned to his platoon. They had been flown in the day before and they'd be joining him and the others out on a two-night, three-day patrol along the line of control. The LOC was essentially the no man's land between the PLA and the Marines. It ran from Twentynine Palms down in Barstow, linked up with the Sequoia National Forest through Yosemite and Tahoe, and eventually wrapped itself around Shasta-Trinity National Forest all the way to Eureka along the coast.

Ninety thousand US Marines and one hundred and thirty thousand Army National Guardsmen from around the country had managed to bottle up and contain two PLA Army groups operating in state. Twice, the PLA had tried to break through the Mojave Desert and the areas around Fort Irwin and Edwards Air Force Base. In both cases, the PLA armor had been thoroughly trounced. The desert area had been the perfect terrain for two of America's top weapon platforms. the M1 Abrams battle tank and the newest version of the MQ-9B Reaper Drone. The new Reapers had become tank-busting machines; the improved versions were now able to carry eight Hellfire missiles.

Between the venerable Abrams and the Reapers, the PLA never stood a chance. The terrain was too wide open, and while they scored aerial victories, they had never been able to wrestle air superiority away from the Americans. Now, the battle lines had been drawn again, and it was becoming a war of logistics. Whichever side was able to equip and field its army faster would defeat the other.

Gunny Mack stuck his head outside of his tent flap, looking for his new recruits. When he saw a gaggle of Marines over by the LOC, he grabbed his patrol cap and his rifle and made his way over to them.

While he walked, he looked around the camp. *I do really like it here*, he admitted to himself.

Their company had set their base camp on a nice plateau just below the top of a ridgeline. They had a number of fighting positions built on the opposite side of the ridge and around their little makeshift combat outpost. Two platoons would rotate guard duty on the COP while another platoon was out on roving patrols. The fourth platoon was on QRF duty, ready to come to the aid of the platoon on patrol or one of the other nearby COPs. This allowed each of the platoons a bit of downtime and still kept them fresh should the enemy decide to do more than probe their positions.

As Mack approached the replacements, they stopped their joking around and stood a bit taller, ready for his inspection. When they had arrived the night before, he'd made it clear to the NCOs that he'd inspect their gear and weapons after morning chow before they went out on patrol. He wanted them to be ready for whatever was coming, and that meant making sure their gear was ready when they needed it.

As he walked up to the front of the group, he cleared his throat. In his loudest Marine voice, he bellowed, "I'm Gunnery Sergeant Mack. I'm your platoon sergeant until the enemy kills me or I get promoted. Last night, Staff Sergeant Rider went over what was going to happen today with you. He also gave you some specific instructions on how to pack your gear and fit your kits out. Before I hand you over to your squad leaders, I want to take a moment to see if you cherries can listen and do as you're told."

Mack walked up to the first guy in line and began his inspection. He got about halfway through when he cocked his head to one side as he looked at the setup of one of the Marines. The kid must have had his parents sign the waiver for him to get in because he didn't look a day older than sixteen. His kit was all jacked up.

The other cherries should have helped him out before this inspection, Mack thought.

He looked at the young Marine's name tape. "Private Morgan, come stand next to Staff Sergeant Rider," he ordered.

The young Marine blushed at being called forward but didn't hesitate. He stood at attention next to Staff Sergeant Rider, facing the rest of the new recruits.

"What is wrong with this Marine's kit?" Gunny Mack asked.

A couple of them laughed quietly. One of the Marines poked his friend and said something Mack couldn't hear. Mack moved with lightning speed, getting in the guy's face, his nose inches away as he yelled, "You think this is funny? Some sort of joke at Private Morgan's expense?"

The laughing stopped immediately. Mack began to pace in front of them, then walked up to one of the other guys who'd laughed at Morgan's setup. "Private...Blount, is it?"

"Yes, Gunnery Sergeant," he replied without hesitation.

"Look at Private Morgan. What's wrong with his kit?" Mack asked.

The private looked at Morgan for a brief second before returning his gaze to Mack. "His tourniquet pouch is on upside down. His magazine pouch is in the wrong location and he only has two grenades on his chest rig."

Mack nodded in satisfaction. "Outstanding, Private Blount. Now, explain to me how you knew all that and Private Morgan here didn't."

The Marine looked at him nervously and then tried to look to one of his friends for support before Mack snapped his fingers in front of him to get his attention. "Don't look to your friends for help. I asked you a damn question, Marine. Why do you know his kit is wrong and yours is right, and Morgan apparently didn't know the difference?"

"I, um…Private Morgan arrived in the second helicopter from brigade, so he wasn't around when Staff Sergeant Rider showed everyone how our kits and rucks needed to be packed for the patrol."

"Outstanding, Private Blount," Mack replied before dropping several f-bombs for effect. "Now, perhaps you can explain to me why Private Morgan wasn't informed of this information when he arrived in your tent last night."

A look of fear spread across Private Blount's face. "We—I mean I—didn't show him," he admitted. His face was now beet red.

"Really? You don't say," Gunny Mack said sarcastically. "So, why didn't you show him?" he asked.

Mack was enjoying this little grilling. He was hoping this would turn into a good teaching moment for his new replacements.

"I, um—we thought it'd be a funny joke," Blount stammered.

Reaching his right hand over to grab the back handle of Private Blount's body armor, Mack proceeded to drag him to the front of the cherries and then threw him to the ground in front of Private Morgan. Then he turned to face the fourteen new recruits.

"Listen up, Marines," he said before swearing in several of the recruits' faces. "This isn't a joke out here. You get me?" he yelled.

"Yes, Gunnery Sergeant!" everyone replied.

"Get this through your thick skulls. You are *replacements*," Mack hissed. "You are here because other Marines before you are either dead, wounded, or Chinese prisoners. You are here because we needed to replace the losses we've taken. The only original people in my platoon from the beginning of the war are me and nine other guys. That's ten guys from an entire platoon.

"When information is handed down to you, it is *your* job to make sure everyone else in your fireteam, squad, and platoon knows it. If you see a Marine whose kit isn't the way it's supposed to be, then take the damn time to help him get it right. Don't try and play a joke on him to get him in trouble with me, because I won't take that crap. What if our COP had been hit this morning and we all had to rush to our fighting positions? Morgan here wouldn't have been ready. He could have gotten killed or he could have gotten several of the rest of us killed."

He stared at them icily without saying a word. He felt that he had appropriately gotten their attention at that point.

"Now, you all have ten minutes to get Private Morgan's gear ready to go out on patrol. When I get back here with the lieutenant and the rest of the platoon, I had better see Morgan's gear looking like everyone else's!"

With his introduction and inspection of their new replacements completed, Mack turned around and headed over to the mess tent. As he walked toward breakfast, his eyes were drawn to a few of the Marines working on a couple of the new BigDogs they'd been given. He made a quick stop to check on Corporal Pyro, who'd been assigned one of the machines.

Just before the war began, the Marines had purchased a few hundred of these quadpedal advanced rough-terrain robots from a company called Boston Dynamics. They were the next gen in robotics, meant to help the infantry carry heavy loads in rough terrain like Afghanistan. They were essentially a twenty-first-century version of a pack mule for patrols, something DARPA had been working on for more than a decade.

The robots could carry up to 330 pounds of ammo, water, food, or whatever else the infantry squads needed, and lug it through some really rugged terrain, but all Mack really cared about with the BigDog was that they had finally fixed the loud buzzing noise the first generation made. Because the original BigDogs were gas-operated robots, they had an exhaust system, which was rather loud. Through additional iterations, DARPA had eventually found a way to make the thing pretty quiet.

Sadly, Boston Dynamics had only been able to deliver a few hundred of these machines before the war started. The company quickly fell behind enemy lines, so DARPA and the engineers from the company had to find another facility to get them built. Eventually, a facility had been settled on in Central Florida, near the two leading robotics universities in Florida: USF in Tampa and UCF in Orlando. Now they were busy cranking these devices out for the Army and the Marines. Mack's company had been issued four of them, one per platoon. This would mark only the third time they'd taken the machines out with them on patrol.

Mack checked on Pyro and made sure he'd packed additional ammo and SMAW rockets. Then he made his way over to the tent to grab some morning chow.

Nothing like some hot food delivered from battalion in the good old-fashioned mermite container, he thought.

When Gunny Mack entered the tent, he saw most of his guys were finishing up their breakfast. Many of them had heard his little rant, and a few applauded him when he entered. Some even let out a few cheers and jeers.

Mack felt proud that the men liked him. Of course, he'd come up through the ranks and knew what he was doing. He always did his best to make sure every Marine made it home, no matter how badly they'd been wounded. Twice, Mack could have gone to the rear when he'd been hit by shrapnel, but he'd chosen to have the platoon medic remove the metal from his arm and his leg and drive on. He'd already been awarded a Bronze and a Silver Star for his actions, which was saying something.

Mack made his way to the mermite container and grabbed four strips of bacon to go along with two biscuits and some sausage gravy. Next, he walked to the table with a thermos of coffee and filled a Styrofoam cup up with the black gold. He found a couple of empty seats near the rear of the tent and took a seat.

Captain Ambrose, who had just been promoted to take over their company a month ago, plopped down in the chair next to him with his own plate of biscuits and gravy.

"You getting our new replacements all settled in?" Ambrose asked with a smile.

Mack doubted anyone on the COP hadn't heard his little beratement of the replacements. "Just breaking them in," Mack replied with a smirk as he dug into his food. "We getting a new first sergeant one of these days?" he asked between bites.

"I asked the battalion CG if he could promote Master Sergeant Freeman. We need a first sergeant, and I'm tired of waiting on a replacement. Freeman's the senior guy in the company right now so it makes sense to promote him. Freeman's been trying to get the sergeant major to keep him a master, but I think even he knows we need a first sergeant and he'd make a good Top."

Mack laughed. "Freeman's just lazy. He's good at his job, but he doesn't want to take over as Top. No one does. It takes him away from the fighting and instantly makes him the admin boy for you."

Ambrose chuckled before he worked on finishing off his food. Mack did the same.

After a moment, Ambrose changed his tone. "Mack, I wanted to talk with you about your patrol you're about to head out on. I just got back from battalion twenty minutes ago, and word has it the PLA is going to start probing our positions sometime today. The S2 says the PLA is sending penal battalions forward to get us to show ourselves. Then they'll send their regular army units in once we've spent ourselves slaughtering the penal battalions."

Mack shook his head in disgust. "That's pretty wicked stuff, sir. Is there any truth to it or could it just be a rumor?"

Ambrose shrugged. "The S2 said the PLA just started implementing this strategy about a week ago. They tried it yesterday further up the line. In any case, I'm not taking any chances. I'm going to send out Third Platoon with you. If you guys run into any trouble or you spot this kind of thing happening, then call it in. You can always fall back, but make sure you communicate what you guys are doing, OK?"

"OK, thanks for the heads-up, sir," Mack replied. "Do we have any mortar or artillery support yet?"

Ambrose shook his head. "No. The artillery that was slated for RCT One got sent down to Twentynine Palms. Apparently, they need it more than we do." He shrugged his shoulders. "How much good would artillery do in this environment anyways, Mack?" he asked. "I mean, these trees are huge, and any round we fired into them would most likely just explode in the canopies. There's a higher chance of fragging our own guys than actually hitting the enemy. I think swapping out the mortars with extra AT4s and SMAWs is probably going to be more effective fire support, don't you?"

Mack finished off the last of his bacon before he nodded in agreement. "Yeah. You're probably right on that count, sir. Still, I just worry that if we run into a large force, we'll run out of rounds or not be able to call for fire support when we need it most."

"If things get really bad, we do have Cobras we can call on," Ambrose countered. "Again, it's a little hard with the dense tree cover, but it's an option."

Mack scratched his chin. "Not that I mind getting the chance to catch up, but now that you're the company CO and not our platoon leader, why are you telling me all this and not the LT?"

"Yeah, about that, Gunny," Ambrose said in a tone that foretold a hammer about to drop. "LT Mitchem got reassigned to battalion this morning during commander's call. So, you're in charge of the platoon for the moment. Lieutenant Greggs from Third Platoon will be the only officer on patrol with you, but you've got seniority over his platoon sergeant."

"Man. You'd think they'd let us keep a lieutenant for more than a week before they poach 'em on us." Mack downed the last of his coffee.

"Yeah, tell me about it. I can't seem to keep these lieutenants alive long enough to get them some practical experience where they won't get themselves or their Marines killed, and battalion steals them from me if they do survive."

"Well, if you want, sir, you can come out with us. It'd be just like old times," Mack said half-jokingly.

Captain Ray Ambrose was one of those really likable officers. He actually listened to his NCOs and didn't just brush them off because he was an officer. Everyone in the company was glad he had taken over as the CO when their last commander had been promoted up. They'd lost a lot of officers and NCOs since the start of the war, and it was good to keep the ones they liked around, if possible.

Ambrose looked at him with a wry grin on his face. "You know what, Gunny, I think I will," he announced. "I'm going to have Greggs stay here and I'll go out with you guys." Then he got up to go make it happen, leaving Gunny Mack sitting there in shock.

****

Two hours later, the platoon had hoofed it down the side of the ridge their COP was built on and began to make their way through the underbrush and foliage of the National Park. Other than the thousands of nearby Chinese soldiers hell-bent on killing them, the patrols were often a time to escape the war. The hours-long patrols through the redwood trees and underbrush of the double canopy forest were peaceful. The hikes were beautiful, so long as they could keep it in perspective and realize an ambush could happen at the drop of a hat.

So far, they'd managed to travel about two kilometers, which placed them right up to the edge of the LOC, the unofficial demarcation line between the two sides. Once they reached the line, which was Waypoint Alpha, they'd report in and then continue down the LOC to the next waypoint. Along the way, they'd spread the platoon out into squads as they began their slow and methodical patrol through their portion of the forest.

The higher-ups at brigade had divided the National Forest up into boxes. Each battalion had been assigned a set of them to patrol. This helped the powers that be know where an enemy probe was happening and what forces could be shifted around to deal with it should the probe turn into an actual attack. With hundreds of miles to protect, this was the most efficient way to break it down into manageable chunks.

As they continued their steady pace through the woods, Gunny Mack looked back from time to time. Each time he did, he almost did a double take when he'd spot one of the BigDogs. This was only his third time on patrol with one of them, and it just seemed so odd having a mechanical robot along on a patrol with them like this. It was almost like something out of a sci-fi book. Mack had to admit, though, that little robot was a beast. It was carrying more than three hundred pounds of ammo, water, and extra SMAW rockets for the platoon.

While Mack's company patrolled their portion of the LOC, the other companies in the battalion took to their own. It was seldom that they'd spot a platoon from another company. When they did, the two groups would usually talk for a few minutes with each other before going their separate ways.

Just in front of the demarcation line the Marines patrolled was a platoon of two-man scout sniper teams. The two-man teams were scattered all across the front lines and would typically act as the battalion and brigade trip flare should a large PLA force make its way towards them.

By midafternoon, the platoon had passed Waypoints Alpha, Bravo, and Charlie, effectively reaching the halfway point of their daily patrol. When they made it to Waypoint Foxtrot, they had been directed to stop for the night and set up a night ambush along one of the park service roads. The next day, they'd repeat the process and travel back to Waypoint Alpha, where they'd set up another night ambush on another park service road before handing off their patrol to the next platoon. This meant there was a platoon always on patrol along the LOC should the enemy decide to probe their defense.

As they walked towards the next waypoint, where they'd stop for lunch, Mack had to admit, aside from the fact that Chinese soldiers were roaming these woods looking to kill him, he really loved these patrols. It was a chance to walk amongst some of the oldest and tallest trees in the world. Being able to listen to the various birds and wildlife during the day and the owls and nocturnal animals at night was a treasured memory of this bloody war he'd hold on to for the rest of his life.

When the war had started, his sergeant major had told him, "You need to find the happy moments in this terrible chaos and death and hold on to those moments. They'll get you through the dark times, but more importantly, when this war is over, it'll give you something good to look back on besides all the death and destruction." It had been sound advice, and he'd passed it on to everyone in his platoon as well.

The platoon reached the next waypoint and settled down to each lunch. One squad stayed on watch while the others broke out their MREs and ate. Then they switched positions and let the other squad have a few minutes to chill and eat before they moved out again.

Just as they were finishing their MREs and getting ready to head back out on patrol, Gunny Mack heard a single rifle crack. The new replacement Marines immediately grabbed their rifles and sought cover. The veterans in the platoon only paused eating long enough to make sure the round hadn't been aimed in their direction before finishing their lunch.

Captain Ambrose, who had been sitting near Gunny Mack, signaled for his RTO to hand him the radio handset. "Loki Base, this is Loki Actual. We just heard what sounded like a shot coming from one of the scout sniper teams near Waypoint Charlie. Break."

"Is there any activity in the area we should know about? Over."

While they waited for a response, they heard another rifle crack. A second later, they heard the chattering of at least two or three Type 56 rifles, which were the Chinese version of the old, venerable AK-47. The AK had a very distinctive sound when fired, so Mack immediately knew what type of rifle it was. He also reasoned that if the enemy was using the older weapons, the gunfire probably came from a militia unit or perhaps one of those penal battalions their intel shop had warned them about.

The radio beeped, letting them know the SINGCARS had synched. "Loki Actual, Loki Base. Scout Team Eight is reporting a large contingent of PLA forces heading toward Waypoint Delta. Recommend you move your platoons to intercept and assess the size of the enemy unit. How copy?"

Mack nodded his head in approval. It was a good call. They should have plenty of time to get over there, and Third Platoon was just a few hundred meters behind them for backup. Eighty-six Marines should be more than enough to handle whatever skirmishers the PLA was probing them with.

Mack stood up. "Everybody up," he shouted to his Marines. "We have an enemy probe moving to Waypoint Delta. I want all squads in a line formation. We're going to move quick to set up an ambush point before they get there. Now let's *move!*"

Gunny Mack turned to Captain Ambrose. "Sir, I'm going to move with First Squad if you need me," he said.

"Go ahead, Gunny. I'll stick with Third Squad. Holler if you run into anything." He grinned as he got up.

"Follow me, Marines. Let's move," Gunny Mack ordered. He fell in next to their point man. They didn't even bother burying their MREs; they just left everything where it was. Time was of the essence if they were going to set up an ambush. They had to cover at least eight hundred meters to get in front of that probing force.

Ten minutes into their movement, they heard several additional cracks from the scout sniper team, which were followed by a series of AK-47 rounds being fired right back at them. This only spurred them on to move faster.

Chances were, the enemy soldiers had no idea where the snipers were. They were just firing at whatever they thought was the sniper, or maybe they were firing just to feel like they were doing something.

His point man turned to whisper to him. "Gunny, if we move much faster, they're going to hear us coming."

"Maybe, but we need to get there before those guys get past our sniper team," Mack insisted. "Our guys are only a few hundred meters across the LOC. That means the enemy force isn't that far away from crossing it. I want to get in position so we can use our claymores."

At this rate, they were trotting through the woods at a brisk jog, barreling through a lot of the underbrush. When they reached a decent position near Waypoint Delta, Mack had the platoon fan out and take a knee. He'd let them catch their breath while he grabbed his four squad leaders to figure out where they'd build up their ambush.

Captain Ambrose had come with them, but he was largely letting Mack figure out how he wanted to organize the platoon's defense. He'd then relay that information back to Third Platoon and have them stand by to come to their aid should they need it.

Mack pointed to a spot on their left flank. "I want First Squad there," he directed. "Get your claymores out and be ready. Make sure you place guys on either side of that massive redwood. The enemy will try to use those trees to their advantage to get around your flanks. That whole arc is your lane."

Gunny Mack turned to his next squad leader. "I want Second Squad on the right flank. Same as before, get your claymores out and cover this arc. Make sure you place at least two guys on the far side by that fallen log. I don't want the enemy trying to circle around your right side and flank you without someone spotting them first.

"Third Squad is going to have the center. Have your guys place their claymores there, there, and there," Mack ordered, pointing. "Chances are, you'll be facing the brunt of whatever's coming our way, so be ready."

That left Fourth Squad, his heavy weapons squad. "Get your rocket teams interspersed with the other three squads and make sure you have your M240Gs spaced out so they can provide solid interlocking fields of fire," Mack ordered, "Get their replacement barrels ready and start unpacking the extra ammo and SMAWs for the rocket teams, OK?"

His heavy weapons squad leader nodded.

Captain Ambrose came up to him with his RTO. "Do you think we should bring up Third Platoon to reinforce our positions?" he asked.

"Not yet," Mack replied. "I need to see how large this enemy force is first, sir. It could just be a platoon like us, but let's find out."

"I'm going to have Corporal Pyro launch his scout drones, then," Ambrose countered. "He's been begging to use them, and we could use some eyes on what we're facing." He then got up and left with his RTO to go find

Pyro. When they'd been given several surveillance scout drones, Mack had picked Corporal Pyro to be the guy who'd get trained up on how to use them. He'd already been trained on how to operate the BigDogs, so it was easy for him to pick up the drone operations as well.

The next few minutes went by in a blur of activity as everyone got ready for whatever was coming toward them. Mack asked one of the Marines where Corporal Pyro had ended up, and he was directed to an area behind one of the big redwoods.

As Gunny Mack approached Pyro and Ambrose, he admired the massive trees around him again. He felt sad that in less than an hour, bullets, high explosives, and shrapnel could transform this entire place into something less than beautiful. As he thought about it, his anger welled up inside him at having to fight a war inside his country like this. It incensed him that so much of California's beauty was being ripped apart by this awful war.

Mack rounded the tree and fallen log where Pyro and the captain were, and he found Pyro wearing his VR headset and holding the drone controller in his right hand. The captain had what looked like an Amazon Kindle Fire device sitting in his lap, and he was looking at footage of whatever

Pyro was seeing. Ambrose looked up and motioned for Mack to take a seat next to him.

Gunny Mack plopped himself down and Captain Ambrose handed him the display. Pyro had piloted the drone high enough to fly above the towering redwoods. These trees could reach heights of three hundred feet and have stumps as wide as twenty feet in diameter, which was the number one reason why mortar and artillery support was essentially worthless. An arcing round would most likely hit the upper branches or trunks before it'd land where it was needed.

Pyro moved the drone a bit further away from their current location before he guided it back down through the canopy. Mack saw something that made his skin crawl. Beneath the cover of the dense forest, the enemy had moved hundreds if not thousands of soldiers toward the various Marine positions.

Ambrose whispered, "This isn't a probing attack—this is an all-out assault. I'm thinking we should order everyone back to the COP. We can probably defend ourselves from that position better than we can here. Thoughts?"

Mack looked at the enemy soldiers heading toward them and thought about their own position. He shook his head. "I think we should move Third Platoon up here ASAP.

Have Fourth and First Platoon get things ready at the COP, and have battalion send the QRF to the base camp. We can hold the enemy here for a little while to give battalion time to get the QRF relocated and get us some gunship support. We don't need to make this our Alamo, but I think we should try and buy battalion some more time by at least bloodying the enemy up."

"That's a big risk, Gunny," responded Ambrose. "What if we aren't able to disengage?"

Mack pointed to the screen. "Look at that, sir. On the edges and the rear of those large formations, everyone in the big cluster of soldiers appears to be holding an AK and not much else. None of them are wearing body armor or carrying rucks. At the edges of the formation and to the rear, some of the other soldiers are kitted out with body armor and modern weapons. This has to be one of those penal battalions the two-shop told you about."

Ambrose shook his head in disbelief. "I—I didn't think that was real. Wow. What kind of fight do you think they'll put up?" he asked.

"Those aren't going to be motivated soldiers," Mack insisted. "I remember reading about the Soviets using penal battalions in World War II. They didn't have enough weapons for everyone, so they gave a rifle and one magazine's worth of ammo to every other man. Then they gave one magazine to the other soldiers without a rifle and told them to pick up the rifles of the dead men around them and keep charging. It was pretty brutal, but that's how they'd overrun the German positions. I don't see any of those soldiers carrying extra ammo pouches. My money says they gave everyone a rifle but only gave them one, maybe two or three magazines worth of ammo."

"No way. They wouldn't do that. They'd run out of ammo," Ambrose quickly countered.

Mack held a hand up. "Think about it. These are prisoners. They aren't going to give them a full load of ammo, grenades, and body armor. They could just as easily use that on the guards that are holding them there. No. I'd wager they gave them one, maybe two magazines, telling them they could get more from the dead bodies of their comrades."

While the two of them were talking, the enemy continued to get closer. Pyro broke in. "Hey, while you guys are arguing about how much ammo these guys have, they've gotten within three hundred meters of our position. What do you want me to do with the drone, and are we staying and fighting or running?"

"We're staying," Ambrose confirmed. "As to what you should do with the drone—go further behind their lines and see what else you can find. Maybe there are more units moving in behind them. If there are, we need to know about it."

Ambrose then grabbed the radio handset from his RTO and put things in motion. His first call was to the COP to have them get ready for the incoming battle. Next, he called battalion and then brigade, letting them know what was happening. In a few more minutes, the battle would start, and it'd be chaos.

Third Platoon began filtering into their lines just as the enemy approached. The birds all took flight. There was a sudden shift by the animals in the forest; where there had been a constant din of squirrels and other woodland creatures, there was now only silence. Then Mack heard the large group of soldiers moving through the underbrush nearby. A few of them spoke in Chinese, but they remained quiet.

Corporal Pyro signaled to Captain Ambrose, who immediately grabbed the tablet to see what he was getting excited about. When Mack saw the image being shown on it, his heart tightened. Behind the initial wave of attackers were at least two more waves of penal battalion troops.

Further behind them were regular army soldiers, outfitted with body armor and modern rifles.

"Pyro, make sure this feed is getting sent back to the COP and link it to battalion if you can," Ambrose whispered. "We need to make sure they're seeing this. Once that's done, set the drones on autopilot and pack your stuff up. We'll need you with your rifle; plus, when we do start to fall back, I want you ready to move." Then he got up and headed over to the center of their position to help coordinate the two platoons' efforts.

Gunny Mack watched as the enemy soldiers came into view. They were now no more than a hundred and twenty meters from their position.

Mack had the men wait until the bulk of the enemy soldiers had emerged from some of the thicker underbrush and presented a solid target for their guns. Then he yelled, "Fire!"

The entire area around them erupted in gunfire. The M240 gunners raked the enemy positions with controlled two and five-second bursts from their weapons while the riflemen took well-aimed shots at them.

The first three or four rows of enemy soldiers collapsed as bullets punched right through their bodies and continued on into the man behind them. Without any body armor, the enemy soldiers were torn apart by the Marine's projectiles.

Loud whistles shrieked as the guards for the penal battalions ordered the prisoners forward. The return fire from the enemy soldiers steadily picked up until the Marines were being assaulted by several hundred terrified Chinese inmates. Mack heard someone grab a bullhorn and shout something angrily at the men in Chinese.

Suddenly, whatever underbrush hadn't been cut down from all the gunfire parted like the Red Sea. Wave after wave of frantic Chinese soldiers screamed at the top of their lungs, charging right at the Marine positions.

The first few swells of enemy soldiers fell to the ground before they even had a chance to get close to the Marines, cut down by the fuselage of gunfire. Another group of incoming prisoners managed to get within thirty meters of the Marine positions before the Marines started triggering their claymore mines. Rows of humanity that had just moments before been about to overrun them disappeared in a pink mist of blood and gore as their bodies were ripped apart by the thousands of steel ball bearings that were thrown at them from point-blank range.

When those three waves of enemy soldiers disappeared, Captain Ambrose yelled out, "Everyone, fall back to the COP!"

The Marines didn't waste a second, falling back in good order as they broke contact with the enemy, just like they had trained and done many times before during this war. One by one, each squad laid down a volley of suppressive fire while the other squads fell back about thirty meters. The Marines hurried out of there, hoping to get out of Dodge before their stunned enemy had time to figure out what had hit them.

Mack and his men had run maybe two hundred meters when he heard the PLA officers' whistles shriek again. Someone yelled at the men with the bullhorn again.

Gunny Mack ran toward his heavy weapons squad, which was getting ready for their turn to lay down suppressive fire. "Start lobbing some SMAWs at the Chinese!" he ordered. He hoped that might get the prisoners to hesitate.

He stayed with the heavy weapons crew for a few minutes while four of his Marines got their launchers ready. They fired off three rockets each and then turned around to beat feet back to their outpost, which was still about two thousand meters to their rear.

As Mack sprinted through the woods, he spotted two of the BigDog robots moving at a quick pace ahead of the Marines. He shook his head in disbelief. It was almost like he was on a set of a *Terminator* movie or something, fighting a battle with these robotic warriors.

Several Marines helped their wounded comrades, carrying them to the COP, where they could be medevacked to a higher-level trauma center. As they approached the base camp, Mack's men started calling out to the guards to make sure they didn't get lit up by their own guys.

Nearly all of the fighting positions were being manned by the remaining two platoons, but as Mack's Marines emerged from the underbrush, they ran up the designated trails and filtered into the empty positions. Then they did their best to prepare themselves for what they knew was coming their way. The two robotic ammo dogs that hadn't come out on patrol with them also made the rounds, allowing all the Marines who'd just arrived to grab more ammo and water.

Gunnery Sergeant Mack made his way over to one of the fortified bunkers they'd built on the side of the COP's defenses. When he walked in, he saw five Marines manning their weapons, ready for whatever was coming next.

He walked up to the Marine manning the M2 .50-caliber machine gun. "They're going to be coming from that direction," Mack explained, pointing. "When they do, I want you to focus your fire along that portion of the forest, not the front rows of enemy soldiers, OK?"

The gunner crinkled his eyebrows at the odd request but responded, "Sure thing, Gunny." Then he clarified, "You want me to focus further behind the enemy soldiers?"

Mack nodded. "Exactly. Look, when we set up our ambush, the first couple of waves of Chinese just ran headlong into our guns. We smoked 'em. But there were additional waves behind them. So, let the guys in the fighting positions handle the first wave or two. I want you guys to send your rounds into the echelons stacked up behind them. That way, you'll bloody them up before they even get to us."

The Marines nearby all nodded, grinning mischievously. It was obvious that some of them were looking forward to the opportunity to slaughter some of the incoming enemy soldiers.

Mack left the bunker and made a beeline back to the command post bunker to find Captain Ambrose. When he walked in, he spotted the captain on the radio, talking to someone. Corporal Pyro was using his drone and had it synced with one of the larger monitors on the command post.

Looking at the images, Mack saw that the enemy had recovered from the ambush and had already closed the gap on them. They were probably less than a kilometer from them now and steadily moving toward them, like a human tsunami that wouldn't be denied its ability to wash over them.

Ambrose snapped his fingers to break Mack's fixation on the impending threat. "We've got several attack helicopters on the way," the captain said. "Battalion is sending the QRF and so is brigade. Reinforcements are about sixty minutes out. Gunship support is about twenty."

"Copy that, sir. We'll hold 'em here," Mack replied. Then he headed out to the line to make sure everyone was as prepared as they could be.

Gunny Mack hopped down into one of the fighting positions with a couple of Marines. "You guys ready?" he asked. "You have plenty of ammo?"

"Yes, Gunny. We're good to go."

Before Mack could say anything else, he heard a higher-pitched whizzing noise and immediately looked up. He spotted a quadcopter drone. It was just like the one their platoon regularly used, only this drone was painted in a slightly different color pattern. Once the drone had spotted them, it quickly shot up several thousand feet, before any of the Marines could take a shot at it.

Then he heard several more of the little whizzing drones flying toward them. This time, the Marines were ready for them. However, these drones didn't fly in like they were looking for them. They flew in like high-speed racing drones. The first one flew right at the Marines, slamming right into the dirt between two fighting positions and summarily exploding. The blast threw dirt, rocks, and tree parts in every direction.

Several of the Marines that had been attacked by the drone called out for a medic, while others just moaned and cried in agony from their injuries.

Mack didn't even have time to curse or formulate what to do next when a second one of these high-speed little kamikazes slammed right into the fortified bunker on their left flank. The bunker blew apart, showering chunks of its material in all directions. Several corpses and body parts flew into the air along with the debris from the bunkers.

"Holy crap! Did you see that, Gunny?" asked one of the Marines near him, utterly terrified. "How the hell are we supposed to fight that kind of thing?"

"Shoot the drones if you see them!" Gunny Mack screamed, hoping everyone would hear.

Then the same loud shrieking whistle he'd been hearing all day screeched, and the Chinese soldiers came running right at them.

"Open fire!" screamed one of the other gunnery sergeants down in the first row of fighting positions.

Ratatat, pop, pop, pop.

The roar of gunfire began in earnest as both sides waged a desperate struggle of life and death. The drone above provided an incredible observer's perspective of what was almost a continuous wall of lead mixed with red and green tracers zipping in both directions as thousands of enemy soldiers assaulted the nearly one-kilometer-long position the Marines were manning.

More explosions rippled amongst the Marine positions as RPG rockets impacted against some of their positions or against the nearby redwoods. The Marines lobbed their own rockets and grenade gun rounds into the enemy positions, adding their own carnage. When the PLA soldiers reached a certain distance from their lines, some of the Marines detonated a series of IEDs they'd jerry-rigged in the areas between the trees and heavy underbrush they'd cleared out. Their hope had been to get the PLA to funnel large numbers of their troops through the more easily passable sections of the forest and then blow them up. As the explosions rippled inside the enemy line, bodies were blown into the air, screams of pain, agony and sheer terror adding to the chaos.

The machine-gun bunker that hadn't been blown up opened fire with its heavy .50-caliber slugs, ripping huge holes in the enemy lines. The gunners did exactly what Mack had told them to do, focusing on hammering the second echelon of troops. Mack smiled when he realized what a great job they were doing at ravaging the enemy lines.

Then he saw one of those little kamikaze drones zipping right for the bunker. He brought his M27 to his shoulder and fired several rounds at it. He had to lead the little drone a bit because it was really moving. One of Mack's bullets got lucky and nailed the drone when it was less than twenty meters from the bunker. The drone blew up in spectacular fashion, but it also sprayed some of the Marines below it with shrapnel, injuring a few of them.

Mack dropped his now-empty magazine and slapped a fresh one in place. He slapped the bolt release and quickly had his rifle back against his shoulder, his cheek flush against the side of the stock. He took aim at several PLA soldiers who were doing everything they could to cut a hole in the concertina wire at the base of their outpost. If the PLA could get through this obstacle, it'd be a straight run up the ridge and into their positions.

"Trigger the claymores!" one of their lieutenants shouted.

Boom, boom, boom.

One by one, the claymores detonated, obliterating the attacking enemy soldiers. The shotgun blasts of steel ball bearings cut the enemy soldiers like a scythe. Three rows of attackers fell to the ground, carpeting the forest floor with more bodies and blood.

Then, instead of a whistle signaling more enemy soldiers to charge forward, a green flare shot up through the forest and exploded above the canopy. Mack wasn't sure exactly what that meant, but he knew it probably wasn't good.

A wave of those nasty little kamikaze drones zipped through the forest, headed right for their positions. A couple of them were destroyed by some of the Marines as they shot at them, but several more got through, blowing a couple more of the Marines' positions up and killing and injuring many of them.

Next, Mack heard a loud roar as hundreds, maybe even thousands of voices echoed through the redwood forest. The next batch of enemy soldiers to emerge were no longer members of the penal battalions or the poorly equipped militia soldiers—these were the regular PLA grunts, outfitted with modern body armor and the best assault rifles China had.

The Chinese soldiers charged headlong into the Marine positions, seemingly aware that the Americans had already expended their most deadly defensive weapon available, their claymore antipersonnel mines. Without the mines or their other IEDs they'd blown up earlier, the regular army soldiers had a real fighting chance. It was all down to speed and tenacity now.

"Hold the line. Hold the line, Marines!" Mack yelled out several times. He got out of his fighting position and did his best to move up and down the line his platoon was hunkered down on.

Every now and then, Mack would stop and take aim at a cluster of enemy soldiers. He'd aim for one or two of them and squeeze off a few rounds. He'd see some of them drop like a switch had been turned off before he'd either move on to another target or stop to help a wounded Marine get back into the fight.

One Marine had lost his left hand and tried desperately to get a tourniquet tied on it. Mack stopped shooting long enough to get the medical device situated on his wrist above the wound and tie it off tight enough to stop the bleeding. Then he changed the magazine out for the wounded man and gave his rifle back to him. He pulled a couple more magazines and two grenades out for him and put them in front of his fighting hole.

He looked at the Marine, who was fighting between going into shock and wanting to kill the enemy. Mack placed his face right in the young man's face. "I need you to keep fighting, Marine," he directed. "Everyone is counting on you right now. Keep killing them and we'll get you some help as soon as we can. Will you do that for your brothers?"

The Marine suddenly had a look of hate and determination burning in his eyes. "You can count on me, Gunny!" he exclaimed. Then he turned to face the attackers. Using his one good hand to hold the pistol grip, the young man used his arm with the missing hand to balance the front half of his rifle. Then he started shooting at the enemy soldiers, who were now no more than forty or fifty meters from him.

Mack saw that the first row of fighting positions was about to get overrun. He aimed his rifle at several PLA soldiers who were charging forward and fired off several controlled bursts with his infantry assault rifle, hitting two of them. He then moved slightly and squeezed off another few rounds, hitting two more enemy soldiers.

Dropping his now-empty magazine, Mack grabbed for a fresh one and slapped it in place. Just as he was about to bring his rifle to bear, something hit him in the center of his chest plate. He was stunned by the sudden punch to his chest, and another object slammed into his helmet, which threw him backwards off his feet.

When Gunny Mack fell to the ground, he wasn't sure what the hell had just happened. All he knew was his head was swimming and he was having an incredibly hard time trying to focus on what was going on around him. Despite what he knew must have been an intense amount of gunfire and shooting going on, it all sounded distant—almost like he was underwater listening to it from a faraway place.

Then he saw something truly unique. It almost looked like a red finger of God had reached down from the sky above them. His vision faded, and he could barely see what was happening, but two more red fingers appeared from the clouds above.

Before he could process what was going on, Mack's world started to turn dark. His blurred vision became more and more tunneled. Then he slipped into the darkness.

Chapter Twenty-One
Texas Invasion

Gulf of Mexico

Near Corpus Christi, Texas

Beads of sweat formed on Staff Sergeant Haverty's face as he finished his set of reps on the bench press. He sat up, and the sweat ran down his face until it dripped off his chin. Haverty stood and took the weights off the bar, placing them back where they belonged.

It feels good to get a decent workout in, he thought.

India Company had been back on the USS *Bataan* now for a few days as they made their way to the next battlefield. While they had a few days on the ship, Haverty was taking advantage of the gym on the ship. He was running the guys in his platoon through it as well. It was important to stay physically fit and let off some steam. The Cuba campaign had been a tough fight, and the Marines had largely been on their own for most of it. A Florida Army National Guard brigade had come to help them towards the end of the campaign, but it had largely been a Marine fight. Now the Guard was staying behind to garrison the island nation while the Marines moved to the next major battle.

As he finished placing the last of his weights away, Haverty saw one of the elliptical machines open up and he made a beeline for it. After cranking the resistance all the way up, he started moving as fast and as hard as he could. His thighs were burning, but he didn't care. The harder he worked them now, the less they'd hurt when he was packed down with body armor and weapons.

Haverty looked up at the TV that was airing AFN and saw that the show that was on had just ended. Now one of the AFN newscasters came on to bring them the hourly news. As Haverty listened, the commentator spoke about some massive battle taking place against several US positions in California, where the PLA forces sought to break out of the state. As the broadcast continued, Haverty's attention shifted much more to what the commentator was saying and less on his burning thighs. He knew his fellow Marine brothers were really the ones keeping the Chinese bottled up in California.

The commentator went on for a while about the heavy fighting in the Sequoia National Forest, highlighting some sort of new terror drone the Chinese had just integrated into their units. He briefly mentioned casualties but stopped short of listing how many service members had been killed or wounded.

That means the death toll is high and the government just doesn't want to disclose the actual number yet, he thought. Over the course of the war, Haverty had learned to read between the lines of what was told to the public and what was being said inside military circles.

The commentator spoke for another ten minutes before they did a quick wrap-up of what was going on around the world and in the United States. When the news was done, AFN put on a rerun of *Family Guy*, a cartoon Haverty found both stupid and funny.

After twenty minutes on the elliptical, Staff Sergeant Haverty finished his workout and made his way over to the shower room. He turned on the water and just let it run across his body. It felt good to have running water again, to really scrub himself down in soap and know he had enough water to get it all off. It was even better was knowing he had time to do all this and didn't have to worry about some sniper shooting at him or a random mortar attack.

While many of the Russian and Cuban forces had surrendered a few weeks ago, some of the more radical units of the Cuban military had been a little more reluctant to accept the end of the communist regime. Some of those die-hard holdouts had cost Haverty's unit a few KIAs. Once the war in Cuba was over, Haverty and his men had been placed on occupation duty. It should have been a low-risk assignment, but several of his Marines had been killed in action, including their platoon sergeant, Gunnery Sergeant Mann. That guy had survived so much death and killing, only to get taken out by a random mortar round.

When his shower was done, Haverty got dressed. He made his way to their training room to see what the lieutenant had in mind for the day's training. Until a replacement showed up, Haverty was filling in as the platoon sergeant.

When Haverty entered the room, their battalion commander, Lieutenant Colonel Wallace, spotted him right away. "Ah. There you are, Staff Sergeant," he called.

Wallace was a well-liked commander. He'd been an enlisted guy before he became an officer, so he seemed to have a special affinity for his NCOs that not all officers shared.

Haverty stood at ease and smiled. "Yes, sir. Just running my guys through the gym and having everyone get a solid workout before our next mission."

"Well, this afternoon we're going to do a quick awards and promotion ceremony in the hangar bay," Wallace announced. "It's been six months since we last held one of these and it's time we get our paperwork caught back up and make sure our Marines are getting recognized…I mentioned that we have a lot of promotions to hand out as well. This last campaign was tough on our regiment and the MEF in general. We may not be slugging it out against the Chinese like our brothers on the West Coast, but we've taken our own licks."

Haverty nodded solemnly.

"Your company in particular took a lot of hits—Gunnery Sergeant Mann being the most recent one," said Wallace somberly. After a pause out of respect, he continued. "First Lieutenant Lacey here is going to take over as the company CO. He's being promoted to captain this afternoon. That means we're going to be short two gunnery sergeants and three lieutenants in the unit. I asked the lieutenant here who'd he'd like to recommend to fill some of these positions. Now, before word gets out, I want you to know that we considered picking you to replace Gunny Mann, but in the end, we opted not to."

Haverty's heart sank. He was almost angry at being passed over. He'd done everything right. He had a perfect record in the Corps thus far.

Wallace must have seen the look of disappointment on his face, because he quickly added, "Lieutenant Lacey said you were far too qualified to fill Mann's position. He said your leadership skills in the platoon are beyond reproach, and you'd make an exceptional platoon leader. As such, this afternoon you'll be given a battlefield promotion to second lieutenant."

Haverty was taken aback. He hadn't expected that. He'd hoped to make gunny during the next selection period and would focus on moving up to first sergeant and then maybe sergeant major before he retired. But a direct promotion to lieutenant—that opened up a whole new career track for him.

"You've earned it, Staff Sergeant. I couldn't think of a better man to lead the platoon I'm leaving," Lieutenant Lacey said as he extended his hand.

Haverty shook hands with the lieutenant and Wallace before they filled him in on who else was getting promoted and some of the awards. Everyone in his platoon was getting a naval commendation medal with valor device, along with a newly created Cuban campaign medal. Nine of his guys were getting a Purple Heart, eight were getting Bronze Stars with V devices and four were getting Silver Stars. One of his guys had been put in for, and was going to receive, the Navy Cross.

Before Haverty was left to go inform his platoon of the afternoon awards and promotion ceremony, Lieutenant

Colonel Wallace leaned in. "I wanted to be the one to tell you I've personally recommended you for a Silver Star for your actions during the blitz on Havana. You saved a lot of guys when you led that charge into that village and took that machine gunner out. You earned that medal. Now, go get your guys ready for this afternoon."

Haverty left the room feeling like he was walking on a cloud. He was being promoted to lieutenant. He was losing one of his staff sergeants to another platoon, but he was also gaining twelve new Marines, fresh from training. Many of his Marines were getting a one-grade promotion as well. He felt good that his first act as lieutenant was going to be promoting many of his Marines and presenting them with their awards.

They've earned it, he thought. *They all have.*

****

Three Days Later

Off the Coast of Brownsville, Texas

Lieutenant Haverty's platoon was loaded up into two of the V-22 Ospreys on the flight deck, along with two of the newly issued robotic BigDogs. As the engines spun up, Haverty felt a heightened sense of uncertainty.

The engines hit a new pitch and the rotors picked up more speed. Soon, the tiltrotor aircraft lifted off the flight deck of the *Bataan*. It gained altitude and moved away from the task force of amphibious assault ships and guided missile destroyers. Looking out the rear of the aircraft, Haverty saw a mix of landing crafts: LCACs, LCMs, and LCUs, all disembarking from their motherships to begin the process of ferrying the Marines' vehicles and other heavy equipment to shore. It was official—the men of the 24th Marine Expeditionary Unit were finally going to join the fight against the Chinese that had invaded their country.

Steadily, the Ospreys gained altitude until they were flying around four thousand feet above the water. Their attack helicopters, the venerable Super Cobra gunships, flew below and in front of them. Above and in front of them were the MEU's Harrier jets, which would swoop in and pulverize whatever the Marines directed them to.

This was a full-court combined arms attack deep behind enemy lines. The MEU's objective was to liberate Naval Air Station Corpus Christi and the surrounding area. Once they had captured the naval base and the city, the rest of II MEF would pour into Texas and they'd begin their offensive to liberate San Antonio and lift the siege of Houston. It was a gamble sending the Marines in—the PLA had just transferred eight divisions of fresh troops to Texas in hopes of finally achieving a breakout.

Ten minutes into their flight, the Ospreys began to fly a lot closer to the water. They also banked from right to left, taking evasive maneuvers as the coast neared. Eventually, the air armada swung around towards the old abandoned airfield at Walden Field.

Looking out the rear of the aircraft, Haverty saw strings of tracer fire flying up to meet them from NAS Corpus Christi. He watched as a couple of missiles flew in from the Harriers as they tried to silence some of the AA guns.

"Here we go!" shouted the crew chief near the rear of the aircraft.

The Osprey flared up slightly as it bled off some speed, and then they gently set down on the abandoned runway.

"Go, go, go!" Haverty yelled to his Marines as they all ran off the Osprey.

They immediately took a defensive position. Not seeing any urgent threats around them, Haverty shouted at his Marines to form up and move out to their objective.

His platoon had been charged with the south gate entrance and the surrounding area. The rest of the company would then move in and capture the rest of the airfield. While their company was completing these tasks, the rest of the battalion would capture the international airport in town and the port facilities. Then the rest of their gear and their reinforcements would start to arrive, and they'd mop up whatever resistance remained in the city.

"Let's move!" Haverty shouted, pointing where he wanted his squads to go. They were slated to travel down Waldron Road, which was a three-and-a-half kilometer straight shot to their objective. Haverty didn't think it should take them more than twenty-five minutes to get there, assuming they didn't meet any resistance.

As his platoon moved onto the road, Haverty split them up so he had two squads on each side of the street. They all kept their heads on a swivel, especially considering the occasional explosion they'd hear coming from the base. The sounds of AA fire slowly faded away as more of the enemy gun positions were taken out. Seeing the plumes of black smoke rising over a quintessential American city was a strange experience for Haverty and the rest of the Marines. Thus far, all of their fighting had been in the Caribbean—not in American cities and the countryside like so many of the other military units in the war.

As they continued moving down the road at a good clip, some of the people that lived in the houses and worked the businesses along the road came out to greet them. Many of the men and women cried. Some of them walked up to the Marines and tried to shake their hands. A few of the women even tried to give them a hug.

It was a surreal scene unfolding around them. More and more civilians came out to greet them, looking skinny and emaciated. This wasn't something Haverty had expected, and he was almost at a loss as to what to do or how to respond. Clearly, their countrymen had been through hell, and now they felt like their saviors had finally arrived. But Haverty had a mission to complete. He couldn't just stop.

"Keep moving, Marines, keep moving. We have to hit our objective in twenty mikes!" he shouted, loud enough for his guys to hear him, and hopefully some of the civilians too. He hoped they'd get the message and try to stay out of their way.

Then he heard the sound of a helicopter coming from the direction of the base. Looking to where the noise was coming from, Haverty spotted a lone helicopter lifting off and heading toward them.

That doesn't look friendly, he realized.

The helicopter was practically on top of them when it angled its nose down, which meant it was getting ready to start shooting. Haverty's new platoon sergeant started barking out orders and his Marines scattered to either side of the road, looking for some cover. The civilians sensed the danger and they, too, ran to hide.

Then the helicopter's chin gun opened fire. Parts of the paved road they'd been walking on exploded from the impact of the machine-gun bullets.

A couple of Haverty's M240G gunners returned fire on the helicopter as it neared them. Probably two dozen other Marines joined in sending as much hot lead at the helicopter as they could. The helicopter flew past them unhindered, as if it could shrug off the bullets.

Instead of turning back to attack Haverty's platoon, the gunship fired off some rockets at one of the other platoons. Haverty heard more gunfire from their comrades as the helicopter flew near them. So far, none of the platoons had managed to shoot it down with their rifles or machine guns. That meant the helicopter was probably armored.

Haverty was about to call out for his RTO so he could place a call back to the fleet for some air support to take it out when a missile streaked through the sky, obliterating the enemy helicopter. Either someone else had beat him to the punch, or they already had a fighter loitering nearby. In either case, the immediate threat had been neutralized.

"Keep moving!" shouted his platoon sergeant.

The Marines got back up and continued their advance to the base. When they neared the facility, a few of the men spotted something and signaled for everyone to take cover.

Haverty made his way over to the platoon sergeant and their point man. "What we got, fellas?" he asked.

His gunnery sergeant pointed to a spot near the gate. "Looks like a couple of APCs and at least two squads of soldiers," he explained. "Judging by their uniforms, I'd make them out to be PLA naval infantry."

"OK, Gunny. I want you to take First Squad and move around into the woods near that power transmission lot," said Lieutenant Haverty. He pulled out a map. "See if a couple of our guys with the SMAWs can take out those armored vehicles. Once you do, we'll engage them from this position over here." He pointed to a couple of positions on the map.

His gunny nodded and motioned for First Squad to follow him as they took off to get in position.

Haverty directed the other squads to fan out along a couple of the side roads about a block away from the main gate. This would place them a few hundred meters from the

PLA soldiers, ready to assist First Squad as they engaged them.

Five minutes went by, and the tension of what was about to happen grew. Haverty got a short message, letting him know First Squad was ready to start things on their end. He gave them the go-ahead.

A second later, two rockets flew out from the woods to their right and slammed into the two armored personnel carriers. The missiles blew the armored vehicles apart. The enemy soldiers took cover and fired into the tree line where the rockets had come from.

Haverty signaled his other squad leaders to start firing. The rest of the platoon's Marines and machine gunners opened fire on the enemy soldiers who were shooting at First Squad. They had the Chinese soldiers caught in a halfway decent crossfire. In seconds, they had cut down nearly half of the defenders. A couple of civilian trucks drove toward them with additional soldiers in the back bay. The Marines turned their guns on the two trucks and riddled them with bullets.

The drivers must have been hit because both vehicles spun off the road and rolled out. Whatever soldiers weren't injured or killed after the accidents used the crashed trucks for cover and returned fire on the Marines.

"Second Squad, move!" shouted one of Haverty's squad leaders.

The thirteen Marines jumped up and bounded toward the enemy position while the other squads laid down suppressive fire. Haverty dashed forward with them, firing off a couple of shots at the Chinese soldiers. A couple of bullets zipped past his head. He'd nearly made it to the next covered position when a Marine to his right was shot in both of his legs. The guy went down hard.

Haverty stopped next to the Marine and aimed at a PLA soldier that was still shooting at them. He squeezed the trigger of his M27 and let loose a three-second burst of automatic fire into the Chinese soldier. The man staggered backward as a series of rounds slammed into the guy's chest plate. He went down and didn't appear to be getting up.

Lieutenant Haverty looked down at his wounded Marine. The wound in his left leg looked to be a bit more urgent. Spurts of blood squirted out with each heartbeat.

Haverty knew if he didn't stop the bleeder, the guy would be dead before he pulled him back to cover. He placed his rifle on the ground, reached down, grabbed the tourniquet from the man's chest rig and got it situated on his left leg. Then he tightened the strap until the blood stopped squirting out.

"Hang on," he told the Marine. Haverty picked his rifle back up, grabbed the drag handle behind the man's body armor and started pulling him to cover.

One of the Navy corpsmen ran up to them and immediately started working on the Marine's other leg. With his wounded trooper taken care of, Haverty scanned the area to see what enemy soldiers were still left. At this point, it looked like only a few of them were still shooting at his men.

By now, First Squad had bounded forward and was almost to the burning wrecks of the Chinese APCs. The three remaining PLA soldiers threw their weapons down and held up their hands to surrender. Haverty's platoon sergeant was closest to them, so he ran forward with several Marines. They kicked the soldiers' rifles away and zip-tied their hands behind their backs.

While First Squad was securing the three prisoners, Haverty called out for the rest of his platoon. "Follow me! We're going to advance to the base and help secure it."

He left First Squad and his platoon sergeant at the south gate. A medevac helicopter would come in and pick up their wounded.

The other platoons from the company had moved forward and had fanned out as everyone advanced on the naval air station. Steadily, the Marines advanced through the base, clearing building after building. Then they progressed to the airfield and cleared the hangars and everything else. By midafternoon, they had secured the entire air station.

A steady stream of Marine and Navy helicopters flew in from the fleet, bringing mechanics, munitions, and additional fuel for the attack helicopters. Their helicopters would be relocated from the ships offshore to the naval air station so they could provide faster support to the ground units.

As Lieutenant Haverty's platoon and company secured the air station, the rest of the battalion had come ashore at Breaker Avenue Beach Park and air assaulted into the international airport. By the time the sun set that day, they had fifteen hundred Marines on land. The city of Corpus Christi, Texas, was officially liberated.

Chapter Twenty-Two
Sea Trials

January 2022
Hampton Roads, Virginia

Vice Admiral Ingalls stood under the open-air tent along with dozens of other naval officers and senior enlisted personnel in their dress white uniforms, waiting for the ceremony to get started. The Secretary of the Navy, the Chairman of the Joint Chiefs, the Chief of Naval Operations, and even the President were in attendance for the christening of America's newest warships. The group was filled with hope that these warships would forever change the landscape of naval warfare.

Sachs walked to the lectern and made some brief remarks about American ingenuity and how these two warships represented the very essence of the country. Admiral Ingalls wasn't so sure about that, but he did have to admit, these warships were by far the most advanced warships to have ever put to sea.

When the President was done with his speech, a few others came forward and gave their own remarks. Admiral Ingalls felt that the worst of the speeches were from the

Senators and members of Congress; they liked to go on and on about how they'd fought tooth and nail to get these ships funded and built. In reality, Ingalls knew they'd had no idea these ships were even being constructed until well after the war had broken out. Now they were all lining up trying to do whatever they could to be a part of the project that was being hailed as the superweapon that would win the war.

When the ceremony neared the final moment of christening the ship, Vice Admiral Ingalls was asked to come forward and give a brief speech. He stood and made his way over to the lectern, surveying those in attendance. When he reached his post, he noted the position of the TV cameras and made sure to speak to them and not the crowd.

This thing never should have been televised, he thought. He'd advocated keeping the launch of the ships under wraps, but ultimately, his advice had been shot down.

Ingalls took a deep breath and stood tall as he began his speech. "Today marks the first day in a new and dangerous evolution in warfare. The ship behind me is the culmination of nearly one hundred years of lessons learned in naval combat. It incorporates the latest in scientific breakthroughs and cutting-edge technology. This ship and her sister ship will not only win this war, they will allow the

United States to project power well beyond our shores for generations to come.

"These two ships represent the newest warships in America's arsenal of freedom, the Manhattan class arsenal ship. I won't go into the exact specifications of what this warship is capable of, but suffice it to say, its technology and weapon systems are unlike any ever seen before. It relegates all other warships, including our current inventory of ships, to the ash heaps of history. With that said, I welcome the First Lady to officially christen first of the *Arsenal*-class ships, the USS *Warhammer* and the USS *Spartan*."

The people in attendance stood and clapped as the First Lady stepped forward and did the honors, breaking a bottle of champagne against the bow of the massive warship.
****

Two Weeks Later

Vice Admiral Ingalls stood on the bridge of the USS *Warhammer* as the ship prepared to fire its vertical launch missiles for the first time. He wanted to make sure they had the conventional system operational before they moved on to the next-generation weapons.

The visitors to the ship stood on the bridge along with the ship's captain, watching the bow of the ship where the missile pods were positioned. A minute later the first missile fired straight up into the air before its rocket motor directed it off towards its target. Sixty seconds after the first missile fired, a second one emerged from the same pod. The reusable VLS tube had successfully proven it could fire a missile, reload a new one from its magazine, and fire again.

Developing a reloadable VLS system meant the ship could carry a large number of missiles without having to obscure a large portion of the deck space with missile pods. Instead, the front of the ship had been outfitted with one hundred reloadable missile pods. The magazine well could hold an additional twelve hundred missiles, ranging from SM2s, SM3s, SM4s, and SM6s to Tomahawk cruise missiles.

Behind the VLS pods, the turrets housed the dual-barreled sixteen-inch railguns. The turrets were dome-shaped, allowing more room for the barrels to elevate to a higher angle. This enabled the gun to arc its projectiles to hit more distant targets. To the rear of the turrets, the phased-array radar and tracking system allowed the battleship to find, identify, and engage hostile targets. This part of the ship looked like an *Arleigh Burke*-class destroyer.

To the rear of the forward section sat two structures on either side of the ship—the direct energy weapon pods. Having them situated on either side of the ship and at different positions allowed them to provide an exceptional bubble of protection. They could both be brought to bear against a host of targets and angle low enough that they could engage smaller ships or boats that might try to get close to the *Warhammer*'s hull.

Also along the sides of the ship were four turrets, two on each side. These turrets consisted of dual .50-caliber railguns, designed specifically to engage enemy aircraft, missiles, and UAVs. They were the ship's point-defense systems should a hostile threat enter the *Warhammer*'s protective bubble.

A two-lane flight deck protruded from the sides of the ship like a twenty-five-degree-angled V. Like the *Ford*-class carriers, this ship would also use a magnetic catapult system, eliminating the need for a steam-generated system. To the rear of the flight deck was a fairly large rear parking ramp. There was also a large hangar that connected to the superstructure, which would house the ship's helicopters. To the rear of the parking ramp were two large elevators that connected the flight deck with the hangar deck below.

From all outward appearances, the *Arsenal* ships looked like a cross between an *Arleigh Burke* destroyer, a World War II battleship, and a supercarrier. They were towering giants with eighteen decks, stretching 1,106 feet in length and 134 feet in width. Most of the ship's internal guts housed the missile magazines and the aircraft.

The unique thing about having the flight deck split in a V shape was that it allowed the ship to launch either four aircraft at a time or recover two aircraft at a time. They could also recover aircraft on one side while launching them on the other. It really changed the way a carrier could operate. However, the landing was going to require some new training, especially because the ship would be launching fighters at the same time.

While the *Arsenal* ships weren't primarily intended to be aircraft carriers, they did have a hangar deck large enough to accommodate twenty-seven aircraft in addition to six helicopters. The *Warhammer*'s airwing consisted of sixteen F-35Cs, four EA-18G Growlers, three E-2 Hawkeyes, four MQ-25 Stingray UAVs, and six ASW SH-60 Seahawk helicopters. The complement of aircraft and helicopters allowed the ship to be a true multirole, multipurpose weapon platform for the twenty-first century.

The first day of tests went by quickly as the crew ran through the various system checks on the different weapon platforms. They identified glitches in the targeting software, ghost targets on the radar screens and numerous other electrical, mechanical, and technological problems on the ship. However, by the end of the fifth day of sea trials, the engineers believed they'd found most of the issues that would need to get fixed.

The air side of testing had also been completed, with only minor changes needing to be made. Most of the changes revolved around the pilots needing to learn how to land in the reverse direction of how they'd been doing it in the past.

Now that the engineers had identified the various glitches and problems throughout the ship that needed to be worked on, they'd head back to port and spend the next few months running through each item, making sure they were fixed before they'd head out for their next battery of tests. Normally this process could take the better part of a year and three or four tests at sea before they'd run it through a full shakedown cruise, but they didn't have that kind of time. They had less than four months to get her ready for war.

Chapter Twenty-Three
Recovery

Bethesda, Maryland

Walter Reed National Military Medical Center

Who's that voice belong to? Gunnery Sergeant Mack wondered. He could barely tell if the voice came from a woman or a man. *Where the hell am I?*

He questioned why he couldn't see and suddenly realized his eyes were closed. *I need to open my eyes...*

Mack's eyes hurt. The lights seemed so bright. He raised his right hand to rub the crust that had formed around his eyes and then used his hand to shield his eyes while they adjusted to the light. Steadily, his eyes began to focus. He saw that he was in some sort of hospital. He saw other beds with bodies lying in them nearby.

A nurse walked by his bed. "Excuse me," he called out. "Where am I?"

The woman, who was probably in her midtwenties, turned and smiled, then walked over to the side of his bed. "Gunnery Sergeant Mack, you're awake," she remarked. Her tone was filled with surprise and happiness. "I'm so glad you've woken up. I have to admit, we weren't sure if you were going to pull through when you came in."

He tried to figure out how to respond. "I, um, yes. I'm awake," he stammered. "How long have I been out, and where am I?"

"I'm sure you have a lot of questions, hun," she said with a smile. "I'll go get one of the doctors. He'll be able to explain more." Then she dashed off.

Damn it. All I wanted was an answer to my question, he thought. As far as he was concerned, they could figure out the rest later.

Mack turned to look around and take more of his surroundings in. He was obviously in some sort of big medical ward. There were two rows of ten soldiers in this room. More than half of them appeared to be asleep. He couldn't tell what was wrong with them from where he was situated.

A few minutes went by. Mack hoped someone would walk near his bed so he could try and call out to ask them some questions. While he waited, he did a quick mental check of his body. Clearly, he could move his arms and fingers. Next, he wiggled the toes on both feet before he tried moving his legs. Thankfully, everything seemed to be working, which was a huge relief. He'd heard horror stories of guys waking up and suddenly realizing they didn't have legs or that they had some other terrible injury. He didn't seem to fit that description just yet.

A doctor walked up to his bed and greeted him with a warm smile. "Gunnery Sergeant, it's good to see you awake. I wasn't sure how long you'd be out."

Not wanting to waste time, Mack got down to business. "Thank you, Doc. Can you tell me where I am?" he asked. "How long have I been out, and what the hell happened to me and my unit?"

The doctor nodded. "You're at Walter Reed. You've been in a coma for nearly two months. As to what happened, you were shot in the chest multiple times. Fortunately, you only suffered a few broken ribs since your body armor stopped the rounds. However, you were also shot in the head. Your helmet absorbed most of the impact, but the bullet did penetrate the helmet and it entered your head around this point here," he explained, gesturing. "We were lucky that the bullet stayed mostly above your brain and settled just under the skull. You had a lot of brain swelling during the first few days after you were medevacked. Eventually, they flew you here and we opened your skull up and removed the bullet. Unfortunately, we had to put you into a medically induced coma to help reduce the brain swelling. That was six weeks ago."

Mack lay there stunned as he took all the information in. It was a lot to digest. He'd been shot in the head and somehow survived. That was pretty impressive if he did say so himself.

"Am I going to be OK?" he asked. "Is there anything else wrong with me?"

"You mean, will you be able to go back to your unit?" the doctor clarified.

"You read my mind," Mack said with a smile.

"Well, I did see into your brain, so there is that," the doctor said, laughing at his own joke.

Mack just stared at him, not saying anything while the doctor chuckled at his expense.

The doctor noticed Mack's sour response and pulled himself together quickly. "Sorry," he said. "I don't get a lot of chances to laugh around here." He waved his arm around the ward and then cleared his throat. "Now that you're awake, we'll assess you to see if there are any long-term problems. You can clearly move your limbs and control them, so that's a big one. You appear to be able to talk just fine and process information, so that means you probably don't have any significant brain damage, which is also good.

We'll put you through a battery of cognitive and physical tests to see exactly where you are."

The doctor paused for a moment. "I'm not sure you can go back to your unit, Gunny," he explained softly, trying to lessen the blow. "Even if you pass all these tests, the fact of the matter is you were shot in the head. You had to have brain surgery to remove the bullet. For better or worse, you've suffered a serious traumatic brain injury. You may make a full recovery, but you may have substantial problems that we don't know about just yet. My advice after seeing tens of thousands of patients is that you take things a bit slow. You can push yourself, but you need to focus on getting better. The war will go on with or without you. They'll win while you recover."

That wasn't exactly what Mack wanted to hear, but he understood what the doctor meant. "Do you know what happened to my unit in California?" he asked.

The doc shrugged his shoulders. "I'm honestly not sure, Gunny. I know there's been a lot of heavy fighting out there, but there's been a lot of heavy fighting all over the country. What I can tell you is that the Marines just landed troops along the Texas coast and our forces in Colorado broke through the main Chinese lines. We seem to be turning the tide in the war, but that's about all I can say."

Mack nodded and thanked the doctor, who left to go attend to other patients.

After the doc left, an orderly came by with a cart and asked him if he'd like something to eat. Mack hadn't thought about food just yet, but the smell coming from the cart suddenly made him incredibly hungry. He eagerly accepted the food. However, as he munched on a turkey sandwich and some cherry Jell-O, all he could think about was figuring out a way to contact his old unit to see how they were doing.

Chapter Twenty-Four
Kidnapping & Mass Murder

Washington, D.C.

White House, Situation Room

The Director of the CIA, Marcus Ryerson, explained to a horrifying discovery to everyone in the room. "Mr. President, there can't be any doubt about what's going on in the occupied zones. For months, the Chinese have been removing nearly all the healthy women between the ages of sixteen and thirty-five and taking them back to China. We've had dozens of Special Forces teams on the ground providing us with video and still images of the women being moved from central processing centers and sent back to China. One of our SEAL teams in LA managed to land a surveillance drone on one of the transports before it left California.

"The drone stayed dormant for a month on the journey to China. The NSA was then able to take remote control of it and provide solid footage of what was happening on the other end. They beamed footage back to a series of drones we set up to relay the information for about a week before the Chinese realized what was happening. During that time, we saw our American women being taken to large internment camps. What was going on in those camps we can't be sure of, but it's odd that they would only abduct the women from the occupied zones."

Secretary of State Kagel chimed in. "I believe I know what the Chinese are doing," she asserted. All eyes shifted to her.

"OK. Why don't you explain what you mean by that?" the President asked.

She lifted her chin. "It's about their population demographics."

"You can't be serious," blurted the President's National Security Advisor, Robert Grey.

Undeterred, she replied, "Deadly." She then turned to the President, the only person in the room who really mattered, as she expounded on her proclamation. "The Chinese have a disproportionate number of men to women in their country. Frankly, they are about seventy million women short when it comes to single men of marrying age. This is a direct consequence of their one-child policy they had in place for decades. Not having enough women has created an unstable environment inside the country. I think our women are being taken back to China to be indoctrinated into their culture and will one day be given as brides to their 'conquering army.'" She was surprised no one else had put it together—everyone looked so shocked.

The President held a hand up. "Whoa. That is a hell of a claim to make," he countered. "What kind of facts do you have to back that assertion up with?"

She pointed to the information the CIA still had displayed on the monitor. "Isn't it obvious, Mr. President? Why else would the Chinese have abducted hundreds of thousands of our women and brought them to China? The longer this war goes on and they maintain control of the captured territory, the more women they are going to kidnap and take to China."

Everyone in the room sat there in stunned silence for a moment, digesting what she had said. Many of them seemed to be having a very hard time accepting this possibility.

Finally, the President turned to General Markus. "The Chinese are clearly carrying out a terror campaign in our country. They've kidnapped possibly half a million of our women, maybe more. We already know they killed several million more of our civilians and appear to be destroying every town and city they withdraw from. What can we do to bring this same level of fight and destruction to Chinese cities? I want their civilians, their people, to feel the same anguish and terror our people are feeling on a daily basis."

Sachs had clearly lost his sense of restraint as the full scope of what was going on in the occupied zones became more and more apparent every day. People would be demanding vengeance as this information got out.

Secretary Kagel jumped back into the conversation before the general could reply. "If I could, Mr. President, let me speak with my Chinese counterpart. Let me lay the cards on the table and let them know we know what they've been doing. If they won't agree to return our people and stop this genocide in the occupied zones, then I'll inform him that America will begin its own terror campaign, bombing high-density civilian populations all across China. Let me at least try to avert a further escalation if possible," she pleaded.

General Markus stayed silent. Based on what she knew of his views, Markus hoped the President would heed her words. He too, wanted to avoid escalating things if possible.

If they could work out some sort of arrangement with the Chinese, then all the better. If not, then the Chinese would feel the weight of America's newest bomber, the B-21 Raider, as it rained death on their cities.

****

Lima, Peru
Belmond Miraflores Park

When Secretary of State Haley Kagel's plane finally touched down at the Jorge Chavez International Airport, she breathed a sigh of relief. She'd never admit it publicly, but she was a bit concerned flying anywhere near a country where the Chinese military was in control. She could just see the headlines: *US Secretary of State's Plane Accidentally Shot Down by PLA Forces.* That would thoroughly wreck her day.

As the plane came to a halt, she looked out the window and saw they had pulled up near a large hangar and were being guided into it. Once inside, she saw dozens of diplomatic security officers and Suburban SUVs waiting to greet her. When the pilot powered down their engines, one of the crew members disengaged the locking mechanism on the door and opened it. Next, some ground crew members moved a set of stairs to allow her to get off.

The first thing she felt when she got off the plane was the immediate temperature difference between Washington and Lima. While it had been in the midnineties in D.C., it was a cool sixty-something in the capital of Peru. It was refreshing to be away from the stifling humid weather of Washington, where the air felt sticky because it had essentially been built on a swamp hundreds of years ago.

"Good morning, Madam Secretary. How was your flight?" asked her Head of Security.

Secretary Kagel smiled warmly at the man who was charged with protecting her. It was not an easy job given the Chinese had already killed off a third of the Congress and wiped out the Supreme Court at the outset of the war.

"I'm doing good, Charley," she responded. "Thank you for arranging this on such short notice."

"It was no problem at all, Madam Secretary. The Peruvians have been exceptional hosts." His right hand gently clasped the shoulder of Mauro Medina, the Peruvian Deputy Ministry of the Interior. Charley and Mauro had worked together in the past on a couple of other projects in Peru, Afghanistan, and Iraq, so he had a good working relationship with the man, even if his nation had decided to remain neutral in the conflict.

"It was no trouble at all, Madam Secretary," Mauro said with a laugh. "When my good friend Charley said you wanted to host a summit with the Chinese in my nation, I was elated and willing to do whatever I could to help make it happen. My government would love nothing more than for this terrible war to come to an end. We are still appalled at what took place with the United Nations. From the bottom of my heart, I am glad Peru never participated in that evil scheme against your nation." Secretary Kagel thought his response appeared to be genuine.

She sighed. "OK. Then let's get going to the hotel," she replied. "If possible, I'd like to get a couple of hours of sleep in a real bed before we have any further meetings. My understanding is the Chinese are going to be staying at the hotel as well, and they arrive tonight. I suspect they'll want to meet sometime tomorrow, once Foreign Minister Jiang Yi has had a chance to rest."

"Agreed. We'll get you to the hotel right away, then," Charley responded. "Madam Secretary, President Tasso would like to meet with you tonight at his residence for dinner. He has some items he'd like to discuss with you if you are willing." He guided her to the waiting vehicles as he spoke.

Kagel paused for a moment and then turned to face Deputy Minister Medina. "Tell the President I would be happy to meet with him tonight at his residence. That's very thoughtful of him. There are a few issues I'd like to discuss with him as well."

The next twenty minutes went by swiftly as her motorcade made its way through the city. Then they pulled into the exquisite Belmond Miraflores Park Hotel, a beautiful five-star lodging near the water. It wasn't a particularly large hotel, but it was ornately decorated and had several amazing conference rooms and side rooms the delegations could meet in to discuss the urgent business at hand.

The government of Peru had gone ahead and taken the necessary precautions of booking the entire hotel. The only people that would be staying there would be the American and Chinese delegations, so talks could be held in private and without distractions.

Once Secretary Kagel had had a few hours to sleep in the overstuffed bed of her exquisite suite, she got ready for her evening dinner with the Peruvian President, Mr. Pedro Tasso.

When her car pulled up to the ornate Neobaroque façade of the Government Palace, Secretary Kagel's Head of Security moved around the SUV and opened the door for her. As she exited the vehicle, she saw Tasso standing in front of the capitol building with his wife, waiting to greet her. Kagel walked over to the two of them; they briefly shook hands as they exchanged pleasantries. The trio then walked into the grand entrance that led into a two-level Great Hall lined with Roman columns, which was how they entered the Peruvian President's residence.

Secretary Kagel followed Tasso and his wife as they wove deftly through the hallways. When they reached a doorway, the Peruvian First Lady excused herself. "I'll let you all talk alone for a while. There's about ninety minutes until dinner."

Kagel tipped her head in deference to Mrs. Tasso, and then walked through the door to the Sevillian Patio. Kagel realized that she was joining a rare club, since this courtyard was only accessible from the residence and Tasso was not known to take all of his visitors there. She liked the glazed tiles that adorned the patio with coats of arms. They stopped at a bench near the fig tree in the center.

"Is it true that this thing was planted by Pizarro?" Kagel asked.

Tasso laughed. "I don't know. But it sure makes a great story, doesn't it?"

A steward came and brought them drinks. When they'd had a few sips, Tasso began the conversation in earnest. "Madam Secretary, I'm pleased that you were able to meet with me tonight. I know you must be tired from your long journey, and you have a lot to prepare for tomorrow."

She smiled. "Mr. President, you may call me Haley when we meet in private. I prefer to keep things more personal and less formal when it's just the two of us."

He nodded and quickly added, "Likewise, you may call me Pedro."

"Pedro, I'm not going to play political games. We have uncovered some horrific atrocities being committed by the Chinese in the occupied territories of my country. I am here to meet with Foreign Minister Jiang to discuss this with him and attempt to convince him that these barbaric activities need to stop."

"If you don't mind me asking, what kind of atrocities are you talking about?" asked President Tasso.

She proceeded to explain to him exactly what was happening. He looked disgusted and horrified that such an evil plan could be carried out against any nation. The sheer number of people that had been killed was appalling.

After a brief pause, he asked, "So, what is President Sachs going to do if the Chinese do not stop these terrible acts?"

Haley paused for a moment, wondering how much she should reveal to him. Since she had been honest with him up to this point, she figured she'd tell him the rest.

"Should the Chinese not agree to end this vicious plan of theirs, then our President is going to exact America's revenge on the Chinese civilian population."

His expression turned sad. "Didn't Sachs already do that by bombing the Three Gorges Dam, though? Millions of people died during that terrible attack. Isn't that enough?"

"That bombing was in retaliation for the Chinese vaporizing our citizens and military facilities on Guam, Arizona, and Oklahoma. More than four hundred thousand Americans died in those nuclear attacks. Then they used an enhanced EMP weapon on San Diego and Hawaii."

She paused, taking a sip of her predinner cocktail. "No. This is different," she insisted. They are committing genocide on a massive scale in our country. It's estimated that more than three million civilians in California alone have been killed." She shook her head as she continued. "This next round of attacks would be on the Chinese industrial centers. However, we are really hoping they'll stop this madness before it escalates any further."

The Peruvian President urged caution in dealing with the Chinese but also recognized that the US would do what was necessary to protect its country and people. When they had talked a bit more, the rest of their guests arrived and the dinner started. Secretary Kagel was fortunate that no one tried to pry any information out of her. It became a pleasant evening of breaking bread with friends, just talking about nothing and everything.

****

The following morning at the hotel, Secretary Kagel received a message from Foreign Minister Jiang that he would like to meet for lunch so they could go over some bullet points for their conversation. He wanted to settle upon an outline of what they were going to talk about prior to their discussions. She sent a message back accepting the invitation and set to work preparing for a working lunch at noon.

When Kagel walked into the formal dining room at the Belmond Milaflores Park Hotel, she saw Minister Jiang sitting at a table for eight, along with three other men from his delegation. Kagel, for her part, had only brought one aide with her to be a part of her delegation. From her perspective, there wasn't a lot to talk about. She was really there more or less to deliver a set of demands she knew the Chinese were most likely going to reject.

When Minister Jiang saw Secretary Kagel, he stood and motioned for her to come join him.

The two shook hands and bowed slightly. Jiang then held her seat out for her as she sat down. Jiang was always a gentleman toward her, even if their nations were currently at war. Under normal circumstances, she might be insulted by the gesture, but frankly, she and Jiang have built up a decent working relationship over the last five years. She knew he wasn't necessarily a Chinese hardliner, but he had his orders from Beijing, just as she had hers from Washington.

"Madam Secretary, thank you for arranging this meeting," Jiang began. "It has been nearly nine months since we last spoke face-to-face. We have lots to discuss."

"I agree, Minister Jiang," she said with a nod. "We do have a lot to discuss. I know you had wanted to develop some sort of outline for our discussions, but if you'd be willing to, I'd like to just get down to business here and now and go over the specific reason I asked to meet with you in a neutral country."

Jiang smiled at her bluntness. He'd been educated in America, so it was well known that he appreciated people who were direct and to the point. Many of his fellow countrymen would have been put off by Kagel's manner of speaking, but he just motioned for her to continue.

"Minister Jiang, I'm not going to mince words. Over the last several months, we have uncovered some very disturbing things happening in the occupied parts of my country."

His left eyebrow rose in surprise. "Really?" he asked. "We have done our best to accommodate your citizens that are now in Chinese-controlled areas."

She smiled coyly at the comment. "I wouldn't call eliminating the sick and elderly accommodating behavior, would you?" she inquired.

Kagel studied every movement of his facial expressions. His face flushed a bit, and his eyes darted down to the left as he responded, "I'm not sure I know what you are talking about." She was not at all fooled by his attempt to feign ignorance.

"Let's just cut to the chase, shall we? We have verifiable evidence in the form of videos and still images of sick and elderly people being driven off to mass grave sites in the occupied zones," she said forcefully. "We have firsthand accounts of people who have escaped the occupied zones telling us of this as well. Worse, we have recently learned that your forces are kidnapping healthy women between the ages of sixteen and thirty-five and sending them back to China. We've seen the reeducation camps in China. You've systematically kidnapped citizens of *our* country and transported them back to your country. I understand this is war, but what your nation is doing is abhorrent; it's a genocide of our people, and it needs to stop."

"You are calling *China's* actions abhorrent?" Jiang asked indignantly. "It was *your* country that bombed the Three Gorges Dam. Millions of Chinese civilians were killed and tens of millions more were injured and left homeless."

"And it was *your* country that used nuclear weapons in Arizona, Guam, and Oklahoma," Kagel countered calmly. "You then used an EMP weapon over Southern California and Hawaii. More than half a million Americans died in those attacks. You're lucky we didn't unleash our entire nuclear arsenal on your country."

The two paused for a moment as they continued to eye each other. Finally, Jiang said, "I am not aware of what you are talking about happening in the occupied zones. For all I know, you could be fabricating this as a way of trying to end this war."

She shook her head in anger. She couldn't believe that he would try to obfuscate something like this. She turned to her aide. "George, why don't you go take a smoke break or get a drink at the bar?" she asked. "I think Mr. Jiang and I need to talk in private."

George nodded and got up. A second later, Jiang's people joined him as they headed to the other side of the room where the bar was located.

Now that it was just the two of them, Kagel got up and moved to sit next to him so they could talk in hushed tones.

"Jiang, it's just you and me now," she said in a conciliatory tone. "Seriously…what the hell is going on with these kidnappings and murders?"

Jiang sighed deeply. He pulled a device out of his pocket that made a sound like a waterfall; the white noise was a precautionary device to protect against listening devices. "Haley, when this war first started, I did not know about any of this," he began. "All I knew was what UN Secretary-General Johann Behr and the others said was happening in America. It wasn't until the conflict had already started that I was filled in on my own country's involvement in this grand scheme. By that point, it was too late for even me to try and talk the President out it.

"Once my country invaded yours, I heard about these kidnappings taking place, so I began asking questions. But this whole thing is very compartmentalized. Even *I* don't know everything. What I do know is it has something to do with what they're calling the 'Q program.'"

She furrowed her brow. "Q program—what is it?"

He leaned in closer to her. "You know we have a serious shortage of women in my country. From what I understand of the program, the goal is to transport the healthy women of childbearing age back to China. As an incentive for joining the war and fighting in America, soldiers returning from the war would be given an American woman to be their bride. This would give an incentive for our youth to not only join the military, but to fight hard to earn the right to marry one of these women."

"Holy crap, Jiang. This is terrible," she said. Part of her couldn't believe it was true, even though this had been her theory. "Do you know how much of a pariah this is going to make China appear in the eyes of the world?"

"I do. Sadly, I do. But this is way out of my control," Jiang insisted.

"Do you know how many women have been transported back to China?"

He shook his head slightly. "I do not have an exact number, but I know it is now more than two million."

She crossed her arms. "Look, I've been told to pass a message from President Sachs to your leader. If China does not stop this and return these women back to our country, he is going to launch a terror campaign on your cities the likes of which hasn't been seen since World War II. He's going to order our bombers to systematically level your densely populated cities. He's furious at what's going on, and in his mind, if your military can do this to our people, then he'll do it right back to yours."

A look of despair and defeat spread across Jiang's face before he could resume his poker face. "I can relay the message to Chen," he replied. "But from President Chen's perspective, this will only fuel his message that the Americans mean to destroy the Chinese people. He has the media and the internet under so much censorship. The average person has no idea what's going on and has zero clue about this Q program. They'll continue to blindly support Chen even if it means the end of China."

She paused for a moment before she leaned in again. "What can we do to convince the Chinese people not to support this war?" she asked. "To demand an end to it?"

Jiang snorted. "Keep doing what you're doing," he replied. "The casualties have been horrific. Even President Chen is having a hard time hiding them from the public. Eventually, they'll grow tired of their sons dying in a war far from their shores."

Secretary Kagel sighed. "What can we do to bring an end to all of this?"

Jiang cocked his head slightly to one side. "You could surrender," he replied with a smile.

"You can't be serious?" she asked, not even trying to hide her laughter. "We just captured two hundred thousand Chinese soldiers in Colorado and we're in the process of pushing your forces out of Texas. Why would we surrender now?"

Jiang quickly replied, "Because we've been letting you push us out of those areas. We've moved millions of soldiers into California. Soon, that army will be unleashed, and when it is, we'll control half your country. If you want an end to the war, then you need to surrender now, and we can begin the process of disarming your military and population. America will become a protectorate of Greater China."

The two sat in silence for a moment as each of them thought about what the other had said. Secretary Kagel came to the conclusion that for the time being, there wasn't really anything further for them to discuss. She had delivered her message to President Chen, and he had told her the only terms China would accept to end the war. There really wasn't anything more that could be accomplished.

Turning to look at him, Secretary Kagel announced, "I suppose we should let the others join us again. We can at least have lunch together. But aside from that, I'm not sure there is much left for us to talk about."

Jiang nodded in agreement and the two of them called their aides over so they could order lunch. The rest of the afternoon was spent making small talk while they prodded and probed a few areas the two superpowers might be able to come to an agreement on, but ultimately, the Chinese had their end goal they were working toward, and America was never going to agree to it.

Chapter Twenty-Five
Operation Vengeance

Taylor County, Texas
Dyess Air Force Base

For a while, Colonel Webb thought they were going to evacuate everyone and everything out of Dyess to another air base. The ground fighting had become precariously close. There was a point where Webb could hear the thunderous booms of artillery and the soft whisper of machine guns chattering, which was a new and unique experience for him. His entire time in the military had been as a bomber, high above the actual fighting below. He'd never been on the ground in Afghanistan or Iraq to know what any of this sounded or felt like. His closest brush with death had been during the initial Iraq campaign in 2003, when the night sky around Baghdad had been lit up like the Fourth of July.

As to the current conflict, the Army had finally been able to stop the Chinese from advancing any further and had begun to push them back. Webb felt a certain satisfaction knowing that he had a major hand in all that. He and his copilot and a few other B-2 bombers had carpet-bombed the hell out of the enemy lines in Texas when things were looking pretty dire. Apparently, a few thousand 500-pound bombs falling on the Chinese lines had finally stopped their momentum, at least for the time being.

Now Colonel Webb and his copilot, Major Hawkey, found themselves sitting in an air-conditioned briefing room, looking over a new mission proposal. They didn't like it one bit. They had been assigned to fly to Alaska, where they'd link up with two B-2 bombers. The flight of three aircraft would then be refueled and carry out what was essentially a World War II-style terror bombing as they attempted to fly through some of the most heavily defended airspace in the world.

For this mission, the three bombers would each be outfitted with eighty 500-pound dumb bombs to plaster the Chinese populace. Colonel Webb understood the reasoning, but it still seemed wrong.

Colonel Webb raised his hand and interrupted the briefer. "Major, I have some serious problems with this mission that I feel need to be expressed. This mission does not fit within the parameters outlined in our laws of armed conflict. As the senior officer of this raid, I need to highlight that."

The briefer acknowledged the question, shifting uncomfortably at the mention of the LOAC. The bomber and fighter-bomber pilots had to adhere to these standards when carrying out a mission. It certainly wasn't standard operating procedure to unilaterally bomb civilian targets for the sole purpose of killing civilians.

Brigadier General Arie stepped up to the front of the room and took the place of the briefer to address Webb's concern. "You are correct, Colonel. This mission would have been a direct violation of the LOAC. However, yesterday, by order of the President, the Secretary of Defense and the Secretary of the Air Force, the LOAC for the Global Strike Command have been amended." He paused for a moment, surveying the faces in the room. "What I'm about to tell you is highly classified. It's going to be released to the media soon, but until it is, you all are bound to secrecy."

General Arie proceeded to give them the ten-cent version of what the Chinese had been doing in the occupied zones: the kidnappings, the starvation and genocide. The information was devastating. Nearly everyone knew of someone or had family that was trapped in the occupied zones. To know that so many of them were being killed or starved to death was heartbreaking and disturbing.

When everyone had had a moment to process what they'd just been told, General Arie continued. "Four days ago, the President issued an ultimatum to the Chinese government. They needed to cease the genocide of our citizens and begin the process of returning our people from China. If they failed to do that, then the US would bomb their cities until they complied. That, gentlemen, is why the LOAC have been changed and why you've been asked to carry out this mission. We are going to bring the war to the Chinese people in hopes that their government will stop this genocide in the occupied zones."

Colonel Webb still didn't feel good about the mission, but he understood why it needed to be done. He just hoped the Chinese would get the message and they wouldn't be forced to make this the new normal.

****

Six hours later, Colonel Webb took the plane off autopilot as they came into visual range of the KC-135 Stratotanker.

"You got this, boss, or you want me to handle it?" asked his copilot, sounding a little too eager.

Turning briefly to look at Hawkey, Webb replied, "You know what, why don't you take this one? You'll be taking over command of an aircraft soon enough. Best for you to get ready to handle every aspect of the bomber."

Webb had been doing his best to make sure his copilot was ready to take command when the new bombers started coming off the assembly line. Since there were only two of these planes in existence, the process to get pilots qualified to fly them was difficult.

Hawkey got them lined up behind the tanker, matching his speed and course. The boom operator's signal lights came on, letting him know he should move closer. Steadily, he inched the giant bomber toward the boom behind the refueler until it was just a few feet away from their open fuel receptacle. Now he just had to hold the aircraft steady while the boom operator made a few adjustments on his end and then extended the fuel nozzle. A green light appeared near the boom operator. The two aircraft had successfully connected, and they'd now top off their tanks.

It took a bit of time to take on all the fuel they needed, but eventually they were ready to disconnect and head to the next waypoint. After a few more hours, they skirted by Russia without being detected as they made their way towards South Korea. Then they crossed over the Yellow Sea as they headed toward China's airspace.

I wish this old B-2 wasn't such a slow aircraft, Webb thought. The B-21 could travel more than twice as fast as the

B-2, which meant they could have flown in and out of the hot zone a lot more rapidly.

As the hours droned on, the trio of bombers finally reached visual range of Mainland China. Webb could tell they were approaching China just by the level of smog in the air. Anywhere there was a densely packed city, the air above and around it was brown. The smog was thick, and it was like a plague covering much of the country.

As they neared the coast, Webb and Hawkey started to pick up numerous search radars. Their instruments told them the sky was being scanned by several HQ-9 or Red Banner 9 surface-to-air missile platforms in addition to several ground radar stations. The HQ-9s however, were the real threat. These were state-of-the-art SAMs. They'd proven incredibly effective in the occupied zones of North America, having shot down more than two hundred American aircraft thus far.

When they officially crossed into Chinese airspace, the trio of bombers changed course slightly and adjusted their altitude. They flew a little lower, dropping down to around thirty thousand feet as they entered the commercial aircraft flight lanes.

The only thing showing on their radars at this point was a handful of commercial aircraft around a hundred miles away—no fighters or other aircraft that could pose a danger to them. When they were less than fifteen minutes from the drop zone, the trio descended from thirty thousand feet to roughly twenty thousand feet. Because they were dropping 500-pound dumb bombs, they needed to lower their altitude and speed a bit so they could do their best to keep the sticks of bombs relatively close together. The goal was to blanket an area with them for maximum damage.

"We're three minutes out," Hawkey stated over their internal comms system.

"Stand by to open bomb bay doors," Webb announced. He hoped the other bomber pilots were moving in sync with him. He didn't want one of the bombers to release too early or too late.

"Sixty seconds."

"Open bomb bay doors."

Webb heard a slight mechanical sound and then the aircraft started to buffet a bit from the wind and turbulence as they temporarily lost their sleek aerodynamic profile.

"Over the target in five...four...three...two...release, release, release."

Colonel Webb held the bomber steady as Major Hawkey issued the eighty bombs they were carrying. One by one, the eight racks of ten bombs fell to the ground below.

The other bombers released their bombs in unison. Then the trio of aircraft picked up speed to the maximum a B-2 could travel and increased their altitude to forty thousand feet.

Roughly two minutes went by before the entire horizon lit up with additional search radars. The PLA had probably detected the wall of bombs headed toward one of their major cities and knew the American bombers must be nearby.

Time to split up, Webb thought. Each of the bombers split off on their own path of egress out of the area.

Colonel Webb increased the throttle. They'd burn through a lot more fuel at this increased speed, but it'd get them out of Chinese airspace a hell of a lot faster. The PLA knew they were in the area, and they'd do their best to try and hunt them down, so it was no time to be concerned about fuel economy.

Fifteen minutes after everyone headed off their separate ways, Webb's radar screen showed PLA interceptors taking off.

"What kind of aircraft are those?" he asked, anxious to know what kind of trouble they might be in.

"They look like J-8s," Hawkey replied. "Finbacks. Fast little buggers."

Hmm...as long as they don't get too close to us, we should be fine.

"OK. I want to keep a wide berth," Webb announced. "Make sure they never get more than one hundred miles from us. Their radars are kind of crappy, but we don't need to make it any easier for them by letting them get near us." He noted down on his log what was happening.

Hawkey took a few minutes to enter the new parameters into their navigation computer. The technology would do its best to make sure they stayed outside the aircraft's radar range.

The next sixty minutes was nerve-racking and tense. Twice, Webb thought they had been found out, and twice he'd been proven wrong. Traveling at their maximum speed, they eventually reached the coast, and soon they were outside of Chinese airspace.

As they moved further and further away from China, Webb slowed them down until they reached their optimal cruising speed and altitude. By his calculations, they'd be pretty low on fuel by the time they linked up with the refueler.

Webb looked down at his watch. He figured they still had roughly sixteen hours left in the air. That was a long time, but the hard part was over. Now they just had to stay awake while they flew home.

Chapter Twenty-Six
Traitors

Bedford, Massachusetts

Hanscom Air Force Base

Colonel Patrick "Paddy" Maine stood at the edge of the aircraft hangar with his hands on his hips. As the sun set, ushering in the night, he let a devilish smirk spread across his normally impassive face.

I like the dark, he thought. *It's when the real work gets done.*

He sniffed the air—someone was eating clam chowder. The smell brought back a surge of memories from his childhood. Paddy's mother and father had both been very involved in his life despite their hectic work schedules. His father had worked in consulting for a firm and his mother had been a professor at Harvard.

His father had been one of those alpha males in the corporate world and had instilled a solid work ethic in him when he was young. His mother had been the polar opposite of his dad—she was an academic, a fifty-pound brainiac. Her area of expertise had been applied physics. Between his mother's academic focus and his father's business savvy, they had trained him to be the best at both. With his mother being a professor at Harvard, he had had a slot reserved for him at the university. In the fall of 1996, Paddy started his first year at the Ivy League school, majoring in business and minoring in applied physics. He was in graduate school when tragedy struck in the fall of 2001.

His father and mother had both been killed during the September 11th attacks. They weren't in the towers, though. They had been eating breakfast at a nearby restaurant when parts of the first plane that struck the building fell to the ground, killing them and half a dozen others. Paddy was an only child, so his parents had been the only family he'd had. It was through that immense sorrow and loss that Paddy had determined he wasn't going to go into the corporate world like his father. Instead, he had decided to join the military and exact some sort of revenge on those who had killed his parents.

The Army had accepted him into the ROTC program at Harvard and had encouraged him to finish his MBA. He'd told them he wanted to go into Special Forces and didn't want to wait another year to finish grad school. The Army agreed to send him to officer candidate school and gave Paddy a guaranteed slot in Ranger School. From there, it would be up to him how far he went in the Army.

Paddy had found that he loved the Army and the Rangers. He'd served four years with them before being recruited into the Unit. From there, the rest was history—he'd been with Delta and inside JSOC ever since.

Paddy had been promoted to colonel and placed in charge of hunting down the remaining CDF and Tate administration officials—the last holdouts in putting down this rebellion within the country. To accomplish this task, he'd been given one squadron of Delta Force operators, a battalion from the 160th Special Operations Aviation Regiment or SOAR, and a company of Rangers. While he desperately wanted to fight the Chinese, Paddy knew his current mission was critical to holding the country together and ending the internal fight raging inside the country.

After months of careful analysis, signals intelligence, and good old-fashioned human intelligence, the intelligence community had finally caught the break they'd been looking for, locating Congressman Tim Borq in Chicago. Through him, they'd found one cell leader after another. Now he'd led them to the second-most-wanted person in America—Page Larson, former CIA operations officer and National Security Advisor to Senator Marshall Tate. Since the UN force had collapsed, she'd been busy recruiting and growing insurgent cells all across the Northeast, and in particular in

Boston and New York. She was a key figure in keeping the civil war alive.

A voice broke into Paddy's thoughts. "You ready for this mission, boss?" someone called.

Paddy turned slightly before he recognized the man who'd come up behind him, Lieutenant Colonel Kissinger, the commander of the 3rd Battalion, 160th SOAR. He was Paddy's aerial support for this hunting expedition.

Paddy smiled at him. "It ends tonight, Kissinger," he responded.

Kissinger nodded. "My guys are ready when you are."

Paddy looked at his watch. "Soon, my friend," he replied. "Just keep your crews ready. We should have the location narrowed down shortly."

Kissinger tilted his head forward and to the right as if silently saying, "Yes, sir." Then he walked back to where his pilots were milling about. The men were on edge with all the waiting, and they wanted to get this mission over with. Paddy knew they wanted to get to the real fight— the battle against the Chinese for their homeland.

Paddy made his way into the Ops Center and looked around for his intelligence officer. Finding the person he wanted to see, he walked up to her. "Captain, what is the status of the safe house?" he asked. "Has Congressman Borq arrived yet?"

She cocked her head to one side and shot him a disapproving look. "His convoy just entered the Dorchester neighborhood of South Boston. It won't be long now until we know which house. I've already got my people identifying LZs for the helicopters and we've alerted Homeland of what neighborhood this is going to go down in."

Captain Melissa Ortega was an extremely sharp woman. She'd graduated in the top one percent of her class at West Point six years ago and gone on to become an intelligence officer in the 82nd Airborne, deploying to Afghanistan and Syria. When she'd been assigned temporarily to JSOC, Paddy had immediately recognized her value and gotten her assigned to be one of his intelligence officers in his squadron. She'd done superb work, and in a number of situations she'd utilized her gender as a strength to make headway where a man might not gain entry. Ever since then, Paddy had made sure she was assigned to his unit every time they deployed.

Paddy held a hand up in mock surrender. "Sounds good. Just let me know when we have the safe house identified," he commented. "Everyone's ready to go when you tell us where."

She nodded. "Copy that, Colonel. I'll get back to you shortly," she replied. Then she turned to go find the drone operator that was shadowing Congressman Borq's convoy.

Looking around the room, Paddy had to admire how quickly they had set up their base of operations. They had previously been operating in New York, but after three weeks of tracking Congressman Borq all over the Midwest, he'd finally led them here to Boston. Paddy had had them move their operations to Hanscom Air Force Base so they could launch on a moment's notice and take both Larson and Borq into custody.

Paddy stood in front of a map of the city. He had a hard time wrapping his head around how everything had gone so wrong in his country. He'd grown up in Boston. It had been his home.

"Excuse me, Colonel. We just got confirmation of the location of the safe house," Captain Ortega announced.

Paddy turned to face her. "Really? Where is it?"

A smile spread on her face. "It's located here," she said as she pointed to the neighborhood and the specific house they were meeting in.

Paddy furrowed his brow, then nodded for her to continue.

"Congressman Borq's convoy pulled up to this house. He and his detail got out of the vehicles and headed inside. The automobiles are now camped out about a block away, ready to whisk him to safety if needed."

"OK. I'm going to round up the guys and our pilots," Paddy said. "Get us some close-ups of the house and the area. Identify the LZs for the choppers and have something ready for us in ten mikes. We don't know how long he'll be at the safe house, so we need to launch this mission ASAP." He turned around to go find his shooters and pilots and let them know they had a location. He wanted them suited up and ready to roll as soon as Ortega was ready to give them a down-and-dirty on the location they'd be hitting.

The next ten minutes saw a flurry of activity as the JSOC operators donned their equipment and headed to the hangar.

****

Standing in the cavernous room, Paddy could just make out the sound of helicopter rotor blades starting outside. When he looked at the men standing before him, he felt an immense amount of pride, knowing they were going to be the ones to finally put an end to this civil war.

Paddy walked up to the whiteboard. Once again, he scrutinized the pictures of the house they were going to raid and the surrounding area. Ortega had done a superb job of getting this put together so quickly.

When he turned around, Paddy saw that everyone had stopped talking as they waited for him to say something. "Men, tonight is it," he began. "Tonight, we capture not one but two of our three remaining high-value individuals. Congressman Borq has led us right to Page Larson's safe house. However, that also means we'll have *two* security details to deal with."

Some of the men grumbled a bit, but they largely held their tongues.

"The mission hasn't changed. We just have a few extra hostiles to contend with. With regard to the security details, these aren't going to be some run-of-the-mill poorly trained bodyguards. These are ex-Spetsnaz and Canadian Special Forces. These guys know what they're doing, and they know how to fight."

Paddy turned his attention to his team leaders. "Team Four is already en route," he explained. "They'll continue to stand by for the ground assault when we give them the go.

511

Team Three will land at the intersection of Vinson and Park Street. They'll move in on foot, closing off the west side of the neighborhood. Team Two, you'll land in the Doherty-Gibson baseball field and advance on foot to reinforce Team Four, who'll be assaulting the front of the house. Team Three, you'll insert on the opposite street behind the objective and then advance on foot to the rear of the house. This is it, gentlemen—the biggest mission of your lives. Are there any questions?"

One of the operators raised a hand. "Colonel, has our air support situation changed?" he asked.

Paddy nodded. "It has. We've got one of those new upgraded AC-130Js for support, in addition to our Blackhawks. Beyond that, DHS has a team of one hundred additional personnel on standby in a couple dozen BearCats a few miles away."

Master Sergeant Bruce "Deuce" Wilder chimed in. "I see you have your kit on, Colonel. I assume you're coming with us and not observing in the Ops Center?"

"Boston is my hometown, and this is the mission that's going to end this civil war. You're damn right I'm going with," Paddy asserted.

With no more time, the operators grabbed their weapons and headed out to the waiting Chinooks and

Blackhawks. They were going in with their full unit—twenty-eight Delta operators and eighty-six Rangers. Another twenty Rangers would be flown to the objective when the Chinooks returned from dropping off the first load.

****

Page stared at Congressman Timothy Borq for a moment before she quipped, "That's not good enough, Tim. We've got a nearly endless supply of money to pay people. Why are you having a hard time rallying additional support in the Midwest?"

"My groups continue to carry out attacks against DHS gestapo forces from Milwaukee to Chicago, Detroit on through to Toledo and Cleveland. That's a huge swath of territory, Page," he retorted angrily. "I wouldn't call it sitting on our hands." He ran his fingers through his hair. "You also have to remember that I'm not a soldier; I'm a politician."

Please don't remind me, she thought in frustration.

Page leaned in closer. "It's still not enough," she insisted. "You're talking about five major cities. That's great that you've been able to keep the attacks going there, but you need that discontent and that willingness to take up arms to spread to more of the smaller and mid-sized cities. Right now, DHS is able to keep their forces concentrated where

513

you're most active. We need to force them to contend with uprisings in dozens upon dozens of cities if we're going to keep this dream of President Tate's alive." She spoke with the passion and zeal of a true follower.

Tim sat back in his chair and sighed audibly. "Maybe you should speak with Admiral Hill about this," he suggested, his voice betraying his irritation. "He's supposed to be training more of these special squads to go after the DHS forces."

"I *have* spoken with Admiral Hill," Page countered. "He's got small hit squads carrying out missions all over the Midwest. But it's you, our politician, who needs to keep rallying people to our side. Hill and I are the muscle, but you need to be our political face if we're to make this work, Tim."

Tim let his breath out in a huff of frustration. "Page, I'm tired of living out of a vehicle. I'm tired of constantly being on the run. Marshall's already thrown in the towel. He's encouraged everyone else to do so as well. Why are we still fighting? What hope do we possibly have at achieving victory at this point?"

Page took a deep breath in and held it for five seconds, trying to calm herself before she replied. She had to keep reminding herself that she needed this buffoon.

"Tim, we cannot achieve victory—not since the UN force imploded. That much is true. What we are trying to attain at this point is concessions from the federal government. If they want this insurgency to end, then they need to agree to some of our demands."

"Why would the Feds possibly agree to our demands?" Tim questioned angrily. "They're fighting the Chinese, and they've done a pretty damn good job of hunting down those of us who still remain."

Page spoke through gritted teeth. "That's why you have to grow the insurgency in the Midwest like I'm doing here in the upper East Coast. We have to make this insurgency so costly to them that they'll agree to our demands so that they can focus their entire attention on the Chinese. This is our best chance."

"You really think they'll release Marshall and give everyone involved clemency? A clean slate after all that has transpired?"

She shook her head in disgust. "Of course I don't expect that. God   how could you have been a congressman and not understand anything about negotiations or leverage? Marshall's toast. We can't get him off the hook. Right now, I'm just aiming to get *us* off the hook. I'm also shooting to get a few of our other demands met, but we can't negotiate with them if we don't have a stronger hand. That's why I need you to do your best to get the insurgency to move beyond the cities where you've already stoked it. We need insurrection to rise up in the rural areas."

Before the two of them could argue any further, Ethan Dawa, Borq's Head of Security, walked in hurriedly. He had a look of concern on his face. "Excuse me," he said, bowing slightly as a sort of apology for the interruption. "I just got an urgent message from one of my observers. A small group of helicopters just left Hanscom Air Force Base. He said they appeared to be heading northeast, but they could just be trying to throw off anyone observing the base."

Page wrung her hands. She had to think about that for a moment. It would certainly complicate things if the Feds had somehow found them. "Ethan, keep an eye out and let me know if you hear helicopters or anything out of the ordinary," she directed. "We'll be done talking in five minutes. Then you can get the congressman moved to our next safe house outside the city."

Ethan nodded and then left the room. He held his secured handheld radio to his mouth as he began to issue orders.

Page started passing Tim information as fast as she could. He seemed to be taking most of it in, and he wrote down a few key points. They might need to talk more again at a later date, but right now, the best thing to do was change locations and separate. When Page stood up, she and Tim walked over to the front room, where they exchanged some pleasantries. Then they bade each other farewell.

****

Master Sergeant Bruce "Deuce" Wilder had just exited from the back of the Chinook when he heard the first string of gunshots. Without missing a beat, he sprinted toward the objective, which was less than two hundred meters away.

The crescendo of gunfire only increased as he got closer. Deuce saw the four SUVs for Team Four parked in front of the safe house; the operators were aggressively engaging the shooters inside. As he neared their location, Deuce saw two of the Team Four members get mowed down by bullets in the front yard. They had been trying to move up the stairs to breach the entryway.

A new set of defenders appeared from across the street, firing into the backs of Deuce's comrades. Several of them were hit before they had a chance to seek cover. While Deuce continued his mad dash forward, he raised his SCAR-H rifle to his shoulder and squeezed off a short burst. He saw a string of his bullets tear into the side of the window frame—at least one of his rounds had hit one of the attackers.

Deuce approached the back of a parked car on the side of the street, two houses down from the objective. He stopped long enough to level his rifle at the two other locations where the shooters were firing from and emptied the rest of his magazine into them. Shoving the now-empty magazine into his drop bag, he grabbed his next one, slapped it in place, and hit the bolt release.

Several of his guys ran past him now as they hurried to the aid of their comrades from Team Four. Deuce was about to join them when he saw more movement in the house he had just lit up. He called out to a couple of the guys from his team to follow him as he moved to clear the house. He wanted to make sure no one else got shot in the back like the assault team had.

Deuce raced across the street. He made it to the center divider and stopped next to a large tree just as another shooter fired at him and his three comrades. Deuce waited two or three seconds before he popped around the right side of the tree and fired two short bursts from his SCAR into the second-story window where the hostile was lurking.

"Cover me!" shouted one of his guys.

Deuce moved to the left side of the tree and dropped to a knee as he fired another controlled burst into the room where he knew there was another attacker. His magazine was empty, so he slapped a fresh one in place before he charged toward the house.

Two of his three comrades had already reached the porch and had begun stacking up on the sides of the entryway. One of them had wired the door to breach it before Deuce and his partner made it to the side of the house with them.

"Breaching!" shouted one of the guys as he detonated the small charge affixed to the center of the door. The explosion blew the door apart. One of the other guys threw a flashbang in and they waited a couple seconds for it to go off.

Boom!

The breacher on the team stormed into the house and turned to the first room on the right, with the second guy following behind him. Deuce and his partner then moved into the room on the left and proceeded to clear it.

They progressed swiftly through the ground floor, spotting two dead attackers but no one else. Then they climbed the stairs to the second floor and began to clear the rooms up there. Again, they found three dead bodies, but no one else. Then Deuce heard something moving above them. He signaled to one of the other operators, who tossed a flashbang up the stairs to the entry of the next floor. It went off, rattling the house.

One of the operators sprinted up the stairs with his partner hot on his heels. The first guy made it to the landing and turned to head down the hallway. Deuce was nearly to the top of the landing when he heard a string of gunshots followed by some yelling. He turned to head toward the commotion.

Suddenly, an attacker exited a closet behind him and shot him squarely in the back. The bullet struck Deuce's rear plate and threw him to the floor, knocking the wind out of him. His partner swiftly swung his body around as he dropped to a knee and fired a string of bullets right over Deuce into the chest of the man who had just shot him.

"Deuce. You OK?" his partner asked.

Deuce shook the effects of the gunshot off, looked up at his friend and nodded his head.

Without waiting, his partner moved to clear the next set of rooms as the shouting, cursing, and shooting had ended in the room facing the street.

When Deuce finally got to his feet, he walked into the room and saw one of the attackers lying on the floor dead with a large knife stuck in his chest. One of his other teammates was sitting with his back against the wall and appeared to be a bit shaken.

As he moved to talk to his teammate, Deuce heard the other two guys call out, "Clear!"

Deuce kneeled down next to his comrade. "Are you hurt?" he asked.

The operator just shook his head. "No, I'm not hurt. I've just never killed a guy with a knife before. I stared into his eyes as the life drained from his body."

Deuce placed his hand on the man's shoulder. "It'll be OK. He didn't leave you any other choice. If you hadn't killed him, he would have murdered you and the rest of us. Put it out of your mind for the moment and let's go help the rest of our team secure the safe house."

The roar of gunfire coming from across the street was intense. It ebbed and flowed a bit, but it was certainly picking up pace right now, which meant the assault team had breached the house and they were now clearing it.

****

Congressman Borq had just exited the front of the house when Page heard an engine roaring down the block, which was followed by the sound of car brakes screeching and lots of shouting. Before she knew what was happening, several members of Borq's security team had practically thrown him back into the house.

The guards out front opened fire on the vehicles, peppering them with bullets.

All of a sudden, the panes of glass that had provided the living room with natural light shattered in front of them. One of her own guards tackled her to the ground. Bullets zipped over their heads, impacting against the wall and furniture next to them.

"Quickly, to the basement!" shouted one of the Wagner private military contractors.

The big Russian whipped out his FN P90 submachine gun, spraying a barrage of armor-piercing rounds at several of the attackers as they ran toward the house with their own assault rifles, firing away. Two of the attackers went down before the Russian was riddled with bullets and fell backwards, dead before he even hit the floor.

Page knew if she and Tim didn't get to the safe room right away, they were going to be either killed or captured in a matter of seconds. Turning to Tim, she yelled to be heard above the roar of gunfire. "Follow me to the basement!"

Without waiting for acknowledgment, she turned and immediately started scrambling on her hands and knees, crawling out of the front living room toward the kitchen in the rear of the house. There was a stairwell there that led to the basement, where the safe room was located. She could call for help there.

Page turned to look down the hall as she motioned for Tim to get down the stairs. She saw one of the Canadian guards toss a grenade out the front door and then take a bullet to the head.

Page didn't even wait for the bang. She followed Tim down the stairs and made a beeline for the safe room. She slapped the emergency close button just as she heard the explosion from the grenade upstairs.

The roar of gunfire above them picked up in pace, and so did the shouting. There were voices yelling in Russian and English as the two sides did their best to kill each other. Bangs and booms rattled the house as the attackers breached the front room.

Page grabbed the laptop in the room and turned it on. This was how she'd send out a call for help and keep an eye on what was happening above them.

While she waited for the computer to boot, she glanced up at the congressman. The man was in shambles. He paced his end of the room like a trapped animal.

When the laptop had finished its start sequence, Page connected it to the internal and external video displays so she could get a grasp of what was going on. Then she shared the video feeds of the cameras on the social media platforms her various cells were using.

Page began to livestream to her groups. "People of the Boston CDF, now is your time to rise up," she began. "I need your help. As you can see, our fascist government is attacking my position as we speak. I need you to grab your friends and your weapons and come to my address and help kill these fascist pigs. Do not delay. I'm not sure how much longer my people can hold out."

She turned the camera off and switched the screens back to monitoring what was happening in the house and around them. Page tried to figure out how much longer they had left.

Breaking her concentration, Tim asked, "Do you really think that quick message will help?"

Without taking her eyes off the computer screen, she replied, "For our sakes, you had better hope so. If it doesn't, we're toast."

From what she could see from the cameras, two of the attackers had breached the home. They were pinned down in the front room by a couple of guards shooting down at them from the second-floor staircase. A couple more shooters had them pinned down from the library and the kitchen hallway.

She changed the view to the outside cameras and saw four SUVs parked in front of the house with their doors open. *That must be the initial assault force*, she thought, wondering who else might be ready to show up.

Page saw two attackers lying dead on the ground not far from the stairs that led into the house. She surmised these must have been the two men her bodyguard had taken out before he was killed.

Then she saw several more attackers dead in the street. She smiled when she realized her guards across the street in one of the other homes must have caught them in a crossfire before they knew where the shooting was coming from.

Page caught something; there was movement in the direction of the park. She took control of the camera and panned it to see where the action was. Her heart sank. She saw two CH-47 Chinook helicopters landing. They disgorged dozens of additional soldiers who were headed right for her location.

The pace of the gunfire above them picked up. A couple of loud explosions rattled the safe room as the house shook from whatever had hit it. Then it suddenly grew quiet. Looking at the camera feeds, she saw a lot of smoke in various parts of the house and not much else. Some of her cameras had gone offline, probably destroyed by whatever had gone off upstairs.

Then Page saw a small cadre of soldiers moving through the house, systematically putting a bullet into the head of each defender's body to make sure they were truly dead. A group of them headed towards the stairwell, stopping just short of going down it. One of the soldiers tossed an object down and then stepped aside. She heard a loud boom outside the door of the safe room.

The soldiers moved down the stairs. When they reached the bottom, they stopped in front of the safe room. The soldiers talked on their radio for a minute and then fanned out to search the rest of the basement.

A couple of minutes later, a lone figure walked down the stairs. He made his way over to the metal door and then proceeded to pound on it twice.

"We know you're in there, Ms. Larson," the man announced. "I'm asking that you come out and end this peacefully."

"I think we should surrender," Congressman Borq blurted out. "They've clearly caught us, Page."

She shot him a disapproving look. "In less than thirty minutes, this entire place is going to be crawling with the cells I've created," she retorted. "It'll take them at least that long to cut through the door. So, no. I say we wait it out."

The man outside the door walked over to the camera. He took his helmet off and looked into it. "I know what you're thinking, Page. I want to tell you there is no point in waiting. You're all alone, and no one is coming to save you."

Incensed at this man's arrogance, Page hit the two-way talk button. "I've been livestreaming this to my cells," she announced. They're on their way, along with half of Boston."

The man just smiled. It was one of those devilish smiles that said he knew something she didn't. "Ms. Larson, do you really believe we would have let you broadcast a message to the world?"

Suddenly her chest tightened. *Did they intercept my message?* she wondered. A flurry of obscenities filled her head.

"We hacked your internet, Ms. Larson. The message you thought went out to the world went straight to our ops center. As I said, no one is coming to save you. Now, I've been instructed to take you alive if possible. But if you are unwilling to surrender, then I'll burn this house down with you both trapped inside. It really doesn't bother me which way this goes down."

The congressman looked utterly horrified. The thought of being burned alive was clearly more than he could handle.

Page crinkled her forehead. The man had used the word *both*. "It's just me in here," she countered. "No one else."

The soldier cocked his head to the side and smiled. "Really? I could have sworn Congressman Borq was in there with you."

Page turned to look at Tim. "How could he have known you were here?" she asked.

Tim just shrugged. "I'm a congressman, not an intelligence specialist. You tell me."

She reached for a small metal device inside one of the drawers of the desk, turned it on and then waved it across the congressman's body. As it got near his stomach, the indicator light flashed. A transmitter had been detected. In that moment, she knew exactly how they'd found her. They had somehow chipped Borq—either he didn't know, or he'd cut some sort of deal.

The soldier outside the door spoke again. "I suppose it won't hurt for me to tell you this, Ms. Larson. Perhaps it'll help you see reason and surrender. We placed a tracking device in Congressman Borq's food nearly three weeks ago. You don't have to believe me, but you've been playing this spy game long enough to know it's possible. Now, why don't you come out of the room? Let's talk about your situation."

Tim reached for the arm of the chair as he sat down shakily. Judging by the look on his face, he was oblivious to what had been done to him. Page's stomach sank.

How many rebel leaders did he meet with during the last three weeks? Page asked herself. She wondered how many of them had likely been arrested as a result.

"It's over, Page," Borq said, his voice barely above a whisper. "We did everything we could. Sometimes you just lose."

Page was filled with rage. *It wasn't supposed to be like this. I wasn't supposed to get caught!* With her and the congressman out of the game, that meant only Admiral Hill was left.

She suddenly felt lightheaded. "Did you meet with Admiral Hill in the last several weeks?" she asked.

Congressman Borq's face became ashen. He didn't say anything. He just hung his head low and cried into his hands.

It truly is over, then, she thought.

She shook her head in anger. Page reached behind her back and slipped her hand under her shirt, feeling for the Kimber 1911 she always carried. She pulled it out and while the Congressman was crying in his hands, she shot him in the head. Then she put the gun to her own head and pulled the trigger.

****

Paddy heard two gunshots emanating from within the safe room and just shook his head. He knew it was over. They had killed themselves rather than surrender. *Damn!* he thought. *Why didn't we know about the safe room?*

One of the soldiers came up to him. "Colonel, do you want us to cut our way into the room?"

Paddy just nodded, not taking his eyes off the steel door that stood between him and the two most wanted Americans. "Yeah. Get it opened up," he replied. "We need to recover their bodies, if nothing else."

Then he turned and walked back up to the ground floor of the home. Everywhere Paddy stepped, the floor was covered in spent shell casings. The walls were riddled with bullets and adorned with the occasional splattering of blood or brain matter. Bodies were everywhere, and the floors were nearly covered by pools of blood.

Paddy exited the house, and one of the captains walked up to him. "Sir, you asked for our losses," the man said.

Paddy nodded.

"Six KIA. Eleven wounded. The area is secured."

Paddy shook his head at the losses. *Damn it. We shouldn't have lost that many people.*

"Has the SSE team arrived?" Paddy asked. "I want this place combed over for evidence. Especially their laptops, thumb drives, and cell phones."

"They're arriving on the next Chinook," the captain replied. "We'll be flying our wounded out as well. Oh—the DHS supervisor told me he's deployed his QRF team to help us keep this place on lockdown. It won't take long for what happened here to get out. There could be trouble in a few hours."

Paddy nodded. "True. Make sure the SSE team knows they need to hurry. Grab everything if we have to. We can always exploit it back at the base." Then he walked back to the baseball field. He wanted to check on some of his wounded before they were flown out. It was the least he could do as their commander.

****

York County, Virginia
Camp Peary

After an hour-long briefing with his analytical team, Major General Lancaster was finally alone in his office. He lay down on a couch as he tried to process everything he'd just been told. They'd gone over the results of hundreds of raids being conducted across numerous states. It was a massive dragnet at this point—if all went well, it'd either end the civil war entirely or seriously slow it from spreading further.

A little more than three weeks ago, they had succeeded in chipping Congressman Borq. He had unwittingly led them to more than thirty CDF militia leaders and cells across the Midwest. But more importantly, he had led them to the location of Retired Admiral David Hill, the true mastermind of the insurgency. As each militia leader or cell had been identified, the NSA and FBI did their best to not only track their movements but identify and monitor everyone they were coming into contact with.

Lancaster, along with the national security team at the White House, had determined they'd hold off on arresting everyone until they had Congressman Borq and Page Larson in custody. That way, no one could be tipped off that they had been discovered. Within forty-eight hours of the raid on Page Larson's safe house, they had apprehended more than five hundred militia leaders and members, including Admiral Hill.

Now the FBI was running through the interrogations of the individuals arrested. A few of the more significant leaders had been handed over to Lancaster and his task force—Lieutenant Colonel Mitchell was going to have his hands full interrogating Admiral Hill. Hill had been a Navy SEAL his entire life; the man had been specifically trained to resist during an interrogation.

The issue Lancaster and his team were facing now was what to do about the previously unknown information about this shadowy group of people who seemed to be pulling the puppet strings of the world. It was almost mind-numbing to think about. If Lancaster didn't pay close attention, even he could get lost in all the layers and webs of this global conspiracy.

Mitchell had been peeling back one layer of this onion after another with Erik Jahn. While he continued to believe these were largely compartmentalized discussions between Seth and a few others, they'd been vetting everything—checking every lead and connecting every dot. The longer Seth debriefed the man, the more they found.

Something didn't sit well with Lancaster. During one of Seth's calls on the secured line, he'd mentioned something that sent a chill down Lancaster's spine. Seth had mentioned a case he'd worked in Iraq when he was still assigned to a Special Forces ODA team.

"The tribal chief in the Diyala province had told me he could deliver many of the Al Qaeda leaders in the country, along with people who were working with the Iranian Quds Force, which was part of the IRGC," Seth had shared. "While the man was providing valuable, accurate intelligence, I couldn't shake the feeling that the man was just having us round up his enemies, so he'd have an easier time consolidating power once he was released by Coalition Forces."

"All right, Seth, how does this relate to our current situation?" Lancaster had asked.

"I feel like Erik Jahn might be doing the same thing with us. That's why he's been only too eager to cough up the names of so many people involved in this conspiracy."

As Lancaster was lying there on his couch, thinking about what to do next, his eyes slowly closed and before he knew it, he was down for the count, asleep before his mind or body could fight it.

From the Authors

Miranda and I hope you've enjoyed the fourth book in the Falling Empires Series. We are currently working on the fifth and final book in the series, which is already available for preorder. Simply sign up on Amazon to grab your copy as soon as it's released.

While you are waiting for our next book to be released, we do have several audiobooks that have recently been produced. All six books of the Red Storm Series are now available in audio format, as is our entire World War III series. *Interview with a Terrorist* and *Traitors Within*, which are currently standalone books, are also available for your listening pleasure.

If you would like to stay up to date on new releases and receive emails about any special pricing deals we may make available, please sign up for our email distribution list. Simply go to http://www.author-james-rosone.com and scroll to the bottom of the page.

As independent authors, reviews are very important to us and make a huge difference to other prospective readers. If you enjoyed this book, we humbly ask you to write up a positive review on Amazon and Goodreads. We sincerely appreciate each person that takes the time to write one.

We have really valued connecting with our readers via social media, especially on our Facebook page, https://www.facebook.com/RosoneandWatson/. Sometimes we ask for help from our readers as we write future books—we love to draw upon all your different areas of expertise. We also have a group of beta readers who get to look at the books before they are officially published and help us fine-tune last-minute adjustments. If you would like to be a part of this team, please go to our author website: http://www.author-james-rosone.com, and send us a message through the "Contact" tab. You can also follow us on Twitter: @jamesrosone and @AuthorMirandaW. We look forward to hearing from you.

You may also enjoy some of our other works. A full list can be found below:

Nonfiction:

Iraq Memoir 2006–2007 Troop Surge

Interview with a Terrorist

Fiction:

World War III Series

Prelude to World War III: The Rise of the Islamic Republic and the Rebirth of America

Operation Red Dragon and the Unthinkable

Operation Red Dawn and the Siege of Europe

Cyber Warfare and the New World Order

Michael Stone Series

Traitors Within

The Red Storm Series

Battlefield Ukraine

Battlefield Korea

Battlefield Taiwan

Battlefield Pacific

Battlefield Russia

Battlefield China

The Falling Empires Series

Rigged

Peacekeepers

Invasion

Vengeance

Retribution (available for preorder, currently set to be released June 8, 2020)

Children's Books:

My Daddy has PTSD

My Mommy has PTSD

For the Veterans

I have been pretty open with our fans about the fact that PTSD has had a tremendous direct impact on our lives; it affected my relationship with my wife, job opportunities, finances, parenting—everything. It is also no secret that for me, the help from the VA was not the most ideal form of treatment. Although I am still on this journey, I did find one organization that did assist the healing process for me, and I would like to share that information.

Welcome Home Initiative is a ministry of By His Wounds Ministry, and they run seminars for veterans and their spouses for free. The weekends are a combination of prayer and more traditional counseling and left us with resources to aid in moving forward. The entire cost of the retreat—hotel costs, food, and sessions, are completely free from the moment the veteran and their spouse arrive at the location.

If you feel that you or someone you love might benefit from one of Welcome Home Initiative's sessions, please visit their website to learn more: https://welcomehomeinitiative.org/

We have decided to donate a portion of our profits to this organization, because it made such an impact in our lives and we believe in what they are doing. If you would also like to donate to Welcome Home Initiative and help to keep these weekend retreats going, you can do so by visiting their website:

https://welcomehomeinitiative.org/donate/

Abbreviation Key

AA	Anti-aircraft
AFN	Air Force Network
AG	Attorney General
AI	Artificial Intelligence
AO	Area of Operation
APC	Armored Personnel Carrier
ASAP	As Soon As Possible
AWACS	Airborne Early Warning and Control System
BND	German intelligence, similar to American CIA
Cav	Cavalry
CDF	Civilian Defense Force
CEO	Chief Executive Officer
CG	Commanding General
CIA	Central Intelligence Agency
CIC	Combat Information Center
CNO	Chief of Naval Operations
CO	Commanding Officer
COO	Chief Operations Officer
COP	Combat Outpost
DARPA	Defense Advanced Research Projects Agency

DHS	Department of Homeland Security
DoD	Department of Defense
DOJ	Department of Justice
EMP	Electromagnetic Pulse
EMS	Emergency Medical Services
FAST	Fleet Anti-terrorism Security Team
FBI	Federal Bureau of Investigations
FIST	Fire Support Team
FLIR	Forward-Looking Infrared
FN SCAR-SC	Type of subcompact machine gun
FPS	Federal Protective Service
FSK	Forsvarets Spesialkommando (Norwegian version of Special Forces)
IBA	Individual Body Armor
IED	Improvised Explosive Device
IR	Infrared
JDAM	Joint Direct Attack Munition
JLTV	Joint Light Tactical Vehicle
JSOC	Joint Special Operations Command
JSTARS	Joint Surveillance Target Attack Radar System
KIA	Killed in Action
LAV	Light Armored Vehicles
LCAC	Landing Craft Air Cushion

LCM	Landing Craft Mechanized
LCU	Landing Craft Utility
LNO	Liaison Officer
LOAC	Laws of Armed Conflict
LOC	Line of Control
LRASM	Long-Range Anti-Ship Missile
LT	Lieutenant
LZ	Landing Zone
MANPADS	Man-Portable Air-Defense System
MEF	Marine Expeditionary Force
MEU	Marine Expeditionary Unit
MG	Machine Gun
MRE	Meal Ready to Eat
NAS	Naval Air Station
NCO	Noncommissioned Officer
NMCC	National Military Command Center
NORAD	North American Aerospace Defense Command
NRO	National Reconnaissance Office
NSA	National Security Advisor OR National Security Agency
NSC	National Security Council
NVG	Night Vision Goggles
OCS	Officer Candidate School

ODA	Special Forces Operational Detachment Alpha
OTR	Over-the-Road
OZE	Occupation Zone East
OZW	Occupation Zone West
PAP	People's Armed Police Force
PD	Public Defender
PLA	People's Liberation Army (Chinese army)
PM	Prime Minister
PMC	Private Military Contractor
POW	Prisoner of War
PT	Physical Training
QRF	Quick Reaction Force
R & R	Rest and Relaxation
RCT	Regimental Combat Team
RIB	Rigid Inflatable Boat
RTO	Radiotelephone Operator
S3	Operations Officer
SAM	Surface-to-Air Missile
SAR	Search and Rescue
SB1	Special Warfare Boat Operator One
SF	Special Forces
SINGCARS	Single Channel Ground and Airborne Radio System

SITREP	Situation Report
SMAW	Shoulder-Launched Multipurpose Assault Weapon
SOAR	Special Operations Aviation Regiment
SOCOM	Special Operations Command
SSE	Sensitive Site Exploitation
SUV	Sports Utility Vehicle
SWAT	Special Weapons and Tactics
TF	Task Force
THAAD	Terminal High Altitude Area Defense
TS	Top Secret
UAV	Unmanned Aerial Vehicle
UN	United Nations
VBIED	Vehicle Borne Improvised Explosive Device
VLS	Vertical Launch System
XO	Commanding Officer

Made in the USA
Coppell, TX
28 May 2021

56458334R00299